Before I Knew You

# Before I Knew You

AMANDA BROOKFIELD

PENGUIN BOOKS

PENGUIN BOOKS

Published by the Penguin Group
Penguin Books Ltd, 80 Strand, London WC2R 0RL, England
Penguin Group (USA) Inc., 375 Hudson Street, New York, New York 10014, USA
Penguin Group (Canada), 90 Eglinton Avenue East, Suite 700, Toronto, Ontario, Canada M4P 2Y3
(a division of Pearson Penguin Canada Inc.)
Penguin Ireland, 25 St Stephen's Green, Dublin 2, Ireland (a division of Penguin Books Ltd)
Penguin Group (Australia), 250 Camberwell Road,
Camberwell, Victoria 3124, Australia (a division of Pearson Australia Group Pty Ltd)
Penguin Books India Pvt Ltd, 11 Community Centre,
Panchsheel Park, New Delhi – 110 017, India
Penguin Group (NZ), 67 Apollo Drive, Rosedale, Auckland 0632, New Zealand
(a division of Pearson New Zealand Ltd)
Penguin Books (South Africa) (Pty) Ltd, 24 Sturdee Avenue,
Rosebank, Johannesburg 2196, South Africa

Penguin Books Ltd, Registered Offices: 80 Strand, London WC2R 0RL, England

www.penguin.com

First published 2011
2

Set in 12.5/14.75 pt Garamond MT
Typeset by Ellipsis Books Limited, Glasgow
Printed in England by Clays Ltd, St Ives plc

ISBN: 978-0-141-03994-7

www.greenpenguin.co.uk

For Gilly

'The past is consumed in the present and the present is living only because it brings forth the future'

James Joyce

# PART ONE

# I

The plane remained motionless while its engines roared, being tested, Sophie hoped, for their ability to perform with similar conviction once airborne. Peering through her scratched porthole, she studied the overcast skies of Heathrow, wondering how the Stapletons would feel, landing amid such gloom when they had left behind a heat wave. The entire east coast of America was simmering at only just below 40°C, Andrew had exclaimed over the paper that morning, delivering the information, as he did most things these days, trivial or otherwise, in a tone that demanded some visible effort on her part at celebration.

Sophie had done her best to oblige, rolling her eyes in a show of happy wonderment, suppressing a strong desire to remind her husband of the propensity of his pale, gingery-blond-haired skin to blister and blotch, and an even stronger urge to slice through his newspaper with her toast knife and say she did not wish to holiday anywhere that year, let alone *swap houses* with some people from Connecticut for *four* weeks, three of which would be without their children. But Andrew had looked so pleased – so relieved – that she had held the smile in place, clung to it much as she might have a cliff edge in the dark, telling herself that if he couldn't see the effort then she should be able to overlook it too.

Of course, Andrew was as apprehensive as she was, Sophie reminded herself – about the heat, about New York, about the whole madcap scheme. It had been the brainchild of his old friend and erstwhile best man, Geoffrey Hooper, who had for years lived on the Upper East Side with his wife Ann.

I recently met with this really nice English guy, William Stapleton – in asset management with Latouche – who was lamenting the cost and difficulty of finding a short let on a decent family home in south-west London. He got married last year to an American and has a beautiful property in Connecticut, but is looking for a base in your neck of the woods for August so he can see something of his kids from his first marriage – they live with the first wife in Richmond . . . Hey, pal, I hope you're following this . . . The point is, the man needs to spend a few weeks in west London and you and Sophie need to visit America before your Zimmer frames stop you getting on a plane. So it occurred to me that if you guys simply traded properties for, say, a month this summer everybody would be happy! Well, Ann and I certainly would!

We have always understood why the pair of you might be reluctant to spend time cooped up with us on Manhattan, but Darien is beautiful – right on the coast, so picturesque and rural, but with easy access to New York. William and Beth's

4

house (we visited a couple of Sundays ago) is colonial style, close to Pear Tree Point, with views over Scott's Pond . . . better than any hotel and, of course, totally FREE! There would be no end of activities if you wanted them – water sports, great walks in the nature preserves, tennis, golf. I swear you and the girls would have a ball. Oh, yes, and the joys of NY await you too – great food, fabulous museums, Broadway – Ann and I would so love to show you around. William and Beth have already said they're game if you are. Let me know SOON so we can iron out details. Best, Geoff

The email, printed out by Andrew, had sat next to the telephone in the kitchen for a couple of weeks, gathering dust and splashes of juice and coffee. Every time Sophie glimpsed it she felt a twist of irritation, both for the unappealing invitation it contained and the careless Americanisms woven through the prose. Geoff had been born in Bristol and acquired a blue for cricket at Cambridge. He'd had an edge of old-fashioned Queen's English to his voice that Sophie had once, briefly, found rather enticing. Before retraining as a barrister in his late twenties he had eked out as pauper-like an existence as theirs had been in those days, freelancing in orchestras while Ann worked in a clothes shop. Now he settled disputes between wealthy divorcing couples and said *pal* . . .

Sophie had been lost to such uncharitable thoughts one evening when Andrew had snatched the email from under her nose, saying, 'I'll tell him no.' He had begun, slowly, to tear the piece of paper in two while Sophie watched – momentarily glad and then suddenly afraid that he might be ripping up something infinitely more irrevocable than a tatty piece of A4.

'Let's say yes,' she had murmured, reaching out a hand to stop him. 'A holiday in America. Say yes,' she had repeated, taking a step backwards as an indication that this spurt of positive energy did not extend to taking command of organizing the project. 'Like he says, we'll probably love it.'

As the aeroplane gathered speed down the runway, pressing her into her seat, Sophie's thoughts drifted back wistfully to the easy harmony of their holiday the previous summer: two weeks in Italy – Naples, Positano, Pompeii – sun, sea and Roman ruins, ingredients to keep all the various ages and temperaments of her family happy. For the start of that journey she had sat between the girls, gripping their slim, nail-bitten fingers as the concrete complex of Gatwick shrank to a blur, seeking to ease her own customary terrors about air travel rather than those of her daughters. It had even – perhaps morbidly – occurred to her that it wouldn't be a bad moment to die, with all four of them side by side, chain-linked, Andrew included, thanks to Milly thoughtfully reaching across the aisle for her father's hand as the plane's snout lifted towards the sky.

Andrew's hand was inches from Sophie's now yet she felt no inclination to reach for it. Olivia and Milly were on tour with the London Youth Orchestra, first violin and cello. At the tender ages of seventeen and fifteen respectively, Andrew had been talking to them a lot recently about how to prepare for and what to expect from music college – especially Olivia, whose application to the Royal College of Music and a clutch of the best conservatoires would be submitted that autumn.

Sophie swallowed, wanting both her offspring so badly that all the recently acquired teenage carapaces – the flouncing, the moodiness, the closed doors and antisocial whirring of laptops – seemed too minor even to consider forgiving. She conjured a fond image of Olivia, her violin pinioned under her chin, all flashing elbows and arms and hips as she played, like a sapling in a high wind. Milly, in spite of being younger and the more volatile character, tended to fold herself round her cello as if it literally grew out of her, bowing with smooth, fluid movements as the soft gingery-gold streams of her hair swung across the struts. She was the more restful to watch – and the better musician, Andrew had occasionally, in hushed tones, confided, in spite of both girls' history of excellent grades. The tour was the opportunity of a lifetime – Munich, Vienna, Salzburg . . . and several other places that Sophie could not remember.

'Poor Stapletons,' she murmured, pressing her fingers to her popping ears as the plane continued to rise steeply and the lacklustre sky began to seep flecks of rain.

'Poor?'

'Getting this weather, and our Volvo and grotty carpets and a weedy garden and Barnes traffic and a view of the river only if you climb onto the window-sill in the top bedroom and crane your neck round the tree that probably caused the massive crack in the cellar.'

'When you've quite finished . . .'

'I only meant that from those pictures they sent it's pretty clear who's getting the better deal – detached, double garage, set in all that unspoilt land. A place like that would cost millions over here.'

'A place like that doesn't exist over here – at least, not in south-west London.' Andrew pulled out his briefcase from under his seat, riffling through it for the score to the German Requiem, to which he had somewhat rashly committed the school choir and orchestra for the following term. He wasn't remotely in the mood for work but needed to put up some sort of barrier around himself – against Sophie's relentless gloom, against his own doubts about swapping homes, running riot now that they were actually on their way. He had to fence some of that out or he couldn't think straight.

He thumbed through the Brahms gently, fondly. He had conducted it only once, some twenty years before, during his Cambridge days. The pencil marks were faded but Andrew could still remember, with painful precision, the exuberance with which he had inscribed them, all the certainty and hope of being twenty and talented, the future unfurling at his command, as lush and promising as a red carpet. 'And our house is *ideal* for them, Geoff said,' he burst out, his invisible fence collapsing. 'Being near the first wife and all that stuff, remember? So the man can see his sons? And the garden isn't full of weeds because I paid that overpriced idiot a small fortune to *weed* it and the Volvo has never been so clean and you can see the river from our bathroom window without craning your neck at all. And – ' Andrew jammed his pencil between his teeth in a bid to stop the flow, fearful of what might come out.

An air stewardess with gummy scarlet lips handed them each a menu. Andrew slipped his into the back of the score, letting the anger unfurl inside his head instead. Sophie had seen a doctor, had blood tests, been checked for MS, early menopause and a host of other delights. A brief dalliance with antidepressants had made no difference, she claimed, other than an upset stomach. Six months, it had been now. Six months since January and the break-in, which obviously hadn't helped, and Andrew had been as patient as he could about factoring that in. But patience, like everything, had limits, and lately, lying awake in the dark as she turned her back on him again, he had felt as if his skin was being stretched to the point of rupture; that one more moment of putting up with the dazed looks and the gloominess, he would split open like some dried-out, over-tightened drum.

Sophie, sensing the vibrations of his exasperation, its proximity to anger, pretended to study the in-flight menu: *boeuf bourguignon or fillet of salmon with dill, broccoli florets, potatoes dauphinoise, a selection of French cheeses, tarte au citron, filter coffee and mint chocolate* . . . Such idiotic jargon, such a silly printed card, when everybody knew it would be the usual reheated mulch in plastic tubs, lukewarm, too salty, too sweet, too . . .

Sophie took a deep breath. The negativity, it had to stop. She must try, like Andrew did, like Andrew wanted. 'I'll have the salmon, I think. What about you?' She did her best to sound interested, as if she didn't already know that he would choose the beef.

Before Andrew could answer, the plane lurched, sending his briefcase – spilling papers – sliding off his lap. Sophie dived forwards to catch it, lunging with the same deft reflex with which she had once fielded a priceless vase, toppled by her own careless elbow in an antiques shop, and Milly, rolling off a nappy mat towards a stone-tiled floor.

'Thanks, Soph.'

Their eyes caught, a brief involuntary connection no less intense for its mutual acknowledgement of the distance between them and their powerlessness in the face of it. Sophie was the first to blink and look away. A new wave of dread for Darien, Connecticut, New York – wherever the hell it was – swept over her. Four weeks in the home of strangers: it would be like putting bare feet into someone else's still warm shoes, enduring the ugly sensation of the ridges worn by their toes. Sophie shuddered.

Yet it was true that she dreaded most things, these days. And there was something to admire in the dogged determination with which Andrew had taken charge of the project – not just booking gardeners, but amending car-insurance policies, sorting key collection . . . all this when he was both deputy head and head of music in a large, demanding private London school, keeping on top of admin by the seat of his pants, resorting to charm whenever his shortcomings as an organizer threatened to let him down. He was a singer who had given up singing, Sophie reminded herself, a composer who had no time to compose. They had met when she was a minion behind the scenes at a music festival in Winchester, modelling part-time, drifting after having dropped out of a degree in English at Reading. Andrew had anchored her, pronounced her his muse.

'Andrew, darling . . .' The endearment felt false, but she pressed on. 'I know I'm hard work at the moment, but I promise you I'm fighting it . . . whatever it turns out to be. It's so difficult to describe . . . just not feeling *right* . . . If it continues, I'll have more tests, I promise.'

Andrew sighed, spreading his hand over hers. 'Good girl, that's the spirit.' The tone was back in his voice, the one she hated – the show of kindness but so laced with impatience that it only left her feeling worse.

Sophie extricated her fingers and returned her attention to the porthole, seeing again the young man who had broken into their back garden in January, the unmistakable beauty of his creamy mixed-race skin, the ugly stains on his clothes, the darting dark eyes and a mouth so full-lipped that even in the midst of all the trauma she had sensed the conscious effort to keep it closed, to hide from public view the bright inner wetness of his gums. She traced her finger down the rivulets streaking the outside of the window. In the end nothing bad had happened, as Andrew was so fond of reminding her. A boy with a knife, stealing cash, scared off by a siren. And yet something nearly happening could be just as bad, she reasoned. Like catching Milly that time, inches from the hard-tiled bathroom floor. Afterwards Sophie had found herself struggling for breath and weeping, in spite of her daughter's soft, precious head being safely cradled in her palms.

The stewardess arrived to retrieve her menu cards and take their order. The image of Milly as a baby, of the January intruder, receded, leaving Sophie only with the now familiar hollowness of being too exhausted to care. And that was because she was ill, she consoled herself, with one of those viruses too cunning and invisible to be awarded the honour of a name. Rest, the doctor said, regular meals, lots of sleep, no stress. And she had been doing her best to obey – it was months since she had given up the part-time teaching of English A-level re-sits that passed for a career, and here she was jetting off on a whole month's holiday. What more could she do? Sophie closed her eyes.

Andrew slipped the Brahms score away and took out the in-flight-viewing magazine. A glass of wine, he decided, maybe two. It would be excellent to see Geoff properly after so many years, and to have time to relax, read a few books, even if he did end up barricading himself in under the protection of air-conditioning. In fact, he liked air-conditioning, not just for its power to cool but for its noise, a humming counterpoint to silence; there was music in it, music and rhythm, like there was in most things if one listened hard enough. 'Four weeks away from the grind,' he declared out loud, 'seeing old friends, the girls joining us, sightseeing, money to spend on nice meals, sleeping in a luxurious house, under a different roof, different stars . . .' He rubbed his palms together. 'We're going to have a good time, I promise you, Sophie, a *really* good time.'

Sophie opened her eyes to nod, glad his mood had lifted, managing not to say that, apart from a shift of angle, the stars would be exactly the same.

When the pilot announced that it was raining in London, Beth and William exchanged looks, laughing. They had discussed this very thing during the course of packing up the previous day, the bedroom blinds lowered against the belting afternoon sun, Dido patrolling the half-filled cases, mewing her suspicions. Never once in his entire life had he landed on a runway in his home country in good weather, William had claimed merrily, tossing clothes onto the bed, which Beth refolded into perfect rectangles and arranged in his suitcase. Hers was already done: a neat patchwork of colours, cordoned in by shoes and all the plastic-wrapped toiletries that, these days, were forbidden safer custody in a carry-on bag. Sweaters, swimsuits, sandals, walking boots – even before the weather conversation she had known that every eventuality had to be catered for. London looked like it was going to warm up, dry out – she had been checking the long-range forecast on her laptop – but they would also be going north to visit William's parents in Skipton, which enjoyed its very own micro-climate, he had teased, usually the opposite of what was going on anywhere else.

The British weather! Beth stared happily at the oval of colourless sky next to her seat, delighting that such an international joke – a cliché – was on the verge of becoming real, as important to negotiate as the tiny criss-crossing streets in William's dog-eared map-book of London and the rather more serious prospect of further encounters with her husband's family.

Her *husband*. Beth stole a glance at William's profile, wanting to experience again that first objective glimpse in the New York coffee shop around two years before – the sharp, clear pleasure of the initial spontaneous acknowledgement of how good-looking he was. Thick dark hair, traced with grey, cut short but not so short you couldn't see the waves, the high cheekbones, the sculpted nose with nostrils that flared ever so slightly when he was surprised, the unbelievably perfect mouth, full with-out being feminine, encasing a set of even but faintly crowded teeth. She could have guessed – even before straining her ears hard enough to hear – that he was English: the hint of chaos in his mouth was, of course, a give-away, but so was the suggestion of scruffiness behind the grooming, the suit that was well cut but also a little too well worn, the tie loose, the long-legged body that looked naturally slim rather than rigorously toned by working out in a gym.

With many years on the dating circuit behind her, Beth had, rather to her own regret, become something of an expert at making such assessments. On the plus side there was the compensatory wisdom of having learnt to recognize the importance of such fine differences and to know therefore that the very carelessness of William's good looks was what drew her. Dimitri, her most recent ex, had the sleek, too-good-to-be-true appearance of a model: a sculpted physique, manicured nails, a close, slick haircut, all set off by an impeccable wardrobe of suits and leather shoes. No man could have looked better on a girl's arm. And he was bright too – Princeton, then Yale, followed by a fast trajectory in a top law firm; Beth's mother, Diane, had been smacking her lips in gleeful anticipation – her difficult thirty-six-year-old daughter, properly hooked up at last to a chisel-faced genius! But no man either could have spent longer in front of mirrors than Dimitri, or looked more disapproving on the rare occasions that Beth blew her own careful regime and tucked into a doughnut or a roll of cookie dough. 'Beth, baby, is it really *worth* it?' he would say, with a tenderness that only made her mad, since it was so obviously about what he wanted rather than her. Eighteen months in and she had begun to feel as if she had acquired a guardian more than a lover, a living embodiment of the hateful never-far-away voice inside her head that told her all the things she didn't want to hear, the one that was so adept at making her feel wretched rather than happy.

In the coffee shop that January lunchtime, William had been eating carelessly, spilling forkfuls of chocolate cake and drinking a cappuccino, between enjoying some quick-fire conversation with another man in a suit – a squat American with the wide neck of an ex-football player. Beth, knowing better than to hanker after things she could not have (beautiful, English – a veritable Hugh Grant on the outside – but married, no doubt, or gay, or screwed up), had drained her own skinny latte, settled the check and been on her way to the door when she was accosted by an 'Excuse me' and a very British clearing of the throat. The squat American had gone and William, with his overcoat over his arm, was clearly preparing to leave as well. 'I don't suppose you have the time on you, do you?' he had asked, with the accent that was so enticingly English, a glint of humour flashing in his dark brown eyes.

Beth had scrabbled at her coat sleeve, her cardigan sleeve, her blouse sleeve – layers and layers of sleeves, it seemed, her purse tumbling into the mêlée from her shoulder – before she was able to deliver the answer displayed by her wristwatch. Whereupon William had remarked what a pretty watch it was and where had she got it? Beth replied that it had been a twenty-first birthday gift from her mother and then added the further, un-necessary, faintly intimate, disclosure that since her mother was generally lousy at picking gifts it was an item of which she was especially fond. To which William had replied, how lovely, and wasn't gift-giving a fiendish minefield of raised and dashed hopes, suppositions and misconceptions and did she want another coffee?

In truth that was the last thing Beth had wanted. Thanks to a dull morning in the HR department of the bank that employed her, she had already had more than her quota of caffeine for the day, and could feel the start of a throbbing headache to prove it. But with her antennae telling her that this might be a special moment – a moment only a fool or a coward would turn her back on – she said another coffee was a fine idea, parked her purse under the table-top and clambered with as much elegance as she could manage onto the stool that had been vacated by the wide-necked American.

'I'll lose my job,' she had gasped, staring in disbelief at the same treasured watch an hour later, headache quite forgotten, and then falling silent as William gently took hold of her wrist on the pretext of examining its gold bangle of a strap more closely. He had wide, strong fingers, with clean unfussy nails and a thick gold signet ring, engraved with something she couldn't quite make out . . . a bird or some kind of old-fashioned lion. In a minute or two she would ask about it, Beth had decided, when she could trust her voice, when her arm had recovered from the electric shock of his touch. Glancing through the glass pane next to them into the street, it had struck her as incredible that New Yorkers were still hurrying about their dull lives, faces down, cell phones pressed to their ears, as if the world was something to be kept at bay rather than dived into and embraced for the miracle it truly was.

Beth smiled to herself, feeling through her cardigan for the familiar shape of the watch-strap. The plane was descending steadily now, bringing the English country-side into fuller focus – as green as everybody had promised, in spite of the steely canopy of rain. The cabin crew were trawling the aisle for unfastened seatbelts and last items of rubbish. Beside her, William was popping out a square of gum – the nicotine stuff, she noticed, although she had been doing her best to encourage him to switch to peppermint. 'Sure you don't want some of this instead, honey?' she asked, offering a piece of the sugar-free brand she was already chewing to counter the tightening in her eardrums.

William shook his head, nuzzling the side of her face. 'You know I'll love you till my dying day for this alone, don't you?'

'For what, dummy?'

'Agreeing to spend a month in my rainy homeland with not much prospect of company beyond my three devilish sons and ageing parents.'

Beth laughed. 'They're not devilish, they're cute, your parents too.'

'Cute? What – even Harry?'

'Especially Harry. He looks the most like you.'

'They think you're really cool, you know that, don't you?'

Beth giggled, luxuriating in the praise. That she had no intention of interfering with how William brought up his three teenage sons was something she had made as clear as possible from the start. She had met them on only two occasions, the first during the course of a half-term visit when William had still been living on his own downtown, and she had been able to dip in and out, joining in for treats to pizza parlours and the movies and the park; and the second, rather more briefly, when they had flown over for the wedding. That was when she had met the parents for the first time, two wiry, robust, white-haired creatures – more like twins than a married couple – who came not only in support of William but to look after their grandsons. Given the potential for awkward-ness – officially graduating to the status of stepmother when, with William's concurrence, she had confessed to never wanting kids of her own, not to mention becoming a daughter-in-law to people whom her husband had clearly grown accustomed to keeping at arms' length – the whole event had gone tremendously well. Politeness, effort, cheerfulness: everyone had behaved impeccably, including Diane, her own, tricky, far from arms'-length mother, who, thanks to being almost more in love with William than Beth herself, had fussed between his parents and progeny like a bee between flowers.

'We're getting a taxi, right? A black cab. Heathrow to Richmond.'

'Yes. Except the Chapmans' house is more Barnes . . . Richmond is where Susan and the boys are.' William sat back, tightening his seatbelt as the plane bucked into its final descent.

'And the neighbours have all the keys – doors, car and so on,' persisted Beth who, after almost four decades of being admirably on top of every minor detail in her own life, still sometimes found it hard to accommodate the often slack attitude of her husband to overseeing the logistics of his.

'Neighbour,' William corrected her. 'A Mrs Hemmel. I've got her phone number in case of a hitch.'

Beth pressed her palms together as a fresh wave of excitement rolled through her. 'Oh, *London*, William, I can't believe it, I just can't.'

'Personally, I'd prefer Bermuda,' William remarked drily, by way of a reference to their idyllic two-week honeymoon at the start of the year. Silky pink sands, excellent food, the peace of unwinding with Beth, away from share prices and markets, the luxury of time – for each other, for reading, for conversation. Not even the crippling impact on his bank account had yet diminished the glow. In fifteen years of marriage he and Susan had never managed anything half as heavenly, not even during the early times. They had been broke for one thing and Susan hated beaches – or anywhere that required sitting still. And then Harry and his brothers had arrived, disturbing their already chaotic domestic world with the unrelenting demands and drama of parenthood.

As the plane made contact with the runway William picked Beth's hand out of her lap, squeezing it firmly until the slight bouncing was over and the brakes had kicked in. Her excitement about the trip delighted him. It was understandable, of course, that she should be thrilled at the prospect of seeing London (she had spent most of her adult life, she claimed, not quite getting round to a trip to the UK), but all the less thrilling things, like having to do her bit with the boys, of staying in a decidedly inferior home compared to their own, of having to postpone their next holiday *à deux* until the new year – none of that had received so much as an eyebrow twitch of a complaint. One of Susan's more insidious tricks had been to agree to things she didn't want and then sulk in carrying them out. William still could not quite believe that he had found a woman who was so contrastingly – so wonderfully – *positive*, so actively determined to see the proverbial glass as almost over-flowing, and place priority on his happiness into the bargain. Even losing her job the previous autumn, thanks to a knock-on effect of the sub-prime mortgage crisis, Beth had refused to regard as a setback. Other HR departments would just have to wait until she was ready to run them, she had joked; in the meantime she had a wedding to organize, a new home to decorate and a fiancé to look after. Arriving home from work in recent months, parking under the glossy rivulets of trailing ivy that swarmed over the lemon walls of their beautiful home, being greeted by the faint smell of Beth's delicious cooking and the mews of Dido, her beloved Persian, basking in a last patch of sunshine by the front door,

William almost had to pinch himself that he wasn't immersed in some elaborate dream, conjured from many haphazard years of groping his way down a series of blind alleys.

He ached to see his sons sometimes, of course. But Beth understood that too and he was careful never to rub her nose in it, wanting, as much as she did, to keep in sharp relief the new clean path of their life together, stretching ahead, different and better from all that had gone before. At thirteen, fifteen and seventeen, the boys were now happily close to a level of independence that William hoped would allow them to step on and off that path, consolidating things with him and, in time, building up a decent relationship with his new wife.

They were good kids, easy to like, especially little Alfie, with his specs and earnestness and endearingly boyish wiry body, as eager still to pursue old-fashioned innocent activities, like chasing balls and climbing trees, as the more sedentary pleasures offered by a computer screen. George, the middle one, presented rather more of a challenge, having always been – even before his current state of full-blown simian adolescence – inclined to surliness and silences. Harry, the eldest, was, as Beth had remarked, the most obviously like him, not just in being well over six foot and dark-haired but also in having an easy confidence in his approach to life, not to mention a quick, enquiring intelligence that often left his middle sibling in the shade. August meant exam results for both older boys and William was looking

forward to being around for the follow-through –
giving George the usual pep-talk and helping Harry
prepare for the Oxford college that had offered him a
place.

'Oh, I loved Bermuda,' Beth exclaimed, once the plane
had touched down safely and they were taxiing to a bay.
'It was the best, but I'm not sure I'd want to go back
there. I mean, going back anywhere is usually a bad idea,
don't you think? And, anyway, Bermuda doesn't have
Big Ben, does it? Or the National Gallery, or Trafalgar
Square, or Kew Gardens, or the London Eye, the Dome
. . . Oh, honey, I'm going to be such a *tourist*, I hope you
don't mind.'

William kissed her cheek, said he didn't mind a bit,
but that he might pass when it came to the Dome:
it had been a famous waste of money and there was
nothing to see now except a space that hosted pop
concerts. What he elected not to mention was that it
was also the place where, on a humid day, lost among
the tacky, over-hyped millennium displays, the children
rowdy and miserable and Susan slinging insults about
his failings as a husband and father, he had first made
a private vow to walk away. It had taken five years, as
things turned out, manoeuvring for one of the New
York jobs, hanging on in there for Alfie who at seven
and eight and nine had seemed too young to leave; but
it was no coincidence that the week following that hateful visit had seen the initiation of his first affair – with
his secretary, which was lowly and corny and obviously

doomed, but it had put the spring back in his step, the one he had been missing. And, as William had recognized even at the time, the business of leaving Susan, as with all new journeys, had had to start somewhere.

# 2

The house was so much more striking than even the Stapletons' excellent emailed images had suggested, that the moment they pulled up in front of the double garage Sophie got out of the car to gawp, leaving Andrew rummaging in his bulky file of correspondence for the house keys and alarm code. A colonial *residence*, there was no other word for it: not just 'detached', but a good twenty yards from its only neighbour (a glimpse of white through the trees), nestling among draping maples and ebullient shrubs like the central bud of some luxuriant flower. It looked somehow fresh and cool too, Sophie marvelled, shielding her eyes from the glare of the sun as she studied the house's attractively ivied pale yellow walls and white window shutters, each as serene as a pair of closed eyelids.

The heat was extraordinary, throbbing out of the tarmac and up, under the hem of her skirt. And yet it felt fantastic to be out of the car, separating herself from all the predictable tension of the final leg of the journey – not being able to locate the car, or its keys, or Interstate 95, or, more crucially, Darien itself, buried, as everything in the area seemed to be, by oceans of trees.

'It's three eight four zero,' said Andrew, starting to pull bags from the boot. 'Then the green button.'

As Sophie turned to help him, a man in shorts and a

Hawaiian shirt, hanging loosely over the visible bulge of his stomach, appeared from among the section of forest shrouding the white house. He looked in his late fifties, with skin like tanned leather, apart from the smooth, bald dome of his head. 'Carter Riley.' He offered an outstretched arm well in advance of arrival. 'How are you folks doing? My wife Nancy and I are your neighbours. Welcome to Darien. Here, let me get some of those bags . . .'

'No, we're fine, thanks,' Andrew replied briskly, once the handshakes were done with.

'Sure, okay.' Carter rubbed his hands together, backing away. 'But any problems and you get directly in touch, you hear? I promised Beth and William I'd look out for you. Anything at all. We've got a pool, which the both of you are welcome to use – just say the word.'

'That's so kind,' Sophie cried, feeling the need to make up for Andrew, who had gathered several bags and was heading for the front door. 'Thanks so much, Mr . . . '

'Carter. Call me Carter. And don't take any nonsense from that darn cat of theirs either.' He chuckled, wagging a teasing finger as a vast Persian cat, with fur like thick beige feathers and a wide, flat, comical face, appeared round the side of the house. It paused to study them for a few moments, curling its extravagant boa of a tail round a tendril of ivy before stalking back the way it had come. 'She's a princess and no mistake.' Carter shook his head as he set off towards the trees separating the two properties.

'Well, they could have told us,' Sophie muttered, wheeling the last of the suitcases to the front door. 'I mean, one of us could have been allergic or something, like Tamsin – remember how allergic she was?'

'You mean the cat?' said Andrew, with deliberate obtuseness, more concerned with the keys, which didn't seem to be working, and having no desire to embark on a discussion about Sophie's sister, whose tragically difficult, handicapped life had been brought to an end by an asthma attack ten years before. 'They did mention it, actually. I didn't say anything because I was afraid you wouldn't be keen . . . Ah, there we go.' He pushed the door open with his shoulder and then dropped his bags, cocking his head and frowning. 'Something should be ringing, shouldn't it . . . or at least beeping?' He pulled a crumpled piece of paper from the palm of his hand.

'You knew there was a cat to look after and you didn't tell me?' Sophie exclaimed, aware that she was over-reacting but unable somehow to resist it. 'You *knew* and didn't tell me?' she repeated, when Andrew didn't bother to turn round.

'There's no need to make an issue of it.' He crammed the piece of paper back into his pocket. 'I didn't tell you because I guessed you wouldn't like it –'

'Well, you were wrong,' Sophie snapped. 'It's not being told that I don't like.'

'Look, sorry, okay?' Andrew wiped the sweat off his temples with his forearms. 'It's called Dido. It requires feeding. It's no big deal.' He turned away from her, releasing a low, appreciative whistle at the wide hall, with its polished wooden floorboards, high ceiling and fresh creamy walls, glowing gently in the dim light. 'I'll get some of these shutters open, shall I? Let in some air and sunshine.'

Sophie said nothing. She was too busy pulling into herself, a trick she had mastered in recent months, like tightening a drawstring over her head, closing up, hunkering down inside an invisible bag. She headed for the stairs with her wheeled suitcase, registering but feeling no connection to Andrew's eager darting between windows, or the lines of honey light falling across her path.

Once safely out of view on the landing, she paused to lean on the banisters, fighting a sudden sensation of physical sickness at the thought of trying to coexist with Andrew in this strangely perfect place, trapped in the spotlight of whatever it was that had so mysteriously come between them, all their hollow efforts to enjoy themselves, with nowhere, nothing – no one – behind which to hide.

The passageway was lined with trellised wallpaper, adorned at orderly intervals with tasteful prints and shelves of small china ornaments. A deep pile toffee-coloured carpet ran the length of it and into each of the rooms, as soft underfoot as mossy grass. Everything looked fresh and expensive, and yet Sophie couldn't help thinking the place felt more like a hotel than a home, falsely pristine, impossible to relax in. Although the girls might like it, she conceded, marvelling – as she continued to poke her head round doors – at the kind of woman who had the time, the *energy* to ensure that her curtain ties matched her scatter cushions. In the bathrooms the synchronicity of the décor was especially overwhelming: pink and lilac towel sets and shower curtains, mirror frames harmonized with floor tiles, while the gleaming chrome fixtures looked large enough to start world wars.

There were no poky spaces anywhere, none of the let's-put-that-there-for-the-time-being approach that had governed the evolution of so much of the space in her own home – the blue wardrobe that didn't quite allow the spare-room door to open properly, or the umbrella stand that lived in the music room because of the narrowness of the hall, or the boxes of LPs that had somehow become a support-stand for four mud-encrusted pairs of wellingtons in the cupboard under the stairs.

But it was the Stapletons' main bedroom that depressed Sophie the most – this time for *not* being like a hotel. Three times the size of the others, it was decorated in soft blues and gold, with a miniature *chaise-longue*, upholstered in velvet, parked along the bottom of the widest bed Sophie had ever seen. Covering the bed itself was an exquisitely embroidered Oriental silk spread and two cream taffeta cushions balanced on top of the pillows, stitched, respectively, with the words *HIS* and *HERS*. It was laughably twee, of course, but what Sophie found hardest to bear was the unmistakable tenderness of the attention to detail, the atmosphere of loving care, of a space devoted to restfulness and intimacy.

They were newly-weds, after all, she reminded herself, putting her bag down and perching on the edge of the bedspread. A moment later she sprang guiltily to her feet, feeling like a trespasser – a *voyeuristic* trespasser – as images of the Stapletons locked in limb-knotted acts of mutual pleasuring invaded her mind, inspired by what was obviously a wedding photo, pinned above the head-board: William so tall and angular, Beth so slim and petite, the pair of them tossing their heads back in a mist of confetti. And suddenly the room was spinning, firing pricks of light into the corners of Sophie's eyes. She leant against the wall, wondering if dizziness was to be a new symptom of her nameless malaise or whether, more probably, she had got up too quickly and was just hot and overtired. Once the world had steadied, she slowly made her way into the sumptuous en-suite and held her face under the blast of the basin's colossal cold tap, letting the water bounce out of her mouth and splash up to the edges of her hair.

Downstairs, meanwhile, Andrew had unleashed the afternoon light into the house, searched in vain for an air-conditioning panel and begun riffling through a stack of instructions, composed in what he now recognized – from the bundle that had been left for them in the glove compartment of the Lincoln – as the sloping, smooth handwriting of Beth Stapleton. There was a whole page for the cat.

*Dido loves to be stroked! She would also like a groom from time to time as she has trouble getting all the tangles out for herself. Her brushes are in the wicker box at the bottom of the tall cupboard next to the fridge. Pick a time when she is sleepy – first thing in the morning – or after she has eaten when she will be self-cleaning anyway and therefore in full grooming mode! She likes to eat twice a day: breakfast, which is two scoops of Kitty-Flakes and a saucer of milk, and supper (usually around 6 p.m.) when she will have one of the pouches of food (store cupboard next to the freezer) and some water. (I don't like to give her too much milk as, although all cats are famous for loving it, it is apparently real bad for their digestive tract.) If you could shake out the woollens on her bed (under the TV in the kitchen) from time to time I would so appreciate that too, as with her long coat they do get badly furred up. If you have any concerns, please don't hesitate to give us a call. Dido says a big THANKS!*

*PS The number of our vet in Stamford is on the list of emergency contacts.*

*PPS There is a cat-door, but as you will see, Dido only goes out when she absolutely has to! (Years of living in an apartment, I guess.)*

Underneath the sign-off there was a smiley face, sprouting feline whiskers and two pointy ears.

Hearing Sophie's steps in the hall, Andrew hastily shuffled the piece of paper to the bottom of the pile and continued exploring the kitchen, a magnificent geometric jigsaw of limed-oak cabinets, gadgets and slabs of glittering black marble. An oval island of a worktop-cum-breakfast-bar with two tall stools sat in the middle of this splendour, but there was also a dining table, positioned between large glass doors overlooking the garden, and a fridge the size of a small car.

Andrew strolled over to the doors and peered outside, pressing the edge of one hand on the pane as a visor against the blinding brilliance of the sun. The *yard*, was how William Stapleton had referred to it in his email, summoning for Andrew images of dusty concrete fringed with scrub. But what presented itself through the window was a well-tended rolling, irregular-shaped lawn, dotted with the heads of sprinklers and beds of flowers. The grass petered out after some fifty yards, giving way to the tall, verdant trees that seemed to smother every acre of Connecticut not otherwise occupied by a road or a building. Although there was water too, Andrew re-membered, peering harder at a distant silvery glimmer and recalling mention of some kind of pond.

'There's a piano, did you see?' said Sophie, appearing in the doorway. She was barefoot and wearing a T-shirt and shorts, both visibly crumpled from their sojourn in a suitcase. Her long blonde hair was in its usual loosely clasped ponytail, although the shorter strands at the sides had broken free and were dangling round her ears. 'In a room next to the study. The girls might be glad of that. And you, of course.'

'Possibly.' Andrew tugged open one side of the fridge. 'This thing's full of beer, do you want one?'

Sophie shook her head.

Andrew took out a bottle for himself, exclaiming in delight at the bottle-top remover handily set into the fridge door. 'God, the Americans certainly know how to do things, don't they?' He slumped into a chair, pressing the cool glass of the bottle to his forehead. 'I can't find where to turn the air-con on.'

'We should go shopping probably.'

'Or we could have a walk-about. The pond-lake thing appears to be over there.' He gestured at the glass doors with his bottle. 'Through the trees. What are all these bloody trees, anyway? Birches? Beeches?'

'Maples, I think. But we don't know when the shops shut.' Sophie could feel strands of hair sticking to her cheeks where the water had dried. She felt gritty-eyed, dogged, exhausted.

'We could eat out. They've recommended loads of places – they're on one of that woman's endless lists, numbers, addresses, types of food . . . I tell you, she is scarily thorough.' Andrew rolled his eyes, enjoying the lovely feel of the beer snaking down inside, slaking his thirst, lifting his mood.

'But we'll need stuff for breakfast anyway. And I'm not sure it's a good idea to go out on the first night when we're so tired – and bound to get lost trying to find our way back in the dark.'

Andrew swivelled his head to look at her, his blue eyes dark. 'Do you remember what I said about *trying* to have a good time? Do you remember that, Soph? *Chilling out,* maybe?' He took two more bottles from the fridge and held one out to her, but she shook her head, confessing in a small voice that she would prefer a cup of tea.

'Well, there's no milk, so I guess we'll *have* to go shopping, won't we?' Andrew kicked the fridge door shut and flopped back into his chair. 'If I might be allowed to relax with a drink first?' He ran a hand through his hair, feeling its lankness in the heat. As the silence between them thickened, he squinted, with feigned interest now, in the direction of the garden, reduced to a blur of white and green in the unrelenting slant of the afternoon sun. It occurred to him in the same instant just what an ordeal these temperatures would be: sun cream and his own sweat – the awful sticky mess of it, for four weeks, every time he set foot outside the door.

Sophie watched him down the second beer, weighing up what she could manage, what she still had the energy to care about. In England it would be ten o'clock at night – teeth-cleaning and lights out – the bliss of sleep. 'I don't mind driving if you're tired. It would be good practice – get me used to the wrong side of the road. I saw there's another smaller car in the garage, but we're not insured for that, are we?'

'Nope, just the Lincoln.'

Sophie was aware of her hot feet squeaking as she crossed the tiled floor to the stack of information next to the phone. 'Was there anything in this lot about a supermarket?' Glancing up, she spotted a dial on the wall and turned it towards an image resembling a snowflake.

A quiet whirring started up at once, bringing with it an instant and delicious coolness, a stroking of invisible icy gossamer that seemed to float down from the ceiling.

Andrew threw back his head with a groan. 'Sophie, you angel, you clever angel.' He leapt from his chair and slipped his arms round her waist. 'I'm insufferable in the heat, aren't I?'

'Yes,' Sophie whispered, wishing she could engage with something beyond the sweet beery smell of his breath and the familiar acidity of his sweat. He was being *nice*, he *was* nice. 'Always,' she added, in a bid to sound playful, leaning back into him in a show of the desire for which she knew he so yearned. 'For a big shop we need to go to Stamford.'

She could feel him shrink, not just physically – in the swift release of his light hold on her waist, in the audible clamp of his jaw – but inside too, some soft part of him closing in a reflex against hurt. It was her fault, of course. It was always her fault, these days. She could no longer *feel* the right things, the things that had once made life so effortlessly sweet. How could an illness do that? she wondered despairingly. How could it alter *feelings*?

'The shopping . . . indeed . . .' Andrew muttered bitterly. 'Heaven forbid we should forget the shopping. But nothing big today – we'll find somewhere local. Now, where did I put the car keys?' He patted his pockets, pulling out his phone, which promptly started ringing.

'Geoff!' He swung away from Sophie, tipping his head back and flexing his legs in an involuntary display of delight. 'Yes, mate . . . bloody fantastic.' He flicked his eyes at Sophie. 'We can't believe it – total bloody luxury. What the poor sods are going to make of our place I can only imagine . . . Yes, yes, I know, it does fit the bill exactly, so hopefully they won't be suing for compensation . . . Of course . . . We'd love to meet up but need a few days to settle in . . . Yup . . . Friday? Hang on.' He held the mobile away from his ear and cocked his head at Sophie, his eyes fierce with the challenge of daring her to refuse.

Sophie managed a smile and a nod before quickly turning away to let the inevitable darker reactions flood in. Geoff and Ann: not seen by her since Andrew's thirtieth, jolly, energetic, *Americanized* – just to think of it made her feel faint. Behind her Andrew was still talking, sounding now so jolly and energized that it occurred to Sophie that if she had any residue of love for the man she should probably leave him. Yes, she should leave. Better that than become a millstone of misery, whittling away whatever feelings he had left for her in the process. The girls were so much closer to him, these days, anyway, with their music, and being wary of her, so out of sorts. She had been putting on as good a show as she could, but it was hard, what with the tiredness and having given up her job and the sometimes public harshness of Andrew's impatience.

*Leave Andrew.* Poised now with pen and paper – torn off a block next to the phone – in preparation to compose a list for the supermarket, Sophie almost wrote the two words down. It took some concentration to write *teabags* instead, followed, after some consideration, by *milk*.

'Good start,' Andrew quipped, peering over her shoulder, all his good humour restored by the phone conversation. 'They're going to meet us at Grand Central Station next Friday, for lunch, seeing the sights and so on?' He turned the sentence into a question, so Sophie nodded, trying to mirror his enthusiasm. 'But right now, before we hit the "mall"' – he stretched the vowel, turning it American – 'I thought I might just take a look at that piano you found.' He trotted out of the kitchen, tossing his phone from hand to hand and whistling – some intricate classical tune, as it always was with Andrew; vibrato, perfectly pitched, a sign of total, self-absorbed contentment. It had been one of the earliest things to snag Sophie's heart.

William had declared his intention to sleep for as long his jet-lagged body desired, but Beth, determined to adjust as quickly as possible to the new time zone, had set her cell-phone alarm for seven so that she could go running, as she liked to do on most mornings back home. When the phone trilled, however, it was all she could do to summon the energy to turn it off. Her body and mind felt leaden, thanks to the patchiest of sleeps – initially not being tired enough and then not liking the spongy softness of the mattress, which seemed to suck her downwards rather than offering support. William, a famously efficient and deep sleeper, had been more than noticeably restless too, murmuring a response when she said his name in the small hours but not following it up with the physical comfort for which she had hoped.

Swinging her legs out of bed, Beth sat upright and rubbed her eyes. Through the Chapmans' loose-fitting bedroom curtains there was a promising segment of blue in the screen of grey cloud. She padded to the window for a better look, thinking, as she tweaked the faded fabric, how much fun it would be to take the entire cosy shambles of this borrowed home in hand and give it a thorough face-lift. Thinning carpets, washed-out furnishings, patches of limescale round every accoutrement connected to water – William, at the same time as offering reassurances, had been sweetly concerned that she might be disappointed – but Beth had seen at once the natural elegance of the place and pronounced herself enchanted. Original patterned floor tiles, high ceilings, cute cornices, sash windows: it was like stepping back in time, even if it was all crying out for the chance to shine as its Victorian creators had intended.

Beth dropped the curtain and picked up a blackened silver-framed photograph from among the ornaments crowding the chest of drawers. It contained a picture of the Chapman family – a strikingly beautiful picture – taken, by the look of it, at some classical ruins. The two girls and their parents were sitting on a wall against the backdrop of what appeared to be a Roman amphitheatre, the daughters bewitchingly thin in tiny shorts and strappy tops, one fair-haired, like the mother, the other with the soft, almost rusty hair and startled blue saucer eyes of her father. What a handsome group! And they were clearly having such a good time too – laughing, mouths wide, their heads tipped at different, unrehearsed angles, as if a good joke had been told a second before the click of the camera.

Behind her there was an audible rustle of bedclothes. 'What are you doing? It's the middle of the night, isn't it?'

'No, sweetie, it's morning, and I'm looking at this picture of the Chapmans – the kids, the parents, they're just too perfect.' Beth carefully positioned the photograph back where she had found it. 'Did you say he was a music teacher?'

'Head of the department and deputy head of the school. It's one of those famous old swanky places – far too pricy for my gang.' An arm, its hairs smooth and dark, appeared from among the bedclothes and patted the expanse of empty sheet on her side.

'Uh-huh.' Beth chuckled. 'No, honey, you're tempting, but I'm going to resist you and go for my jog. I thought I might try and find a route along the river. I guess there is one?' Receiving no reply, she set about trying to remember where she had stowed her exercise pants and trainers. It had been something of a challenge, unpacking – a couple of empty drawers here and there, one third of a rail and not many coat-hangers in the closet. 'Is there anything I should watch out for?' she murmured, kissing

William's ear a few minutes later. 'Any local dangers?'

'Only my sons,' quipped William, drowsily, 'but they're a couple of miles away and will be asleep for many hours yet . . . Hey, are you sure you have to go right now? There are other ways of staying fit, you know.' He tried to catch hold of her arm.

Beth dodged, playfully slapping the bedclothes. 'You are corrupting and terrible and I adore you. I'm taking my purse belt so I can buy fresh Danish if I see them. I'll do my usual forty minutes . . . unless I get lost,' she added happily, closing the door behind her.

'Be careful!' William called, raising his head and then dropping it back among the pillows with a groan. So early in the morning Beth would be lucky to find a newsagent open, let alone somewhere selling decent pastries. As always, her energy was remarkable. The last thing he felt like doing was jogging through the grime of London. Arriving via the drab solidity of the M4 traffic, the ugly concrete tower blocks and the murky brown of the Thames streaming under Kew Bridge, William had caught himself wishing Susan could either have stayed put in their marital home in Woking or moved deeper into the countryside. Her parents being in Richmond had been the rationale behind the decision (they had subsequently moved to Devon) – as well as decent schools – but it wasn't a part of the capital William knew well or for which he had ever felt much affinity.

During previous attempts to spend time with his

sons, using hotels and the spare bedrooms of friends, he had often given up on the whole miserable effort and scooped them into a hire-car for a spell up north with his own parents instead. The two elder ones complained vociferously, mainly at the prospect of their grandparents' tiny television, which managed a flickering rendition of the five terrestrial channels and then only if the weather was clear. Once they got there, however, they always seemed to enjoy themselves hugely, wolfing their grandmother's meals like the starving animals they were, accompanying their grandfather on fishing trips or setting up elaborate golf courses round the molehills and rabbit burrows that pitted the rough outer reaches of the garden.

His parents drove William mad in so many ways – opinions like stuck records, ancient, nonsensical, maddening domestic habits, distrust of technology and foreigners, scrimping when money wasn't, and never had been, tight – and yet as a pair of devoted, unquestioning grandparents their qualities were unsurpassed. Even George unfurled a little bit up there, sitting more obviously enthralled than the other two while his grandfather demonstrated the making of a certain fly, or sprawling happily on a riverbank as the four of them watched for water ripples round their lines.

The shrill ring of the bedside phone wrenched William back to full consciousness. Fearing for Beth – thinking suddenly of her purse belt, bulging with her freshly changed money, her open, trusting face, ready to love

41

everything British regardless of its worthiness – he was momentarily relieved to hear the harsh, girls'-boarding-school voice of his ex-wife instead.

'I tried your mobile but it was off. Thank goodness you gave me this number too.'

'Hello, Susan. This is a bit early, even for you.'

'Crisis.'

'Oh, God, what?' William sat up so fast he cricked his neck and then compounded the injury by letting his head thwack back against the bare wall, occupying the space where he was more used to finding a cushioned headboard.

'George got a call late last night asking if he can play cricket in Weybridge this afternoon, filling in for someone with a groin strain or something, because, as you know, or if you don't you *ought* to, he didn't get through the club trials in spite of playing his heart out – he's really good this year and *should* have been selected – but anyway, because of that his first reaction was to say no, but of course that would have been entirely the *wrong* response . . .'

William rubbed his sore neck while Susan talked, trying to rejoice in the fact that he was no longer married to her and might, one day, not many years hence, be able to dispense with the need to correspond with her at all. Except, of course, for the occasional big event, like weddings, funerals, christenings, degree ceremonies . . . His thoughts drifted, conjuring an image of Susan in one of the dreadful hats made by the friend on the Isle of Wight, and Harry goofing round in a gown and mortar board . . .

'William, have you been listening?'

'How could I not?' William replied drily. 'I'm either to drive to Weybridge or to take charge of Alfie. Harry has been poorly but is feeling better now. All three are to come and stay from tomorrow instead of the day after and for as long as I want because you have a mountain of orders to get through and want to go to the Isle of Wight to visit Corinne, who has just had the all-clear on her chemo.'

'There's no need to use that tone of voice . . . as if it's all some massive *chore*, as if . . . '

Again, William let her talk, trying to rise above the urge to get angry. She needed to let off steam. She had, after all, done so much of the parenting alone. He – as she never missed an opportunity to remind him – had been a brute. No one, least of all Susan, seemed prepared to acknowledge that he had been through a lot too. The divorce had been ghoulishly painful but *necessary*; it had taken courage to force that into the open, to see it through. Angling for the transfer to New York might have been selfish, but by the time he had agreed to all Susan's terms for divorce, the extra money had been badly needed. And for the whole three years he had done his level best to make up for the distance, fighting tooth and nail round Susan's endless plans and change of plans, all the subtle scuppering tactics to make things more difficult – to make him feel worse than he did already.

'I miss them,' William cut in, when she was still mid-flow. 'Every day, I miss them. The only reason I have not been on my knees begging to have them under this roof for every minute of my entire four-week stay is for fear that *they* might not want it. Okay? Got that? Now, tell me where this cricket match is, and I'll solve the problem of Alfie by taking him with me.'

Beth cast a last look back at the house as she jogged away, thinking that the line of sturdy red-brick houses looked fine enough but that she had done her time of living next to and on top of other members of the human race. When she had been growing up in Baltimore, their apartment had been shabby and small, with walls thin enough to crumple under a fist-punch. Four years at Georgetown followed by a working life in New York had seen considerable improvements on the accommodation front, but never in Beth's life had she been happier than she was now, with William in the spacious rural splendour of Connecticut.

And London streets were so narrow, she noticed, reducing her jog to a brisk walk as she dodged a solid line of vehicles parked half up on the pavement, bumper to bumper, all sporting the special resident's permit stickers that Andrew Chapman had told William about and William had told her. Except that she hadn't really listened, since driving *per se* was an activity she planned entirely to avoid. Handling a stick-shift, navigating alien one-way systems, congestion charges, indecipherable parking regulations – how would that be a holiday?

Beth turned left out of their street towards the main road and the river, which she knew – from having taken the precaution of checking William's collapsing, yellowed *A–Z* before setting off – lay just beyond. She had the image of the page firmly imprinted on her mind – she was good like that, able to retain pictures and facts for the length of time that they were to be immediately useful. William, in contrast, could remember all sorts of random interesting data effortlessly, like dates of battles and who was president of where and which year a certain vineyard in France had produced a certain wine. Beth loved it that he was so smart, but liked it even more that there was never any smugness about these extra files of knowledge. It added to the joy of having escaped Dimitri, who had taken great delight – sometimes publicly – in probing the chasms in her general knowledge.

It wasn't until Beth had found her way down to the riverside that she began to run properly, looking for the rhythm she knew she would need if she was going to complete the course she had set herself – crossing to the north side at Hammersmith Bridge and then coming back south over Barnes Bridge, which looked like it served trains as well as people. The route was pretty smooth, of compacted mud and empty, apart from the occasional dog-walker and cyclist. Perfect conditions, Beth chivvied herself, as a sharp pain stabbed through her left knee.

Beside her the river darkened as the last patch of blue sky slid from view. A brisk wind was coming off it, thick with the possibility of rain, driving her hair at annoying angles across her face. With the tightness in her left leg worsening, Beth found herself contemplating the sore truth of never having been a natural athlete, of having knees that angled ever so slightly inwards, and hips a tad too wide for her petite frame and a rear-end that – given a glimmer of a chance – sucked up calories like some guzzling incubus. She ran so she could eat and drink things that gave her pleasure, she reminded herself, things like croissants and cheesecake and cookies and William's prized stock of fine wine. She ran so she was never again to be the kid who, through her early teenage years, didn't get picked for anything by anybody except pitying teachers; the kid whose stomach rolls had sat like stacked doughnuts between her hips and chest, prompting frequent, unsubtle eye-rolls of despair from her mother, ruining attempts to wear prom gowns and – worst of all – provoking teasing, painful stomach pinches from her uncle Hal, whose weekend visit for her thirteenth birthday had stretched to an interminable four years.

Oh, yes, she had big reasons to run. Picking up her pace, Beth was rewarded by the knee pain and all the accompanying negativity segueing to a sudden un-expected euphoria – a sense of such *rightness* about her place in the world, on the windy London riverbank, with her hair stinging her eyes, and the map in her head and the tumbledown, homey house to return to, and William, sleepy, unshaven, loving, waiting for her, that it was all she could do not to shout her joy to the gun-metal skies. Instead she grinned at an approaching fellow jogger, an old guy with bandy legs and half-steamed glasses, who managed a brusque British nod in return.

Beth shifted her attention to the river. A pencil of a boat was slicing its way down the middle, its eight occupants labouring with such visible rhythmic fluidity that she found herself increasing her pace still further, out of some dim quest for emulation. The rowers were young and muscled, impossible to copy, of course – but thirty-eight wasn't so old, Beth reasoned cheerfully, not these days, not for her. At the same age her mother had already been in freefall (widowed, propped by bourbon and pills and the dreadful Hal), whereas her own was just taking off.

And there was Hammersmith Bridge already – a fine piece of architecture, but also such a neat staple of a thing compared to the bridges back home that Beth felt a wonderful burst of certainty that London would be easy to conquer, easy to love, that it would lay itself open for her much as William had in the coffee shop nearly two years before. '*Go, girl,*' she breathed, feeling beautiful as she always did when she ran her hardest, when the calories were flying off, and her knock-knees pumping so hard she could almost believe they were straight.

# 3

Standing on the main concourse of Grand Central Station that Friday, Sophie wanted, more than anything, to be alone – not away from the crowds, she liked the crowds, but from Andrew, who had a finger in one ear and his mobile pressed to the other in the hope of locating Geoff. They had only been off the train for a minute or two and Sophie was pretty sure she had already glimpsed the proposed rendezvous spot, a central kiosk crowned with a large brass clock, in snapshots between the hurrying travellers. But Andrew was panicking, just as he had on day one when he hadn't understood the supermarket checkout girl's question about 'paper or plastic', and on day two when they had got lost during a quest to find the country club that was supposed to have a swimming-pool and, that morning, when the cat hadn't shown up for breakfast.

America was making Andrew edgy, Sophie mused, which was a shame, of course, but also something of a relief for her, since it removed the sense of being solely responsible for his disappointments. She moved a little away from him and tipped her head back to admire again the vast cathedral curves of the station's interior: the light alone was transfixing, pouring in through the giant arched, barred windows and streaming off the rows of electric bulbs studding the moulding along the tops of the pillars and walls. It elevated every detail – the soft brown stone, the balustrades along the end staircases and balconies – to the matchless elegance of a colossal ballroom. It had never occurred to Sophie that she would *like* anything on the holiday, (except perhaps the arrival – in eighteen and a half days' time – of her daughters). And yet here it was, a swell of pleasure – and with Andrew making irritating faces at her (now that he had spotted the central kiosk), not to mention the prospect of Ann and Geoff, hale and hearty, in charge of their afternoon.

'Sophie!' His voice throbbed with irritation.

Sophie nodded but hung back for a moment more, not to annoy, as her husband assumed, or because of the arresting spectacle of the station, but simply to relish a final few seconds of being motionless within such a hubbub – the pinprick of stillness within a storm.

Geoff's once thick mop of hair was so closely shaven and bristled with grey that without Andrew falling – in a most un-Andrew-like way – into his arms, Sophie wasn't certain she would have recognized him. She had forgotten how short he was, five eight at the most to Andrew's six two, yet he seemed somehow the stronger presence with his tanned, muscled forearms and calves gleaming like polished wood against the bright yellow of his Ralph Lauren shirt and smartly pressed blue shorts. He exuded an almost tangible aura of self-assurance; a man, clearly, in the prime of his life, with money in his pocket and dominion over his own happiness – a dominion of which Sophie had no recollection during his London years as a jobbing musician.

Ann had changed less, with her auburn hair cut into the same bobbed style she had favoured since her twenties and the heavily made-up face, designed, Sophie had always suspected, to draw attention away from the thick, matronly figure. Yet that suited her now, Sophie realized, as if her late forties were precisely the era Ann's body had been waiting for to come into its own; rounded, strong, *statuesque*. A latecomer to their penurious, post-university group, several years older, fussing and bossy with Geoff, Ann had always been more tolerated than welcomed by his close friends. But there was no denying how well the pair of them looked now, how *aligned*, with their identically confident sweeping embraces and the merry finishing of each other's sentences as they gushed about plans for the visit.

'We thought Ground Zero – you *have* to see Ground Zero – although it's fast disappearing under fresh concrete –'

'And MOMA –'

'And lunch. We know this heavenly Italian place at Thompson and Bleecker –'

'Although the museum restaurant is *excellent*.'

'Moma?' echoed Sophie, as Ann fell into step beside her and the men strode on ahead.

'Museum of Modern Art.'

'Oh, yes, of course.' After the cool of the station the

swamp temperatures of the street were a shock. Belting out of the pavements, shimmering between the sheer towering walls of stone and glass, the heat seemed literally to thicken the air. Even the dense indigo of the sky, visible in geometric shapes above the tops of the buildings, felt part of a conspiracy of compression, like a layer sealing the city in rather than a portal to a wider world. Sophie groped in her bag for her sunglasses, while Andrew hurriedly pulled out the peaked cap he had bought in Naples the year before – dark blue, emblazoned with the words *Ciao Baby*, much to the amusement of his daughters. After only a few steps Sophie could feel the perspiration inching its way down her ribcage, seeping out from her armpits, her bra strap, the top of her neck, up under the hot bundle of her hair. Peering over her sunglasses, she felt a pulse of empathy for Andrew, whose brown shirt was breaking out in dark dots of perspiration, like the surfacing of a sinister rash.

'Isn't it a furnace?' yelped Ann. 'I should think William and Beth were delighted to escape to good old England – wet, as usual, so our daughter informs us. She's there visiting friends from her Cambridge days. You know she went to Geoff's old college, don't you? Third generation, Geoff was so thrilled. She's at Harvard now – a postgrad in biochemistry, of all things. We don't know where she gets it, but it's just wonderful having her down the road.'

'Harvard ... golly ... fantastic ...' Sophie murmured, struggling to picture the petulant baby and toddler, responsible for ruining so many of their early social gatherings, as a grown woman with an intellect.

The further they walked, the more Sophie could feel herself getting used to the heat – surrendering to it – just as she had on an exploratory stroll to the lake the afternoon before. While Andrew had slapped at insects and hopped between patches of shade as if they were stepping stones, Sophie had walked with deliberate, contrasting steadiness in as straight a line as the trees and brambles would allow, keeping her eyes half closed and moving much as she might have swum across the mill-pond stillness of the water ahead of them – slowly, but with strength, giving in to the element that embraced her.

'And your daughters are well?'

'Oh, yes . . . Milly, Olivia. They're joining us in just under three weeks . . . I can't wait.' Sophie felt her throat swell. There had been a text from Olivia that morning:

Glad hse cool. All good here. 200 at concert
last night. Awesome! M sends x

A few moments later, under Geoff's direction, the four of them were wedged into a yellow cab, trying to keep their damp, slippery limbs to themselves while warm air blasted through the windows, opened wide to compensate for the vehicle's lack of air-conditioning. It had been decided that they would take a drive-by tour of Ground Zero and then have lunch. As the taxi lurched its way downtown – an endless stop-start straight line of cross-roads and traffic lights – Andrew, much to Sophie's relief, seemed happy to take charge of the conversation, fielding enquiries about the girls and their music before turning to the indisputable glories of their holiday home. 'It was a genius plan of yours, Geoff, thank you so much for suggesting it.'

'Only too glad to oblige,' Geoff barked, performing a mock salute. 'But I must correct you about one thing: Darien is pronounced Dairy-Ann – unlike its namesake in Central America. It's petty but the locals care about that stuff.'

'Like the way you say my name – *Ann*,' chirruped Ann, waving her red-taloned nails out of the window and exclaiming in the same bright tone, 'Oh, look, here we are. This is it. Zero as in *Ground*.'

Sophie sensed Andrew repressing an urge to catch her eye as they both peered gingerly – dutifully – out of the cab window. Ann was terrible – they were united in that at least. Cranes, keep-out signs, men in hard hats, the hum of machinery – for a moment it seemed no more than a massive building site, like the ones that appeared to have taken up permanent residence at Scotch Corner or Waterloo Bridge. It took a few moments for the other, older, images to filter through – the Hollywood clarity of the TV coverage, the grainier shots of falling bodies.

'I always think it's like a tooth has been pulled out,' exclaimed Geoff, in the same cheery tone as his wife, 'such a clean extraction. I mean, look at all those other skyscrapers – functional, untouched. You've got to admire the precision of the destruction.'

*The precision of the destruction* . . . Sophie tried to hold on to the phrase. It seemed such a terrible thing to say. And yet within a moment her thoughts had slipped to the sheer, tediously self-centred business of being unhappy. She was at a place where thousands had died – *thousands* – and all she could manage was self-pity. It was laughable, disgusting. She glanced across the taxi at Andrew. No wonder he was visibly close to giving up on her. No bloody wonder.

'We were so sorry, Sophie,' Ann said softly, once they were settled in the much-praised Italian restaurant and their husbands lost to a conversation about mutual friends, 'to hear that you have been unwell.'

'Unwell?' Sophie carefully returned her full spoon of fish and sauce to its bowl.

'It's all right. You don't want to talk about it and I totally respect that. A friend of mine had ME . . .' Ann paused to twirl a heap of pasta threads round the prongs of her fork '. . . and it lasted for *years*. Not enough energy even to watch telly, let alone run a house . . . She never did go back to work. Though she is much better now,' she added hastily, 'totally *normal*, just as I'm sure you will be after this lovely holiday Andrew has arranged for you.' She crinkled her forehead in sympathy, misinterpreting Sophie's lack of response as a licence to go further. 'I just want you to know that Geoff and I are totally here for you, okay? Anything we can do – absolutely anything – you have only to ask.'

Sophie responded by excusing herself and sprinting to the Ladies, where she leant against the locked door breathing so fast that pins and needles pricked her fingers. That Andrew had said anything, to Ann and Geoff of all people, felt like betrayal. Even her parents, resident for many years now in southern Portugal, knew only that she was taking time off work – a well-deserved break from the labour of trying to hammer a few literary facts into students on final ultimatums from despairing parents. The ignominy of being in some sort of nameless crisis was something she had imagined only she and Andrew shared. What else had he told them? Who else?

Restored with the energy of indignation, Sophie strode back to the table only to find her anger shrivelling under the inescapable realization that the three of them had been discussing her – the sudden silence, Andrew's sheepish avoidance of her gaze. It made her want to weep.

'We've been formulating a plan,' declared Geoff, attempting to cover the moment with a display of gallantry – leaping up to pull back her chair, topping up her glass, offering her another bread roll. 'The pair of you are going to stay the night in town with us, so we can take in a show and then head out to Green Hills, our country club, tomorrow. It's this side of Greenwich – a half-hour drive. We tend to go every weekend in the summer. There's a great pool where you ladies can sun yourselves while I introduce Andrew to the golf course and –'

'But we do not have our things.' Sophie spoke steadily, trying to contain her horror.

'Hey, that's no problem – we have spares of everything, and you girls can sort out some clothes, I'm sure. And if there are any toiletries you need, we can pick them up at the drug store. It just seems crazy posting the pair of you back on the train, with this heat and it being Saturday tomorrow and –'

'No.' Sophie fixed her gaze on her bowl of chowder, lumpy with uneaten seafood. 'No . . .' She could feel some of the resolve seeping back into her. She even managed a small, apologetic smile. 'As you know, I . . . I tire easily at the moment. But Andrew – he would love to, wouldn't you, darling? So, what I suggest – what I would prefer – is to make my way back to Connecticut this afternoon, after MOMA . . .' she smiled again, brilliantly, at Ann '. . . to which I am *so* looking forward, and let Andrew stay with you tonight and do the golf tomorrow, which he would *love*, wouldn't you, Andrew? That is what I would very much *like* to do,' she concluded firmly, 'if you all don't mind.' She placed a morsel of bread in her mouth and chewed slowly, while looks were exchanged and air inhaled.

When the protests came she was ready for them, reiterating that Andrew needed time on his own with his oldest friend and that she needed rest. 'And, of course, there's the cat,' she added, with all the slow relish of a poker player turning over a winning card. 'I would hate to think how the Stapletons would feel if we let Dido miss supper as well as breakfast.'

He really was uncannily like his father, Beth decided, admiring the rangy limbs and thick dark hair at the back of Harry's head as he scrambled out of the taxi in front of her. But still only a boy, she reminded herself, as he immediately wandered off, lost in communication with his cell, while she took charge of payment – of what seemed an exorbitant amount, given that they had spent much of this second taxi journey sitting in traffic so motionless it had made her almost nostalgic for New York.

'More time for seeing the sights,' Harry had urged, by way of persuading her to choose cabs over the subway once a bus had ferried them from Barnes to Hammersmith. And yet, when it came to putting names to those sights, her stepson had proved comically ill-equipped. By the time Beth had pointed out the Albert Hall as proof that what he had called St James's was more likely to be Hyde Park, he was hunched against the window, visibly disconcerted.

He had no difficulty identifying Harrods, though, which had been their first port of call and one of the promised objectives of the day – even if his lassitude upon entering the place had quickly persuaded Beth to defer exploring its wonders properly until a second visit, either with William or on her own.

Her priority that morning was Harry, she reminded herself, hurrying to catch him up once the taxi had edged back into the traffic. 'So here we are . . . the King's Road . . . What exactly was it you needed to buy?'

'Er . . . shoes.'

'Shoes . . . okay . . .' Beth glanced up and down what seemed to her to be the most uninspiring of streets, given all Harry's excited chatter about celebrities. 'What kind of shoes?'

'Trainers?' Harry offered, but without conviction, rechecking his phone. 'But,' he went on, with a charm that reminded Beth again of his father, 'I'm sure you would like to go window shopping and stuff, so maybe we should split for a bit and meet up at Sloane Square.'

'Sloane Square . . . and where would that be?'

'That way – we came through it just now. It's got trees in the middle, and this big shop called Peter Jones right on the corner – like Harrods but a bit smaller. I could meet you outside the main entrance in, say, an hour?'

Beth smiled, shaking her head in a manner designed to mask the faint hurt that he should prefer time alone to being with her. 'Are you okay for money?'

Harry looked momentarily uncertain and then joyful as she produced two crisp twenty-pound notes. 'Don't tell your father, okay? We wouldn't want him to think I was *spoiling* you, now, would we? That's to help you buy some really cool sneakers. I'll see you outside this Peter Jones place in one hour exactly. Is that a deal?'

'Totally – brilliant. Thanks.'

As Harry took off into the crowds of shoppers, Beth allowed herself a moment of private congratulation. Who said bribery didn't work? She wanted the kid to like her and she had bought some time for herself – much-needed time, given the shape the week had taken. She had yet to see a single one of the cultural sights on her hit list. This was partly because managing everyday basics in these unfamiliar surroundings – shopping, cooking, laundry – was proving alarmingly time-consuming, and partly because there had been numerous extra chores to cope with, like getting sets of house keys cut for the boys, contacting the helpline when Sky crashed, not to mention enduring a couple of practice driving sessions in the Volvo, since William insisted it was mad to be reliant on the vagaries of public transport when they had the use of a car. As a result, the first nine days of the holiday had slipped by at extraordinary speed, exposing in the process the naïvety of her original hope of remaining on the fringes of the logistics of her husband's interaction with his sons. For the purposes of the trip at least, she was in the thick of it, whether she liked it or not.

And, to her surprise, Beth did quite like it – so far – in bursts. Knowing it was only for a few weeks helped enormously, as did the scruffy comforts of the house – the large deep-cushioned furniture, the unfussy bathrooms, which lent themselves perfectly to three lounging teenagers, content to graze for hours between the sofa and the fridge, clad only in boxers and T-shirts until commanded otherwise by their father. Beth let William do the commanding. She stuck to the role of half-involved spectator, enjoying the temporary business of playing at family life, especially under the watchful gazes of the oh-so-perfect Chapmans, whose blue eyes peered out of photographs in every niche of the house.

But keeping her own needs on hold had its limits, as Beth had realized the night before, when a pleasant – if noisy – evening of TV and take-out had been interrupted by a dictatorial phone call from Susan, announcing yet more cricket for George the following day (a twenty-twenty tournament, whatever that was) and a paint-balling party for Alfie two hours out of town. Beth had listened with mounting frustration and disbelief as William acceded, waiting in vain for him to point out that the five of them had already made plans to spend the day going down the Thames by boat, taking in both Tate galleries and Greenwich, as her guidebook recommended. The improbable notion of her and Harry spending the day as shopping companions had arisen out of the rubble of these dashed hopes, agreed to by both out of a tacit mutual desire not to upset William, who had been noticeably mute and edgy by the end of the call.

'I thought the boys were with *you* now,' Beth had ventured, once they were safely in their bedroom with the elder two sworn to quietness in front of a late movie and Alfie asleep along the corridor. 'I mean, just to phone like that and switch everything around ... I just don't think it's acceptable.'

William, sitting on the edge of the bed tugging off his socks, had nodded balefully, muttering, 'That's Susan for you', before going on to talk with a little more of his customary exuberance about how thrilling it was to have George – at last – doing better at something than his elder brother, even if it was only cricket, and how, (relaxing now, into affectionate chuckles), no one's life would have been worth living if Alfie had discovered he'd missed a paint-balling party.

'But now you're going to spend the whole day in Hambringham!' Beth had exclaimed, the injustice bursting out of her.

'Hambledon.'

'Whatever . . . '

'Look, Beth, I'm sorry it's like this – all a bit chaotic. Things will quieten, I promise – especially during our spell up north. We'll have loads of time to ourselves then.'

'It's just that I'm starting to feel kind of *deprived* of you,' Beth had confessed, pressing her anger away. 'Cricket, parties . . . they are kind of demanding, you've got to admit . . .' She stepped over the discarded socks and knelt in front of him. 'Alfie in your lap all evening – that's my place, baby . . .' she added softly, feeling with her fingers for the buckle on his belt.

William released exactly the sort of sigh she had been hoping for and bent to kiss her hair, tucked in its usual silky-smooth neatness behind her ears. 'Silly,' he growled, sighing again, more heavily this time, as the belt slid free and dropped to the floor.

'Dad . . .'

They were on their feet in an instant, William so hastily that his elbow caught Beth in the ribs, knocking her sideways. 'Hey, big man, what's up?'

Alfie rubbed his eyes, which looked wider and paler without the habitual protection of his glasses. 'I was in bed but in my clothes . . . ?'

'Yeah, because you fell asleep on the sofa and I didn't want to wake you . . . In fact, I think you still are asleep. Come on, mate.'

William had shot Beth a rueful look as he steered his son back out into the hallway and she had done her very best to look rueful back – as opposed to pissed, which was how she felt, in spite of knowing that such a reaction was graceless and altogether beneath her. She was thirty-eight, for God's sake, married to a man who not only loved her but who, according to his own selection of heartbreakingly moving marital vows, *worshipped* her, body and soul. She had *saved* him, William had said then and on a few precious occasions since. She had given him his life back. So to feel even partially sidelined by his thirteen-year-old son was plainly dumb, especially since the kid was so pitifully clinging and babyish, with a voice still several pitches higher than her own, and a need to clamber onto his father's lap and be tucked up like a toddler. When she was thirteen, Beth had reflected bitterly, she couldn't wait for the night-time seclusion of her bedroom, the safety of being in her nightgown without scrutiny, away from the tipsy lovingness that came when that evening's bottle of bourbon was almost gone.

Annoyed with herself, anxious as always not to dwell on any aspect of her unsatisfactory upbringing, Beth had settled into bed to wait for William, quelling her bad mood by examining a dusty stack of books parked behind her bedside table. *Mozart, Man or Genius?*, Graham Greene, *A Life in Letters*, *The Beauties of the Baroque*, *A History of King's College, Cambridge*. So she slept on the husband's side, she had mused, experiencing a trace of unease at the weird intimacy of two couples occupying each other's beds and then being diverted by the thought of the musical Andrew Chapman possibly tinkling some life into her piano in Connecticut – an unused millstone of an heirloom that had received more attention from removals men over the years than it ever had from her. He would have some proper elbow room there too, Beth speculated smugly, unlike the cramped study-cum-music room off the hall downstairs, so stacked with boxes and music stands that she didn't know how he even picked his way through to the stool.

It was only later, after making love, that Beth realized the day's rearranged plans might well involve meeting Susan, who had said she would field Alfie and leave William to deal with George. Susan Stapleton, the ex, in the flesh at last. A restless night had followed, in spite of William's baffled, sleepy attempts at reassurance.

Beth paused in front of a window display, studying an attractive pyramid of strappy summer shoes. When did one really grow up? she wondered. When did all the childish stuff finally drop away? She had endured a lousy night, fighting ancient insecurities, and all for a blowsy, overweight woman with brittle over-bleached hair and a strident voice. With William upstairs and Alfie still half asleep over a bowl of cereal, Beth had been the one to open the door. *I can never like you*, had been her first and then recurring thought through the mutually polite, stiff greetings, the offers and rejections of refreshment, followed by a joint drawn-out quest to locate Alfie's sneakers.

The distinctive deep set of George's eyes came from their mother, Beth had observed, during the course of these trials, as did Alfie's Cupid's bow mouth and small nose. And she felt duty bound to acknowledge, privately, that Susan did a good job of disguising her ample figure with attractive loose-fitting layers of creamy silk and linen, which probably came from the organic-clothes business William had told her about – describing on one occasion the chaos of looms and wool and swatches that had gradually taken over the ground floor of the Woking home, ghoulishly underscoring the inner disintegration of their last few years.

The King's Road was okay, Beth decided, having succumbed to a pair of high-heeled yellow sandals in the shoe shop. She ambled next in the direction of the square Harry had indicated, wishing she had brought her guidebook so she could make better use of her time. For all she knew she was a stone's throw from the best gallery or monument in town; it seemed such a waste. Spotting the trees Harry had mentioned and with a good twenty minutes left until their rendezvous, she decided to give in to temptation for once and treat herself to a hot chocolate and a cookie. She needed warming up too, thickening cloud and a wind she hadn't anticipated having made her unbelievably – in spite of pants, sweater and jacket – *cold*.

A few minutes later a Starbucks obligingly appeared. Beth purchased her calorific treats and took a seat by the window, thinking how she could have been in New York, except for the weather, which, after nine solid days of squall and cloud, was starting not to feel like such a joke after all. During the time she had spent in the queue, fat dollops of rain had begun pouring from the heavy clouds, battering the pavement like bullets. Beth peered through her section of the window, feeling mild concern for Harry, who had neither a jacket nor an umbrella. No sooner had the thought formed than she glimpsed Harry himself, sauntering among the streams of hurrying shoppers, not only visibly wet, as she had feared, but with a cigarette in one hand and the other across the shoulders of a tall, bony girl with a half-shaved head, a bare midriff and tattoos snaking round her elbows and upper arms.

Beth got up from her chair and then sat down again. She should wait till they met up, she decided, see how Harry played it. Her thoughts flew to William, boasting of his health-conscious beloved eldest, even more of a star on the rugby pitch than he was in the classroom.

There had been something about a junior national swimming squad once too. Beth stared after her stepson as he disappeared into the sheets of rain, wondering also about her forty pounds. But the kid was nearly eighteen and the last thing she wanted was an ugly scene.

Beth finished every crumb of her cookie and then bought another, eating fast. Halfway out of the door, working at the release on her umbrella, she suddenly remembered the small bag of yellow shoes and ran back inside. Wet from the pavement, the soles of her loafers slid upon contact with the hard, polished floor, propelling her legs forwards while her body flailed behind. *Crap*, she thought, then said, out loud, as a lunge for the back of an empty chair to prevent the inevitable, only succeeded in bringing it down on top of her.

# 4

The golf course was a surreally perfect, sumptuous composition of undulating green velvet, pitted here and there with neatly scooped bunkers and small, variously shaped lakes, each a glassy reflection of the seamless azure sky. Even the patches of rough were carefully landscaped, comprising attractive clusters of tall, lean trees, manicured shrubbery and grass clearly nurtured into long lush carpets instead of having arrived in such a state by being left to grow as it pleased. Threaded through these splendours was a narrow sandy road designed for golf buggies, beaded at irregular intervals with rustic benches and vending machines, offering snacks as well as juice, Coke and water, all trussed up in wooden casings so as to blend in with the natural beauty of the surroundings.

Except none of it was natural, Andrew mused, blinking in disbelief as Geoff led the way out of the club house, his mind balking at what such a triumph of man over nature must cost to maintain, let alone build. It was beautiful, of course, but also – he couldn't help thinking, given the current global context of food, energy and water shortages – faintly obscene.

And it made him jealous of Geoff, which wasn't pleasant

either. Good old live-for-the-moment, saxophone-playing, beer-swilling, last-to-leave-a-party Geoff, who had somehow spent a decade and a half replacing these fondly remembered attributes with level-headedness, excellent business sense and the luck of the devil. Andrew was aware that his oldest friend had been doing well for himself, from Christmas-card comments, emailed photographs from the decks of boats and the balconies of skiing chalets, not to mention the immaculate cut of his clothes at the college gaudy he had attended a couple of years before; he had unsheathed his own fat post-prandial cigar and talked about the profits and pleasure of investing in modern art. Life was treating him handsomely, that much had been clear.

But exactly *how* handsomely had been a shock reserved for Andrew's arrival at Geoff and Ann's West Side apartment after they had seen Sophie back onto the train. On the fourteenth floor of an elegant greystone block that looked no different from its two neighbours, Andrew was totally unprepared for the open-plan, lofty-roofed grandeur that swung into view as Geoff pushed open the door: oil paintings spread across the walls, marbled floors, huge silk carpets, a long mahogany dining table with fourteen matching chairs (he counted), casually placed Oriental vases – as large as cellos some of them and probably ten times as valuable – and, most stunning of all, an L-shaped sitting room lined with soft tan leather furniture and views over Central Park.

'You like?' Geoff had pressed, grinning, as he placed a bottle of beer in Andrew's hands.

'You scumbag,' Andrew had murmured, shaking his head in wonderment, forgiving his friend's blatant smugness for the fact of it being so justified. 'It's out of this world.'

After a few more beers Ann had served a splendid meal, as good as in any restaurant, of tomatoes, mozzarella and fresh basil, followed by paunchy fillet steaks with creamy mashed potato and fried zucchini (as his hosts insisted on referring to the succulent breaded slivers of courgette). Geoff had opened one bottle of Montrachet and then a second. Andrew could not remember the last time he had enjoyed himself so much. And part of it, he knew – like some guilty secret – stemmed from the pleasure of being away from Sophie, away from the burden of her hideous low spirits and his helplessness in the face of them.

'Ready, pal?' Geoff slapped the empty seat of the golf buggy – an accoutrement that, in other circumstances, Andrew might have been tempted to dismiss as a laughable extravagance. In Connecticut in August in a heat-wave, however, it was walking the course that would clearly have been laughable. Already the blue polo shirt Geoff had lent him was clinging uncomfortably to his sweat-soaked chest, while the thin canvas of his Italian cap felt no match for the sun, which was pounding – although the day had barely started – with an intensity that made his ears throb.

'You know I'm rusty, don't you?' he warned. 'Not a stroke since nine holes at a Suffolk links two summers ago.'

'So you keep saying. Got any other excuses to add – like, say, a broken leg? Blindness? That can be impeding, so I'm told. I've offered you ten shots. Are you saying you want more?'

'I just don't want you to be disappointed . . . '

'Like hell . . . You're a bandit, Chapman, you always were. And those clubs you've hired are the dog's bollocks, so we'll see, shall we? And there's nothing like one of Ann's fry-ups to start the day, is there?'

Andrew responded with an appreciative pat to his stomach. The plate of sizzling egg, bacon and fried potatoes had been just the thing, not only for his appetite but for his head, which, with a malt following the Montrachet, had not been feeling too robust even before they had left the ice-box cool of the apartment.

At Geoff's invitation Andrew drove off at the first tee and managed what would have been an adequate strike had his hot hands not slipped on the grip, sending the ball woefully off course. After a few more similar misshots and the aggravation of thinly disguised chuckling from over his shoulder, Andrew ventured to enquire – with some venom – whether his companion's huge, zip-infested golf bag housed such a thing as a spare glove.

'Of course. Why didn't you ask before?' The item was duly handed over, along with a dry remark about poor workmen and their tools and various more-hesitant quips as Andrew, fired by irritation and his new non-stick palm, began to play well. It was like singing or playing an instrument, he decided, each ball soaring obediently at his touch, as he fell into the trance of performance, letting instinct override intellect, having the courage to fly blind. And not having Sophie, the millstone, that was helping too.

It took Geoff – visibly digging deeper into the recesses of his concentration with every hole, drawing, perhaps, on the hours of fine-tuning he had boasted of receiving from the club's resident golf pro – to the very last putt on the eighteenth before his friend was finally beaten. They shook hands, exhilarated with each other and themselves, Andrew relishing the fact not just of having played the best round of golf in his life but of being properly in touch at last with that holiday feeling – unwinding, having *fun*.

After a couple of beers they joined Ann at the pool and messed around like teenagers – ducking, diving and racing – until lunch, which they chose to eat under an air-conditioned awning adjoining the main restaurant. Andrew triggered much mirth by ordering shrimp, and then exclaiming in surprise when he was served not the modest dish of prawns he had expected but three sprawling clawed creatures the size of small lobsters. They drank a Chardonnay and then something Californian to go with desserts and a board of cheese. Interrogated about himself properly for the first time, Andrew talked expansively about the increase in distinguished musicians among the pupils since his time at the school, how he was putting several – including Olivia – forward for the RCM, how there weren't many schools capable of nailing the Brahms Requiem, let alone in one term. He even confessed to the stop-start composing, the promising violin and piano concerto in the bottom of his desk drawer, just waiting to be retackled and pushed to the finishing post, when he had the time, when Sophie was more herself.

Just saying her name broke the spell.

'Hey, she'll pick up.' Geoff patted Andrew's hand. '*Women* . . . it's probably a time-of-life thing, eh?' He rolled his eyes.

'Geoffrey, that's hardly appropriate. She's barely forty,' Ann scolded. 'What is she, Andrew, forty-three?'

'Forty-one.'

'There you are.' She made a face at Geoff. 'But she's not *right*, is she? You can see that a mile off,' she continued, returning her attention to Andrew, her plump face crumpling with sympathetic concern. 'And I can't help thinking, since you said they'd done tests for all the obvious things, that . . . well . . . she did have that sister with all those problems, didn't she? So maybe there's something that . . . you know . . . runs in the family.'

'Sophie's sister was deprived of oxygen at birth,' said Andrew, after a long moment, his voice strangled. Several men, probably, had fallen in love with Sophie Weston during the course of the Winchester festival, twenty years before: the uncertain smile, the mane of thick fair hair, cornflower-blue eyes, the curves of her long model legs in drainpipe jeans. But for Andrew it had been meeting the younger sister a few weeks later that had been the turning point. Wheelchair-bound, mute, saucer-eyed, with a skinny, lop-sided rag-doll of a body that needed to be shifted and propped up and turned – the first sight of Tamsin had triggered in him an avalanche of shamefully clichéd, pitying, knee-jerk responses. It was Sophie who had instantly transformed those reactions, then and for ever afterwards, launching into an effortless flow of sisterly chatter, and teasing, and gentle tending, allowing Tamsin to emerge, rather than the limitations of her circumstances. An enactment of love – there was no other way to describe it – so wonderful, so inspiring, that Andrew's certainty about making a proposal of marriage had blossomed directly out of it.

'And there's nothing *genetic* about oxygen deprivation, is there?' Andrew continued, painfully aware suddenly of the full force of all the alcohol he had consumed and the hot concrete burning through the soles of his shoes.

'No, Andrew, of course there isn't . . . I was only saying that I remembered there had been something *wrong* with her.'

'Tamsin . . . She was called Tamsin. She died ten years ago.' Andrew stopped, appalled to find that he was on the verge of tears, not for his dead sister-in-law, as his companions – exchanging anxious glances – supposed, but for the version of Sophie from those early years, the version he had lost.

'Andrew, I'm so sorry, that's terrible,' Ann flapped and folded her napkin, smoothing her fingers over the food-stains and imprints left by her pink lipstick. 'And I didn't mean . . . in fact, I . . . Excuse me.' She cast Geoff an imploring look and left the table in search of the Ladies.

Geoff responded by rushing off to seek out a waiter for the check, thereby giving Andrew time to collect himself. 'Ann meant no offence, as I'm sure you understand,' he said, squeezing Andrew's shoulder when he got back to the table. 'What you need is time out, mate, and I'm going to make damn sure you get it. Okay?'

Andrew nodded vehemently, still too overcome to speak, not just on account of his friend's kindness but the unsettling revelation of how thinly layered his self-composure had grown. He experienced in the same instant a burst of resentment at Sophie for allowing such a thing to happen. He needed caring for. He needed tenderness. Once upon a time she had known that. These days, she was too wrapped up in herself to care. Or maybe he was just drunk, Andrew reflected darkly, so nearly losing his balance as he stood up that he took very small, careful steps behind Geoff for the walk back to the pool.

For the first time since arriving Sophie awoke fully cognizant of the fact that the blurry fall of the tall blue curtains opposite her, their outline burnt with electric precision by the early-morning sun, was real, rather than the lingering image of some strange dream. She was in Connecticut, not Barnes. And she was alone. As this last thought registered, she rolled onto her back and stretched her arms and legs into a star-shape of luxuriating celebration, before closing her eyes and falling instantly back to sleep.

It was the heat that woke her next (unlike Andrew, she preferred nights without the background hum of air-conditioning), coupled with the pleasurable guilt of the truant. She had got away from Geoff and Ann! She had seen it through, stayed strong in the face of the numerous pleadings and counter-arguments that had pitted the afternoon. Would she manage the train ride? Or the drive from Darien station? Or the sticky lock on the front door? Wouldn't she mind being alone? At times, Sophie had been close to caving in because she *had* been nervous, of course, especially of navigating her way back to the house in the tank-sized automatic car, with the roads all looking the same, the names of areas and streets either non-existent or dangling in unexpected places.

Having successfully negotiated all such obstacles, however, Sophie had found herself in a state of near-joy. She was in a bubble of time in which nothing mattered, she had realized, closing the front door and leaning against it with a sigh. *Nothing*. Kicking off her shoes, unzipping her skirt, peeling off her shirt, she had floated around the house in her bra and pants, swinging her arms, even singing a little – normally an unheard-of indulgence, thanks to her being in possession of a voice that, compared to the rest of her talented family, was woefully thin and off-key.

For supper she had crumbled several chocolate-chip cookies into a half-eaten tub of vanilla ice cream, poured herself a glass of white wine and stretched out on the sofa in front of the Stapletons' large plasma TV. She had watched the movie channel – half of one film about a haunted house and then half of another about a high-powered career woman having a baby. She had eaten directly from the ice-cream tub, using a long spoon, letting each mouthful melt on her tongue before swallowing. When Andrew phoned, yelping into his mobile about how amazing the Hoopers' apartment was, saying she had been a fool not to stay, sounding drunk, Sophie had felt so *interrupted* that it was all she could do not to cut the call short.

With the glow of last night's good mood still upon her, Sophie showered and dressed and went downstairs. After retrieving the plastic-wrapped *New York Times* from the front lawn, she sat at the kitchen table to eat breakfast, starting and then abandoning a bowl of the too-sweet cinnamon wheat flakes masquerading as cereal and having a slice of toast instead, thinly coated with the blueberry 'jelly' upon which they had settled after having searched in vain for marmalade. Or by 'blueberry' did the Americans mean blackberry? Or maybe blackcurrant? Sophie studied the label on the jar, thinking of

Andrew: he was finding the differences in language so interesting he had started a maddening list – Jell-O for jelly, jelly for jam, pants for trousers, pantyhose for tights, sneakers for trainers, traffic circles for roundabouts. He had recited it for Ann and Geoff in the MOMA café, inviting additions. Sophie had torn her paper napkin into thin strips, unable to think of any contribution beyond the fact that being understood had little to do with a common vocabulary.

Starving, thanks to her lacklustre supper, Sophie smothered a thick layer of the blue stuff on a second piece of toast and got up to look out of the garden doors while she ate it. They had yet to find a switch for the sprinkler system (a mystifying omission from the copious notes left next to the phone) and in consequence the grass had taken on a visibly sickly yellow hue. Soon it would be dead, Sophie reflected, trying to evoke a sense of urgency at the prospect as she squinted through the glass. It occurred to her in the same instant that, having used the cat as the clinching pretext for her early return from New York, she had yet to see any sign of it.

Maybe the animal simply didn't like them, she mused, fighting a dim sense of insult as she unlocked the doors and called its name into the hot silence of the garden. It certainly hadn't liked Andrew's desultory effort at 'grooming' a couple of days before, leaping away in a flurry of spitting indignation the moment he had touched it with the comb. They had had no practice with pets, that was the trouble. They had seen off phases of supplication for puppies and ponies from the girls, making do with the regular visits of Mrs Hemmel's lovely ginger tom, until a speeding car had managed to crush his dear tiger-striped body between its tyres and the kerb.

Sophie fetched her sunglasses and embarked on a proper search, covering the drive and several hundred yards of road before working her way from the front round to the back garden. The heat pricked her eyes and burnt her gums and throat, reducing her already suspect efforts at mewing to something even less convincing. But she licked her lips and pressed on. The animal simply had to be found.

Behind some shrubbery on the garden's furthest perimeter, she came upon a small Wendy House-style shed, ghoulish, industrial-sized cobwebs dangling from its low ceiling like loose knitting. Inside, it was hot enough to bake bread, no resting place for any creature, let alone a cat with Dido's extravagant fur covering, Sophie observed, hastily withdrawing. The shed produced one worthwhile discovery, though, in the form of a tank and a tap hidden in the same cluster of shrubs. One cautious half-turn of the tap and Sophie was rewarded by the sight of bubbling fountains of water breaking out all over the lawn, fizzing and spurting as they gathered power.

She watched, transfixed, elated. The grass wouldn't die! And she did care, she really did, she realized, skipping through the jets of water to continue her search in the stretch of woodland separating the house from the lake.

The cat would be in the cool of the trees, of course it would. Or maybe *up* a tree. Possibly even stuck up a tree – yes, that made sense. Sophie tipped her head back, pushing her legs through the thin straggles of under-growth, enjoying the springy feel of the forest's pine-needled floor under her flip-flops. This is good, she thought. This is *enjoyable*.

But then a branch snapped and she spun like a cornered animal herself, her pulse wild. There was nothing there. Nobody. Just the endless dark towers of the trees, and the buzz of insects and tricks of lights where sun dappled shade. Sophie's heart thumped as she checked and re-checked her surroundings, trying now to see behind the lift of every leaf, the rustle of every branch. It had to have been some harmless scuttling creature – possibly even the cat, she told herself, labouring to filter out the panic. Instead, it grew worse, a dread, the like of which she had never known, reaching through her ribs to squeeze her heart, taking her back, it seemed, to every fear she had ever known – a maniacal demon in a film when she was a child, Tamsin's rigid, trusting, twisted face as she fought and failed to breathe, her baby daughter falling like a stone, the tom's mashed tiger fur stuck to the road. It was like a fast-forward of horrors, slowing only when it reached the boy-intruder, in his mud-encrusted trainers, the laces trailing and stiff with dirt.

Sophie had recalled the events of the afternoon countless times, but this was different, deeper, as if she was living it again, smelling the faint, stale odour of his skin, seeing the flecks of black in his bright brown eyes. Bad things happened when you least expected them, that was the awfulness. They happened when you felt safe. She had been sorting laundry, standing at the over-stuffed airing cupboard, so maddeningly positioned on the turn in the stairs. The first she had known of anything amiss was when Andrew called for her to come down.

Except, no, she hadn't known, or guessed from his voice, that anything was wrong. She had said, 'Hang on,' and finished putting the pillowcases on top of the sheets, trying to compress them next to a pagoda of clothes without ruining all her hard work at the ironing board. She had said, 'Hang on,' and then gone downstairs to the kitchen to find the cold tap running and nobody there. Challenged with regard to his presence in the garden, the boy had asked for a drink, Andrew explained later, to her and then to the police. He had asked for water. So Andrew had *invited him inside*.

When Andrew called her name again, Sophie had traced him to the dining room. Andrew was sitting on one of the chairs and the boy was standing behind him. As she entered, the boy reached into his pocket and pulled out a small knife, clicking it open and pointing it in the direction of Andrew's neck.

Sophie found that she had shuffled backwards against a tree. It felt solid, cool, reliable – a sentinel watching her back. It felt the best place to be, in the circumstances, with the echo of the snapping branch in her ears – and this unlooked-for, unwanted onrush of the past it seemed to have released, washing up details that had never seemed to matter before. Like how young and small – how *assailable* – their assailant had looked, clearly still so much more of a child than a man, and so visibly slight beside Andrew's six-foot-two frame, folded obediently into the dining-room chair.

And there was the fact of Andrew calling for her – Sophie hadn't really thought that through before, at least not the timing of it – which was what she found so overwhelming now, with the ridges of the bark digging into her spine. Had the boy produced the knife before Andrew called? Or had it been afterwards, when she entered the dining room? Why wasn't she sure? Why did it matter?

Sophie dug her nails through the tree's matting of ivy, feeling for the comforting crust of the bark, closing her eyes as she tried to think beyond the fear, still washing through her in waves. It mattered because before the knife Andrew might have done something. It mattered because Andrew had invited the boy in, allowed a bad situation to develop and then summoned her into the thick of it.

'Watch out!'

The shout ricocheted her back to the present with all the impact of a gunshot. She felt a fingernail rip as she clung on and twisted round. A shadowy figure was lumbering towards her through the trees ... Sophie pressed her eyes shut, moaning softly.

'Mrs Chapman – Sophie – I'm sorry to butt in, but you should get right away from there.'

It was the neighbour, Carter, in dark shorts and a black T-shirt, stretched tight over his belly. Sophie blinked stupidly, embarrassed, but still too shaken to move.

'Poison ivy?' Carter wheezed, dropping his hands to his knees to catch his breath. 'This place is crawling with it. Seriously . . .' He stepped towards her, placing one sandalled foot carefully among the undergrowth and offering his hand. 'I'm sorry if I alarmed you, but you should get right away from there now. Although I'm afraid it might already be too late,' he added, shaking his head as Sophie at last allowed herself to be led to a clearer patch of ground. 'Look, right there.' He pointed to the greenery entwining the body of her tree. 'Clusters of three, no thorns, those white flowers – I was taught to look out for that as a kid. We're going to have to get you washed up – and fast.'

'Washed up?' Sophie echoed, her mind still reeling.

'Yeah – and with soap. You gotta scrub like no to-morrow – not just a jump in my pool, though you look like you could do with that too.' Carter started to chuckle but checked himself when the Englishwoman set off back towards the house without a word, her eyes fixed open, like she had seen a ghoul or taken too much of something illegal – or perhaps prescribed, he mused, his mind darting to a battle Nancy had fought for a time, with substances channelled to her between doctors and drugstores.

'I was looking for the cat . . . for Dido,' Sophie muttered, when he caught up with her, the embarrassment settling in properly now. He was nimble in his sandals, she noticed, in spite of the swell of his belly, as evident as a pregnancy in the too-tight black T-shirt. 'She's not been around for a couple of days and I was worried. This poison ivy, what will it do?' She thrust out her arms for a cursory examination and then dropped them back to her sides.

Andrew had called her before the knife appeared. That was the thing. The boy had only produced it when Andrew had succeeded in summoning her. He had held it awkwardly too, unconvincingly, although that had done nothing to stop her scrambling to do his bidding – cash from every nook she could think of – all the while issuing silent prayers of gratitude that the girls were safely bowing their instruments at a parish hall in Sheen, rehearsing for a fund-raiser that evening. Fauré's Requiem, to help rebuild a church spire. The tickets had been sticking out of Andrew's breast pocket – Sophie remembered that too, suddenly, along with the thump of fear it had caused her, as if the girls themselves, rather than evidence of the concert, were half in view.

Must be around a week gone and still the woman's arms were pale, Carter observed, although not white like the husband's. The colouring was because they were British, he knew, although it had occurred to him during the brief encounter on the day of their arrival that there was something deeply washed out about the Stapletons' temporary tenants, like once-vivid book jackets or paintings drained to insipidity by daylight. 'Poison ivy is a bummer,' he explained, as they walked, hoping to break the intensity of her expression. 'It contains this stuff called urushiol, which is toxic and invisible. That's the deal with the soap – it's the only way to get rid of it. Even so I'm afraid you're going to have rashes on your hands and legs by tomorrow, which will itch like hell and maybe even blister and weep.'

'Weep?'

'You know . . . like when the blisters burst?'

'Oh, I see. Well, thanks.' They had reached the garden boundary at an angle that allowed a glimpse of his house through the trees: white with blue shutters and twice the size of the Stapletons'. Sophie squinted, making out a low white picket fence and what looked like the surround of the swimming-pool.

'You should hurry. And wash your clothes too – the slightest trace of that urushiol and you're cooked. Some say human urine works the best but that's not my experience.' He tried a grin, which was rewarded by a smile – the first he'd seen. A pretty girl, once, he noted, real pretty, and still not bad either with the thick wheaten hair, which looked like it still grew that colour of its own accord, and such a tall, slim figure – too slim in his view, though Nancy, battling with her weight-loss programmes, would be sure to disagree.

'Urine? Really?' She was still smiling. 'You've tried it?'

'As a kid – sure. You try anything as a kid, don't you?

Hey, come over for a swim once you're done . . . you and your husband.'

'Andrew's not here.'

'Hell, just you, then. Nancy would love that. We can offer you a soda or tea or whatever the hell you guys drink at this time of day. And we can have a look for the princess too, if you like.'

'Thank you, but . . .'

Carter watched her struggling with the decision. Nancy was at an audition and the cat never came near them. Their old dog Buz saw to that, not deliberately – he was docile and deaf – but by the mere fact of his presence. So he was being deceiving, but only in a good way, Carter reasoned, since he was in the mood for company and this woman looked like she could do with some cheering up too, unless he had mistaken the expression behind the big sunglasses and tree-hugging was a regular hobby of hers back home.

'The fact is, I'm not a great one for swimming, and if I was, I could always use the lake.'

'The *lake*?' Carter released a snort of amazement. 'Well, I guess you could, but nobody swims in that – it's kinda cold and real muddy round the edges and normally just used for boating and looking at and, besides, it's quite a hike and a *hazardous* one at that,' he concluded, with some triumph, nodding at her hands. 'Are you feeling anything yet?'

'I'm not sure.' Sophie studied her fingers, which looked pinkish anyway through her dark lenses.

'Hell, what am I doing yakking like this? Go this instant and get washed up – with soap, remember? They say you have fifteen minutes and I reckon you've already used ten. And then come by for that swim, okay? I – we shall expect you momentarily. Don't bother with the front entrance – just come right around the side. And no need to bring a towel, we've got plenty,' he added, striding off before she could compose a refusal.

## 5

Beth raised her leg and tried, gingerly, to circle her foot. Five days on and the swelling was half its original, horrible watermelon proportions, but the bruising was still a rich blue lake, fringed with pink, red, violet – and a hint of yellow, too, this morning, she observed grimly, carefully lowering her ankle back onto the cushion that William had thoughtfully provided for her. He had brought her a cup of coffee too, holding his smeary butter knife out of the way as he paused to plant a tender kiss on her forehead before rushing back to the kitchen. He was making a picnic and had paid an early visit to the supermarket to prepare, taking Alfie with him and shouting at the elder two through their bedroom doors to be breakfasted and ready on his return. They hadn't been, even though Beth, hobbling her way down to the sofa, had banged on both bedroom doors with her crutches.

After the shopping trip the house had pulsed with noise – yelling, feet thundering, the play-fighting that always got out of control. Beth had breathed a sigh of relief when the door finally slammed, vibrating in the silence. They were off to yet more cricket, this time to watch it at a place called Lords, which Harry had gleefully explained had nothing to do with the Houses of

Parliament. They had a thing now, her and Harry, ever since the aftermath of her ridiculous accident in the coffee shop. Embarrassed, surrounded by well-intentioned strangers gathering up her things, offering her cups of water, Beth had almost wept with relief at the sight of her stepson striding in from the street, shaking the rain from his hair, looking so sweetly anxious after her phone call. Smelling of smoke, but with no sign of his unsavoury-looking companion, Harry had half carried her to a taxi and then waited with remarkable patience during the drawn-out business of getting X-rays and doctors' verdicts in the Accident and Emergency department of a nearby hospital – all performed for *free*, which had seemed to Beth remarkable, but done nothing to impress Harry, who said the NHS was crap and full of bugs that killed people. It was only when they were finally on their way home, when she had recouped some of her wits and resilience (a week on crutches, the last doctor had advised, which meant the dearly bought yellow shoes wouldn't get an outing for a while but she would at least be fit for the trip up north), that she had ventured to remark that she had caught sight of him in the street after they had separated and how sore William would be to know his eldest son had taken up smoking.

Harry had scowled at the rain streaming down the taxi window. 'Yeah, well, he can talk, can't he?'

'Adults usually know what's best even if they can't always manage it themselves. Besides, he's trying hard, your father, with the nicotine gum.'

Harry snorted.

'What concerns me more,' she had pressed on, 'is that I gave you money to buy sneakers.'

'Here. Have it back.' Harry had started plucking notes out of his trouser pockets – a five and a ten.

'I don't want it back. It was a gift. It's just . . . Look, Harry, I'm okay with most things except . . .' Beth had paused, hoping he would drag his gaze from the taxi window. 'Except being taken for a ride. The point being that if you had wanted to meet your girlfriend you should have said straight out. I could have gone to the Victoria and Albert Gallery or somewhere. Then we'd all have been happy, wouldn't we? And maybe I wouldn't have sprained this darned ankle.'

'Dad wanted you and me to spend the day together, didn't he?' Harry had mumbled, still talking into the hand on which he was resting his averted head. 'So he'd have been pissed off about me doing anything else. And now he's going to be *really* pissed off.'

'Not necessarily,' Beth had ventured, gaining his full attention at last.

She still felt a small surge of pride at how she had handled the conversation, treating the seventeen-year-old like the young adult he was, explaining the error of his ways but then securing his affections by promising to keep the minor episode of his deceit entirely to herself. On getting home, she had – loudly and publicly – sung Harry's praises to William, who had responded by letting his eldest out three nights in a row without a curfew, which meant the boy looked like a walking ghost and his middle brother was too jealous to speak to him, but then, as Beth had spent a lifetime reasoning to herself, few things in any kid's life were ever perfect.

The day was grey – again – but not raining. Beth read the papers and her book, a disappointingly dull yarn about a quirky female detective, until the sofa felt lumpy. Shifting onto her side, she flicked the television on and tried to memorize a lean, wiry-haired chef's demonstration of how to make the perfect cheese soufflé. Her appetite stirred, she hopped into the kitchen and ate the croissant she had promised herself she wouldn't touch – even though William had fought the boys off it on her behalf – followed by a wedge of delicious crumbly white cheese threaded through with diced apricots. English cheese, like English bread, was proving a revelation; and all fruit was good, she reasoned, as was dairy, in sensible quantities.

Breaking off a hunk of the cheese that was not remotely sensible, and squeezing it into a soft granary bap, she then laboured upstairs with the crutches, stopping to take bites of her snack and to poke at items of laundry strewn along the stairs and landing. She found the messiness of William's children astonishing. She was not to clear up after them, he had thundered several times – loud enough to shame the boys into spurts of action – but the mess would build up again, within minutes, it seemed, and Beth, for whom orderliness was integral to sanity, was finding it increasingly difficult not to mind.

Having planned the trip upstairs to seek diversion on her laptop, plugged in next to Andrew Chapman's pile of bedside books, Beth found herself hobbling first into the passageway bathroom that housed a weighing scale. Leaning the crutches up against the wall, she stepped warily into position, only to fall against the toilet cistern with a howl. Seven pounds. Oh, God, *seven pounds* in only ten days.

Spitting expletives, Beth seized the crutches and propelled herself into the bedroom where she threw herself onto the carpet and began a series of frenzied exercises learnt at the body-sculpting class she attended in Stamford. She worked frantically, ignoring both the jolts of pain in her injured ankle and the dim, dispiriting notion of trying, like the king in the legend, to command back an unstoppable tide. How had she let things slip so badly? How many millions of crunches would it take just to get rid of the calories she had ingested that morning, let alone all the others packed into the construction of the hateful hefty holiday weight-gain?

'I bet you don't have to do this,' she gasped, catching the soft blue eyes of Sophie Chapman watching from a small oval picture frame on the window-sill. 'You and your beautiful English-rose looks and your exquisite skinny daughters and handsome husband and this wonderful *casual* old house you live in, all messed up but *nicely* . . . like none of you has to *try* . . . ' Beth pushed out the words to the rhythm of her sit-ups, finding it helped to take her mind off her cramping muscles. 'Well, some of us do have to try,' she hissed through gritted teeth. 'Some of us have *always* had to.' After managing a final agonizing ten, she rolled onto her stomach to recover, her eyes level with the dusty underside of the bed.

She sneezed violently, disturbing the body of a dead moth. In fact, Beth saw, looking more intently – enjoying a spurt of distaste – the state of the carpeted area under the bed was nothing short of disgusting. The moth was one in a veritable graveyard of stiff dusty insects, caught in the neglected dirt and fluff of the carpet. Scattered among them were other offending items – a small grey sock, a shoelace (at least, Beth hoped very much it was a shoelace), a teaspoon, furred with grime, and a small cardboard box, tucked against the skirting board. Beth reached for the spoon and then, simply to postpone the uncomfortable necessity of continuing her workout, wriggled further under the bed to retrieve the box. She lifted the lid without hesitating, but then paused, her eyes wide. Inside was what looked like a bundle of letters, secured by a desiccated elastic band.

Beth licked her lips, which were salty and dry from her exertions. She put the lid back on the box and then took it off again. The Right Thing to Do was not at issue. As she had said to Harry in the taxi, there were ways to behave that were acceptable and others that were not. She replaced the lid for a second time and reached for her laptop. Still lying on her stomach, she switched it on and summoned her emails. There was a grand total of five: three notifications of special offers from her favourite direct-mail companies, a newsletter from her New York cat-lovers group and a letter from her mother.

Hi, honey,

Are you having a wonderful time? Have you visited Buckingham Palace? They say you can go right inside these days. If my blood pressure were better I might have invited myself along too, but I guess I'll just have to be content with the happy memories of visiting London with Hal all those years ago, when you were at summer camp, and we saw the royal guards on their horses and walked till the soles of our shoes wore thin.

I quite understand that you can't call, with it being someone else's phone and the cost of using a cell abroad – I look forward to hearing all about it on your return.

The reason I am writing is to say that I would like to stay a full week for Thanksgiving this year, from Tuesday to Tuesday, if that's all right by you and that darling husband of yours. The journey wears me out so and my new specialist says I would be crazy not to allow my body some time for readjustment both sides of the Holiday. He's called Larry and I am really thrilled with the quality of his care, though it does not come cheaply, of course. As usual, it's thanks to Hal that I can manage.

Let me know soon about the dates, honey, won't you? Airplanes from Florida to NY are always so busy in the holiday season – and pricier too, if you leave it to the last minute.

Mom

Beth posted a brief reply, saying the holiday was going great and she was sure the dates for Thanksgiving would be fine. The references to Hal she ignored, apart from fleeting irritation that they had been made at all. Her antipathy towards her uncle, together with her mother's continuing financial dependence on the man, were old battlegrounds, for many years now as mutually avoided as they were irrefutable.

Elbows aching, Beth rolled over onto her back and studied the darkening skies through the bedroom window. The impregnable carapace of good cheer with which she had arrived in England was, she knew, wearing dangerously thin. She had seen no sights to speak of. She had almost broken her ankle. Her body was ballooning. She was bored. And, worst of all, William just didn't – ever – seem to have time for her.

As if on cue the bedroom phone rang and the voice of William himself burst onto the line, asking if she was okay, but in a rushed way that seemed to Beth to preclude the possibility of saying no. It was spitting with rain and the light was bad, he reported from the cricket match, but they were going to sit it out. Harry had bumped into a friend and temporarily disappeared, which was annoying, but the younger two were being easier as a result.

After the call the house felt even quieter. And cold. Beth put on another sweater and then – with the sigh of one giving in to the inevitable – reached under the bed for the box of letters. Turning her back on the quizzical gaze of Sophie Chapman, she began to ease off the elastic band only to find it snapping between her fingers, intensifying the no-going-back feeling that had already taken hold. Her hands trembled pleasantly as she picked out the first envelope. It was like being in one of those nineteenth-century dramas broadcast on PBS. What secrets lay cradled in her palms? What hilarious revelations?

*My dearest darling Sophie,*

*I should be writing a symphony not a measly letter – so great are the things I want to say! It has even crossed my mind to get my friend Geoff, who is much cleverer with words, to put something on paper on my behalf (like in that French story where the ugly guy with the long nose gets his mate to do the wooing . . . except that's the other way round, isn't it, because the ugly one could at least write the words and I think you rather like the way I look . . . at least that was the impression you left me with at the end of Winchester and if that has changed then please, for God's sake, tell me right away before I make even more of a total idiot of myself than I have already. Christ, I'm writing DRIVEL and it's all YOUR fault – four weeks, three days, two hours since we met and I appear to be out of my mind . . . ).*

*Where was I? Wanting to say great things – but I'm clearly incapable, or at least in no fit state, so let me say instead that OF COURSE I want to come and stay with you! Yes, I would love to get to know your family and those dates look fine. I'll come by train. There's one that arrives at 4.45 p.m. Is there any chance you could be at the station so we can have a little time together – before (I admit I am terrified) I meet your parents? Any tips on how to win them round? Any pitfalls to avoid? Write soon — I'll need all the help I can get!*

*Yours hopelessly,*

*Andrew*

*PS I AM writing a symphony as it happens . . . I vowed not to tell anyone until it was done, but since you are the reason behind it — my muse (I am sorry, but it seems only fair that you should know the very worst) — I couldn't resist.*

*PPS Of course phone if you prefer, but during this miserable period of needing to live at home there is always the danger that you will be subjected to a grilling from my mother, who knows I have met SOMEONE and is horribly curious. I am certain your parents must be nice (they have to be pretty special to have produced you!) but I'm afraid mine are pretty terrible — annoying, embarrassing, etc. At my last concert they clapped BETWEEN movements — aagh!*

What was it with Englishmen? Beth marvelled, clambering onto the bed and settling back among the pillows with the remaining letters. All that charm and romance and endearing muddle-headedness — how had the Pilgrim Fathers lost such things on a single voyage? She read each letter slowly, avidly, her heart swelling just as Sophie Chapman's must have done by the end of that summer two decades before. They were all from Andrew, each a little more ardent, each a little more intimate. He met her and then longed to meet her again, and again and again. Interspersed with the passion there were tantalizing references to fragments of their lives — the sick younger sister, Tamsin, a dog called Boodle, a house in Cornwall, a stolen bike, endless rehearsals and concerts. The only consistent thread was to be found in the expressions of love, blossoming in a manner suggestive of total reciprocation.

'I was kind of down today,' Beth confessed later that night, keen to catch William before he fell asleep, which she could tell he was eager to do from all the sighs and pillow-punching as he clambered into bed.

He rolled over to look at her, pushing a strand of hair off her cheek. He had a red mark across his forehead where his cricket-watching hat had bitten into the skin. 'Really? Because of your ankle?'

'Yup, I guess, and ... if I'm honest, I was sort of lonely.'

'Oh, darling, I'm sorry. I felt terrible leaving you, but last-minute tickets to Test matches are impossible to come by and when I bought them we agreed you wouldn't come ...'

'I know.'

'You would have hated it if you had.'

'I know that too.' Beth pressed her forehead against his chest.

'Hey, you really have had a bad day, haven't you?'

'It was just long, that's all.' Beth swallowed till the threat of tears had subsided. 'Nothing but an email from my mom for company, asking about Thanksgiving, of all things – *Thanksgiving*. When I last looked we were only in mid-August ... and I guess I do kind of miss home.'

'Me too.'

'I don't know if I'm *homesick*, exactly, just a little frustrated.' Beth reached for a tissue from the box on the bedside table and dabbed her nose.

William pulled her more tightly into the crook of his arm. 'My poor darling, that ankle sprain was such bad luck. But everything will get better from now, I promise. We've got a celebration lunch tomorrow, for starters.'

'Celebration?'

'Harry's results – I've booked a noodle house in Richmond that Susan says is very good.'

'Susan?'

'She's not coming, obviously – but she does know the local haunts pretty well. Then we've got the long weekend up north to look forward to – I've decided we'll drive rather than go by train because of your poor leg – and once we're there my parents will just take the boys over. You'll see – it'll be brilliant, loads of time to ourselves.' William disentangled himself from her with a kiss and turned off his bedside light.

Beth waited a moment, fighting the knowledge that he wanted to be allowed to sleep, that the comforting of her was done with. 'William, I love it that you want to spend time with your kids – I love how you are with your kids. The whole *family* thing, it's so . . . impressive . . . but it's also hard for me sometimes not to feel on the outside of it all.'

'Silly.' He groped through the bedclothes for her arm and patted it.

Beth lay still, her hands resting on the new hateful thickness of her stomach. After a few minutes she whispered, 'William, would you write me a letter one day – you know, like a real old-fashioned love letter?'

But he was already asleep, and she was a dummy who needed to remember to buy a fresh pack of elastic bands, Beth scolded herself, aware of the stiffness in her over-worked abdominal muscles as she shifted onto her side. As she closed her eyes, a sliver of envy for Sophie Chapman slid into her heart and lodged there, like an invisible splinter. Willowy, smugly contented, no doubt, with her romantic English husband and their pretty children, and this clever trade-up of holiday homes – swapping the dog-muck and Styrofoam-littered streets of west London for the clean, green environs of her own beautiful Darien . . .

Beth hurriedly stoppered her thoughts, releasing a gasp of disbelief into the dark. What was wrong with her? She had her own dashing Englishman, after all, and a life that, current minor inconveniences aside, was equally perfect, just so long as she kept a firm grip on it . . . made sure none of the ancient bad stuff crept back in.

Sophie looked at her legs dangling in the swimming-pool next to Carter's and giggled. They looked so disconnected through the prism of the water, and so weirdly white compared to his. In fact, after ten days of daily sunbath-ing, she was more tanned than she had been for years, with such a stark imprint of the outline of her main bathing costume that catching sight of her naked reflection in the Stapletons' bedroom mirror was like glimpsing a hybrid creature inhabiting two entirely different skins – one pasty and old, the other polished and new.

'When will he get back this time?'

Sophie interlocked her hands and stretched, peering at the American over her sunglasses. 'Late.' Lowering her arms, she leant backwards until her upper body was flat on the ground, letting the heat of the poolside stone burn her wet skin. The effects of the joint they had shared were wearing off now, although there was still the lovely feeling of weightlessness in her limbs and a musty taste in her mouth – faintly acrid, but not unpleasant.

Carter lay down next to her, turning to rest his weight on one elbow. 'More golf?'

Sophie shook her head, flicking droplets of water across his face. 'Nope. More music ... thanks to the loathsome Ann and her Goody Two Shoes charity concert. The pull-out by the conductor is looking permanent, so Andrew – ridiculously, in my view, since he is supposed to be on *holiday* – has agreed to step in. The last couple of sessions were with the choir. Today is the first rehearsal with the orchestra there too ... the first, no doubt, of many. It's always like that with Andrew – full-on or not at all. The actual concert is on the last day of the holiday and, of course, the girls and I will have to go. Handel's *Messiah*, which is an odd choice, you must admit, given that we are, thank God, still several months off Christmas . . .'

Carter sat up, extracting his legs from the pool. 'I like Handel, especially *Messiah*.' He got to his feet, offering a hand for Sophie to follow suit. 'The guy could write.'

Sophie laughed as he helped her up. 'I know – of course. In fact, of the many trillion concerts I've attended over the years, *Messiah* is probably my favourite. It's just that woman' – she pulled a face – 'sticking her nose in, getting Andrew to run around.'

Carter went behind his poolside bar and pulled a jug of the iced tea to which he had introduced her out of the fridge, jangling it to shake the ice cubes. 'Ready for more tea?'

Sophie sang, 'More tea, Vicar?' and laughed again because the phrase had made Carter look so puzzled. He did puzzlement very well, she decided, settling back on the lounger with the tall glass he handed her. He had a way of appearing like some endearingly gormless bear, with his wide, pleasant face and thick-set body, the arms hanging at a little distance from his sides, as if the sheer width of his torso prevented them making contact with his hips. But there was the grace that Sophie kept noticing too, a grace that spoke of the college baseball he had now told her about and which was still visible in the neat, bouncing dives he occasionally performed off the short board protruding over the deep end of his swimming-pool, legs and arms straight, hanging in the air for an instant before making a smooth, near-splashless entry into the water.

Witnessing it for the first time, on the afternoon when he had rescued her from the poison ivy and persuaded her to swim, Sophie had burst into a spontaneous round of clapping, at which Carter had grinned like a bashful schoolboy, burying his smiles in his swimming-towel. He had produced the first jug of iced tea shortly afterwards along with a tub of lumpy ointment (oatmeal, apparently, being the key ingredient), which he had gruffly insisted on smoothing over the affected areas himself, going on bended knee when it came to her ankles.

Sophie had regarded these attentions with incurious detachment. The wife not being there wasn't right, she knew. A last-minute summons to a casting had been Carter's explanation, the dog being taken – as apparently was the norm – for luck. And yet, with the shock of her private trauma among the trees still upon her, whether Nancy – or indeed the dog – even existed hadn't seemed to matter much. It was as if the world had tilted, taking her already precarious sense of balance with it.

'It could have been a lot worse,' Carter had clucked, scooping out and gently rubbing the cream over the livid rashes. 'You must have some resistance or something.'

Sophie had watched, like a meek patient, grateful for the kindness, almost to the point of tears. She felt so delicate – so fragile – and he seemed to know it. Yet more kindness had followed in the form of a towelling robe and an invitation to escape the heat into the ice-box cool of a state-of-the-art den of a cinema built onto the side of the pool house.

'I'm a scriptwriter – or at least I *used* to be,' he had explained, plucking *Casablanca* from a floor-to-ceiling unit of DVDs after she had backed away from the suggestion of choosing something herself. She curled onto the sofa to watch the film, tucking what she could of her bare legs under the hem of the robe, glad that he had his own separate chair for viewing, a deep, weathered leather bed of a contraption that had clearly seen many hours – years – of use. The first spliff had been produced, to the accompaniment of a companionable wink a few minutes later, from an attractive ornamental box parked on the table between their chairs. 'If it won't bother you.'

Sophie had said not at all and then accepted a few turns herself, aware even with her amateurish efforts to inhale of the drug's deeply relaxing effect. The horror among the trees, the astonishing rush of anger and understanding that had followed, had instantly – pleasantly – begun to recede. Of far more concern had been the fictional events unfolding on widescreen in front of her: from the initial 'Play it, Sam,' to Rick's square-jawed decision to sacrifice personal happiness for the greater good, she was spellbound. And there had been many fascinating interjections from Carter throughout the film too, about how certain lines had been cut and added, why one character was standing on the left or the right, how each small scene was called a 'beat', action triggering reaction and so on,

'Like pearls on a string,' he had murmured, as the final credits rolled, adding reverently, 'All to prove in the case of this particular movie that love can exist without the presence of the other person.'

'So are you a *retired* scriptwriter?' Sophie had pressed cosily, dreamy from the dope, the itchy patches on her skin soothed and forgotten.

Carter had shot her a dark look from under the grey thickets of his eyebrows. 'I'll only answer that if you promise to tell me why you were hugging that darned tree like your life depended on it.'

'A panic attack,' said Sophie, promptly, aware that while the figure of Carter himself appeared to be moving in and out of focus, her mind, thanks to the dope, had ascended to a level of astonishing and glorious lucidity. 'Difficult things ... converging ... yes, that was it – *converging*.'

'Wow – sounds tough.' Having posted the *Casablanca* DVD back into its correct slot, Carter returned to his TV chair and perched on its arm, facing her. 'Would it be wrong of me to ask what those "difficult things" might be?'

Sophie had hesitated, fiddling with the tie on her robe, torn between the desire to talk and a dim awareness that it would indeed be wrong, just as the man's kindness and being there in the delicious cool cinema were wrong. But then she started and it was impossible to stop. She had told him everything – much of it in the wrong order – about Tamsin, about having been happy and then suddenly not, of the intruder and the months of living under some dark invisible cloud. 'We were all fine, nothing damaged, and yet nothing has been quite the same ever since. It's like I lost something that day, my confidence – *something*. But the worst of it – what had just dawned on me before the "tree-hugging", as you put it – was that all along I had been blaming Andrew for letting the horrible boy into our house, into our lives, as if he could have done something to prevent it, which of course he couldn't. And he senses it – poor Andrew – I know he does. There's been this distance between us, you see,' she had confessed, in a small voice. 'That's part of what's changed, why we came out here – the house swap. It's to try and sort things out.' She had laughed, nervously, as sense and sobriety came flooding back in, bringing the room and her recklessness into sharp relief. 'Really, I should go . . . I shouldn't have come . . .'

'Well, I'm glad you did.'

The frankness of the remark, its quiet intensity, was like an alarm bell. Colouring, Sophie hastily got up from the sofa, holding the edges of the robe tightly across her chest. 'Well, that's nice, obviously, and thank you, Carter – for listening and so on, but now I really should be getting back . . .'

'Hey, no need to run.' Carter had raised both arms in the manner of one professing himself to be devoid of weapons. 'That lotion has sunk in nicely – you could have another swim first.'

'Thanks, but I don't think so. And thank you for being

so kind. The swimming, the oatmeal stuff – you've been great,' Sophie had jabbered, fighting the door handle and a sudden absurd terror that it might be locked.

'Enough with the thanking,' Carter had replied drily, reaching past her to manoeuvre the handle, which she had been twisting in the wrong direction. 'Only people who aren't friends thank each other all the time.'

'Friends?' Sophie had turned to squint at him as they stepped back out into the eye-aching brilliance of the sun.

'Sure . . . at least I hope so. And Nancy and Andrew – I want all of us to get along. Next time make sure he comes, okay?'

Sophie had fled through the little gate in the picket fencing that surrounded the pool and into the trees, ignoring Carter's shouts about forgotten promises to help look for the cat.

It seemed incredible, Sophie mused now, smiling to herself as she jangled the melted shingle of ice cubes in the bottom of her glass, that only a week and a half had passed since all the high drama of that first encounter – her running off like some madwoman wanted for a monstrous crime. She had waited for Andrew's return that evening with dread, certain that he would detect some new and terrible change in her. Smoking a joint of all things (even as a teenager, drugs had never held any allure for her), not to mention the private film-watching, the wild, disloyal talk – he would see it all, surely, somehow, flashing in the guilty flints of her eyes.

But Andrew had arrived back from his overnight stay and golf game in the most unexpected of moods – sombre, sheepish, almost to the point of penitence. Playing down what had clearly been a marvellous time with Geoff and Ann, he had listened intently to Sophie's somewhat edited version of the day's events, asking all sorts of uncharacteristically detailed and polite questions. When she showed him the rashes on her hands and legs, describing their neighbour's timely intervention, he had said only how fortunate for her that Carter had been around and well done for allaying some of the man's bullying need to be of service by at last taking a dip in his pool.

While Sophie had prepared supper he had sat down for his now customary evening session at the Stapletons' piano, galloping through a few familiar old favourites before slipping into an experimental style she hadn't heard in years, trying chords and key changes with different snatches of tune in between.

They had eaten in front of the television, exchanging surprisingly effortless, companionable remarks – snippets of text-news from the girls, the triumph with the water sprinklers, the worrying absence of the cat – before retreating to bed where Andrew, instead of emitting his usual silent electrical storm of disappointment at her lack of interest in sex, had for once been the first to fall asleep, his mouth open, his glasses down his nose, his book on his chest.

Aware of a shadow across her body, Sophie opened

her eyes from her reverie to find Carter standing next to her lounger. They had spent so many hours together now that in her mind they had all merged into one: a thick, hazy layer of sun and conversation, tea and silence, all of it as restorative as it had been unexpected. Through his slightly bowed legs she could see the grizzled snout of Buz, the dog, which had heaved its sagging old body into the baking shade offered by the outdoor dining table.

'He hates it when she's gone,' Carter commented, by way of reference to the pet and the continuing absence of Nancy, whose casting session had not only proved genuine but had resulted in a guest appearance in a soap, tying her to a new, hectic schedule. He squeezed an inch of sun cream into each palm and held out both hands with a questioning nod.

'Yes, please.' Sophie rolled over and tugged the straps of her costume off her shoulders.

Carter leant over her to perform what had become a favourite task, glad she could not see the extra, unflattering sag the position gave his belly. 'Things still going better with that husband of yours?' He spread the cream slowly, smoothing it in even sweeps over her shoulder-blades.

'Oh, yes.' Sophie sighed, her voice full of the happiness and perplexity that this fact afforded her, while her body relaxed under the now familiar pleasure of Carter's big, kind hands moving across her hot skin. 'It's so weird – nothing has been *said* but it just feels as if there's no pretence any more. We're each doing our own thing –

meeting up like half-strangers in the evening and managing to be pleasant as a result. Andrew can't believe how happy I am to be left alone while he goes gallivanting with Geoff and Ann. After each excursion – golf, music, whatever it is – he walks into the house wearing a guilty expression, like the girls when they were little and had done something fun but terrible and were awaiting a telling-off. But he can also see how much more relaxed I am and thinks it's time on my own that's doing the trick – reading lots of novels, popping over here for the occasional swim.'

'Well, that's the truth, isn't it?' Carter murmured.

'Hmm, not quite . . . or, at least, there are a few gaping holes in that truth, aren't there? Like the reason I'm more relaxed is because that panic attack made me realize – at long last – how angry I was with him . . .' Sophie paused, amazed at how simple things could be when one dared to spell them out. 'Oh, yes, and the minor detail of having poured my heart out to a total stranger, then allowed him to ply me with drugs . . .'

'Hey now, let's not exaggerate,' Carter protested, laughing. 'Three spliffs in two weeks hardly constitutes *plying* . . . at least, not in my book. The point is, you needed a friend and I just happened to be available for the job.' Carter tried and failed to keep the huskiness from creeping into his voice. Her back was so long and slim. Working in the cream, he could feel the indentations of her ribcage; and her pleasure at his touch, he could feel that too. God, he had forgotten that – the simple sweetness of skin on skin. Nancy worked at their sex life like she worked at everything else – vocalizing, negotiating, analysing, as hell-bent upon maintenance and improvement as she was with regard to her own body: surgery, regular shots into her face, she did the whole deal. And as an actress in her mid-fifties, Carter didn't blame her. It was the toughest of professions for older women and he admired her fighting spirit. But there was no eroticism to it, no vulnerability, no *need* . . .

'Hey, thanks, I think that will do.'

'Sure.' Carter hastily retreated to his own sun-bed. The deal was friendship, he reminded himself; confidants who hugged and trusted and told each other their worst and best thoughts. He had sold her the idea himself, during the charm offensive that had persuaded her into a second visit – a door-stepping encounter that she'd thought had just happened to coincide with the husband being absent, when in fact it had been the worthwhile product of two hours' uncomfortable surveillance, hovering with binoculars between the thinnest clumps of trees at the end of his drive. And she had bought into it like a trusting kid, telling him more details, not just about the recent ups and downs of her marriage but also about her childhood and the wheelchair-bound sister with allergies whom she had loved so dearly.

So far Carter had done his best to buy into it too, showing Sophie round the place, telling all the stories behind his belongings – from the tackiest ornament to the framed Oscar nomination that hung next to his desk in the office. One afternoon he had guided her around every inch of his huge yard and its environs, proudly pointing out and naming the orange-gold *Helenium*, the rainbow colours of the *Echinacea* beds, the black-eyed Susans stalking the edges of the dusty pink hydrangeas and electric purple-blue *Caryopteris*, shyly saving his favourites – the proud sentinels of the Casablanca lilies – till last, in the hope that she would make the same irresistible connections that were firing in his own mind; that she, too, would feel how the beauty of what they were sharing went way beyond flowers. Out loud he had admitted only that the land-scaper did the heavy work, but that the choices and design were all his. Sophie had been so admiring, so attentive that he couldn't even bring himself to add the sorry truth that the discovery of his green thumb had only come about because of the dust gathering on his notebooks, the yawning blankness where once there had been torrents of words. Without the yard to work on he would have gone mad.

'Still no sign of the princess?' he ventured now, closing his eyes in a bid not to stare too greedily. Instead the image of her near-naked body shimmered across his retina, as clearly emblazoned as a brand on a hide. She had brought a novel this time and he already felt jealous of it.

Sophie lowered her book with a groan. 'Not a peep. Except that I keep putting out food and every morning it's gone . . . '

'Crazy lady – that will be raccoons or skunks or coyotes . . .'

'*Coyotes?*'

'Beth and William – you're going to have to tell them.'

'I know. I've been putting it off. I just didn't want to ruin their holiday, that's all. I'll get Andrew to give them a call tonight.'

'Coward.'

'You think?'

'Sure. A beautiful one, though.' Carter grinned, show-ing off the dental work that had kept his face young. 'That's my favourite of your swimsuits, by the way – high on the hips. You look great, even if the white bits from the other one make it kind of weird.'

Sophie threw her towel at him and did a running dive into the pool. When she surfaced he was in the water next to her, his face close, his eyelashes dripping. 'What?' he gasped, as she stared.

'I was just wondering. You and Nancy . . . couldn't you have children or . . . ?'

'We moved here to start a family but Nancy's career took off and then suddenly it was too late.' Carter ducked back under the water, not to hide his tortured thwarted-father emotions, as Sophie supposed, but to escape the temptation of placing his mouth against hers, which, darkened by the pool water, looked good enough to bite clean through.

# 6

Andrew studied the rows of singers and musicians while he conducted, noting with some dismay how old most of them were and hoping they were all too lost in the challenge of trying to follow his baton to guess they were being scrutinized. The choir, apart from being thin on tenors, had already proved itself to be basically sound, most having performed the piece before. Ann, in the front row of the altos, was working hard as usual and professional to a fault, her mouth wide, her eyes glued either on him or her score. The orchestra, too, were indisputably accomplished, barely missing a note, and yet, as so often happened during the first combined session of music and vocals, the cohesion felt shallow, while the pace – even in the fastest movements – was woefully uncertain and lacking punch.

After 'His Yoke Is Easy' had laboured to its end in a plodding, methodical manner entirely contradictory to the intentions of its creator, Andrew clapped his hands to call a halt to the run-through, risking a quip about the yoke sounding pretty cumbersome from where he was standing. To his delight there were gales of good-hearted laughter. 'And at times the choir and orchestra appeared to be pulling the yoke in entirely different directions ... I don't suppose anyone here could stay an extra half-hour, could they?' he ventured next, as more ripples of amusement died away. 'If we're not going to get booted out of this hall, that is.' He shot a questioning look at Ann, who responded with a thumbs-up. Meanwhile all heads seemed to be nodding to indicate a willingness to stay.

It was certainly different, Andrew mused, garnering another laugh as he rolled up his shirtsleeves and pulled a devilish face before raising his baton again. In England choirs might practise for a few weeks before such events, but orchestras, like soloists, tended to pride themselves on requiring one run-through just a couple of hours prior to performance. But this was New York and a word-of-mouth gathering of volunteer musicians assembled in a high-school hall by Ann. There would be two more rehearsals at least, and no one was receiving a fee, not even the soloists, who were various music students he had yet to meet, apparently grateful for any chance to showcase their talents. The proceeds of the event were destined for a small charity working with street children in Peru, a cause all the more poignant for the fact that the original conductor (now in hospital with a diagnosis of severe pneumonia) had adopted two little girls from that part of the world.

As Andrew pressed on with the rehearsal, any sense of the limitations of the assembled throng of musicians fell away, as did the fact of being packed into a school hall on the Upper West Side on a baking Friday, with the smell of floor polish in his nose and beads of sweat sliding down his temples. He was a conductor – a conduit, literally – for some of the greatest music ever written. Of advanced ages the players might have been, but compared to many of the schoolchildren he had to work with back in London, with their short attention span and crammed curricula (music squeezed in for a lot of them, often as the last priority), they were workhorses, Trojans, heroes to the last man and woman. By the time they got to the end of the extra half-hour the 'yoke' section had lightened to a tight, breathtaking gallop, which made even the hairs on his own neck stand on end, while the 'Hallelujah' had reached a volume and energy that seemed to shake the very rafters of the hall.

Afterwards coffee, tea and orange juice were served by Ann and a group of her friends from a trestle table in the corridor outside the hall. The singers and musicians clustered round him, all exuding the warmth and openness that Geoff had cited as the reason he and Ann had found it so easy to make America their home. They thought Andrew's skills were considerable and queued up to tell him so, interrupting each other with their compliments.

'We might not let you go back to England,' teased one of the flautists, a woman of such width that during some particularly impassioned playing Andrew had feared for the security of her narrow school chair.

'I told you I'd found the answer to our prayers,' Ann crowed, bestowing a proprietorial congratulatory pat to Andrew's sweat-dampened back, wondering if she had yet done enough to make up for the early dreadful *faux pas* about the handicapped sister. Seldom had Geoff given her such a roasting. Deeply shamed, she had begged to be allowed to offer an outright apology; but Geoff had talked her out of it, insisting that with someone as sensitive as Andrew (so much the quintessential buttoned-up Englishman), it would only make things worse. So Ann had simply devoted her energies during all their subsequent encounters to being as nice as she possibly could, aware that with the flaky Sophie in the background, the poor man needed all the looking after she could manage. Asking him to step in on the *chicos perdidos* cause had turned into a particularly inspired triumph, not just because Andrew had been so visibly flattered, but because he was a magnificent conductor – she had forgotten quite how magnificent and had remarked on the fact with sufficient frequency for Geoff to grumble that he had once been rather good on the saxophone, *if* she could be bothered to remember. 'Yes, sweetie, and now you're good at lots of other things,' she had quipped, tugging her husband's chin between her forefinger and thumb, enjoying the rare display of possessiveness.

It certainly *felt* as if he had forgiven her, Ann mused happily, glancing from Andrew to the rest of their little group, which had been joined by the flautist's daughter, a tall, skinny creature with long thick chestnut hair and gazelle eyes. 'Andrew, meet your soprano solo – Meredith Chambers, ex-Juilliard, now finishing a post-grad in composition at Columbia.' Ann squeezed the girl's hand affectionately as she introduced her. 'She'll be doing her bit at the next rehearsal, won't you, Meredith? With the other three soloists too, I hope, though apparently the bass is recovering from a bout of laryngitis.'

'That was so great,' Meredith exclaimed, with singsong exuberance, once she had kissed her mother and reached for a glass of orange juice. 'I got here in time for "Worthy Is the Lamb" and the last Amen . . . They were both so moving.'

'I'm pleased you thought so. And I am very much looking forward to hearing you at our next rehearsal,' replied Andrew warmly, privately amazed at the girl's youth – no older than Olivia by the look of her, although from what Ann had said about her being near the end of her second degree she had to be twenty-five at least. Her mane of dark hair had been tied with artistic in-souciance entirely to one side of her head so that the entire bundle tumbled over her shoulder. She was dressed just as his daughters now did in hot weather, in a skimpy T-shirt and short skirt that made no secret of her long legs – of so little obvious genetic resemblance to the bulging limbs of the parent standing next to her that it was hard not to marvel.

'Ann and Mom said you were, like, a music scholar at King's College in Cambridge,' Meredith chattered on excitedly, 'which is, like, the *best* place for music in England, isn't it? I mean, that's where Benjamin Britten and, like, *every* famous twentieth-century composer went, isn't it?'

Andrew, flattered enough to blush, was diverted from the need to respond by a tap on the shoulder from one of the trumpeters, a wiry elderly man with ebony skin and a head peppered with grey, who was eager, like so many others, to shake the English conductor by the hand and pronounce – with some formality – on the pleasure of working with him.

Such attention and praise were thrilling, of course, but it was the joy of the music that lingered in Andrew's heart as he sat on the train back to Darien. How had he lost touch with that? he wondered, watching the glorious colours of high summer glide past the window, seeing a depth to them that he was sure didn't exist in England. And there was more sky too, he was certain of it – higher, wider, bigger. Maybe that was why he felt so much freer, so much more himself. He had thought Sophie was the one who needed to right herself, but maybe it had been him all along.

And yet Sophie had been undergoing some sort of transformation on the holiday too – so visibly that Andrew, in recent days, had had to bite his tongue to stop himself angling for some acknowledgement – some credit – for bringing it about. The holiday had only happened thanks to him, after all, hacking his way through all the recent, hateful months of her negativity. A conversational gambit along the lines of *I told you so* hardly seemed unreasonable. But on the other hand he was too grateful for the change in his wife to want to risk scaring it into retreat, even with some joking demand for congratulation.

Whistling softly, Andrew slid the Lincoln into its side of the garage and skipped up to the front door, pausing to yank a tendril of ivy that had entwined itself around an outside light. He had done nothing about the house-alarm not working, so it seemed particularly important to make sure that such minor security measures could flick into action, should the necessity arise – although it was hard to conceive of such a necessity: the quietness, the tree-muffled seclusion, only the occasional car driving by, let alone a pedestrian. Andrew had never encountered anywhere that, while part of a busy community, still managed to exude a sense of such tranquillity. The only regular familiar faces were those of the newspaper boy, hurling his plastic-wrapped delivery straight from his bicycle carrier into the drive, and the postman, a moustachioed chunky man dressed in a Boy Scout-style uniform of shorts and shirt, who called, 'Howdy,' if spotted delivering items into the mailbox, before roaring off in his regulation golf buggy of a car to the next address. In fact, after almost three weeks, the place, for him at least, was beginning to feel a little *too* secluded. Sophie was clearly thriving, but lately Andrew had relished every pretext that came his way for diving back into the hubbub of New York.

Once in the house, Andrew dropped his music case at the bottom of the stairs and headed along the hall to the kitchen. In the doorway he paused, momentarily awe-struck by the sight of the tanned, slender woman in a sleeveless white cotton dress and bare feet bending over a chopping board, her knife slicing expertly through an orderly array of vegetables.

'Good music-making?' She looked up, smiling briefly, the blade poised over a wide, velvet-gilled mushroom. Her hair, freshly washed and now streaked near white in places by the sun, hung loosely round her face, heightening the blue of her eyes and the strong ridges of her cheekbones.

'You look amazing. That dress, is it new?'

'Nope . . . ancient. M&S *circa* 1995.' She pulled a face. 'Incredible what a bit of sunbathing can do.'

Andrew crossed the room and put his hands over hers. She looked up, taken aback, but also, he judged, quite pleased. 'Sophie, I just want to say that . . . well . . . coming home to you like this – cooking, happy . . . it's nice.' And then suddenly, without having planned it, he was kissing her, with a tender intent not attempted for so long that it felt new. To his surprise – and rather to Sophie's, from what he could tell – she responded in kind, breaking away after several long moments with a shy, girlish laugh. 'I've lit the barbecue,' she pressed the back of her hand to her mouth, as if remembering the kiss, 'or, at least, turned it on – it's a gas one. I decided it was about time we ate outside.' She gestured at the halved mushrooms, lying alongside chunks of onion, red pepper and a heap of chopped moist pink chicken breast. 'Kebabs, I thought.'

Andrew nodded absently. They might make love that night; the possibility had been there, hanging in the sweetness of the kiss, for him to take . . . if he still wanted it. What had it been now? Four months? Six? He pushed open the kitchen door and stumbled outside. It took a few moments for his eyes to adjust to the dark. The music from the rehearsal was still swirling in his head, pumping in time to his heart. The air was balmy from the heat of the afternoon and thick with the clack and hum of insects. In the corner of the patio he could see, from the flicker of blue flame, that Sophie had indeed lit the barbecue – a square metal contraption with as many grills and knobs as the stove in the kitchen. Above it, an outside light was attracting a miniature universe of bugs, some of such alarming shape and size that Andrew decided to search for some candles with which to illuminate the meal instead. He was rummaging in drawers when Sophie came to stand next to him, carrying the kebabs, now assembled and arranged cross-wise along the chopping board. 'Can I help?'

'Candles, I thought.'

'Down there.' She pointed to two candlesticks – containing two new dark blue candles. They sat on a low shelf next to the empty cat basket, a sight that caused both of them to stop in their tracks.

'Bloody animal.'

'I know,' Sophie murmured, 'I feel terrible too . . . so terrible that I took the plunge and phoned them.'

'The Stapletons? Blimey. Well done. What did they say?'

'There was no answer – I tried everything, home,

mobiles, so I've left messages. I said we'd looked and called and informed the SPCA and was there anything else they wanted us to do. I apologized too, of course – as best I could – saying the only reason we had left it so long was because we hadn't wanted to worry them.'

'Quite right. Well done. At least they know now, eh? There really isn't anything more we can do.'

Sophie nodded, her thoughts shifting guiltily to Carter, not because his teasing accusation of cowardice had stirred her to take action about the cat, but because of all that had happened afterwards.

She had ended it. That was the main thing. A boundary had been crossed, but she had pulled back. And now all she cared about was building on the good, unexpected things that the holiday had produced – her own peace of mind, the mending of feelings between her and Andrew, not to mention a mounting, irrepressible excitement at the prospect of seeing the girls. Just the thought of hearing their voices again brought a lump to her throat, to watch how they ate and laughed and lounged, just *being* in the way that teenagers seemed to manage so effortlessly – she would savour every moment.

'Tell me about the rehearsal,' she said, returning her focus to Andrew, noting with a twist of delight how handsome he still looked in the soft light of the candles, how much twinkle there still was in his forty-three-year-old grey-blue eyes. While she stood over the kebabs he had opened a bottle of wine and assembled the salad, whistling like a songbird – because of the kiss, Sophie guessed; because of the kiss, which had felt extraordinary to her too, like a door opening, a door that – to her joy and relief – she still wanted to walk through.

Andrew responded to her enquiry with boyish eagerness, describing – through mouthfuls of food – the commitment and deftness of the musicians, and Ann, bossy as ever but still impressively in touch with her music, and Meredith, so rake thin and young, but with a reputation that apparently made her more than equal to the exquisite vocal demands of 'I Know That My Redeemer Liveth', the toughest by far of the many solo soprano treasures he had yet to hear her perform. Delighted by his wife's rapt expression, Andrew gave the fullest account of everything, daring – needing – to let her glimpse the intensity that had made the day so special and burnt inside him still, like faith restored.

'And did you do any more hard work on the neighbourly front?' he prompted, once their plates were empty and he feared he had hogged the conversation for too long. 'Any more swimming to promote the cause of Anglo-American relations?'

'I . . . yes, but only briefly.' Sophie blinked, aware of the blood rushing to her face. 'And I got another one for your damn list,' she rushed on, groping for safer territory. '"Green thumb".'

'Hmm?'

'The American for "green fingers" is "green thumb". And this is "flatware",' she added, picking up her fork.

'But I already . . . Hey, what's the matter? Sophie?' She

had leapt off her seat and was crouching by the table. 'What on earth . . . ?'

'There – did you see it?' she shrieked, clutching her head now and pointing. 'Oh, God, this is hideous, I've got to get inside.'

'Christ, it's bats – loads of them,' Andrew exclaimed, getting to his feet, enthralled, as a thick dark silent swarm – like one long spectral animal instead of a pack of many thousands – swept over their heads. 'Hey, Soph, it's okay. They're coming close, but they won't touch – the best radar systems in the world, remember?'

Sophie had grabbed his leg and worked her way to a standing position, pressing her face into his shirt. 'Ugh . . . I can't bear it,' she said shakily.

'Dessert inside, then, is it?' Andrew teased, keeping a protective arm across her head until he had steered her into the kitchen.

Sophie smiled sheepishly. 'There's ice cream and fruit, but I think I might just have lost my appetite.'

'Bed, then?'

'I guess.' Sophie turned away, smoothing imaginary creases in her sundress. 'We can clear up in the morning.' She stretched, opening her mouth for a yawn that then didn't arrive.

'No, I'll do it now.' Andrew spoke brusquely, aware of a sudden, curious reluctance to see the evening through to what now seemed like its obvious conclusion. She had shunned him for so long, after all, *neglected* him. Why should he suddenly dance to her tune? 'You cooked so it's only fair.'

He went back outside to blow out the candles and gather up the dirty crockery. To his surprise the bats had gone and the insects had fallen silent. A swelling suspense seemed to fill the darkness instead, as if not just he but the world was holding its breath. He stacked the plates and glasses and then paused, watching Sophie through the glass panes as she carefully folded a tea-towel and hesitated in the doorway of the kitchen, as if torn between waiting for him and going upstairs alone.

# 7

William wasn't sure he could have confessed, even to Beth, how soothed he felt at the sight of the slate-grey stone Yorkshire farmhouse in which he had spent the first twenty years of his life; how he loved it for being so obstinately unchanged, from the rusted cockerel weathervane that never spun, to the lichen-studded wooden gate of the driveway, propped open for so many years that plumes of grass had lashed themselves over the lower slats, as if making their own bid to bind it where it stood.

And his parents too – after the first momentary shock of the deepening stoop in his father's tall frame, the thickening furrows in his mother's once smooth, pearly complexion, the thinning sweeps of their robust white hair – were still so comfortingly as they had always been, emerging from round the side of the house in matching mud-caked wellingtons and padded green jerkins, glove-fingers and trowels sprouting from the pockets. Moving in unconscious unison, they crossed to the edge of the front lawn, smiling and waving their arms in needless hand-signals to assist in the easy business of parking. William pulled up, as he always did, along the low dry-stone wall that began by the disused gate and ran round the perimeter of the entire garden. In the neighbouring field a cluster of sheep brayed their distaste before trotting off to graze at a safer distance.

The moment William switched off the engine, Alfie and George tumbled out of the passenger doors like released springs, trailing food wrappings and the wires of the various technological entertainments that had kept them more or less quiet for the long slog up the M1.

'Two not three?' called his mother, even as she was receiving George's cursory entry between her arms, while Alfie leapt with his usual boyish enthusiasm at his grandfather.

'Er . . . this time, yes.' William stole a guarded look at Beth, still levering herself out of the car. It wasn't the moment to talk about Harry and he hoped she knew that. The crutches had gone, thank God, but she was still walking very unsteadily, putting as little weight as she could on her bad foot and spending large proportions of each day lying on her back or side, doing leg and ankle exercises with a thin stretchy purple rubber band given to her by Susan's physiotherapist – a man cursed for the source of the recommendation, but in whom she nonetheless seemed to have acquired a certain wary trust.

'Where *is* Harry, then?' barked his father, releasing Alfie and approaching the boot to help with luggage.

'Don't, Dad – the boys and I can manage.'

Anthony Stapleton ignored the admonition and seized the two largest bags. 'Parties preferred to grandparents now, is it?'

'In a manner of speaking . . . Beth, are you all right there?'

'Yes, William, thank you.' Beth had safely extricated herself from the car and was leaning against the stone wall for support while closing the door. But then two bold sheep, their stubby tails twitching, the straggly fringes of their thick coats dangling with mud-clods, made a darting approach and she hastily moved away. William's mother was hovering by the bonnet, waiting to offer a proper greeting. 'Hey, Mrs Stapleton – it's just great to be here.'

'It's Jill and Tony, please.' Jill kissed Beth on both cheeks and then stood back, shaking her head in concern as her daughter-in-law hobbled towards the front door. 'William, I thought you said the ankle was better. The poor love. Tony's got a walking-stick, haven't you, Tony, from that time you twisted your knee? Shall I find it for you, dear?' she cried, hurrying ahead of Beth and holding open the door.

'Oh, no, I'm fine . . . really.' Beth, who had felt her ankle swelling during the long confinement of the journey and who wanted only to be able to lie down somewhere, preferably with her foot raised above her hips, managed a smile. 'This is so beautiful – this house, all these *hills* and so *green*.'

'Yes, well, that's the rain, I'm afraid,' admitted Jill, cheerily, shaking a limp fist at the overcast sky as she ushered Beth inside. 'Worst summer on record – but, then, they seem to say that every year, don't they?' She took Beth on a tour of the ground floor – a labyrinth of small, low-ceilinged rooms full of fireplaces and decorated in shades of mustard, orange and brown – before starting up a set of steep, narrow stairs, which Beth managed only with considerable assistance from the spindly banisters.

'I've put you two in the guest room rather than William's,' she explained, her voice fading as she trotted, with enviable sprightliness, along the passageway. 'That's for the boys, these days – fun for them, I always think, to admire their father's model aeroplanes and have the *Beano* annuals and such. This is you.' She pushed open a door at the end of the narrowing corridor, revealing a room barely larger than the double bed it housed. 'Such a shame Harry's not with you ... As the eldest, he normally gets the box room upstairs.'

A look of such steely questioning accompanied this last remark that Beth, ensnared now in the tiny bedroom, felt bound to respond. 'I guess you may as well know – I mean, William will tell you himself –'

Jill stepped closer, releasing her grip on the door latch. 'My dear, what is it? Has something happened?'

'Not like that, no ... It's just those summer exams Harry took – they didn't go so well. We heard last Thursday. It's not a system I'm familiar with, but he got D grades instead of As.' Beth hesitated, thinking not of her stepson's disappointing results, or the boy's brief, pitiful attempts to conceal them with a series of stumbling lies, first about the grades themselves and then with

some smoke-and-mirrors talk about the school sub-
mitting papers for reappraisal, but of William who, after
cancelling the prematurely arranged 'celebration' lunch,
had unplugged Harry's early-eighteenth-birthday-present
laptop and hurled it across the sitting room with such
force that one of its corners had punctured a splintering
hole in the Chapmans' ancient television – much as
a bullet might have left, Beth had thought. The long
moment of spellbound horror that followed broke with
Alfie bursting into tears, Harry storming upstairs and
William out of the house, slamming the door with
sufficient violence to make the light fittings shake. Beth
had remained in the sitting room with George, who
had said, 'Fuck,' first to the carpet and then to her, so
bleakly – and with such indisputable aptness – that rather
than offering some sort of stepmotherly reprimand she
had merely nodded in agreement.

'So William got kind of mad,' she explained to Jill,
adding loyally, 'as he had every right to, and Harry has
gone back to his mother's.' She sighed, managing not to
add that the impasse had shown no signs of a break-
through, not even on Harry's actual birthday. He had spent
the night clubbing with friends, Susan had reported –
enjoying the rift, William said, rather than offering any
constructive help on what was a truly dire situation.

'Oh dear, oh dear . . .' Jill wrung her hands. 'But he
was supposed to do so *well*, wasn't he? Oxford, William
said.'

'Yeah, well, with those grades, William says it's retakes

or nothing, but – and this is what has been driving him really crazy – Harry is apparently refusing ever to take another exam as long as he lives, which is insane, of course, and I'm sure the kid will come round ... but, hey, you know what? George got *his* grades yesterday and it was top marks across the board!' Beth clapped her hands together, trying to boost her own spirits as much as her mother-in-law's. She had felt rather sorry for George (normally the least easy to like of the three), for having his own unexpected academic triumph so cruelly blighted by the lingering shadow of his elder brother's disgrace. William had said well done a couple of times, but there had been no celebration lunch in a noodle house.

But the person for whom Beth felt the greatest sympathy was herself. She found the intensity of these family wrangles both alienating and abhorrent. Worse still, they were continuing to make the man she loved not only unhappy but unreachable. Since the day of Harry's results there had been several more front-door-slamming walks. He returned from each one smelling of smoke and with a grimace etched so deep into his pale, handsome face that Beth was beginning to fear it might never dissolve. No solace she offered seemed to help: comforting words, comforting meals, not even sex, which, although now taking place with something like its usual reassuring frequency, did not quite lead to the dreamy post-coital peacefulness that she had once so treasured. She detected a new urgency to William's lovemaking too, a sense of desperation almost, that seemed to linger even after their climaxes, as if he had been seeking something that remained unfound.

'So here you are!' William exclaimed, bursting into the little bedroom.

'Beth has just told me about Harry,' said Jill at once. 'I'm sorry, love – what a worry for you.'

'Yes, it is,' William agreed briskly. 'But, do you know, I'm fed up of letting that child bring everything down. Beth and I are on *holiday* . . .' William slipped an arm around her waist and dropped a kiss on her head '. . . a fact I know that I, for one, have been in danger of forgetting. So what we both badly need, Mum, is lots of that restorative Yorkshire air you and Dad like to brag about, not to mention some of your even more restorative home cooking. Don't we, darling?' William kissed Beth again, more tenderly this time, his face crinkled with smiles.

'Oh, we so do . . .' Beth found that she was almost too choked to speak. This was her man, back again, her beloved, loving, attentive man. If the oxygen of northern England could perform that in the space of ten minutes, she would be indebted to it for life.

'And George's GCSE results were *unbelievable* –'

'Oh, yes,' Jill interrupted excitedly, 'Beth mentioned that too. Haven't I always said he was the clever one, the dark horse who would do well? Middle children, now they're the ones to watch. Like that sister of yours – running her own language school in France, if you please, while Lizzy never set her sights so high . . . although I'm not saying you're not a high-achiever, love – all those share-options you talk about. I'll never understand them, no matter how many times you explain.' Clucking fondly, she turned to Beth. 'And where are you in the family pecking order, dear? I'm sure William must have told me but I'm afraid I've forgotten.'

'Oh . . . well, actually there was just me.'

'Well, that can be good too.' Jill shifted her attention to the bedroom window, tweaking at a pleat in its floral curtains. 'Oh, look, Will.' She pointed through the pane. 'We've got a visitor.'

William left Beth's side and went to peer over his mother's shoulder. 'Oh, God, not Henrietta. I'm not in the mood for her, I really am not.'

'And who is Henrietta?' ventured Beth, glancing with some longing now at the lovely linen dome of fresh white bedding next to her, thinking how enticing it looked compared to the prospect of milky English tea and the labour of conversing with people she knew barely or not at all.

'She's the daughter of the Purleys who own the farm next door,' Jill explained, smoothing her manly crop of white hair with the palms of both hands as she squeezed past Beth to get to the door. 'They're away and she's up here to keep an eye on the place. She and William grew up together – birthday teas and the Pony Club. Lizzy was more her age but they never really saw eye to eye, those two . . . Come on, William dear, she'll want a cup of tea and I think your father's already taken off with the boys to the river – the fish are jumping early, he says, now the days are shortening.'

William pulled a comical, reassuring face as he followed his mother out of the room, but Beth, left to edge her way along the passage and down the stairs, felt childishly stranded. A guest with an unpleasantly strident voice, she decided, even before she caught up with the gathering in the kitchen and found herself being introduced to a tall, muscular woman clad in an obscenely tight pair of riding pants and a T-shirt, carelessly flecked with mud and wisps of straw. She moved around the kitchen with enviable familiarity too, pulling mugs and plates and cake tins out of cupboards, her auburn ponytail as thick and swinging as the very thing from which it had acquired its name, her ruddy, handsome face working energetically as she talked and smiled. There was a masculinity to her that Beth couldn't help being glad of, but her eyes were large and vibrantly blue and seemed, every time she looked at William at least, to dance with knowing amusement.

'You've slept with her,' Beth accused, the moment they were alone, perhaps because the moment itself had been so long in coming, what with wedges of fruit cake to succumb to first, over talk of things and people of whom she had never heard, followed by a frenzy of vegetable-peeling and table-laying into which she had jettisoned herself purely to appear like the dutiful daughter-in-law she so knew she wasn't.

With three pheasant roasting under layers of bacon, dishes warming and the redoubtable Henrietta pressed into returning for dinner, they had escaped upstairs at last, to 'freshen up' before the meal. Beth had changed into a smart black skirt and coral shirt and was doing what she had so longed for three hours before – lying on the plump, freshly laundered bed, her bad foot propped on a pillow. William was leaning out of the window, smoking a cigarette.

'Henrietta?' He turned to laugh, rills of smoke floating round his mouth. 'Er, no, thank you.'

'Well, something, then ... *something*,' Beth muttered, turning her head away, hating herself. Along the landing she could hear sloshing noises from the cottage's one and only bathroom as the boys took shifts at washing off the mud. The fishing had produced merriment rather than fish, with a long, convoluted tale about both boys ending up half clothed in the freezing river and then being commanded by their grandfather into a variety of sprinting races to warm up. The trio had returned damp and breathless, exuding a joy that was evident still in the sploshing and joshing coming along the corridor and which, instead of lightening Beth's spirits, only served to heighten her sense of being out of things, of not belonging, not even to William. 'Honey, I just hate that you feel the need to smoke,' she ventured, in an effort to crush the feeling into non-existence, as William hurled his stub into the grey evening air and ducked back inside the little bedroom. 'If you're stressed you should bring it on to *me*.'

William laughed. 'And why on earth would I do that?'

'Because that's my job – as it's any wife's job – to be there for her husband to lean on.'

'Well, that's very sweet, Beth, but I think you've got enough on your plate as it is. And much as I love you, nicotine gives me a hit you cannot quite provide.'

William had spoken lightly but to Beth's fragile state of mind the remark felt like a smack across the face, an outright declaration of her inadequacy. 'Have you even looked at that book I got you?' she snapped. '*How to Quit in One Day* . . . Have you even *looked*?'

William, who had started to massage the toes of her sore foot, stopped abruptly. 'No, Beth, I haven't. Now, leave it, okay? Just *leave* it.'

Beth caught her breath and held it, seeing again the flying laptop, the jewels of glass spraying out of the TV screen. It wasn't the violence of the act that had frightened her, she realized, so much as the sense of something breaking, something special and irrevocable, something between her and William. 'It's because I care for you,' she murmured, slowly releasing the air in her lungs. 'I can't remember my dad's voice – or even his face that well – but I can hear him coughing every morning, *every* morning, William, making way for that day's pack.'

William stood still, doing his best to look compassionate rather than irritated. Although Beth made few references to what he knew had been a tough childhood, he had heard about the coughing father before, several times. A drinker, a gambler, a womanizer, Beth's dad had finally left for good when Beth was five, leaving no money or fond memories. A phone call from a hospital a few years later revealed that he had met his death in as ugly a fashion as he had lived his life, under the impact of a jack-knifing lorry on a Missouri freeway. Recalling this now, William tightened his expression, fighting the urge to point out that coughing was neither a sin nor a sure indication of the manner of a man's impending death. But Beth was already moving the conversation on, saying something about Harry and the tragedy of getting hooked so young.

'Harry?' William laughed sharply, scornfully. 'Making a hash of his A levels is one thing, but as I've told you, that child is too sensible – too vain for that matter – about being fit and playing rugby ever to take up smoking.'

Beth looked at her hands, the fingers interlaced across her stomach, the nails trimmed into perfect smooth semi-circles and shining with her favourite light pink polish. Lying on sofas was good for manicures, she had discovered, if nothing else. She liked it when her hands looked good and pretty. Unlike other body parts – not to say people – hands never let you down. William was leaning against the window-sill, clearly waiting for her to respond, arms and legs crossed in a show of relaxation that contradicted the tension in his face. This arguing was new, hateful, but worse still, Beth reasoned, would be not telling the truth. Harry was in so much trouble already, it was hardly like it was going to make a big difference. And William being mad at Harry was preferable to him being mad at her. Anything was preferable to that. 'That day I twisted my ankle . . .' She took a deep breath before going on to describe the details she had hitherto withheld – namely, Harry's familiar casualness both with the cigarette and the Goth girlfriend.

'Why didn't you tell me this before?' William pushed off from the window-sill and advanced on the bed.

'I'm not sure . . . I guess . . . Well, the truth is, I promised Harry I wouldn't.'

'You promised *Harry*? Well, that's nice.' William spun away with a look of disgust.

'I'm sorry,' Beth cried, in a tone that was accusatory rather than apologetic. 'I just didn't think it was such a big deal.'

William folded his arms, glaring at her. 'Well, that's where we differ. He is my son. For him to behave so out of character *is* a big deal, as I think recent events testify. And you putting loyalty to him over me,' William shook his head, releasing a dry, bitter laugh, 'call me petty, but that doesn't feel insignificant either.'

'I was just trying to get along with him,' Beth pleaded, appalled both that they were rowing and at the stance William was taking. 'You know – trying not to be the wicked stepmother. And anyway,' she continued, frustration getting the better of her, 'it's hardly like it would have made a difference to anything, is it? He's eighteen, for Christ's sake, at an age when he can do what he likes, regardless of what you think. What's gotten you really upset, I reckon, are those D grades. Or are you going to blame me for those too – ?' She broke off as a faint, trilling voice floated up from the ground floor, announcing supper. 'Oh, William, don't be mad,' Beth whispered. 'I do understand, really I do. And of course I shouldn't have made that pact with Harry over you . . . I see that now.'

'It's dinner – we'd better go down.'

'William . . .' Beth tried to seize his arm as he walked past the bed. 'Please, baby, it's too horrible to argue – '

'Forgive me if I overreacted. It's been something of a testing week.'

'I love you so much.'

'And I love you,' replied William, in a dull voice, holding the door open till she was on her feet but then striding ahead of her to the stairs.

Beth started after him and then stopped, overcome by a body-blow of longing to be back within the spacious, orderly, beautiful confines of their marital home, with its pretty pitched roof and tidy yard, and all the towering maples guarding it like a private army. Widely acknowledged as an area famous for its excellent public schools, Darien as a choice of location had surprised some of the work colleagues who doubled as friends and who therefore knew Beth well enough to suspect that having kids might not be high on her and William's agenda. But Darien was also in the heart of the state she had been brought up to revere for its affluent beauty –

rural but *tamed*, boasting some of the most fabulous real estate money could buy; a veritable picket-fenced paradise, interspersed with parks and ponds, which, like the handsome fringes of Long Island Sound along its coast, bobbed with sleek yachts and motorboats the size of small houses. For years Beth had drooled over magazine snapshots of such images, vowing that if the world were ever to become her oyster it was this particular corner of it that she would choose.

How, she wondered now, had she ever agreed to let trespassing strangers onto such hallowed ground? Sophie and Andrew Chapman, in *her* precious corner of the world, still so newly acquired, so treasured – and with their kids, too, no doubt fouling the place up. Had she been out of her mind?

Glancing down, Beth saw that her ankle, although feeling a little better, was still bulging visibly over the edge of her smart heeled shoe. In warmer, dryer temperatures it would have ached less, she was sure. Downstairs, a rapping of the door knocker was followed by Henrietta's confident high-pitched tones ringing through the hall.

Beth edged back into the bedroom and fished her cell phone out of the bottom of her purse. Only a little more than a week remained but it felt like a lifetime. She needed at least to hear an American voice, garner some news from home, no matter if that news came from Florida instead of Connecticut. She wasn't herself in England, Beth reflected bleakly. It didn't *suit* her. And neither was William. The place was bad for both of them, very bad. She started to punch in her mother's number and then stopped, recalling William's merry warnings about the impossibility of getting signals for anything among all the dales and valleys – or whatever the hell they were. He had described the area as a geographical conspiracy against anything technological and Beth had laughed, never imagining how personal that conspiracy could feel, how hostile.

'Fucking country!' She flung the phone onto the bed, where it bounced once before landing with a clatter on a section of bare floorboard peeking between the two thin rugs that passed for carpeting. For a moment Beth held her breath, imagining a break in the jolly conversation downstairs, heads tipping to the ceiling, eyes rolling in mutual critical concern at what the *foreigner* was playing at.

More likely, they hadn't even noticed her absence, she decided miserably, feeling the too-tight cut of her skirt as she retrieved the phone and then groaning at the sight of her reflection in the narrow mirror pinned to the wall. There was no escaping it: she had gone up an entire size – and all on her lower half as usual: hips, stomach, ass. Her skirt was straining so hard the stitches on the seams showed. It was a miracle William hadn't said anything, a total miracle. Although love-making *was* always in the dark, these days . . . could that be why? Had she grown hideous?

Beth forced herself to look again at the mirror, this time turning sideways and sucking in her stomach. She breathed deeply, holding her head high, drawing on ancient, hard-fought lessons for inducing calm, lessons she hadn't needed for years. No, not hideous, she reminded herself, but . . . *beautiful*, like all God's creatures. And in just over a week's time this cold, damp, hateful experience would be behind her, boxed safely, as memories could be if one worked at them hard enough.

On the top stair she faltered again at a wild whoop of laughter from the kitchen. She should have checked on her choice of clothes with William. Maybe her skirt and blouse would be too formal. *Why* hadn't she checked with William? He was wearing chinos and a clean shirt. But then William invariably wore chinos and a shirt. It was different for women . . . It was always different for women.

Beth took another deep breath, telling herself that her spry, business-like mother-in-law was bound to have smartened up for dinner, as would the dreadful, meaty, hearty Henrietta, even if it was into an outfit that made as big a deal of her peachy ass as the gross riding pants. Of course the skirt was fine. *She* was fine. Beth spread both her arms for balance as she started down the stairs, gripping the banister with one hand and pressing the other against the wall. Her ankle might have been feeling better for its rest, but with other, older, deeper frailties stirring, no measure of self-protection felt too great.

Life had got complicated again, William reflected bitterly, slumping down the following morning on the crest of the hill that reduced the valley to a green fold in the earth, containing homes no bigger than scattered pebbles and a glassy slit of a river, which from this distance appeared to run an inch from his parents' front door instead of a good mile. Sheep dotted the surrounding fields with all the simple innocence of a child's collage of cotton-wool buds on green felt. Overhead, cartoon-warship clouds patrolled the skies, the sun bobbing between their steely prows like a perky buoy flashing its brilliant light.

'Hey, Dad, check this out.'

William turned in time to see Alfie swinging at a tatty tennis ball with an old putter of his grandfather's that he had brought along for the walk. The ball sailed high and veered left on a gust of wind, landing among some yellow speckled gorse clumped round a lone tree, billowing on the sky-line like a schooner in full sail. Alfie didn't see the wild beauty of the place, William knew, just as he hadn't at that age. It was simply somewhere in which it was easy to be happy, somewhere open and large enough to swallow all the noise and energy he could hurl into it.

'Nice shot!' William waved, then returned his attention to the view, thinking wistfully of days when how far one could hit a ball had meant the world, when staring at the dots of human occupation of a valley would not have prompted yearnings for a similar distancing perspective on his own life. Getting to know Beth had been close to retrieving some of that innocence, William saw now; falling in love – the delight of finding that he still could

– had made the world seem so splendid again, so easy to forgive and believe in. Buying the Darien house had stretched his finances to the hilt, but it had been worth it for the sheer pleasure of Beth's pleasure, making her wildest dream come true, she had said more times than he could count, always adding that it was only their shared occupation of it that made the dream complete.

But since they had come to England there was no denying that some of that splendour had been stripped away. Beth might have been a fresh start in one sense, but the last few weeks had woken William up to the fact that she could not be kept separate from all that had gone before, no matter how much either of them wished it to be so. The past might seem to slide out of view, but it was always there, always knitted to the present, whether that involved Harry screwing up his exams, Susan (unbelievably, in the midst of this new crisis) angling for more money, or Henrietta gate-crashing the dinner table, making eyes over a glass or three under the mistaken apprehension that a limping, glum-faced wife was sufficient pretext for persuading William to re-enact some old times.

Once, not that long ago, it might even have been fun to confess rather than lie about the very brief, indisputably desperate, pre- and post-Susan phases that had encompassed shagging his childhood playmate – invariably when they had both had too much to drink and usually (at least on William's part) to sobering disappointment. The ability to rugby-tackle sheep for dipping had proved no qualification either for erotic athletics between the sheets or interesting pillow-talk afterwards. Of equal disappointment had been the discovery of just how quickly Henrietta's trademark show of feisty, cheery independence collapsed under the joint assault of alcohol and intimacy, exposing a sobbing neediness that William had found as repellent as it was pitiful.

In her current frame of mind William knew that Beth would have been unlikely to see the funny side of such admissions. Indeed, her resentful dislike of Henrietta during the course of dinner the previous evening had been palpable almost to the point of embarrassment – even after he had whispered heartfelt apologies for the row about Harry. She was clearly (in spite of denying it) itching to turn her back on England and the whole house-swapping project. And William could hardly blame her: what with her ankle injury, Susan playing hard-ball and the shenanigans over Harry, their supposed holiday had been bumpy enough to make life back in Connecticut look even rosier than when they had left it. Thinking of Darien now, he couldn't conjure any memory of stress other than friendly tussles about which steak house to choose for a night out and whether to rent two movies from Netflicks or three.

Only a fool wouldn't yearn to return to such simple pleasures. Yet such a long spell in England had also served to remind William just how fond he still was of his homeland: cricket, pubs, real beer, the option of

TV without adverts, not to mention the undulating countryside, spread beneath his feet that morning like a glorious feast. But the real, crucial tie, surpassing all such superficial pleasures, was of course his sons. To have the chance to spend so much time with them had been as wonderful as it was unprecedented: he had managed two straight weeks before, but never four, and never in such logistically trouble-free circumstances. The thought of that ending, of stepping back into a flimsy, intermittent pattern of emails and often unsatisfactory phone calls, especially with the unresolved issues now surrounding Harry, was like a knife slicing through his heart.

'Guess who!'

William jumped as a pair of muddy palms was clamped over his eyes. 'Tiger Woods? A member of the SAS? An annoying thirteen-year-old trying to give a parent a heart-attack?' William spun round, grabbing his youngest under his protuberant, boyish ribs and wrestling him onto his back on the ground where he pinned him under one knee. 'Surrender?'

Alfie jerked his head from side to side, his glasses jiggling, helpless with giggles.

'Surrender?' William repeated, but hoarsely this time for his attention had drifted to the freckles on his son's nose, the wisp of down on the upper lip, the new band of muscles under the ribcage. Only the arms and legs were still childishly skinny, as well as being endearingly criss-crossed with evidence of a good summer holiday – scratches, grazes, dirt, interspersed with clusters of mosquito bites. 'My God, your glasses are filthy,' William muttered, amazed that the eyes regarding him through such grimy lenses could still manage to be such a mischievous, heartbreaking blue.

'But I don't surrender,' prompted Alfie, sensing that some vital impetus to the game was in danger of being lost.

'Then you shall *die*,' William snarled obligingly, flipping him onto his stomach and starting a session of merciless tickling that ended only when an accidental elbow caught his cheekbone.

Afterwards they lay side by side on their backs in the grass, watching the warships, which had spread and thickened into continents.

'I don't want you to go back to America, Dad. I like it better when you're here.'

'I'm not going for ages yet.'

'Eight days. You're going in eight days.'

'To a huge house with a huge garden that you're going to visit in the Christmas holidays and every holidays after that.' William held his breath, hoping that Alfie wouldn't look sideways and see the rogue tear that had trickled out of the corner of his eye and down his temple. George, Harry – the idiot – he could manage, but not this, not this.

'When we come out to stay, we won't have to call her "Mummy", will we?'

'Of course not.'

'Never?'

'Never ever ever.'

'And are you going to get a swimming-pool built, like you said?'

'Too bloody right I am.' William sat up, delivering a playful finger-poke into the gap between Alfie's shorts and T-shirt. 'Okay?'

'Okay.'

'Good. Well, I'm glad we've got that settled.' William got to his feet, blinking away a swarm of unhelpful images of the figures on his recent credit-card statements. His end-of-year bonus should set things straight, as it always did, but in the meantime things were tight, as he had tried, with mounting exasperation, to explain to Susan. 'Come on, mate, we should be getting back.'

'Maybe not yet . . . Look.' Alfie pointed down the hill.

'Blimey . . .' William put his hand to his eyes, squinting as the sun burst through one of the sky's now thinning plates of cloud. Beth was making her way towards them, thrashing through the clumps of sharp-bladed grass and thistles with the aid of his father's walking-stick. William's heart swelled. It was a hell of a walk, even for someone fully fit. He had forgotten how resilient she was, how keen to bounce back. 'Hey, Beth . . . Beth.' He swung both arms above his head, but she kept on climbing, hauling herself with long, lop-sided strides, barely glancing up. 'Wow.' William grinned, reaching out to ruffle more chaos into Alfie's haystack hair. 'We could roll to meet her. What about that, eh?'

'Roll?'

'A race.' William had already thrown himself back onto the grass, parking his body for release down the hill.

'But it's prickly . . .'

'Sissy.'

A moment later they had both set off, a few feet apart, their arms crossed over their chests, their faces clenched against any hostilities lurking in the ground. Laughing, crashing, restarting, crashing again, it was several minutes before they were close enough to Beth for William, sitting up between tumbles, to notice that the determination in his wife's uneven stride was grim rather than cheerful. Alfie set off on another roll, but William stayed where he was, his own cheerfulness subsiding under the realization that she was cross. No, not cross . . . upset. She was wiping her face . . . crying.

'Beth . . . darling . . . what is it?' William stumbled towards her, almost twisting his own ankles in his haste, his heart surging with terrors. His mother? His father? Harry, God forbid? He had never seen her so distraught.

Alfie, realizing the fun and games really were over, got to his feet with a sigh and started back up the hill for the putter.

'Beth, darling, what is it? What on earth has happened?'

She stopped to wait for him, flinging the stick to the ground, her shoulders heaving. 'She's gone! She's gone. They've lost her! For DAYS she's been gone and they never said . . . they NEVER SAID. Those fuckers . . . they've LOST her. They left a phone message. I went with your mother to the shops and got a signal and . . .' She dropped to her knees, sobbing.

'You mean . . . ?'

'DIDO! Who else could I mean, William? Oh, God, we should never have done it – letting those people into our home. I *knew* it was wrong, in my heart, I knew it and I never said . . .'

'Hey, darling, calm down . . .' William crouched next to her, stroking her shoulders, inwardly relieved but recognizing that it was no moment to confess as much. 'Let's get a little perspective here, shall we? You're over-wrought and upset and no wonder, but if Dido has gone walkabout she may yet come back and –'

'I need to return now.'

For a moment William thought she was talking about his parents' grey-brick cottage, its dark slate roof just peeping into view from a patch of trees in the valley below.

'I need to look for her. The Chapmans must leave our home.' She had stopped crying and was talking with the calmness of one believing their words made sense.

'Beth, for heaven's sake . . .'

'I *need* to, William. I'll phone Virgin – I'm sure I have the number in my purse . . . Maybe I can get a signal up here, do you think?' She stood up, fumbling with the catch on her bag, which she had strung across her chest like a satchel.

William took a deep breath. Above them, Alfie was making his way back down the hill, thwacking the golf club at clumps of grass. 'Sweetheart, you're not thinking straight.'

'Oh, but I am . . . very straight, straighter than I have for weeks.' Beth swallowed. Her mouth was dry and still tasted horrible from the post-breakfast throwing up that had preceded the excursion into Skipton. A drastic measure, not resorted to for many years, the relief of evicting her mother-in-law's irresistible heaped plates of sausages, bacon and scrambled egg had been euphoric. And with the hideous news about Dido she was even gladder she had done it. She could cope with many things, but not getting fat . . . not now, on top of everything else. 'I need to look for Dido. If that family won't move out then I'll ask if I can stay with Carter and Nancy, or perhaps use the Travelodge. I need to call to her, William, she knows my voice. The longer we leave it the less likely –'

She broke off, overcome by more tears. Alfie, back within earshot, blushed and darted off in a different direction, jumping on molehills and hoping to look like he didn't think anything was wrong.

'Beth, baby . . .' William hugged her, half amused, half moved by the violence of her reaction. It was mad, but sweet. That she had a big heart was one of the things he adored about her. It was the same heart, after all, that was so possessively crazy about him. And Dido was aptly named, a queen of cats who would be a great loss to their small household, particularly for Beth whom the creature made no secret of loving above all other. 'There is no way you're going back early – this is our holiday and I *need* you. And we couldn't possibly boot out the Chapmans, could we? Or impose on Nancy and Carter . . . It's only a few more days and, besides, cats are famously brilliant at finding their way home, aren't they? Mum has this story about one that got stuck in a removals van and walked back to Clapham from Lands End.' He kept his arm firmly across her shoulders, half supporting, half propelling her for the walk back down the hill.

Beth, calmer for her outburst but still muttering, leant on him heavily, allowing herself to be led. 'People said I should have had her claws removed, to stop her straying, but she was such a *house* cat, wasn't she, from those two years in my apartment, that I never saw the need . . . and how cruel anyway to remove an animal's claws – I just couldn't do it, and she didn't scratch too much, did she?'

'No, sweetheart, she didn't. Hey, you know what? Dido probably just didn't like the look of the Chapmans and is holed up somewhere waiting for your return.'

Beth managed a bleak smile. 'Yeah, maybe . . . I'm sorry, honey, I guess it would be crazy to go back early, but I just feel so sad, so helpless . . .'

'Of course you do,' William soothed hurriedly, fearing more tears, 'but we'll be home soon enough – with everything back to normal, Dido included . . . I say, what about a piggy-back for the rest of the way?'

'Ride on your back? I don't think so.'

'Come on, it'll be quicker – and better for your poor ankle.'

'But, William, I weigh a *ton*.'

'Silly, you're a bird. Get on.' William bent his knees and took hold of her legs to help her clamber aboard. 'Hey, Alfie, take the stick, could you?'

Alfie obeyed, trying not to look at his stepmother's puffy eyes, but the stick was pleasingly smooth and solid with a curved brass handle and soon he was whirling it in the air along with the putter, barking equestrian commands.

'Tally-ho,' shouted William, breaking into a canter.

'You're mad,' Beth shrieked, clinging on, laughing in spite of herself.

William galloped faster, suffused with a sudden glorious certainty that his world would right itself again; that the people he loved would love each other; that worries about money, cats and exam results would dissolve as quickly as they had appeared.

When they finally reached the road his arms and legs were burning. 'There we are, my lady.' He set Beth down gently, breathing hard. 'Your knight is forever at your bidding.' Alfie handed back the stick without being asked and ran on ahead to open the gate that offered a short-cut along a wooded path to his grandparents' back garden. The sun, meanwhile, had come out in full strength, making the tarmac gleam like treacle and the hedgerows look bejewelled instead of merely wet. William was happy to keep pace with Beth and the stick, linking arms on her good side, revelling in his restored faith in the world and its power to give pleasure.

They reached the gate to find Alfie squatting in front of a large spider's web strung between two lower slats. 'It's midway through its lunch.' He pointed gleefully at the occupant of the web, a creature as large as a hazelnut, busy masticating through the corpse of a fat fly.

'Ohmygod.' Beth bent down, clapping her hand to her mouth. 'That is so gross . . . would you *look* at that, William?' She clutched her throat, exchanging eye-rolls with Alfie.

William did look, but not at the web. It was his wife and his son that he found so transfixing, crouching together, joined in the simple unity of shared wonderment. *His wife and his son* . . . As the image burnt before his eyes an idea exploded inside William's head, an idea so huge, so right, that he felt dizzy just from trying to accommodate it.

'Hey, Dad, don't you want to see?'

'Yes, of course. I – I was just wishing I had my camera . . . You two and that spider – it would make such a great shot,' William bluffed, stepping up for a closer look.

'But I've already taken some pictures with my phone.'

William laughed. 'Oh, good. Of course you have.'

A few minutes later they were almost at the house, Alfie out of earshot.

'Beth?'

She turned sharply, her expression taut and distracted, the arresting spectacle on the gate clearly forgotten.

'I love you,' William mouthed, reining in the urge to

say what was really on his mind. It was a massive idea after all, a total *volte-face*, in fact. It would need the most finely tuned moment for release, the gentlest persuasion.

# 8

'A white doughnut,' was Olivia's pronouncement on the Guggenheim as she followed her mother across the foyer out into the street. Through the glass wall, Andrew and Milly were just visible, deep in the long queue for the checkout in the gift shop. And all for three postcards – of a cardboard sculpture, a Van Gogh and a Jackson Pollock – so painstakingly chosen that Sophie caught herself wondering if it was the recent immersion in some of Europe's oldest cities that had suddenly bestowed on her younger child such a precise certainty of her cultural preferences. The tour had already produced an endearingly meticulous scrapbook, comprising not just the predictable photographs of friends posing on hostel beds and at café tables, but programmes and tickets from venues, all interspersed with snaps of monuments and neat blocks of handwritten description.

Olivia, in contrast, appeared to have developed a new determination not to be impressed by anything. 'A doughnut, eh?' Sophie turned away from the glare of the museum's curved white walls to slip on her sunglasses.

'Yeah, a white *ugly* doughnut.'

'So you preferred all that classical stuff in Vienna and Salzburg, did you?' They had moved away from the busy entrance to an empty stretch of pavement, where Olivia plucked her phone out of her shorts pocket and quickly settled into a tidy cross-legged position against the wall. 'Huh?' She looked up blankly.

Sophie laughed. 'We haven't been able to get Milly to stop talking about it and you've barely said a word. It's almost like the pair of you went on different trips.' She peered fondly at her elder daughter over the rims of her glasses, relishing the easy family cohesion that had returned in full force during the course of the final week of the holiday. Across the road, the reservoir in Central Park glinted invitingly through the trees. It made her think of Carter's pool, all those long, secret afternoons of talk over iced tea and dope. It felt incredible now, like the behaviour of someone she didn't know.

She hadn't seen the American since the day everything had slipped out of control, an extraordinary day for many reasons, the most significant being that she and Andrew – after surviving the swarm of bats – had made love, embracing with an intimacy that had felt all the more intense for having been so glaringly absent. Sophie had swum on several occasions since, but only at a place called Pear Tree Point, which she and Andrew, building on their new-found closeness, had discovered together and to which they had subsequently and eagerly introduced their daughters. A mere fifteen-minute drive from the Stapletons', it was a breathtakingly picturesque spot on Long Island Sound, with plenty of room for parking and its own dear pristine little stretch of sandy beach, frequented by friendly locals, but never too populated for the easy accommodation of four extra somewhat faded British towels. Sophie's happiest memories of the holiday were already rooted there, a marker in her own mind for all the trouble being done with, for equilibrium – her own and the family's – properly restored.

'Different tours? What a weird thing to say.' Olivia caught a bunch of her long hair and squinted at the ends. 'I just don't *go on* about everything the whole time like Milly, that's all. Anyway, you and Dad are the ones who look like you've been in different places. You're, like, *black* while he is still the whitest, weediest white.'

Sophie cast a sharp glance at her daughter. 'Dad has to be careful on summer holidays, as you well know. It's either that or third-degree burns.'

But, of course, in a sense they *had* been on different holidays, at least to begin with, Sophie mused, turning her gaze back to the park as a tingle of shame tiptoed up her spine at the recollection of how willingly she had soaked up the American's kindness. From the first gentle massage of oatmeal ointment into her inflamed hands it was as if something inside her had surrendered, something exhausted and needy. It had felt wrong, yet also deeply therapeutic. Attentive, older, warm-hearted, full of wisdom, Carter had appeared like some sort of rock-solid receptacle, ready to have anything poured into it that she chose. And she had taken full advantage, because she sensed he wanted her to and because it had felt so good.

But then, when things had got out of hand, all that

goodness had vanished in an instant. And although Sophie had hitherto done a remarkable job of blocking it from her mind, aided by the wonderful night of reconciliation with Andrew and the arrival of the girls, on this last full day on American soil she was finding herself assailed by flashbacks to that fateful afternoon. On the face of it, she had done nothing wrong. She and Carter had simply been having one of their long, deep talks, lying side by side on the loungers. The American had accused her of being one of life's 'carers' – a type, he claimed, who were notoriously bad at taking care of themselves. 'Tamsin took away your right to complain,' he had drawled, like some veteran analyst, knitting his brows against the sunshine as he fired one of his affectionate challenging stares. 'She was so sick you couldn't compete. Over time that stuff builds up, sometimes finding the weirdest reasons to come out. Like your scare with that kid breaking into your home. Maybe something in you broke that day, something that had nothing to do with the burglary.'

Sophie had got off the lounger and sauntered to the edge of the pool, pondering the truth of these bald assessments and whether explanations for entire lives could be so easy. Carter, stepping up behind her, had caught her off-guard.

'Oh, Sophie . . .' Before she could move he was running his fingers back through the mess of her hair, tenderly raking the strands off her face.

Instead of resisting Sophie had leant against him,

letting her back rest on the swell of his belly, thinking that a man who could be so kind – so fearless, so wise – deserved no less. The next instant his mouth was on her neck and then over her lips, his tongue probing feverishly for hers. For a few minutes – five? Ten? – Sophie had committed the sin of responding fully, so amazed at the American's urgency that it seemed only right to try to match it. Until it dawned on her that the physical desire stirring deep inside her, after months of dormancy, was not for the large, hectic hands already sliding under the stretchy fabric of her bathing costume but for the gentler, familiar touch of the man she had married.

'But I love you,' Carter had groaned, when she eventually found the wherewithal to twist away, gasping protests. 'You must have known that, you *must*.'

She had done wrong, Sophie reflected now, waiting for her heart to stop pounding as she watched Olivia's slim musician's fingers working furiously across the tiny panel of her phone, but good had come of it. Carter knew where he stood – she had spelt that out plainly enough during the course of scrambling for her book, her sun cream, explaining that, grateful as she was for their friendship, it was at an end; that what had just happened had never once been her intention and she was sorry if she had allowed him to believe otherwise. And her reward had been Andrew, arriving home from the rehearsal that night with a new light in his eyes, a light that had seemed to see her instead of looking through her, a light that, once his lips touched hers, had drawn all the suppressed, misplaced desire of the afternoon back to what felt like its rightful place.

And now, in just twenty-four hours, they would be returning to the familiar, welcoming clutches of their own home. As would the Stapletons to theirs. Sophie tipped her face to the portions of sky visible above the skyscrapers – the same dense indigo it had been for every day of the four weeks – conjuring an image of the two planes passing mid-way across the Atlantic. If England had proved half as magical as Darien had been for her and Andrew, they would be a happy couple indeed. William Stapleton, phoning the previous week for more details about the missing cat, had certainly sounded cheerful enough, saying not to worry and such things happened and how perfectly her and Andrew's house had suited their needs.

'Hey.' Sophie poked her toe into Olivia's leg. 'You might want to go easy on that thing. We are still in America, you know, and your phone bill must already be astronomical.'

'Not necessarily, because they only charge *per text*, don't they? So all I've been doing is writing extra long messages.'

'Okay, clever clogs.' Sophie pulled a face, wondering how she could ever have allowed herself to lose enthusiasm for the relentless and wonderfully energizing business of being a parent. Normality – who would have thought it could feel so special?

A moment later Andrew emerged from the museum entrance, hands in his pockets, whistling. Milly trotted at his heels, twirling a small plastic bag containing her postcards.

'Apparently, while on tour, Olivia acquired a *boyfriend*,' he whispered, as they drew near. 'Milly's been telling me about it.'

'Oh, God.'

'A worrying development, I agree. A percussionist too – they're always untrustworthy.'

Sophie giggled, looping her arm through his as they set off down the street, the girls a few paces ahead.

'So – a last shopping session for you lot while I bash through a final rehearsal. There'll be three reserved seats in the front row, did I say?'

'Yes, you did.' Sophie squeezed his arm. He was as excited as she had ever seen him. For whatever reasons he might have agreed to do the favour, the obnoxious Ann's charity concert had clearly become a real source of joy. 'Andrew, this holiday, you were a genius for organizing it.'

He grinned. 'I know.'

'And how I was . . . before . . . I think it was some sort of *phase*, tied up with my immune system being under par, of course, like Dr Murray said, but also something else . . . something perhaps unleashed by that horrible thug of a child breaking into the house –'

'I always said that, didn't I?' Andrew patted her hand, scanning the street for taxis.

'Yes, yes, you did . . . ' Sophie swallowed, gripping his arm a little harder, needing to get the rest of it out – not Carter's version of events, but her own. 'I think the whole business made me feel fundamentally *unsafe* . . . but also – and, Andrew, here's the really awful thing – I realized that there was this huge part of me that had been blaming you . . . '

'Me?' He wrested his gaze from the traffic with a grimace. 'Of course you *blamed* me. I invited the little shit in, didn't I? Offered him a glass of water . . . Christ . . . ' He flicked his attention back to the street, which was streaming with traffic, but none of it the right kind, muttering, 'And I thought every second car in New York was supposed to be a cab.'

'He was such a *boy*, you see,' Sophie pressed on, 'so I think there was this old-fashioned-damsel side of me that thought you should have wrestled him to the ground and –'

'With a knife in his hand? I might be a romantic, but I'm not stupid.'

No, she was the stupid one, Sophie saw suddenly, wanting a knight in shining armour instead of a real man – a man sensible enough to be scared. It didn't matter *when* the knife had appeared: the threat of it had been there all along. Andrew had stayed calm and co-operative, and if big situations were tests of character then hers was the one that had failed – perhaps because of what Carter had said: some overstretched, coping part of her caving in.

'Forgive me,' she urged, tugging on his arm. 'Andrew, say out loud that you forgive me for how I've been . . . for *everything*.' She had meant to utter the last word with real force but it died on her lips, thanks to a familiar figure emerging from the park across the street, arms hanging loose and wide, the slight bow in his legs visible even though he was wearing trousers rather than shorts.

'Hey! Wait up!' Carter yelled, hurling himself into breaks in the traffic, light on his feet as always, in spite of his girth.

If Andrew murmured his forgiveness, Sophie never heard it. He was too busy stepping forward to greet their holiday neighbour, surprise lighting his face and then pride as he introduced his daughters. Sophie hung back, looking at the middle of Carter's forehead rather than his pleading eyes, offering a stiff windscreen wipe of an arm by way of a greeting.

'I phoned a couple of times to try and entice you over, but your mother said you were too busy,' Carter joked at the girls.

'As, indeed, we have been,' exclaimed Andrew, loyally, adding, 'But what a coincidence, bumping into you.'

'Well, sir, New York is a very small place.'

Sophie looked at the pavement, wondering if the rest of her family could hear the intensity in his voice.

'You guys leave tomorrow, right? Well, Nancy and I will sure miss having you around. Hey, Sophie, you know what?' He clicked his fingers, as if just remembering something. 'You left a book at our place, which I've been meaning to return. I'll leave it on your porch tonight, okay?'

Sophie looked at him then, hard. All her books were packed, layered between clothes to spread the weight. 'Okay, thanks.'

'Is there a trick to finding a taxi round here?' Andrew interjected, with an anxious glance at his watch. 'We need two – one for downtown, as this lot are going shopping, the other for the Upper West Side, where I am supposed to be conducting a rehearsal.'

'Retail therapy, eh, ladies?' Carter grinned at the girls, thrusting his hands into his front pockets and rocking on his heels, as if the five of them had all the time in the world. 'I wish you well, though the pound–dollar exchange rate isn't so good these days, is it? As for taxis . . . ' He pulled one hand free and looked at his own watch, a heavy chain-linked, multi-knobbed contraption that he had once instructed Sophie to use for timing how long it took him to swim four lengths of his pool. He had asked her to fasten it back on, she remembered now, turning his wrist to reveal soft, boyish white skin streaming with long black hairs. She had struggled to work the catch and he had laughed.

'Sorry, folks, but it's a quarter of four, coming up to shift-change time, which means you could have quite a wait . . .'

'There's one!' Sophie shrieked, hugging Andrew with wild relief when he insisted she and the girls get into it.

As they sped away, she kept her gaze fixed through

the front windscreen. Flanked by its shimmering sky-scrapers, the busy avenue stretching ahead looked more like a tunnel than a road. Even when the girls turned to wave at their father she remained stiff-necked, fearing that one swivel and Carter would be there waiting for her, his big, bear-like body radiating desolation.

Sophie wished with all her heart that they were *en route* to the airport. A mounting restlessness to get home had been brewing anyway, but now that restlessness felt closer to panic. The American might have played a key role in restoring her sense of well-being, but the hateful chance encounter had made her see that he had the power to remove it too. So visibly, intensely forlorn, lying about some book – who knew what else he might do? Maybe bumping into him hadn't been chance at all.

Carter's image haunted her all afternoon: every other shopper seemed to be a man with a bald head or loose swinging arms. Entering the concert venue on the Columbia campus three hours later, she found herself nervously scanning the rows as they made their way to their reserved seats. Even in the restaurant afterwards, waiting while a flock of waiters moved tables and flapped tablecloths to accommodate the fact that they were eight not six (the soloist Meredith and her mother having been persuaded to join what Geoff and Ann were insisting was to be the Chapmans' farewell treat), Sophie strained for glimpses of every face in the room, half expecting to see Carter huddled over a bottle, keeping his hopes alive.

It wasn't until after a couple of glasses of wine that

the world came properly back into focus, aided by excellent food and an irresistible atmosphere of mutual good cheer. Andrew was the hero of the hour, followed closely by Ann (the takings were apparently fantastic) and Meredith, the quality of whose voice (it was volubly agreed) had easily outshone the efforts of her three fellow soloists and electrified the hall. Even Olivia seemed a little star-struck by the young soprano who, with her soft blue eyes and breathy voice, seemed to have time for everyone, and who looked so undeniably resplendent in her long midnight blue chiffon dress, her glossy curtain of hair pinned up off her slender neck. It was Milly, seated on Meredith's left, who hogged the singer's attention most, bombarding her with questions throughout the meal and at one point pulling out a dog-eared programme and asking for an autograph.

'*You*,' said Ann, meanwhile, wagging a fond, accusing finger at Sophie the moment the other three adults were absorbed in conversation, 'are a different woman from the one who arrived a month ago.'

'I am indeed,' Sophie conceded, smiling sheepishly, aware that the prospect of saying goodbye to Ann made it a lot easier to feel warmly towards her. And how could one not like someone who had gone to so much effort on behalf of homeless infants? She had made an excellent speech at the close of the concert, looking almost as stunning as her star soloist, in towering heels and a black silk cocktail dress, topped with a black velvet choker that emphasized the impressive plunging triangle of her *décolletage*. Andrew was to be kidnapped, she had joked to the audience, so eager were his adoptive choir and orchestra to persuade him to stay. She had concluded with heartfelt thanks to all ticket-buyers, not just for helping the worthy cause of *chicos perdidos*, but for proving that the most famous choral work in the world could be summoned for good use a little earlier than was seasonally traditional.

'And you and Geoff have given Andrew the time of his life,' said Sophie, eager to shift the spotlight from herself. 'He's the one who is different – so much happier.'

'But he's made *us* so happy,' Ann cried. 'The kidnap joke was real, you know. We'd all keep him if we could.' The index finger was wagging again. 'You are one lucky lady there, Sophie, as I hope you know.'

Recalling the remark during the taxi ride back to Connecticut (a pre-paid treat organized by Ann to round off the evening), Sophie experienced a frisson of irritation, although there was no denying that seeing Andrew through the eyes of others had indeed served as a reminder of just what a gifted and extraordinary man she had married. Spilling out into the street after the meal, with the girls engaged in a last-minute flurry of exchanging email addresses, he and Geoff had hugged like parting lovers, while first Ann, then Meredith's mother and finally Meredith herself had swamped him with embraces and effusions of praise and gratitude.

As the taxi joined the freeway, Sophie let her head flop

back and closed her eyes. The girls, on either side of her, snuggled against her shoulders.

'I'd like to live in America,' said Milly, through a yawn.

'Would you, darling?' Sophie kissed her head.

'So I could go to the Juilliard School like Meredith.'

'Yeah, *sure* . . .' sneered Olivia, sleepily.

'The Juilliard, eh?' Andrew, in the front next to the driver, had turned to flash an admiring smile at his younger daughter. 'That would be even harder than the Royal College, Millikins.'

'So?' Milly nestled more closely against her mother. 'I'm going to Google it when I get home.'

Both girls were sound asleep by the time the car pulled up the drive. The outside light came on at once, intensifying the glow of the house's soft yellow walls in the moonlit dark. 'Come on, you two.' Sophie nudged her daughters, reaching across them for the door handles. 'A happy house,' she murmured, holding back as the rest of the family launched themselves at the front door, feeling the urge to offer a private thankful farewell for the healing powers of the holiday and knowing that their morning departure would be too hectic for such niceties.

'And this must be your book,' exclaimed Andrew, holding up a carrier bag as she approached the door. 'That was good of him, wasn't it? Which one was it, then?' He peered into the bag but then was diverted by Olivia, shrieking from inside the hall that she had seen a cockroach.

Sophie took the bag but resisted looking inside

until the girls were in their beds and Andrew noisily performing ablutions in the bathroom, whistling between mouthfuls of water and toothpaste.

The book was nothing but an old paperback with an innocuous title by someone she had never heard of. Puzzled, but relieved – even wondering if Carter had made a genuine mistake – Sophie was on the point of dropping it into her open suitcase when a piece of folded paper fell out from between the pages.

*Sophie, you have stolen my heart. Remember when I said, 'Love does not need the presence of the other person'? Well, I lied. I need you and always shall. Carter*

It seemed to Beth the final, inevitable insult that their day of departure should present them with the best weather of the entire holiday. Tugging back the faded, loose-fitting bedroom curtains for what she hoped, most sincerely, would be the last time, she only just managed to refrain from remarking on the fact. William had grown defensive enough about the trip as it was, without her making things worse. And she no longer cared about the weather anyway. All she wanted was to get on the airplane, to get home. The desire for it had been burning for days now, a constant, invisible, shameful fire, gobbling up her ability to appreciate anything. Even the crammed sightseeing upon which William had gallantly insisted during the final week – the National Gallery, the postponed boat-ride on the Thames, the Tower of London, dragging George and Alfie in their wake – had rolled past her like some sort of a slide-show rather than an experience of the real thing.

'Honey, you awake over there?' She spoke softly, a tremor of inexplicable, terrible sadness sweeping through her at the sight of William, still in bed, hugging a pillow to his chest like a child with a comforter. He looked so vulnerable. And since their return from Skipton he had been noticeably subdued. The smoking had gotten worse too, although she had bitten her tongue and not said a thing. He was leaving his kids, after all, she reminded herself, with an ex who, for all her good clothes sense and ethical garment-stitching, was a money-grasping, whining bitch. And then there was his last conversation with Harry, a shouting match over the phone the previous evening, which had left William too sore to talk. Beth ached to get him away from it all, back to the place where he could be his wry, merry self again, waking up happy just because he had her.

When William didn't answer she returned her gaze to the window. It was going to be hot, you could tell, from the gauzy look of the sky. Absently, she picked up the photo of the Chapman family that had once so impressed her, aware of how dramatically her feelings had changed, not just towards England but towards this gently dilapidated borrowed house and its owners. Especially the woman, Sophie. Beth brought the photo closer, frowning. The sharp gaze and high cheekbones, the beautiful daughters and romantic musician husband, the dusty box of love-letters so carelessly hidden – how readily she had lapped it all up, such a willing slave to envy and admiration. But now she knew better. Now she knew that the friendly, smiling photos, the scruffy comforts of the house, had been part of a subtle conspiracy – a conspiracy to lure her trust and then stamp on it. Four weeks of misery. And Dido . . . Beth dropped the picture and wiped her hands on her nightie, as if fearing contamination. The whole place was jinxed. She couldn't wait to leave it, to reclaim her own home, find her beloved pet and forget the whole damn trip ever happened.

An airplane had appeared in the sky, thunderously close. Not far behind it was another. There were too many airplanes in west London, William had muttered recently, but Beth had secretly decided she loved every one of them – noise and all – for being reminders that the world was small, that escape from what had turned into one of the most insidiously unpleasant months of her life was just at hand.

'Better get up, honey, we ordered the car for nine thirty – remember?' Beth started pulling on the clothes she had laid out for travel the night before, noting with a burst of joy that the tightness of the trousers' waistband had eased. Her ankle was better, her weight was better, only an hour till the taxi – life was really getting back on course. Bending down to lace up her trainers (chosen because her still tender ankle was bound to swell once they were airborne), she peered at the shoebox under the bed to make sure she hadn't dreamt sliding it back into its cobwebbed corner. She had even fixed a new elastic band round the letters, a little thicker, but red like the one that had crumbled in her fingers.

Upright, ready to go, she was staring with despairing affection at William, his face still plunged deep in the folds of the pillow, when the doorbell rang. 'William – it must be the taxi. William!' She thumped the bedclothes and hobbled down the stairs.

But it was a uniformed young policewoman, one novice enough to assume she was speaking to the owner of the house and to launch, therefore, into an invitation for Beth to attend an identity session at the police station.

'We have a youth in custody for a burglary similar to the one you experienced in January. It's all done on video,' she added helpfully, misinterpreting Beth's blank expression as reluctance. 'You won't be face to face or anything.'

'No, you don't understand, I'm not Mrs Chapman, I'm . . . a house-guest.'

At which point William – still pulling on a T-shirt – took over, offering to leave a note to explain the development to the Chapmans, even though the policewoman, visibly fighting mortification at her mistake, insisted they would get in touch in person anyway.

'I think they should have told us,' Beth remarked stoutly, returning to the subject once they were finally – blissfully – speeding towards Heathrow along an almost empty motorway. 'I mean to say . . . a *break-in*? As future tenants we had every right to know. Can you imagine if something like that had happened while we were there . . . and with your kids too?' she added, adopting a tone of horror that had more to do with her now settled antipathy towards the house – and the visit in general – than concern for the welfare of her stepsons. 'William? Don't you think it might even have made us think twice about the whole plan to swap houses?'

'So, better not to have known, then,' murmured William, who had been staring in a dazed way out of the window, not really playing ball on this conversation or any other. 'I'm sorry it wasn't better,' he added quietly, 'the holiday . . . You had such high hopes, I know.'

'Don't be *dumb* . . . it was great.' Beth managed a breezy laugh. 'A few set-backs along the way, maybe . . .' She pulled a face that was trying to be funny but he didn't see.

Once in the terminal, they were among the first passengers to check in, a satisfaction that proved short-lived when it was announced that the flight, thanks to a minor technical problem, would be delayed by at least two hours. Beth sought consolation in the consumption of three chocolate croissants. Shortly afterwards she left William to go and throw them up into a toilet, a process that took quite a while, given the need to disguise the noise of vomiting with flushes and then clean her teeth and touch up her face with powder and lip gloss.

'I thought you were never coming out,' William exclaimed, when she returned to him.

'I'm a *girl*, remember?' Beth shot back, pleased to hear an echo of the old playfulness in his tone.

He had his iPhone in his lap and was scrolling through messages. 'I've just sent Harry an email, saying maybe I could fix him up with a work-experience thing in New York. An attempt at an olive branch. What do you think?'

'Oh, baby, that is *such* a good idea. Do you think you could?'

William shrugged. 'The way things are it will certainly be difficult. But it's worth a try . . . Anything's worth a try, given that Harry's only plan appears to be playing drums and signing on for a job seeker's allowance.'

'Harry plays the *drums*?'

William scowled. 'Badly, but yes. That's mostly what our delightful chat was about last night, since he has formed – God help me – a *rock band*. Susan's made him keep his kit in the basement for so long – between all her boxes of wool samples – I thought he'd lost interest. Or, at least, I hoped he had.' He smiled ruefully. 'But then maybe he's the next Ringo Starr and I don't know.'

'Maybe.' They caught each other's eye and laughed, aware that lately such moments had been rare. William's eyes grew moist – from mirth, Beth assumed, until suddenly, astonishingly, a few real tears were spilling down his cheeks. 'Honey? My God, William, what is it? Is it Harry? He'll be fine. He's just a kid finding his way.' Beth picked up his hands and pressed them to her lips, close to tears herself. 'Oh, you know what we both need right now? A *holiday* . . . '

And then they were laughing again and hugging like the fledgling lovers they were, two instruments in the same key, playing the same tune.

'Oh, look, look, this is my favourite,' said William, sniffing and smiling, extricating himself from the embrace to stroke the screen of his phone to get to his photos. 'There. Look at that. Beautiful or what?'

Beth was somewhat bemused to find herself staring not at an image of her and William, but one of her with George and Alfie, sitting on a wall outside the Tate Modern. She had her arms round both boys and their heads were tipped in towards hers. It was a good, clear shot, with all of them grinning yet managing to look natural. 'Yeah, that is a really nice one. They're such great kids – I loved getting to know them better . . .'

'And you're so good with them, *so* good . . .'

'I don't know about that. I'm just myself, I guess.'

'Exactly.' William turned towards her, knitting the fingers of both their hands. 'Beth, listen, there's something I want to say, but I need to know that you'll forgive me before I say it.'

'Forgive you?' She smiled uncertainly, her mind darting to a host of possible horrors.

'Not that there's anything really to forgive,' William gabbled, seeing from her expression that he was in danger of losing her before he had even started. 'Except that we had agreed something and now I want to revise that decision – or at least *revisit* it. And I know you're going to be shocked so please do your best not to be.'

'William, at this rate we're going to miss our flight-call,' Beth murmured, still nervous but faintly exasperated too.

'A baby. Our baby. We could have one. Maybe. To complete us.'

In the silence that followed Beth was aware of her emptied stomach grumbling. It even occurred to her that one of the other more obvious fears might have been easier to react to. A grope with the peachy-assed Henrietta, perhaps . . . an old-times'-sake fuck with Susan . . . Yeah, both those would have been a whole lot easier.

'But . . . we are complete,' she said at last, her voice small.

William dropped his head. 'Yes, we are. And I've upset you. I didn't mean to upset you. It's just that . . .' And instead of backing off he was in full advance again. 'You cannot imagine what it's like to have a child – the love, the joy. It's worth all the heartache a million times over. I want you to know that love, Beth. You deserve to know it. It will, quite simply, blow your mind. But more than that, I keep thinking how wonderful it would be to see the bit of you that would be in *our* child and the bit of me that would be in *your* child. It was such a screw-up with Susan, but with you I – we – could get it right . . .' He pulled his hands free suddenly and sat up. 'Okay, that's it. I'll stop there. Don't say anything,' he added, slapping his thighs in a manner that Beth hoped meant the matter was closed.

But then he was off again, his voice calm, his eyes ablaze. 'Don't say anything now, that is. I promised it was something we never needed to discuss and I've gone and broken that promise and for that I apologize. But there are reasons I've broken it and so all I'm asking for the moment, Beth, my love, is for you to agree to think about it. Just to think about it. Okay?'

Beth nodded, already not thinking about it. He shouldn't have asked and she felt mad at him for that. But he was so wound up, so emotional, that it seemed unfair to judge him too harshly. Time alone was what they needed, back in their own space, their own home.

When their flight was called at last they walked slowly, William because of the conflicting emotions tugging at his heart and Beth because she was over-compensating for the unedifying desire to run.

'Hey, you do forgive me, don't you?' he murmured, placing his hand on her lap as the plane taxied towards the runway, bouncing on the ruts in the tarmac. 'What I asked you to think about back there – you're not cross?'

'I was just surprised, that's all.' Beth kissed the side of his face. How could she be cross now, with the plane pointing home? She relaxed back into her seat, so enjoying the push of engine acceleration against her chest that they were in the air and her head bursting before she remembered to feed herself a stick of gum.

# PART TWO

# 9

Email to: Bethstapleton@aol.com
 8 September
From: Sophiechapman@hotmail.com

Dear Beth,

This is just to offer you my own personal HUGE thank-you
(I know Andrew has written separately to William) both for
looking after our own home so well and for allowing us the most
fantastic holiday in yours. Your house was so beautiful – I can't
put into words what a wonderful time we had. Everything was
just perfect – and so much more relaxing than being in a hotel.
(Not to mention a lot cheaper!) We were able to see our old
friends in New York and do lots of sightseeing, but also to soak
up the tranquillity of Darien . . . I can honestly say that every
member of our family was thrilled by the whole experience.

The one big sadness, of course, was the disappearance of
your lovely cat Dido. I just don't know what can have
happened to her and cannot apologize enough. Every time I
think about it I still feel terrible. I know that Persian cats are
very expensive so I would like to say now that if she doesn't
turn up and you decide that you would like to replace her,
Andrew and I would be honoured if you would allow us to
pay. Just let us know.

William assured me over the phone that our own, much more humble dwelling suited your needs well, so I am truly glad about that. I gather the weather was pretty terrible, which was a shame for you – the dampest August on record, according to our tireless weather pundits. It seems grossly unfair to confess therefore that I acquired (and still have!) the most fantastic suntan. The girls are brown as berries too, but even Andrew, who has the palest of skins and never tans, has more than a hint of a healthy glow!

So THANK YOU. The holiday of a lifetime. We shall treasure it always.

With warmest wishes,

Sophie Chapman

PS If we have left anything behind, apologies – I haven't noticed anything yet but we are a bit of a messy family! Please could you put any stray socks etc. in the post – we will reimburse you, of course.

Email to: Zoëwatson@btinternet.com
8 September
From: Sophiechapman@hotmail.com

Dear Zoë,

I simply CANNOT believe it is eight months since we last had a proper get-together. Where has the year gone? Of course, with the girls being older and not needing quite so much chaperoning, we don't have all those chances to bump into each other . . . but still, that's no excuse! Having just returned from a wonderful family holiday (in Darien, Connecticut – we SWAPPED houses with some Americans!) I am determined to turn over a new leaf and make an effort to see the friends I care about. To which end, can you and Pete come to dinner a week on Friday (26 Sept), say eight o'clock? Let me know.

All best in meantime,

Sophie

PS I have asked Karen and Jeremy too. I know they were planning to move south, but I think the credit crunch scotched that, didn't it?

Email to : WFCCollege@tiscali.co.uk
8 September
From: Sophiechapman@hotmail.com

Dear Gareth,

Many thanks for being so understanding over the phone. I am writing now, as we agreed, to confirm that I would very much like to resume teaching at WFC this term in a similar freelance capacity as before, i.e. doing twelve hours a week but, as I said, having mucked you around, I am happy to do more or less than that, depending on what suits. I am in your hands! I appreciate that, so late in the day, you already have tutors lined up for this term and will wait patiently to see what you can offer.

I would also like to assure you that (touching wood), my health seems thoroughly restored. I entered the year suffering from what seems in retrospect to have been a form of exhaustion, but as I said on the phone, six months off – culminating in a glorious four-week holiday in the USA – have set me right back on my feet.

With best wishes and thanks,

Yours sincerely,

Sophie Chapman

The computer, like the entire house, was extraordinarily – spookily – clean, Sophie noticed, pressing the exit button and then tracing a finger lightly across the screen in a manner that, five weeks before, would have left a trammel of dusty evidence. When her finger squeaked, she sat back in the chair, smiling in fresh wonderment that their extraordinary holiday should have concluded with the icing-on-the-cake finale of returning to a home that sparkled in every corner. Either Beth Stapleton had slaved for hours, or they had paid one of those spring-cleaning companies that cost the earth.

Even Andrew, normally blind to the most striking domestic alteration, had been impressed without prompting at the new, pristine state of their surroundings; while the girls had reacted by bursting out of their bedrooms, complaining of rearranged items and the audacity of whoever was behind it. A more fiercely house-proud creature than Sophie might well have joined them in taking offence. As it was, she could muster nothing except delight that Beth Stapleton had gone to such trouble. While not having warmed to the over-prissy condition of the house in Connecticut, returning to so polished a version of her own family home somehow underlined exactly the fresh start on which she and Andrew appeared – much to her joy – to have embarked. And it was a useful woman-to-woman jolt too, like seeing socks pulled up and recognizing one's own had been round one's ankles.

Sophie's fingers hovered over the keyboard, toying with the idea of getting back online to send Beth a more thorough, separate thanks about the cleaning. Leaving Darien, she had done nothing more than run a cloth over the kitchen surfaces and a brush round the lavatories, not because she was lazy but because of a squat, raven-haired woman called Ana who – in accordance with Beth Stapleton's instructions – had come twice a week to clean and do the laundry. It was only during the course of the cleaner's final visit – on their last morning – that Sophie had discovered the poor woman's wages were funding five young children in the Philippines, a fact that had sent her scrabbling through her purse for every last spare dollar, while Andrew chuckled that it was nothing but a cleverly timed sob-story and she was a fool for falling for it.

Faith in people: that was what mattered, Sophie decided, pulling the front door shut five minutes later and setting off at a brisk pace in the direction of the police station. It was a good mile away, but it seemed too nice a morning not to walk, with the sun high and a slight bite of early-morning chill still hanging in the air. *Not* walking had been one of the few down-sides of their family week in Connecticut. Trying it once, in single file because of the absence of a 'sidewalk', with the girls reluctantly trailing behind and the sweat pouring off them all in rivers, they had ended up feeling not so much like tourists as a species from another planet – an endangered species, thanks to the swerving of passing cars and the looks of intrigued bafflement from their occupants.

By the time the square concrete front of the police station came into sight, Sophie had taken off her cardigan and was rather wishing she had worn flip-flops instead of socks and shoes. The bite had gone and the sun blazed. An Indian summer, the papers were calling it – pay-back for the thoroughly foul August. Sophie smiled to herself, hoping for the Stapletons' sake that such a description didn't make it into the *New York Times*.

Carter had preferred the *Washington Post*, she remembered suddenly, trying out the thought of the American much as she might have tiptoed onto a patch of thin ice. The love-note tucked into the paperback had been a horrible shock. When she had tried to drop it into the bedroom wastepaper basket, it had seemed to cling to her fingers. It was still mid-air when Andrew emerged from his teeth-cleaning, patting his face with a hand towel and singing 'Unto Us A Boy Is Born' in a comedic but note-perfect falsetto. Any dim notion of a confession had died in Sophie at that instant. Andrew's happiness

– hers – had simply felt too full, too raw, too precious to risk. And it wasn't as if the situation with Carter would have been easy to explain either, threaded as it was with complicated elements, some good and some bad, some her fault, some not. 'I can't wait to get home,' she had blurted instead, falling against her husband with a prayer of longing for their speedy and safe passage back to England the following day, picturing how the vast, wonderful buffer of the Atlantic would protect her from Carter's unwanted passions – the one outcome of the holiday she regretted terribly.

One prayer answered, one to go, Sophie told herself now, pushing through the station's heavy front doors and introducing herself in clear, fearless terms at the front desk. When a skeletal young policeman with a shaved head arrived to usher her down the corridor, she followed with her shoulders back and her chin high. She was to watch a videotape of mug-shots, labelled with numbers, to see if she could pick out the youth who had conned his way into their home in January. Bumping into the boy himself was out of the question, she had been assured, since he was being held at a different location.

It would be easy. Sophie clenched her fists, cursing the emergency pre-school-inspection meeting that had necessitated Andrew postponing his attendance till the following day. He had been so busy since their return that they had had most of their conversations passing in the hall or over the phone. 'What if I'm not sure?'

she asked the policeman. 'Will that mean he gets off?'

'Not necessarily. A victim of a more recent crime will be watching the same tape. And there's your husband to come too. We only need two positive IDs to have a good shot at a successful prosecution.'

Sophie perched on a lilac chair in a small grey room, while her angular companion fired the controls at a large television and DVD player. Once so haunting, she now couldn't picture the intruder's face at all, she realized, panicking; the slight frame, the full mouth – none of it was real any more. But then the tape began to roll and there he was, the first picture, as sorry a mug-shot as one could imagine, the face full-on, but the body language slouched and reluctant, the eyes seething.

'That's him.' She pointed a finger, feeling fantastic.

'Are you sure?'

'One hundred per cent. Number twelve. That's him.' Sophie leant closer to the screen, frowning. 'Why isn't he number one if he's the first?'

'We change the numbers for each ID session to rule out the possibility of conferring, like with your husband, say.'

'Wow, that's clever.' Sophie exhaled, the exultation coursing through her. Life went through bad phases, of course, but never had she emerged from the thick of one so bad or been so certain that it was at an end. A couple of days before, wanting to test Carter's theory, she had paid a visit to the south London cemetery that housed her younger sister's remains, a once regular habit that had lapsed when her parents moved to the Algarve. If her nameless crisis had been about grief and guilt, going underground, tangling with other things, she would know it there, surely. She had taken a miniature white winter cyclamen with her, scooping it out of its plastic pot and planting it with her bare hands. Afterwards, she sat back on her heels, picking out the clogged dirt from her nails, aware not so much of sadness or understanding as a new resolve. Whatever the elements were that had led to all those months of unhappiness – the distance between her and Andrew, the melt-down in the hot Darien woods – it was a phase of her life that was done with, she decided joyfully, leaving her stronger, as bad things so often did.

And now this hateful child-criminal, so insidiously linked to that phase, would go to jail – or Borstal, or wherever they sent young offenders, these days. It was the perfect finishing touch. Sophie reached for her bag, grinning at the policeman.

'You have to watch the whole tape.'

'Oh, yes, of course, whatever you say.' She sat back down, wriggling herself into as comfortable a position as the hard lilac chair would allow.

'There's tea or coffee in the machine.'

'No, thanks. I'm all right. Thanks so much.'

There was a small window in the room overlooking an alleyway, stacked with boxes and bags of rubbish. As the grim on-screen parade continued, Sophie kept glancing through it, not at the rubbish but at the small square of blue sky in its top corner, deepening in colour as the morning wore on. She would change her shoes and go into Richmond, she decided, have a coffee at a pavement table, maybe buy herself a new skirt – she could certainly do with one if she was going back to work – and possibly a top too, something white or cream to maximize the glow of her fading tan. In New York that last afternoon she had indulged both her daughters in a variety of department stores, but with the shadow of Carter still stalking her, she had been in no mood to make any purchases for herself.

And maybe she would buy something for Andrew too. He was hopeless at choosing clothes – too disinterested and impatient. She could perhaps get him a new shirt, smartish but not for work, bright colour, something he might decide to wear for their little dinner party, Sophie speculated happily. Picking up with old friends was all part of her new resolve and she was really looking forward to it. Once upon a time she, Karen and Zoë had lived in and out of each other's houses, exchanging domestic triumphs and woes over biscuits and cups of tea. Where had those days gone? Sophie wondered suddenly. Why had she let them go?

After her skinny custodian had led her back down the corridor to the front desk, Sophie glided out into the sunshine. She bought herself a small bottle of water from a newsagent and then dawdled on her way home, pausing every so often to try Andrew on his mobile. Getting on well again meant not minding sharing him

with the outside world, she reminded herself wryly,
leaving a message on her eighth attempt to say the ID
session had gone really well and could he give her a
call?

## 10

Since they had got married and moved to Connecticut, breakfast with William had become one of Beth's
favourite times of day, with the view of the garden
through the glass doors and the table laid just as it should
be – a jug of juice, a basket of fresh pastries, a steaming
pot of coffee, yoghurt, a dish of sliced fruit, strawberries,
mango, kiwi, whatever had looked nicest that week in
their excellent Darien grocery store. It was as perfect a
start to any day as she could imagine, with her darling
seated opposite her, offering companionable comments
on the headlines before handing over the inner sections
and turning his attention to whether stocks were up or
down. With William's commute, it meant getting up early,
but she didn't mind since it fitted in with her running.
William was the one who needed encouragement sometimes, clinging to the bedclothes, dear sleepy-head that
he was, always putting off the plunge under the shower.

Two weeks after their return from the UK, however,
it seemed to Beth, tapping her knees together under the
breakfast table, picking at a slice of kiwi, that some glow
– or innocence – about such treasured routines had slid
out of reach. There were shadows between them now,
clouds on the once pure canvas of their love.

The holiday, laced with its various misfortunes, was

responsible, of course. Difficulties had arisen that would take a while to iron out. Yet something in Beth sought a darker level of blame too, based on the dim but irrepressible sense that the English family's recent occupation of their precious home had somehow corrupted it. Ana had done her usual good job – every room had been tidy and spotless, only a few things were out of place (mostly in the kitchen) – and nothing had changed, yet nothing felt quite the same either. Worst of all, Beth kept finding herself arrested by sudden vivid images, invariably of Sophie, filling the same precious space, breathing the same air, changing it. Sometimes she was even sure she picked up a hint of the Englishwoman's scent, in the en-suite or the main bedroom, seeping out of a towel or buried deep in the pressed cotton of a pillowcase.

It didn't help that, by the cruellest coincidence, the east coast heatwave had ended on the day of their return – minutes after they had pulled their suitcases into the hall, in fact, almost as if William's turn of the key in the front door had been the trigger for the deluge. The rain had fallen in torrents for three straight days, to the accompaniment of plummeting temperatures and a blackened sky. When the sun did reappear it was still only a washed-out smudge, patchy, reticent, a spent force, ready always to segue to the re-amassing clouds. That morning fat dollops of rain were again thudding against the garden doors, while the wind rattled the panes and handles like a fearless stranger determined to break in. William was holding the newspaper high, as if to shield himself from the sight, while absently chewing his way through the slices of banana.

'More coffee, honey?'

'No, I must go.' He folded the paper into his briefcase and patted his pocket to check for his wallet and cell phone. 'Are you busy today?'

'Sure.' Beth looked out of the window. It was her body-sculpting day but she had already decided not to go.

'Because . . .' William hesitated, his face flexing in agitation '. . . I don't think you should spend another day looking, that's all,' he blurted. 'You've worn yourself ragged with it. You've asked around, put up notices, checked countless times with the SPCA – there is nothing more you can do. Dido has gone, Beth. Best to face it, let it go – busy yourself with other things. Maybe even . . .' he paused, chewing his lower lip '. . . could it be a good time to start looking for another job?'

'Okay, right. And is that before or after I'm to get pregnant?' Beth caught her breath, astonished by the comment that had fired out of her like some kind of involuntary gun shot. What kind of a dumb idiot was she, raising the subject she most wished him to forget?

William bounded round the kitchen table, knocking chairs with his briefcase. 'Is that a yes? Tell me, my darling, is that a *yes*?'

'No, it's not . . .'

He stopped short of her, his eyes wide with the effort of reining his hopes. 'But you're still thinking about it, aren't you? Tell me you're still thinking about it.'

'I guess.' Beth folded her arms and looked back out at the rain. William could say what he liked about Dido. It wouldn't stop her heading off in her car the moment he was gone, winding the window down so that her voice could carry, cruising every street, wearing the spectacles she only just needed to be sure she didn't miss the slightest movement behind every tree shadow, every clump of grass. Whenever she was tempted to give up, she thought of her beloved pet, disoriented and trembling in a nook somewhere, her beautiful fur matted, her green eyes dim.

'I still don't get it,' she murmured, sufficiently calm to wrest her attention to William, who was gripping the back of a kitchen chair as if his life depended on it. 'Like me, you were so sure about not wanting kids.' She frowned, remembering the horrible shock of his convulsion at the airport, the evangelical blaze in his eye. 'What has changed?'

William shifted his weight from one foot to the other. 'It's . . . it's hard to put into words . . . I've probably not done it that well . . .' He traced his finger round the heart carved into the back of the chair. 'I guess the bottom line is about wanting to be a family rather than just a couple . . .'

'*Just* a couple? Wow, that makes me feel really good.' Beth noisily stacked their plates and marched to the dishwasher. 'So I was right. I'm no longer enough for you.' She dropped the fruit fork, points down, into the cutlery rack, where it stuck fast. 'And anyway . . .' she cast him a sly look from under her lashes '. . . what about money? Since getting back you keep saying how tight things are. So tell me, how would having a kid help that?'

'But this is so much more important,' William cried. 'And money will be fine soon. It's just a question of hanging on till bonus time. You are already more than I ever dreamt of, Beth,' he pressed more gently, 'but to have our own child would give us *more* of each other, don't you see? Bits of you and me bundled together – it's such an everyday commonplace thing that people forget the wonder of it . . . *I* had forgotten the wonder of it. Hey. Stop doing that and come here a second.'

He held out his arms and she stepped between them with a sigh. She had grown thinner, William noticed, feeling the gentle undulations of her ribcage under his palms; from the lamentable hours of cat-hunting, he supposed, since, if anything, she had been eating more since their return from holiday – even having seconds sometimes, a habit she had once laughingly declared to be out of bounds. The desire to protect her – to make her happy – swelled inside him. 'I know you're hurting about Dido. It's so sad. I miss her too –' William broke off, swallowing the urge to point out that such proven capacity to mourn a lost pet was the perfect reassurance – if she needed it – of the intensity with which she would love a child.

He had to be patient, William told himself, picking over the conversation as his train pulled out of Darien station twenty minutes later, sliding past the parking lot and into the town's woody surrounds. Beth was only thirty-eight, after all – a spring chicken, given the age some women had babies these days, well into their forties and fifties. And changing her mind-set would take time, knitted as it was to the kind of childhood she had endured: being so shy, with the unloving bolting father, and an embittered lonely mother, not to mention the uncle who had visited and tried to take over. Little wonder, then, that the desire not to experience parenthood – confessed to and explained during the early days of sharing personal histories – had become so ingrained.

It was clear that his boyhood, with loving, no-nonsense parents, had been a paradise in comparison. Reconnecting with that remained, for William, the greatest wonder of the holiday. The desire for another chance to be a good father himself had sprung as a direct result. With Harry, George and Alfie he had got so much wrong. How obvious, how irresistible then, to want to do it all again, *better*, with a woman he truly loved. The only really astonishing thing was how long it had taken him to realize it.

He would win Beth round, William vowed. In the meantime, what had he been thinking with the impulsive off-beam suggestion about job-hunting, increasing Beth's stress levels instead of reducing them? She had been noticeably fragile since their trip, brittle-tempered, inclined to tears, letting the Dido business get on top of her. And hadn't Susan's grim determination to run a cottage industry between breast-feeding and nappy-changing been one of the earliest factors to trip them up? His arrival home to over-tired, hungry, squabbling toddlers because his wife had been too busy 'working' had always guaranteed rows that made the walls shake.

No, Beth needed a new focus, but not in the form of a job . . . William closed his eyes, smiling to himself as he toyed with a boyishly simple plan of hiding the yellow pack of little pills she kept in her bedside table. The smile deepened into a sigh as he allowed his imagination to conjure an image of his petite wife transformed by the wild voluptuousness of pregnancy – such a turn-on first time around that Susan, during close moments, had liked to tease him for being a perv.

Slipping his phone out of his pocket, William called home and then Beth's cell, only to be greeted by messages on both. 'Hey, darling, it's me . . .' he whispered. Through the window the brown and grey scenery of New Rochelle was coming into view, looking drabber than usual under the screen of rain. 'Just to say you were quite right about job-hunting. I wasn't thinking straight. Sorry, baby. Given everything else, it would clearly be a mad undertaking right now. Forgive me, won't you? And I'm afraid I'll be late again tonight – I've got a five o'clock that's bound to run on. In fact, it's going to be like that for a while . . . tough times and having to make up lost ground for being away, et cetera. But you are beautiful and wonderful and I love you and don't ever forget it.'

For the remaining twenty minutes of the journey

William wrote emails to his sons, managing – in spite of his full heart – to strike a jocular note with the younger two (how hopeless they were as correspondents, how he would be signing up forthwith to Facebook to keep track of them) before adopting a much more serious tough-love tone with Harry.

Since you still haven't replied to any of my messages, I have gone ahead and put out a few feelers re work experience for you over here – for which you should have the decency to be grateful. However much you might wish it, Harry, life does not arrive on the proverbial plate – it has to be sought out and worked at.

Maybe Mum could pull her finger out and help you find something closer to home – I would be fine with that. In the meantime I have no intention of 'cutting you off without a penny', as you so dramatically put it when we spoke that last night in London. Surely you can understand why I would be a lot happier to continue forking out an allowance while you do something USEFUL, as opposed to just meeting up with your mates to beat drums. (That's called a hobby in my book – great for weekends and evenings.)

Sorry for sounding harsh, but if your own father can't give you a reality check then who can? For the record, I still think retakes (then university) are the way to go – there are loads of places in London that I'm sure would take you, but with the academic year about to start, time is running out. Think of it this way: given the recession, jobs are hard to come by so it's a brilliant time to be a student. And you would love it, I know you would. Why not apply for English next time instead of History? You always said you found that easy. Just a thought. Dad

PS And please reply to this, fella. You've made your point. No need to take it too far.

After a two-hour search Beth arrived home despondent and wet, desperation having driven her to explore various sections of parkland on foot in only her thin raincoat, without a hat or gumboots. She had also stopped at the mall in Darien and spent thirty minutes hurrying in and out of stores to check for sightings, doing her best not to be knocked back by the glimmers of pity in the eyes of those not too busy to offer a response. Leaving the drug store she had walked right into Carter and Nancy, hurrying through the parking lot under an umbrella, bags of groceries in their arms and their fat old dog wheezing on its lead.

'Any news?' Nancy asked at once, clutching Beth's wrist with her usual theatricality before somehow steering the conversation to her new 'wonderfully challenging' role in a day-time drama.

'We're getting wet here, honey,' Carter eventually interjected, casting Beth a look that seemed to suggest he shared some of her darker thoughts. 'They were good people, the Chapmans,' he had added, ducking out from under the umbrella to make sure Beth heard the comment. 'I can tell you, they felt real bad about the princess taking off – especially Sophie. She looked and called for hours every day.'

Reflecting on the conversation as she stood, dripping, inside her front hall, Beth found her discomfort and disappointment merging with a fresh, irrational spurt of vitriol towards the Englishwoman. What use was the looking if she hadn't found anything? And what could a creature like Sophie Chapman know anyway – so pretty and privileged, with her sheltered, fairytale life – about feeling 'bad'?

Beth shook off her coat and shoes, but then slipped in her wet socks, tweaking her still weak ankle and thumping her hip painfully against the banister post. The antipathy surged with the pain, returning her to the dark, irrepressible suspicion that her recent tenant, not content to leave strands of her long hair lurking across the undersides of chair cushions and down plug-holes, had somehow sucked the happiness out of the house too – taken it back to England with her, along with tacky mementoes of New York and a suitcase of dirty clothes.

She clung to the banister as the waves of pain and mad thoughts receded. She had to breathe deeply and stay calm. Too much, lately, had been slipping from her grasp – that was the trouble. She needed to throw up. Yes, that would help – it always helped: the blissful emptiness, the total control. Since the trip she had been trying to do it less, but really, what could be so bad about something that had so many benefits? A mere brushing of the back of the throat with her fingertip sufficed, not like when she had first started twenty-odd years before, jabbing with the toothbrush while the tap ran, every sinew strained for the sound of Uncle Hal's breathing on the other side of the door.

Wanting the security of her own bathroom, Beth forced herself upstairs, gripping the rail like she had when her ankle had been at its worst. Inside the en-suite, she dropped to her knees and hugged the bowl. Moments later her breakfast was swirling out of her, brown liquid dotted with black – pips from the kiwi, she knew, having puzzled over exactly the same sight on previous occasions. A second violent retch made her eyes water, but nothing came out this time. Beth sat back on her heels, blinking, waiting for the onset of the euphoria that made it all worth while – the brief, giddy rush of relief, the delicious hollowness. Instead her throat ached and the pounding between her temples quickened and thickened, feeling like the countdown to something unspeakable even before the figure of her uncle had slid back into her mind.

The bulge of his gut, so hefty it hid his belt. Beth whimpered, but the image was already moving on, ex-panding.

*Are you sick, Bethan?* The toilet in the apartment was so small her nose had been level with his fly. She was sure she had locked the door – fed the little hook into the brass loop on the door jamb – and yet here he was, standing next to her, his zipper so close the gold of it blurred in front of her eyes. She could sense him liking it – the power of that proximity – but she didn't yet know why.

*If you're sick we need to get you to a doctor. Or is it something else? Bethan, is it something else? There are other signs. Have you had other signs? Have you been a dirty girl? If you've been dirty you must tell your uncle Hal . . .*

He had always breathed heavily – his thick lips were dry with it, peeling round the edges. While chewing food, the breath came out in snorts down his nose. Asleep, the snores rumbled through the apartment's thin walls. But that was the first time, aged fourteen, that Beth had heard the quick rushes of air coming from the back of his throat, so thick they fugged up his words.

*No, I'm not sick.* She had fought her way out into the narrow corridor, half hoping, half dreading to see her mother emerging from the bedroom where she had lived out her life in those days. *I ate too much, okay? A whole bag of cookies – they made me sick to my stomach.*

He had laughed then, catching hold of her elbow as she squirmed away. *Don't you go wasting away on me, you hear? You're good just as you are.* His free hand had fumbled for her waistline, squeezing its ugly loose folds in a way that hurt more if she tried to pull away; the way he called tickling but which had always felt to Beth like pain.

Beth stood up and pressed the shining chrome flush on the toilet. The roar of water drowned the throbbing in her head. She was going to be okay. Uncle Hal was a prick. The world was full of pricks and she had learnt to ignore them. William was her world now; William who, after their tricky exchanges at breakfast, had left her the dearest message any girl could hope for. She pushed her hair back off her face and tore off some toilet roll to wipe her mouth. As she did so, she noticed that the bedroom wastepaper basket had somehow strayed into a corner under the washbasin. Of attractive wicker-work, it had an inner silk lining, which was coming loose. Beth picked it up and clutched it under one arm as she made her way back into the bedroom. The dizziness was setting in now, forcing her to grope through her damp socks for the start of the carpet for fear of tripping over. She might even lie down, she decided, or perhaps fix herself a herbal tea to sip while she visited a few retail websites – nothing reckless. A spot of online shopping never failed to soothe.

The tip of Carter's note was sticking out of the loose fold in the lining of the wastepaper basket, snagged between the silk and the outer wicker shell with sufficient firmness to have survived both Sophie and Ana's assumptions that they had emptied it. As she plucked it free merely with the intention of dropping a stray piece of trash where it belonged, it was the unfamiliar handwriting that first caught Beth's eye. And on closer glance, it was to Andrew Chapman's beguiling letters of courtship that her thoughts initially swung: Sophie Chapman – irksome, enviable object of husbandly adulation – triumphs again. When her eyes had properly registered the author's name, Beth – still untrusting of her state of mind – stared at it for several long moments, before she shuffled to the edge of the bed and sat down.

That it was funny took several more readings to sink in. *Carter* – dull, fat, grumpy, *old* Carter, as bow-legged as his ancient dog – and *Sophie Chapman* . . . Beth flopped back onto the bed, her arms spread wide, hooting out loud as her emotions, near to breaking point just a few minutes before, ricocheted back upwards. Not so perfect then, the Englishwoman, and not so clever . . . no, not clever at all. To be that unguarded – signing his *name*, for Christ's sake, not to mention hers – they had to have been smitten indeed. Oh, boy, it was delicious.

Beth sat up, wiping her eyes as the hysteria drained away. Other people's failings were always heartening. What to do, that was the thing. She tapped the note against her leg and then propped it against her bedside light before going downstairs to boil water for her tea.

To: chapmanandrew@stjosephs.sch.org.uk
25 September
From: annhooper@googlemail.com

Dear Andrew,

How lovely to hear from you. I know we're well into the fall now, but I am not exaggerating when I say that you are still spoken of in hallowed tones as 'that great conductor from London'! Seriously, the fund-raiser was such a triumph and it was all thanks to you. Geoff has been missing you too – even less communicative than usual with his wife – and throwing himself back into work in the way that he always does when life is getting him down.

So you can only imagine my joy at your suggestion. Yes! Yes! Yes! (As Meg Ryan would say.) I have already started speaking to people about possible venues – high schools being the obvious starting point, but I hope to get some more challenging 'gigs' for your choir as well. A capella is such a popular form of singing over here – although they're usually all-male 'barber shop' groups, so your mix will have added appeal, especially given the kind of modern-classic programme you sketched out. Your dates don't give us that much time – and the Christmas holidays are invariably busy – but I've always liked a challenge! Presumably you have to raise money, find sponsors or whatever . . . unless the St Joseph's music budget easily stretches to encompass such things? (Given what I recall you telling me of the general excellence of the school, maybe it does?)

Now we get to the Juilliard and Milly – of course I will find out anything helpful I can about 'foreign' applications. How delightful that she should feel so strongly. So many kids these days are content just to drift or follow obvious paths. That's one of the reasons we were so thrilled when Katherine decided to take her biochemistry studies to the post-grad level – she turned down some excellent job opportunities en route but that subject is her passion and we totally respect that. And who would pass up on the chance to go to Harvard – right?! As to making sure none of this gets back to Sophie,

you have my word. Like you say, at this very early stage it's
only fact-finding, isn't it? So I'll use this email address from
now on, as you suggest.

I miss you, Andrew. Can I say that, without it sounding weird?
(I sincerely hope so since I already have!)

I promise to be in touch again soon.

With love as ever,

Ann x

Andrew shifted his gaze from the computer screen to the
view of the school playground, two storeys below. With
the tarmac and high fences it looked like some sort of
giant outdoor cage, which it was, really, he mused, given
the close watch kept upon its occupants and all the rules
about running and kicking balls. A group of younger boys
were trading high fives and football cards in one corner,
while in another some of their female counterparts
looked as if they were practising dance-steps. Older
pupils of both sexes – including Olivia, he noted, spotting
his daughter easily amid a gaggle of chatting girls – were
engaged in less strenuous forms of recreation, most of
them involving the chance to plug into music or tele-
phones. Some, like Milly, were at lunchtime clubs –
St Joseph's priding itself, among its many other virtues,
on the broadest spectrum of extra-curricular activities,
everything from tiddly-winks to fencing, and the students
were encouraged to take full advantage.

It was a wonderful school, Andrew reminded himself, turning his gaze from the caged playground to the faded print of Monet's *Water Lilies* that hung above his desk. Private, co-educational, fiercely competitive, with a reputation for achieving excellent results on all fronts, music included, there would have been no question of affording it for the girls without the considerable discount that came with his position. Indeed, that had been a primary motive behind Andrew's application for the job, since the boys' prep school where he had been head of music previously had offered no financial advantage to a man with two daughters. Seven years on, and now the rumour mill had it that when the current head resigned (a move said to be imminent) the job of running the school would be Andrew's for the taking.

Andrew frowned at *Water Lilies*. Waiting for anything wasn't pleasant, especially when one wasn't even certain it would happen. The governors were bound to advertise the post. A host of better contenders would want the same prize. And if he was successful, it would mean appointing someone else to take over running the music department, cutting himself off from what had always been his natural area of strength – his source of joy, even if it was at second hand, these days, accessed via flashes of talent in students rather than himself. He already had an encouraging number of subscribers for the tour, Milly, happily, being one of them, although Olivia had yet to be persuaded. Blessed as they were with perfect pitch, Andrew knew that his girls would be a vital asset to his troupe and was determined to recruit both.

'What's up?' said Sophie, the moment he answered the phone.

'Oh, nothing much . . .' Andrew cast another look down at the fenced tarmac of the playground. 'Feeling a bit hemmed in, I think – inspectors breathing down our necks, cock-ups on the timetable, pushy parents, all the usual joys of running a department at the beginning of a busy term. At this very moment I'd give anything to rewind the clock and be back across the Pond.'

'Well, you'll be there soon, won't you,' Sophie pointed out, 'with this choir tour thingy?'

'Indeed I will.' Andrew matched her light tone, not wishing to provoke further discussion of a subject that had already produced dispiriting quantities of wifely bafflement: scooting back to a place from which they had only just returned, all with the added hassle of finance to sort out and fifteen teenagers to keep in check? Was he out of his mind? Connections needed to be exploited before they went cold, Andrew had countered, using logic to explain a pull he hardly understood himself, other than the desire not to lose touch with all that had happened in August, the renewed sense of inspiration, of self-belief – a portcullis lifting, one he hadn't even known was there.

'Well, my news,' continued Sophie, brightly, obligingly moving away from the topic, 'is that Karen and Jeremy have just phoned to pull out of dinner. Her mother is sick, apparently.'

Andrew laughed. 'Why "apparently"? They wouldn't say that if it wasn't true, surely?'

'I don't know. She sounded funny on the phone and people make up all sorts of stuff when they're trying to hide something, don't they? Anyway,' she continued quickly, 'I've asked Gareth instead . . . and his new partner – I could hardly say no, could I?' she cried, when Andrew groaned. 'He landscapes gardens and is called Lewis and I'm sure he's jolly nice. Besides, I've just bought six lamb steaks, so it would be a shame not to use them.'

'We could have had seconds,' remarked Andrew, drily.

'Pardon? Oh, I see – without Lewis, you mean?' It was Sophie's turn to laugh, still so much her old happy self since the holiday that Andrew could feel some of his own restlessness retreat. They were back on an even keel and he should do everything to keep them there.

'Oh, and that nice policeman phoned,' she chattered on, 'the one with no hair, you saw him too. He says they've now got enough to take that horrible boy to court. We don't have to do another thing.'

'That is indeed brilliant news.'

'And Gareth has asked me to cover for someone tomorrow morning – an hour of Shakespeare at ten pounds more than it used to be. And he says a tutor is about to go on maternity leave so there's heaps of work if I want it.'

'Wow – fantastic. I'll hand in my notice this after-noon.'

Sophie giggled. 'Well, that might have to wait a few months yet, but it does feel good, I must say. By the way, Milly has offered to play waitress for us tonight – for a fee, of course. She's saving for the tour, she said, which is so sweet, don't you think?'

Andrew spent what remained of the lunch hour organizing a rescheduling of the Brahms for the follow-ing term, writing up a list of extra singing rehearsals, forwarding various parents' niggling queries to the correct quarters and scrawling some elaborate red-biro comments on a patchy attempt of Olivia's to highlight the musical influences of the Baroque.

By the time he returned to Ann's email, only five minutes remained until he was due in a classroom.

Dearest Ann,

Thank you so much for your email and all those positive responses on every front. I await further reports with interest. (If you think you've got a challenge on your hands, you should teleport yourself into one of my rehearsals!)

Please pass my best wishes on to the whole crew – pit and stalls. You might tell them, confidentially, that England still rather palls after the splendid time we had together. I arrived in New York thinking I wanted a rest (well, I did want one, of course) but actually what I really needed – I see now – was to start to love music again. Forgive me if this sounds dramatic,

Ann, but that's where you helped me more than you could possibly know.

 So THANK YOU. (Don't worry about Geoff – he loves being a cantankerous old sod, but I'll drop a line anyway to cheer him up.)

The sun is shining here, which is more – if my Internet browsing is correct – than can be said for your neck of the woods. But, as it happens, I've never been one to mind the rain . . .

In haste and with love,

Andrew

## 11

Email to: Stapletonw@latouchedawson.com
25 September
From: alfie1234@sky.net.co.uk

Hey dad, I am ok at school and good except that george trod
on my glasses and I tried superglue which didn work so we
are using tape till I can get to the optician. Its still really hot
here. Sorry for not writing much but with school I am busy.
Jake came for tea yesterday and we played Mario which you
know is my favourite. Miss u dad ps hows the pool coming
along here is my plan for the shape of it so we can fit a diving
board in.

Pps I asked harry to write to u like u said but hes not said
definitely he is driving mum mental cos of his drums but I
think hes quite good.

William peered round the side of his computer screen
to scan the office for people he wished to talk to or avoid.
After three hours of trading the markets were still sticky,
nervous, unreadable, edging down and bobbing back up
again, defying pattern and sense as they had so often
since the start of the global recession. It seemed incredible that only a little over a year before he had
sprawled in the same swivel chair watching the same

screen with the confidence of a conjuror in possession of a deep hat. It was a jungle in comparison now – a jungle without a compass.

The atmosphere in his wing of the asset-management team had altered too. The banter, the camaraderie, the gallows humour were still strong, but beneath it some openness had been lost. It didn't help that the close arrangement of desks still sported empty terminals from the frenzy of redundancies that had followed the official confirmation of the downturn twelve months before. No great sense of luck or even survival guilt had built up among those who remained; instead an unacknow-ledged caginess stalked the corridors, a watch-your-back strategy of self-protection, not sharing the best know-ledge or the best tips, as had once always been the case over matters of obvious common interest.

As the end of the calendar year approached there was also the customary growing bubble of tension with regard to bonuses, a dirty word now in many quarters beyond Wall Street, but still of obsessive interest to those whose annual incomes they defined. For fund managers like William, it was already clear that the usual cut of annual profits on the trading of specific accounts would be virtually non-existent, but the company had made money in some areas, a percentage of which, traditionally, was shared out across the board. And there was always the third component of any bonus package – the per-formance reward, recognition of another twelve months' hard slog. It would obviously be down on previous years, but William fell asleep thinking about it most nights now, performing sleepy calculations as to what would be left over once the credit cards had been paid and monthly allocations taken out for his mortgage, a fixed-rate product, which had looked so sensible upon signing but which, in the new world of slashed interest rates, had been increasingly – ball-breakingly – high.

'What's your crystal ball saying this morning, Bill?'

'Cloudy – best advised to take an early lunch.' William shot a grin at his neighbour, a swarthy dynamo of a young man called Walt, who liked to boast of the pounds he could lift and the number of women he laid. Surpassing William on energy but not experience, his bonus – in the two years they had spent sitting next to each other – had traditionally trailed William's by a few thousand or so. Kurt, on the other hand, the German who sat on his left, normally managed to keep his nose ahead of William's. No numbers were ever discussed outright, but somehow the broad facts of expectations versus delivery would seep out anyway, during the course of conversations at odd quiet moments – after Europe had closed, say, or over a few beers on a Friday. Not this year, however. This year, so far, all speculation had been private. No one was giving away a thing.

'And it's really getting to me,' William confessed to Geoff, over their plates of sushi at lunch. 'I mean, who's good, who's bad, who's in, who's out, I just don't know any more. I keep my clients happy – well, as happy as any client can expect in the current climate – my performance is no better or worse than anyone else's and yet, with profits down, there is just no *certainty*.' He slammed down his water glass, rattling the little dishes of sauce. His companion had ordered a large white wine. William had felt envious, but was holding out.

'That's the good thing about divorce,' replied Geoff, glibly, dipping his nose over the rim of the glass before sipping his wine. 'It never goes out of fashion and it always costs ten times as much as the participants imagine.' He posted a sausage of rice and gingered prawn into his mouth, emitting a hum of appreciation as he chewed. 'But to turn to happier matters . . .' he continued, perhaps glimpsing genuine distress in William's usually cheerful, rugged face '. . . I hope my house-swap scheme was as much of a success for you as it was for Sophie and Andrew.' He paused to pinion a cube of raw tuna between his chopsticks. 'Those two ended up having such a great time I thought they might never leave.'

'Oh, yes, like I said on the phone, it went really well for Beth and me too, thanks . . . Wonderful to see so much of my boys, as you might imagine . . .' William faltered, his stomach twisting at the thought of Harry. Five weeks now and there had still been no communication. Phone, text, email, Alfie – he had tried every avenue he could think of. Not even the enticement of a job in Manhattan had worked, although this was just as well since none of the feelers William had put out had yet come up with anything. Susan, during the course of recent phone calls, had sounded as desperate as he had ever known her. Harry came and went, she said, refusing most of the time to say where.

To confess such a sorry state of affairs over their delicate dishes of Japanese food felt impossible. Geoff was really only a friend of a friend after all – a warm enough guy, but primarily one of those eager, tireless Manhattan net-workers, incapable of conversing without a competitive spirit wheedling its way into the dialogue. The daughter, William knew, was high-powered – Harvard, something medical. He quailed at the thought of bringing the hapless Harry up against such a paragon; Harry, who, until so recently, had been such a paragon himself. 'Although you know how it is with trips home,' he pressed on, swallowing the uprush of anxiety, 'there's all that obligation to visit family – if one's not careful one ends up tearing around England trying to keep everyone happy.'

Geoff rolled his eyes. 'Oh, boy, yes. It took Ann and me a few years before we learnt how to stop playing *those* games. Mercifully, we don't have much cause to cross the water, these days, not with Katherine, our daughter, up the road. No roots left.' He grinned. 'We're Yankees through and through.'

William smiled back but with less conviction. He pointed at Geoff's glass. 'I think I might have one of those after all.'

'Good man . . .' Geoff signalled at the waiter. 'But there was the sorry business of the cat, wasn't there? It hasn't turned up, I suppose?'

William shook his head. 'Afraid not. The Chapmans have offered to pay for a replacement.'

'I would expect no less.' Geoff stabbed the air with his chopsticks. 'They were mortified about that animal disappearing – mortified.'

William took a swig of the wine, which was delicious – dry and ice cold. 'Yes, so our neighbours said. And it's a kind offer, but we're not going to accept.' He twirled the stem of his glass, watching the lemony fluid sway. Beth had not liked the idea of a new kitten, not even a Persian. It was a guilt trip, she had claimed, a cheap way for the Chapmans to make themselves feel better. Animals, like humans, could not be 'replaced', she had added, her eyes brimming with tears. William, a little surprised by the vehemence of the refusal, had been happy to go along with it, not just because he could take or leave having a pet but because of a hazy recollection that cats and foetuses weren't an ideal mix. He remembered Susan, who had turned a stray from their doorstep shortly after falling pregnant with Alfie, explaining to their two disappointed toddlers that cats carried an invisible bug with a long name that was capable of making unborn children very sick.

When the bill came William accepted, with a sinking heart, that it was his job to offer to settle it. Geoff might have been the one to suggest the lunch, but he had brokered the holiday. Nonetheless, seeing the cost of their six glasses of wine, foolishly ordered individually rather than as a bottle, he dithered, hoping his companion would intervene. Geoff was loaded, after all – the bespoke silk suit, the soft leather wallet, the suede loafers: it oozed out of every pore. As he had boasted, divorce never went out of fashion.

Geoff, however, embarked on a tactful scrutiny of his BlackBerry, leaving William to perform a quick mental recap as to which of his cards currently bore the lightest load.

In fact, apart from a nod of thanks, his companion didn't speak until they were out in the street, tugging up their collars against the wind, which felt damp in spite of the happy absence of rain. 'He's coming back over, by the way.'

'Who is?'

'Andrew Chapman. He's bringing some choir from that fancy school of his for a pre-Christmas tour in New York. Ann is like a pig in clover. She's organizing the venues, you see.' Geoff grimaced. 'And there's nothing my wife loves more than having a project. Hey, if he does come, we could all meet up – Beth, you, me, Ann and Andrew. How about that? I'll call you,' he promised, miming a phone at his ear as he walked away.

Or not, William had mused, chuckling darkly at Beth's likely reaction to such a prospect. The whole Dido business had made her so anti the Chapmans he couldn't imagine her wanting ever to meet them. That said, she seemed to be happily back into her stride on other fronts – running, taking new classes, including Pilates and one on painting in watercolour: a very passable seascape was already propped on top of the piano, inspired apparently by a group outing to Pear Tree Point.

Her support about Harry continued to be heart-warming too. Seeing his gloom after Susan's call the night before, she had even offered to try and make contact with Harry herself, venturing that there might be a residue of trust left from her and her stepson's mini-allegiance in August. William had been deeply touched, and also impressed, since the offer cleverly took the last trace of a sting out of what had, after all, been one of the worst rows of their marriage. He had turned the idea down – on the grounds that it might work against them for Harry to feel too 'bombarded' – but the result had been a resurgence of all their old natural closeness. They had spent the rest of the evening cuddling on the sofa in front of the TV, as relaxed and happy as they had ever been; and then – as if that wasn't wonderful enough – once they were upstairs preparing for bed, Beth had suddenly tugged open her bedside drawer and flung her pill packets into the wastepaper basket.

'That's my "yes",' she had murmured, keeping her eyes fixed on William's gaze of delighted astonishment as she started to peel off her clothes. She stopped at her bra and pants – an eye-catching set of cream and black lace that he didn't remember seeing before – then crawled towards him across the duvet, her hair swinging across her cheeks, her lips parted with an intensity of intention that had made every worry in his life, financial or other-wise, dissolve into insignificance.

*

Sophie was sitting at her desk in the sprawling comfort of the WFC staff room, a sitting room by original design, with an elegant, corniced high ceiling and a large bay window, when she spotted Olivia hovering by the gate, her messily clipped hair spilling over her shoulders and her school skirt hoicked unevenly to a level that succeeded in revealing most of her thighs. Sophie rapped on the window and hurried to the front door. 'Is everything okay?'

'Yeah, fine. Were you working?'

'No, I've finished, but I need a moment to sort out some paperwork with Gareth.'

'I'll stay out here, then.'

'Don't be silly. Come and wait in the staff room. There's no one there.' Sophie ushered her daughter along the carpeted hall, amused to see how gingerly she peered about her, clutching her schoolbag, as if expecting a teacher to leap out and deliver a scolding. 'Given the afternoon off, were you?'

Olivia wrinkled her nose in a show of offence. 'Friday from lunch I have free periods this year, remember? And don't worry, I've signed out.' She flopped onto the padded bench that ran under the bay window. 'I didn't have my keys and Dad was teaching, and I remembered you said you'd be here. I tried calling but you were turned off.'

'Good. Right. Well, I won't be long.' Sophie hurried up to the first floor, which housed several tutorial rooms and Gareth's office, a handsome library of a room decorated in Wedgwood blue and white, overlooking the back garden. Bookshelves covered three of its four walls, the highest served by a sliding mahogany ladder on brass wheels. Her employer's vast rosewood desk dominated the remaining space, along with three elaborate gold-framed oil paintings, apparently of his ancestors. Like the house itself, the pictures had belonged to the wealthy spinster aunt who had adored Gareth enough to make him the sole beneficiary of her will and alienate, post-humously, every other surviving member of her family. It was a story Sophie had heard several times and which Gareth told well, invariably underplaying the acumen and determination it had taken then to convert the in-heritance into a thriving business. The classic but homely feel of the college reassured parents and students alike, but it was the results that kept the numbers up, results that depended on finding good tutors and keeping them. The woman going on maternity leave had been a bad call, Gareth had confided earlier that day, well advanced in her condition when she applied, but keeping quiet about it until he had signed her up.

'Hah, my favourite freelancer,' he exclaimed, peeling off his wire-rimmed spectacles as Sophie appeared round the door. 'Shakespearean tragedy and gormless eighteen-year-olds – do you reckon you earned your extra tenner?'

'Every penny,' Sophie countered, laughing. The tutorial had worn her out, but had been tremendous fun. Keeping youngsters interested, *teaching*, she had forgotten the buzz of it. '*King Lear* – I forced them to empty their rucksacks so I could see how many were cheating with summarized notes. They hated me.'

'Good girl. And next week you've got Keats and Plath and Steinbeck by way of further cover for my pregnant, mendacious Corpus graduate with a first. No plans for the next three years, she said ... Give me a girl who dropped out of university to be a model any day ... if she's up to it, that is?' Gareth eyed Sophie carefully, pulling back the page of times and dates he had been holding out to her across the desk. 'Are you sure you're ready for all this, my dear?'

'Absolutely.' Sophie met the gaze of his watery blue eyes, unjustly small, she had always thought, for so warm-hearted a man, and faintly reptilian too, thanks to lashes that were the same washed-out shade as his thinning grey hair.

'So what was it, then, that you're so absolutely better from?'

'I told you – exhaustion ... and generally being stressed out. But I'm *fine* now, Gareth, honestly.'

'Good. We shall proceed, in that case.' He handed the piece of paper to her. 'That's just an outline. I've emailed more details, reports and so on. It's the same group in each class, apart from the last – a one-on-one with the Spanish boy I told you about. Nice kid, anxious parents. That'll be more a language-teaching session than anything.'

'This looks great, thanks.' Sophie cast a quick eye over the schedule, her mind skipping to Olivia, waiting downstairs, and the dinner party, its ingredients still in various packages and bags scattered round the kitchen. 'See you at eight, then?'

'Indeed, you shall. Black tie – I've told Lewis.'

It took Sophie a moment to grasp that he was joking. She grinned. 'Tell him black tie is fine – whatever floats his boat.'

'And you,' Gareth slipped out from behind his desk and barred the door, 'are to tell me the moment things feel like they might be getting too much. Promise?'

Sophie rolled her eyes. 'Okay . . . and *enough already*, as they say across the Pond.'

'Our bodies talk to us,' persisted Gareth, gently, stepping aside for her to pass, 'and when they do we should always *listen*.'

'Aye, aye, Captain.' Sophie fired a mock salute as she hurried down the stairs, uncertain whether to feel offended or flattered by such solicitude and hoping the dinner party didn't produce any more of it.

They had waited what felt like an age for a bus and were within a few yards of their stop before Olivia gave any hint that her fifteen-minute walk from the school gates to her mother's place of work might have had a purpose beyond the need for a set of house keys.

'Dad's really on my case at the moment, Mum. I don't suppose you could get him to back off, could you?'

'On your case?' echoed Sophie, amazed. The closeness of Andrew and the girls was something she took for granted.

'Like he wants me to join his stupid *unaccompanied* choir. I hate that singing – it sucks. And, anyway, we've just been to New York so I can't see the point of going back there. In fact, I'm not even sure I want to do music any more,' she blurted. 'All the practising – I'm just fed up with it, to be honest. Like this afternoon, I know I should do loads because I didn't play a note yesterday or the day before, but I've got so much work, not to mention my CUKAS application . . . I'm just so knackered, Mum, but then there's this eighteenth-birthday party I really want to go to . . .' She paused, inspecting and then chewing a fingernail. 'The piano's okay, I suppose, but sometimes I just wish I'd never even started the stupid violin.'

Sophie had had enough experience of parenting to know that it rarely paid dividends to admit to being shocked. It helped that they were trying to get off the bus – fighting past bags and people and then waiting for the doors to hiss open. By the time they were on the pavement, she had even experienced – and dismissed – a pulse of pleasure at having her support sought over Andrew's. She loved her daughters' musical talents – and her husband's – but the struggle not to feel excluded was always hovering.

'That's okay,' she said at length, prompting a glance of incredulity and then suspicion from her daughter. 'Of course you're going to feel like this sometimes. Music has been such a huge part of your life. Now you're older, you want time for other things too.'

'Oh, Mum, that's it *exactly*. But Dad doesn't get it.'

'Don't worry about the choir tour. I'll talk to Dad. As for wishing you'd never started the violin . . . I can't quite believe that.' She dared a smile, which was reciprocated. 'You've just got a lot on your plate at the moment – work, A2s looming, college auditions. Go to your party, have a lovely lie-in, you deserve it, and by Sunday you'll feel better about everything.'

'Thanks, Mum, you're the best.'

'Who's turning eighteen anyway?'

'A friend of Clare's – Clare Anderson. I'll be staying at hers.'

Later, with the front door echoing behind the clack of Olivia's high heels and Milly helping her clear the dining room of the usual detritus that seemed to edge into it – books, laptops, correspondence, stray socks – Sophie probed for a little more information about the percussionist, whom she suspected lay behind this sudden flurry of a desire for more free time.

'Oh, they aren't together any more.'

'Really?'

Milly rubbed at a smear on a placemat with the sleeve of her school jumper. 'He had commitment issues.'

'Did he now?' Sophie suppressed a smile, making a mental note to repeat the phrase to Andrew. 'And is there someone else?'

'*Mum*, how would I know?' Milly snorted, her co-operation snapping.

'And this new choir of Dad's – a capella or whatever it's called – I know Olivia's against it, but what about you? Are you looking forward to the tour?'

Busy placing the mats at exact distances, Milly paused to suck in her cheeks and close her eyes in a show of ecstasy. '*Sooo* much. It's going to be the coolest thing. You know Meredith? She's promised to come and listen.'

'And one out of two isn't bad,' Sophie declared, having got to the end of a précis of the afternoon's conversations while she and Andrew scrambled past each other in the bedroom a few minutes after eight o'clock, her in search of the right – her only functioning – lipstick, Andrew rummaging for a laundered handkerchief to counter what he had announced as the onset of a cold.

'For studying music or the tour?'

'The tour, silly. Of course Olivia won't give up on music. She's just flexing a few muscles, in need of a breather. Ten minutes after our chat she was looking through the RCM prospectus – so it can't be that bad, can it? And life isn't a straight line, is it? I mean, look at me, not even finishing my degree and I turned out okay, didn't I?' Sophie offered an impish expression at her husband in the wardrobe mirror, expecting to receive something similar in return.

But Andrew, having found a hanky, merely grimaced. 'I wish she would bloody come on the tour, though. And you, for that matter.'

'Me?' Sophie, her upper lip pink, swivelled from the dressing-table mirror in astonishment. 'To New York?'

'Yes, of course to New York. Where else?'

An image of Carter flared and died. Sophie turned back to the mirror, pressing her lips together to spread the pink. 'Not to sing?'

'Well, no, obviously not, but as . . . support.'

'Right.' Sophie cleared her throat. 'Well, the thing is, as I've tried to explain, we have only just *been* there, haven't we? And the run-up to Christmas is always *so* busy . . .'

Andrew shook out the handkerchief and blew into it, a mournful trumpeting sound that seemed to underline his disappointment in her.

'Sorry, darling,' Sophie added gently, 'but I thought I'd already made my position clear. And it's not like you'll *need* me over there, is it?'

'Do you love me, Sophie?'

'Of course.' She snapped the lipstick shut and went to kiss him, touched, but also a little bewildered. 'You know I do. How can you doubt that?'

'I need . . . I need to trust you.'

'Andrew, what is this?'

'I'm not sure.' He pressed the handkerchief, a mangled mess now, against his forehead. 'I just feel . . .'

The doorbell rang, followed by the sound of Milly's footsteps hurrying out of the kitchen to answer it. 'False alarm,' she shrieked up the stairs, a moment later. 'Man selling dishcloths.'

'Feel what?'

But the moment had passed. 'A little unwell, to be honest. Flu . . . something. I think it's been building all week.' He pressed his fingertips to his temples. 'I could do without this sodding dinner party, that's for sure.'

'I'll get you something.' Sophie hurried along the landing to the bathroom, trying not to mind that Andrew had turned the once simple, pleasurable prospect of seeing friends into an ordeal. The poor man had every right to be ill, especially given the nameless virus with which she had burdened the family earlier in the year. No, it was the pressure to accompany him to America that had got to her, Sophie realized, shaking a couple of paracetamol into her palm and setting off back down towards the bedroom. The holiday had been incredible but she had no desire to go back to New York, or Connecticut, for that matter. It wasn't even about Carter. She just didn't want to return there. Ever.

Passing the spare room, she saw that Milly – in spite of specific instructions to the contrary – had un-ceremoniously dumped all the items from the dining room onto the bed, including her and Andrew's laptop. Still switched on from her rushed check for Gareth's email, it was teetering at a precarious angle on the edge of the mattress, its screen flickering. A new message had arrived, Sophie noticed, kneeling on the carpet to investigate. And from Beth Stapleton, too – a reply at last, about the cat, no doubt. Sophie's pulse quickened. Who knew what a Persian kitten might cost? Hurriedly, she opened the email.

Dear Sophie,

Thank you for the offer of money but William and I do not
feel that Dido can be replaced so easily. Besides, I still have
this feeling that I will find her one day. Then how would that
be, for her to come home only to see that her place has been
usurped?

Sophie clamped a hand to her mouth to stifle a small
cry of disbelief, almost swallowing Andrew's tablets in
the process. How bad did this woman want them to feel?
If it wasn't sad it would have been hilarious. She shouted
for Andrew before continuing reading.

As to items left behind, I have found only one thing – a note
from our neighbour, Carter, to you. Quite a composition. I see
better now why you had such a great vacation. But did your
husband enjoy it as much? That's what I keep asking myself.
He looked so nice too, in those photos of you and your
beautiful family. And the letters he wrote you – in that box
under your bed (excuse me for snooping, but they weren't
exactly hidden, were they?) – I've never read anything so
moving, so romantic. I thought we were borrowing the home
of the luckiest woman alive. Funny how, for some, being lucky
just isn't enough.

William tells me your husband is paying another visit to New
York soon. His friend Geoffrey has already suggested that we
should all meet up. Now, wouldn't that be fun?

Sophie rocked back on her heels, snapping the laptop shut. Behind her Andrew put his head round the door, saying if he didn't take something that minute his head would explode. Milly called up the stairs to say she could smell something burning. The doorbell rang again.

Sophie uncurled her hand. The tablets, dampened, had shed some of their white coating on her palm. Andrew took them without a word and turned for the door. Downstairs the hall was suddenly full of voices – Gareth's and Zoë's – they must have met on the doorstep. Sophie watched the back of Andrew's head as she followed him along the landing, the gingery boyish down curling over the edge of his shirt collar, the slight thinning on the crown. She should tell him everything, of course. Make a clean breast of it. What had Carter been, after all, other than a misdemeanour, a stepping-stone on a path she had not understood but which circuitously, inexplicably, had helped to make her well?

'Darling . . . you remember that neighbour of the Stapletons, the old fat one with the bow legs? Well, I saw rather more of him than I let on and he fell in love with me . . . Well, yes, I did encourage it a little . . . and, yes, I did respond, a little . . . I was kind of low at the time if you recall – flat out and face down on the proverbial carpet, in fact. The thing is, he made me feel good again – *understood*, interesting, worthwhile . . .'

No. It didn't work. It wouldn't do. Especially not with so many weeks having passed already, so much mutual trust restored, so many good things said and felt. A 'confession' might destroy all that, let alone one triggered by a gun-to-the-head email from a creature mad and monstrous enough to break into private correspondence and conduct finger-searches of her dustbins.

Having reached the top of the stairs, Andrew stopped to swallow his tablets – hurling them at the back of his throat and scowling at the effort of managing without water. 'Into the breach,' he muttered, twisting to offer Sophie a grim smile before heading down the stairs.

Sophie caught up with him and squeezed his shoulder. Beth Stapleton wouldn't really do anything, would she? It was a joke, a bluff . . . insanity. She was simply a pampered, ridiculous woman with too much time on her hands. The best response would be simply to ignore the whole thing. Or, possibly, to write back and say the problem was all Carter's and Andrew knew about it and had she ever heard the phrase 'get a life'?

Sophie's mind whirred as she exchanged pleasantries and cheek-pecks with her dinner guests, then rushed to check on the contents of the oven. The lamb steaks were dark – too dark, but soft and salvageable. She worked fiercely in the blast of heat released by the oven door, scraping up what was left of the juices and spooning them round the pan until the meat glistened.

# I 2

Fall was in full swing. Somehow, at myriad indefinable unobserved moments, green had been turning into yellow, orange, crimson, gold. Trees across the county were on fire with it, swarming the iridescent sky and the dark lustrous evergreens like rampaging flames.

It was enough, almost, to make one believe in God, Beth mused, staring out of the diner window, light-headed still from the all the deep breathing with which they had ended the Pilates class. She was with two fellow attendees and the instructor, a young, taut-bodied girl called Erica, who put them all to shame with her supple-ness and big smile.

'But you're looking in such great shape, Beth,' she exclaimed, drawing Beth's attention away from the win-dow and tossing her sleek ebony ponytail over her shoulder so that it hung like an arrow down the middle of her back. 'Are you on some kind of new regime you should be sharing with the rest of us ladies?'

'Or maybe she wants to keep it a secret,' pitched in a woman called Patty, a certain edge to her voice, perhaps from reputedly being the longest-serving member of the class and still its largest by some way. A professed martyr to calorie-counting, she had made a big deal at the till of asking for a low-fat muffin and double-checking on the 'skinniness' of her latte, while the rest of them had gone for regulars of both.

'Oh, there's no secret,' replied Beth, coyly. 'I keep busy, I guess, and try not to eat outside of meals.' They all looked at their snacks and laughed. 'And the other thing,' Beth continued, smiling, especially at Patty, for whom, double-chinned, barrel-bodied, it was impossible not to feel pity, 'I haven't had kids, have I?' She dropped her eyes quickly. It was so great to start to feel a part of this group (her painting class was so like an exclusive club she was thinking of giving up on it) and she was determined not to make a mess of things by implying any sense of superiority. And, of course, pregnancies did make keeping a figure harder – she knew that and needed them to know how much she respected them for it.

Patty, who had four kids, was fond of laying public blame for the barrel stomach on her youngest – Stewart, a baby so heavy she claimed he had broken a county-hospital record. Cathy, sitting next to her, had three, and only stayed passably trim, she claimed, by being a slave to a cross-trainer in her spare bedroom. Even the lithe Erica had recently had a child, an impossibly cute round baby whom she had brought to show off to the class – along with her restored waistline – a few weeks after giving birth. Famous for its excellent state-funded public schools and spacious quality of life, the Darien area attracted families like bees to a hive. Beth had known this but not really understood the full permutations of it until coming to live there – unforeseeably jobless, and faced with the necessary challenge of making friends. Not being a mother had really set her apart.

'And would you like kids?' ventured Patty now, in spite of the other two women's eyes boring disapprovingly across the table.

'Actually, we are trying,' replied Beth, softly.

'Oh, honey.' Cathy clamped a hand over hers. 'Howard took years – *years* – but the girls came right along when I was ready. Or not ready, I should say . . .'

And soon they were all pitching in with their conception and birth stories – the waits, miscarriages, the false hopes, the early arrivals, the pain. Beth, meeting their gazes now, nodding, listening, smiling, frowning, felt as if she was in a play – a marvellous play she had devised herself, with her in the lead as the tragic mom-in-waiting with her hopes high, the hopes that would surely fail; although no one knew that yet, of course, not these voluble, well-intentioned women whom she wanted as friends, and certainly not William, whose love she needed as much as the air she breathed.

The warmth of it all was still upon her as she drove home. A request for discretion about her small intimate revelation had been agreed to with teary eyes. An invitation to join a cancer fund-raising committee had followed soon after, along with pleas for her painting instructor's phone number, and the promise of a recipe for walnut brownies that *never* came out too dry. Most wonderful, however, had been the sense of inclusion; all they had needed, Beth saw now, was a nudge in the right direction, a clue as to how to place her in their circle, where she fitted in.

Getting the hang of life never stopped, she reflected, slowing, out of habit, to scan the roadside for a stray bundle of fur during the final mile. Several weeks on from her disappearance everyone, including William, assumed the matter of Dido to be closed. And yet, privately, Beth couldn't quite agree with them. A tiny tight inner part of her simply wouldn't allow it, a part born not of optimism so much as a painfully acquired, self-preserving steeliness. Things wanted badly enough could be achieved. Hadn't she proved as much to herself time and time again? Like all the difficult repercussions from the hateful house-swap holiday. Her world, briefly, had been turned upside down, tipping her back to places she didn't want to go – but now she was fighting again, for her happiness, for William, whatever it took.

Being gifted with the wherewithal to rattle Sophie Chapman had been the turning point: realizing the woman was silly, flawed and powerless, and having the courage to let her know it. Pressing 'send' on the email she had composed after finding the ludicrous love-note had been quite a moment – cathartic, vengeful, sweet but, above all, empowering. Beth couldn't imagine now how she had ever let the Englishwoman get under her skin. There had been no reply yet, but there would be, she was certain. In the meantime the prospect of turning on her computer had become one of the highlights of the day.

Indeed, such was her eagerness to check her correspondence on getting home that morning that Beth almost forgot to throw up. The remains of the muffin she had eaten proved unusually resistant to eviction too, eventually requiring some brutal throat-stabbing to get the process under way. By way of reward for the effort, she treated herself to a good long appraisal in the bedroom mirror afterwards, congratulating herself on the slack look of her Pilates pants, hanging in loose pleats off her hips, and replaying in her mind all the admiring comments from her coffee group. With results so good, who cared how they were achieved? And who would want to end up like Patty? she marvelled, shuddering at the recollection of sighting her new friend in the supermarket the week before, all four of her brood hanging off the cart, like pirates dangling from a ship's rigging, yelping and snatching at items in spite of their mother's protests. How could William wish even a fraction of such ugly misery on them? How could he?

Not bothering to change out of the pants, Beth padded downstairs in her socks and fixed herself a camomile tea before curling up between two cushions on the sitting-room sofa and switching on her laptop. As the icons assembled themselves, she peered round the room through the steam of her drink, relishing how absolutely hers it felt once more. And the rest of the house too – not a trace of Chapman anywhere.

There were only two new items in her in-box: confirmation of a recently despatched direct-mail order from her favourite online fashion company and a brief message from her mother, listing the flight times for her Thanksgiving trip, already spelt out so frequently over the phone that Beth could have recited them to the correct minute by heart.

But nothing yet from London. Suppressing disappointment, Beth was about to quit the page when Sophie Chapman's name obligingly appeared in the box announcing the arrival of new mail. Beth glanced at her watch, her heart racing. It was four o'clock in England. The Englishwoman had to be sitting at her own computer at that very minute, in the dank dining room probably, where the carpet was dark with the stains of careless eating and the shades on the wall lights sported bulb-burns the colour of spat tobacco. To be able to picture the scene so vividly was both comforting and compelling. The distance, the connection – the thrill of how she had managed to turn the tables: it was, Beth decided, like being the quiz master of some elaborate reality game.

She was on the point of pressing 'read' when a sound from outside made her look up guiltily. The sun had come out, showing up faint smears on the sitting-room windows. Apart from a few stray leaves and broken branches being pushed around by the wind, the yard, from what she could see of it, was quite empty. Not even William knew of the existence of Carter's sorry little love-note and for the time being Beth wanted to keep things that way. The moment to play her hand might well come, but not yet, not yet.

To: Beth Stapleton

I have not replied to your email until now because I did not know what to say. I still don't know. I cannot imagine why you wrote it or what you are hoping to achieve. You have drawn false conclusions about a situation you could not hope to understand and which I am under no obligation to explain to you.

That you saw fit to read my private correspondence appals me.

Andrew has a punishing schedule during his forthcoming trip to New York and has already told me he won't have time for socializing.

We both remain grateful for the use of your house and deeply regretful for the loss of your pet.

I sincerely hope that this will be an end to our correspondence.

Yours,

Sophie Chapman

Beth pressed her knuckles into her mouth, breathing hard. It wasn't what she had wanted, what she had imagined. It was too clever, too strong. Closing her eyes, she did her best to refocus, summoning an image of Sophie squirming on one of the big, uncomfortable, loose-springed dining-room chairs, her legs twisted under her, anxiety creasing that irksomely smooth, striking face. When she started typing her fingers flew over the keys.

Well, Sophie, how great to hear from you at last. I am only sorry that you wish for our correspondence to end. Maybe you will change your mind when I tell you I saw your good friend Carter the other day. He was with his wife Nancy at the grocery store. They are a fine couple, but I couldn't help noticing that he looked kind of sad. Are you missing him too? Maybe I should put both of you out of your misery. Who was it who said 'the truth will set you free'?

Such a fine saying, I've always thought.

With very best wishes,

Beth

Beth dropped her head back against the edge of the sofa, exhausted. There would be no answer that day, she sensed at once, from the deep silence that seemed to pulse out of the machine. She hoped it meant Sophie was reeling round her ugly dining room, tearing at her hair, gnashing her teeth, the panic rotting her. It was the least the woman deserved, Beth decided bitterly, her heart racing faster as her mind scrambled to justify what she was doing. The Englishwoman had sailed into her happy corner of the world and hijacked it – yes, that was it. She had stolen Nancy and Carter's happiness too, bulldozed it, behaving as if actions did not have consequences. Who did she think she was? Actions always had consequences, especially where sex was concerned.

Beth pressed the points of her index fingers into her temples. Her pulse had grown so wild it was hard to think straight. William loved her – yes, that was all that mattered. She would hold on to that. Instead, the beefy Henrietta popped into her mind, followed by dim memories of conquests to which William had confessed during the honesty of early courtship, behind Susan's back, some of them. The world was so riddled with deceit. How could she trust him? How could anyone trust anyone?

And there suddenly, in spite of all her efforts, was Uncle Hal – the dry lips, the slightly overlapping front teeth, so vivid it was as if he was standing next to her, his fists producing the pounding at her temples.

Beth leapt to her feet and ran upstairs to her bedroom. With fumbling hands, she changed into her jogging clothes, lacing her trainers with extra tight double knots. On the doorstep she collided with Joe, their whistling moustachioed mailman. He handed over her two mail-order packages, saying it was good to see the sun and how she was to have a nice day. Beth retreated into the house to give him time to drive away. She stared hard at the packages before mustering the energy to open them. So must-have at the instant of purchase, she could see nothing but a pair of caramel suede boots with ugly tassels, and a red cashmere dress that would itch because wool dresses always did, no matter how high the price tag.

As she left the house a second time, the hazy lemon button of a sun looked like it was losing its fight to warm the day. Beth set off down the drive with clenched fists, propelling her legs into little more than a fast walk. Her mind had grown dark and blank. The Pilates had left her body feeling pleasantly stretched, but in the cold now her ankle was always cranky. One stumble and she would be back on crutches. She broke into a slow jog, keeping her gaze fixed on the clumps of dead leaves gathered along the edge of the road, aware of just how easily they might disguise potentially hazardous undulations in the ground. And yet, she remembered suddenly, at a similar time the previous year, before the leaf-sucking machines had done their job, she had run shin-deep in leaves and relished every moment.

Beth forced herself to go faster, pumping her arms. A few minutes later she was rewarded by the darkness in her head beginning to lift at last, letting the earlier high spirits from her exercise class back in. Winter would soon be upon them, after all, and she loved winter. The previous year William had taken some of the heaviest snow-days off work, giving them the excuse to nestle like hibernating animals in front of the then still novel luxury of a roaring hearth (the flames gas-powered, but not so as anyone would guess). Soon they would need the heating on all day and the town would be full of pumpkin sales and ghoulish kids' costumes. Hallowe'en, Thanksgiving, the holidays ... William's boys were due to visit, but only for a week, which, surely, would feel like a blink of an eye after the ordeal of the summer.

The trick was to keep looking ahead – not too far – just a bit at a time. And the looking back – that simply had to stop, Beth scolded herself, at least until she had regained the knack of focusing not on the horrors themselves but on the far more important fact of having left them behind.

After the slam of the front door Beth called from the kitchen, asking if he had had a good day.

'Okay. What about you?' William draped his jacket over the banister and then, remembering that Beth preferred it put straight onto a hook, scooped it off again and opened the stair cupboard.

'Fabulous. I did Pilates, I ran, I made brownies.'

'Hmm, I thought something smelt good.'

As he entered the kitchen Beth, laughing, tilted her cheek towards him for a kiss. 'The brownies were earlier. That smell is our dinner – a meat loaf, using up leftovers like the good thrifty girl that I am. And I've put a bottle of that Chardonnay you like so much in the fridge to go with it.'

William managed an appreciative smile. The homely meal, the warmth of his wife's good mood, there was nothing he wanted more, but he had opened a letter from his bank that morning which made the economies inherent in the production of a meat loaf look risibly insignificant. His overdraft either had to be cleared or converted into a loan, the letter said, at rates that had sickened William to the extent that he had spent most of the afternoon on the phone trying to argue a compromise. What was more, there were only three bottles of the Chardonnay left. It was indeed his favourite white and far too good – far too pricy – for a weekday meal. On top of which, he had been planning not to drink that night, so as to be at his most lucid for a day ahead of back-to-back meetings that included a summons from the chief investment officer.

'Hey, what's up?' Beth asked, picking up on his reticence.

'I might save my share of the bottle for the weekend, that's all.'

'Really?'

'Tough day tomorrow.' He pulled a face. 'A string of difficult clients and a summons from Ed Burke.'

'But you like Ed Burke. He got you your job out here, didn't he? After you worked on the same team in London?'

'He did indeed. But he's a political animal and only a fool wouldn't be on their guard.'

'Well, one glass won't harm, surely? In fact, it will do you good.'

'Maybe . . . I'll think about it in the shower. Back soon.' William kissed her again, giving a gentle squeeze to her backside to remind himself of the pleasure of how physically close they were again, making love most nights – with added intensity, too, thanks to their new shared hope of having a child. 'Hey, don't lose too much more of these curves, will you?' he whispered softly. 'You know how I like them.'

'Go clean up,' Beth commanded playfully, shaking him off.

In the shower William sang snatches of opera as he lathered himself, unable to resist rejoicing – as always – in the powerful hot jets of water installed so effortlessly by Americans and beyond the wit of any plumber he had ever come across in England. Maybe he would have a glass of the Chardonnay, he decided; Beth was right, it would relax him and make tackling the thorny subject of money a lot easier. He had been too gentle with regard to the grim reality of their financial situation, he realized, too proud and protective. If he didn't want her to rush back to work – which he didn't – he had to make her see that the extra classes, the online shopping, simply had to stop, at least for the time being.

Finding Beth waiting for him as he stepped out of the bathroom – a towel tied round his slim hips, his hair in dark wet spikes – William almost blurted as much out loud. But she was holding the phone, her face fixed in what he had come to recognize as an effort at inscrutability. 'That was Alfie. He said you agreed to try out Skype tonight. He's logging on now.'

William groaned, and slapped his forehead. 'Oh, God, I forgot. Yes, I did agree.'

'Isn't it a bit late?'

'Yes, it is. But I've already loaded the software and I've

been promising to give it a go for ages. I also thought it might be a brilliant way of bouncing dear Harry into a conversation at long last . . . It won't take long, I promise. Hey, open that wine, why don't you?' William flashed his best rendition of a winning smile as he tugged on a shirt and jeans. 'I'll do it in my study . . . Dinner in ten, I promise.'

Twenty minutes later, William was still at his desk, legs splayed wide on the chair, his head in his hands. After hovering at the open door a few times, Beth ventured inside, bearing a glass of wine for him so as not to betray the impatience fizzing inside. She had guessed from the silence that the Skype session had been over for several minutes. William's computer had withdrawn into its screen-saver mode – a photograph of a much younger version of his sons, sprawled, careless and laughing, on a patch of grass amid the remnants of a picnic and several tennis balls. What Beth knew to be Susan's bare feet, the nails scarlet, protruding from the swirl of a long blue skirt, were just in view to the right of the scene – there, but not there, like always. William, to her surprise, appeared to be writing a letter, using the fat gold fountain pen of which he was so fond that still required a pot of ink and had a habit of leaking onto his fingers.

'Could we eat?' She pressed her palms onto the tops of his shoulders, which felt unresponsively flat and hard.

'In a minute.'

'How did the Skyping go?'

He twisted to look at her then, his eyes dark with a

sadness that made her balk, both on account of its ferocity and for obviously having no connection to her. 'Horrible, if you must know. Alfie cried. There's been some sort of incident at school – bullying – I don't know – I couldn't get to the bottom of it. Susan said it was fine but, God knows, that's little reassurance. George had nothing to say, and I mean *nothing*, like he didn't know me. And Harry . . .' He paused, grimacing. 'It appears that Harry has left home.'

Beth hesitated. It didn't seem such bad news to her. Harry was making his own way. Good for Harry. But of course William was worried – she wasn't so dumb she couldn't see that. 'Where has he gone?'

'Sheen, apparently . . . A basement flat, no phone, heating on a meter. It sounds hideous.'

'And how is he going to afford that?'

'God knows. I just wish something had come up for him over here, but there's nothing. Nothing.' William dropped his head back into his hands, raking his fingers through his hair – pretty grey now, Beth noticed suddenly, underneath the top layers. 'His sixty quid allowance from me isn't going to get him far, is it? Two other members of his so-called band are living in the same hovel. They've been busking, apparently, to raise funds . . . Christ, Susan is *hopeless*,' he shouted, banging the keyboard of his computer so hard that Beth caught her breath, while the screen-saver was momentarily overlaid by columns of options and menus. 'She has no control, no fucking control whatsoever. We agree one thing and then the

247

moment Harry asks she agrees to something else. If I was there . . .'

The sentence hung unfinished, filling the silence with its implications.

'Well, I'm glad you're not,' Beth said tightly, groping for William's free hand while he clicked the mouse to remove the menus and restore the picture of his sons.

'Of course. Me too.' He squeezed her fingers and then pressed the palm of her hand, which was cool and smooth, against his forehead. 'It's just difficult . . . with Harry *rebelling*, or whatever the hell he's doing. But, hey, we'll probably be going through the same sort of thing with our own in a decade or two . . . or not,' he finished lamely, aware of how crass the remark sounded. He released her hand and turned back to his desk. 'So I've decided to use that old-fashioned weapon of last resort,' he picked up the fountain pen and waggled it, 'a letter, appealing – begging – for the little bugger to see sense.' He laughed sharply, lifting the flap on a pad of paper parked next to his keyboard.

Screwing up her eyes, Beth could make out the opening, *Dear Harry,* and then several lines of writing that seemed to consist mainly of crossings-out. 'William, we need to eat – the meal is near ruined as it is.'

'I'm sorry, Beth, I can't – not until I've done this.'

Beth dug her nails into her palms, summoning patience from a well that felt dry. 'What are you going to say? Can I help?'

'I was thinking of bribery,' William muttered, 'except

I can't afford it . . . which reminds me . . . .' He swivelled in his chair to look at her properly at last, his voice and face alert. 'This may not be the best time, my love, but I have been meaning to say, your – our – efforts at cutting back, I'm afraid they've got to get tighter. So no more new classes, or shopping for anything but necessary items, okay? I'm sorry if that sounds harsh but . . .'

'Shall I cancel Thanksgiving, then?'

'Beth, don't be silly.'

'Or get a job after all?'

'Beth, whoa there. All I'm saying . . .'

'I know what you're saying. You have also said that we'll be fine come December and bonus time, that I wasn't to worry. It's not like I'm extravagant . . .' Beth faltered, remembering the dress and the boots, still in their boxes, hastily pushed to the back of her closet. 'And what about those company shares, anyway, the ones you told me about from a previous pay deal that are due to vest in January? I thought you said they were worth thirty thousand, didn't you?'

William raised his eyebrows, impressed in spite of himself. He hadn't been going to bother her with that. 'You're right, they do. But the fact is, with the WFC share price having been on the slide for months, they're not going to be worth anything like that. It would take a miracle . . .'

'Miracles happen,' said Beth, stoutly, and then burst into tears. 'We are a miracle, William,' she sobbed, 'or at least we were until we loaned our house and everything went wrong.'

William put down his pen with a sigh, pushed back his chair and pulled her onto his lap. 'What nonsense . . . eh?' he chided softly, picking the strands of hair off her wet cheeks. 'What balderdash and codswallop . . .' The sentence, comfort-talk from his own childhood, died on his lips. It was what he had wanted to say to Alfie, he reflected bleakly, remembering his youngest's miserable, puckering face on the computer screen, fighting for composure in a manner all the more heart-rending for the dreadful, still-Sellotaped glasses sliding down his small nose, lop-sided, the lenses steamy with grime and tears. 'I want you, Dad,' he had sobbed. 'Mum doesn't understand.'

William hugged Beth harder, inwardly cursing the tidal advance of communications' technology, making loved ones seem so close when they were in fact far away, opening up emotions that for years he had found fairly easy to compartmentalize. 'Life wouldn't be life without its ups and downs, would it now?' he said hoarsely, stroking Beth's hair with his fingertips, slightly unnerved at how like a child she seemed herself, curled up in such a ball on his lap, her head tucked under his chin, her fingers playing with the buttons on his shirt. It was endearing, of course, but also strange, like becoming acquainted with yet another of the new sides to her that had been revealing themselves throughout the summer – the jealousy, the snapping when she felt cornered, the capacity to swing from intense happiness to gloom. She was right: since England things had hardly been plain sailing. But he hadn't exactly been revealing the best of himself either, William reasoned guiltily – and wasn't that what a good marriage was all about? Getting to know each other's strengths and weaknesses – loving each other in spite of them? And his *volte-face* on the decision not to have a child – hadn't she been amazing about that?

'Hey, baby, your heart is beating fast,' Beth whispered. She was composed now, breathing softly with her cheek against his collarbone, one hand pressed against the left side of his chest. 'So fast . . .' She undid two of the shirt buttons and slid her hand onto the same place on his bare skin.

'I've got a letter to write . . .'

'And you've got me,' she murmured, lifting her face, still streaked with tears, the eyes red-rimmed, looking at him in the new bold way she had – the lids heavy, her pupils wide, her lips slightly parted in the suggestion of a kiss planned or recently delivered. 'Nothing matters except us.' She nimbly shifted her position, until the tips of their noses were touching, her legs straddling his waist, their chests pressed close. 'I love you, William Stapleton,' she crooned, brushing her lips against his and starting to press her pelvis in a slow, determined rhythm across his lap.

William moaned softly. He was being manipulated, of course, but who could mind? And there was the possibility of conception too, an added turn-on for him although he hadn't yet had the confidence to reveal to Beth quite how much. Her hands had moved to the lower buttons of his shirt and her hips were moving faster. 'We could go upstairs . . .' The chair tipped and he glimpsed the image of his three sons on the screen behind her. It felt too much, to have the boys there, with their messy, guileless happiness, *watching*. And their dimpled smiling faces were stark, sore reminders, too, of where he had failed . . . where he was continuing to fail. 'Upstairs,' he said again.

'No. Here.' Beth stripped off her T-shirt and tossed it onto the floor. 'I – want – you – here.' She knelt up, hitching her skirt to her hips. 'Say you love me,' she commanded, tugging at the zip on his trousers and then lowering herself back onto his lap. 'Say you'll always love me – and no one else – no matter what. Say you will never leave me – never – never – never –'

It was good sex, of that there was no doubt. Fast, furious – no man, let alone husband, in his right mind, would have complained. And yet even as William succumbed, swearing the words she needed to hear, forgetting, in the heat of his own arousal, the protesting creaks and teetering of his desk chair, there was something disquieting about it too – something connected to the realization that yet another facet of her was emerging, that the task of getting to know the woman he had married had only just begun.

It wasn't until nearly midnight, with more wine inside

him than food (the meat loaf, as Beth had feared, had been well past its best, somehow justifying solace in a second, cheaper bottle), that William again picked up his fountain pen. Tearing up his first efforts, he set upon a new page, writing with fast, alcohol-fuelled fluency.

*My dearest, beloved Harry,*

*You'll hate that opening, I know, but I don't care. This letter is going to say important things – things that are real and true – so please do me the honour of reading every word. You were a long time in entering this world, did you know that? Hours and hours – your poor mother. Not for nothing is it called 'labour'. And then suddenly the room was full of white coats and machines and doctor-speak and I was booted into the corridor. Your heartbeat was getting faint, you see, so they had to move fast to get you out. Christ, I thought, not born and we're going to lose him. To be honest, it was only at that moment I knew how much I loved you. That corridor – the waiting – I promised every deity I could think of that I would guard each precious intake of breath you took, if only you came out of that room alive, bawling your eyes out. Which you did.*

*But the joke is, of course – proof of god(s) aside – that it wasn't a promise I could keep, not just because I've been a crap father (yeah, yeah) but because no parent can offer such protection. You are you, Harry. It's your life, your choices. Being eighteen makes this obvious, but for even the smallest child, there is only so much looking-after a parent can do. It's torture, frankly, and no one warns you, but it is also wonderful and I wouldn't have it any other way.*

*I'm rambling, I know. It's late and I'm not at my best. But stick with me, please, I'm nearly done. As you get older doors close (I've had, for example, finally, to let go my hopes of opening the batting for England, ha ha) but at your age — and for many years to come — they should still be flying open on all sides. If you pack in your education now, that won't happen. It will be hard graft all the way, making any direction change hugely difficult. I'm not saying don't play in a band (maybe you're going to be as big as the Rolling Stones, or the Cure, or whoever you listen to on that iPod of yours) but you can do that at university, you know, while getting a degree . . .*

*The world should be your oyster, Harry, so don't turn your back on it. On me, yes, if you must, though it breaks my heart.*

*Your most loving father*

*PS How about a hundred quid for every A level above a C?*

William deposited the letter (carefully, tenderly, addressed with the hateful new details Susan had given him, *24D Curlew Street, SW14*) in the mailbox at the bottom of the drive. The wetness in his eyes was not just from the sting of the autumn night air. He was drunk, of course, which didn't help – full of sentimentality – but it did seem incredible that he had once fantasized about his sons growing up and moving away and not needing him. How could he have been so naïve to imagine a process so clear-cut, so simple? How could he not have known how much *he* would always need *them*, no matter how many more wives he had or kids he spawned?

Shivering from cold, William fumbled for a final cigarette, huddling close to the mailbox to coax a flame from his flimsy booklet of matches. With his free hand tucked into his armpit for warmth, he studied the night sky as he smoked, automatically identifying the constellations pointed out by his grandfather during idyllic bonding sessions under canvas and round campfires thirty years before, while his sisters – unfairly, he could see now – had been banished indoors. How lucky he had been and how little he had been aware of it – but the very essence of such luck was not *having* to be aware of it, William realized, drying his eyes on his shirt cuff and lifting the little flag on the box to alert Joe to the presence of an item for collection. The most nurtured child took love for granted, as his elemental right.

Tiptoeing through to the bathroom five minutes later, he dropped a light kiss on Beth's sleeping face, wondering fondly – excitedly – if the seed of their own child might have taken root that very night, on the creaking study chair. He couldn't wait to see the effect motherhood would have on her, the focus, the shared, mind-blowing love. Beth stirred, frowning, and then shook her head from side to side, as if banishing a bad dream. William closed the door of the en-suite quietly behind him and soaked a flannel with hot water to wash his face. His skin looked pasty and faintly yellow under the strip light above the basin, as did his teeth, he observed grimly. Too many fags – he had to stop, properly, once and for all . . . soon. When he was safely through to January, he promised himself, glowering at his reflection, when there were clearer waters all around.

Humming softly, he opened the bathroom wall cabinet and scanned the shelves for a tube of whitening toothpaste that he remembered Beth buying after one of her anti-smoking tirades in England. The shelves were narrow and tightly stocked with bottles and packets of this and that – floss, shampoo, soap bars, cotton-wool buds, analgesics. William riffled through it all, trying not to make a mess or a noise but managing both as several items toppled onto the floor. Stopping to gather them up, he noticed a bright yellow oblong box, identical to the one Beth had, with such wonderful drama, hurled out of her bedside drawer.

William picked it up, turning it over in his hands and peering in at the small, foil-encased pills, two rows of which were missing. She would have several such boxes, wouldn't she? Doctors handed out a few months' supply in advance – that was how the system worked, wasn't it? William scowled, trying to summon knowledge from his years with Susan, who had never refrained from acquainting him with all the earthiest aspects of the chore of being female – leg-shaving, eyebrow-plucking, her flabby rubber Dutch cap, the onset and heaviness of her periods – to the point where William had sometimes wondered if she was deliberately challenging his capacity to be repelled. Beth, in contrast, had always been sweetly, protectively – alluringly – reticent about such matters. Girls' business was for girls, she had declared several times early on, by way of a consoling explanation for a locked bathroom door or the nights she turned her back on him instead of pulling him into her arms.

William took out one of the foil rectangles and inspected it. They weren't pills, but capsules, quite unlike the coloured tablets he remembered Susan taking. Turning over the box he studied the small print: *KLB6, containing Kelp, a natural food rich in iodine, helps to maintain a healthy thyroid. Lecithin – an excellent natural source of choline and inositol, two members of the B-complex vitamins, B-6 – functions as a co-enzyme involved in protein and fat metabolism.*

Not contraceptives, then, but vitamins of some kind, helping to speed up the metabolism by the sound of it. He must have got the packets mixed in that case. Two yellows – similar in his memory, but no doubt quite different shades when side by side. Easy mistake to make, especially for a man barely awake he was so tired. Giving up on the whitener, William carefully stowed the fallen items back in the cabinet and cleaned his teeth with ordinary toothpaste, before creeping to bed. His last waking thought was of his letter to Harry, sitting in the cold mailbox, and what a flimsy thing it was for the transport of so much hope.

# 13

To: annhooper@googlemail.com
28 October
From: chapmanandrew@stjosephs.sch.org.uk
Subject: NY Tour

Dear Ann,

Thank you so much for that outline itinerary – it looks as if things are shaping up really nicely. I wish I could say the same for this end! The rehearsals are not yet close to the standard we need and my letter asking parents for final commitment and payment just before half-term has prompted quite a few pull-outs. That said, I have – as I hope you'll agree – made a couple of inspirational additions to the programme: namely, a portion of the Rachmaninov Vespers and, by way of a grand finale, Herbert Howell's tribute to JFK, 'Take Him Back For Cherishing', an exquisite piece of unaccompanied singing, which I expect you know. If we can only pull it off there shouldn't be a dry eye in the house!

Thank you too, for all your kind words with regard to Olivia, understanding so well (unlike Sophie, I regret to say) that it is the wasted potential which upsets me most. She was born with a gift and would, I am certain, have got into the Royal College or one of the other five top conservatoires. Reading music at one of the regular universities – after a gap year, for heaven's sake – just won't be the same. She'll lose her edge, disappear into the crowd, end up doing something menial like so many talented girls seem to . . .

Phew! Sorry to lumber you, Ann, but it is impossible to voice such thoughts at home, partly because Sophie has very much taken Olivia's side and partly because Sophie herself has always had a bit of a chip on her shoulder about not getting a degree, not being musical, etc., etc., which is ridiculous, of course, and should have no bearing on every parent's duty to encourage the very best from their child (as opposed to second best, which is what Olivia is settling for). Thank goodness for dear Milly, is all I can say, practising like a fiend already in anticipation of her secret dream of auditioning for the Juilliard in two years' time!

As to the other thing you mentioned – it blew me away, to be honest. I am tempted of course, but – if I am to be completely truthful – I am also terrified of looking a fool. The competition doesn't bear thinking about. Then, of course, there would be the massive logistical implications to consider too. The only thing I can say with absolute certainty is how deeply grateful I am to you, Ann, for showing such faith in my abilities. As a washed-up has-been of a musician, soul sold to bureaucracy, paperwork and a failing educational system, I can't tell you what it means to be invited even to consider such a possibility. And I will be in your debt for that always, no matter what happens.

In the meantime, the coal-face beckons. Counting the days now till the tour . . . excited but apprehensive!

With love

Andrew

PS Yes, I think it's a brilliant idea to ticket the events and sell as many as possible in advance.

PPS Please thank Meredith for finding the time to send a reply to Milly's emails – she was thrilled.

Autumn had turned ugly, the leaves clogging the gutters, the frosts seeing off the last flowers, but Sophie felt her faith in the world returning in ever greater depth, the old layers of herself – her life – falling back into place, stronger, more certain for having been called into question. The decision to ignore any further communications from the odious Beth Stapleton seemed to have paid off. Weeks had passed without a further word. Indeed, the flurry of panic caused by the woman's two creepy emails had receded into a pinprick of a memory, along with the Darien holiday itself and the suntan that had encouraged the purchase of a white cardigan, ruined on its first outing, thanks to slops from the dinner-party lamb steaks.

Sophie fell into the half-term break with groans of grateful exhaustion, sleeping in as late as the girls on a couple of mornings and, even if she was up, enjoying padding round the house in socks and crumpled clothes, idly catching up on chores between cups of coffee and reading the paper. The tiredness felt natural and good – quite unlike the fretful state of mind that had gnawed away at her earlier in the year – and was as much from demands made within the family as being back at work. There had been hitches – mainly with Olivia – but nothing that had felt beyond Sophie's capabilities; on the contrary, supporting her daughter in her momentous decision to change tack – not just by applying to university rather than music college but waiting until she had secured her A levels before doing so – had wrought a wonderful new bond between them. Andrew was still a little prickly about it – not surprisingly – but privately Sophie felt she had handled her husband well too, pointing out that it wasn't about taking sides so much as having the faith to let their much-loved firstborn find her own way in the world, as opposed to the one they might have mapped out for her.

'I think he's finally recognized that it's Olivia's life, not his,' she told Zoë, when they met in what had become their regular café for a sandwich lunch on the Friday during half-term, 'while all I can think is how *brave* Ollie is being, how honest, daring to plough her own furrow with her father glowering in the background. He's strong, Andrew – sometimes I don't think he realizes quite how strong.'

'Pete too.' Zoë grimaced in sympathy, before going on to recount at great length a recent marital stand-off about the purchase of a new carpet.

With the tone of sharing confidences thus set and the happy sense of being able to discuss a drama that was safely past, Sophie found herself talking about the less exemplary aspects of her time in America. It took a while, both because she left no detail out and because she was at pains to explain the nuances that had led to the folly, the reasons why she had been so vulnerable.

'Or maybe you fancied this American and told him your life history in the hope of having a snog,' Zoë teased, shaking her head in amusement.

'That's monstrous,' Sophie cried, flapping her paper napkin in protest, laughing in spite of herself. 'It wasn't like that at all.'

'So much angst over one embrace,' Zoë scoffed. 'I've never heard anything more ridiculous, even if, as you say, it was quite a *long* embrace and you had done rather a lot to encourage it . . .' She started to laugh but then stopped abruptly, flinching. 'It certainly doesn't compare to the fling Pete had a couple of years ago – six whole months before I found out. Some mother from the football club, if you can believe it. I couldn't tell you before because I couldn't tell anyone. They used to screw in the back of her car, of all sordid things, parked in lay-bys and behind wide trees, like desperate teenagers.'

'Oh, God, Zoë, I'm so sorry . . .'

'No need. We're totally through it now – stronger for having been tested or *something*.' She pulled a face. 'All I'm saying is, this Curtis business –'

'Carter,' Sophie corrected her.

'Whoever. It's a big deal out of nothing. Mountains and molehills. Not telling Andrew from the start, that was your only mistake.'

Sophie frowned, trying to take herself back to the course she had chosen and why. 'I suppose different couples can cope with different things,' she ventured at length. 'Andrew and I had been so rocky and things were going so well . . .'

'And as for that woman and those emails,' Zoë exclaimed, remembering the Beth Stapleton part of the story, 'she's clearly certifiable. Ignore her. I mean, what's the worst that can happen?'

'Exactly, that's what I keep telling myself.'

'This woman of Pete's,' Zoë blurted, lighting a cigarette the moment they were outside and sucking hard, 'it was Karen. That's why they didn't come to your thing. Sorry.'

'Oh, God, I'm the one who's sorry,' Sophie gasped, putting an arm round her friend. 'I had no idea . . .'

'Of course you didn't. How could you? And, like I said, we're fine now.' Zoë drew on her cigarette so hard she made a popping noise with her lips. 'I've told him, one more stunt like that and I'll chop his bollocks off – lob them over the garden fence like that other, even madder American woman . . . What was she called?'

Sophie giggled. 'I know the one you mean, but if I recall correctly it was a different part of his genitalia and afterwards he had a surgical replacement of such impressive proportions that he was able to put it to lucrative use by becoming a porn star.'

'No? Fantastic.' Zoë clapped her hands, all the moroseness gone. 'God, human nature – you couldn't make it up, could you? Oh, Sophie, I love our lunches. Don't let's give them up, ever, okay?'

'Okay.'

'And you're all right, are you, you and Andrew?'

'Brilliant. It turned into a great holiday. There was just that little bit of it when I was an idiot. I want to forget about the whole thing, to be honest – just get on with my life with Andrew, the life we had before I let everything get on top of me.'

'Yeah, why would any wife want to go to the bother of learning to put up with a whole new set of annoying male habits?' Zoë joked, pulling another of her funny faces as she stamped on the stub of her cigarette. 'Farts, belches, smelly socks – best to stick with the ones you know, that's what I say.' She lit another cigarette straight away, batting at the smoke as they kissed goodbye.

Sophie walked home, feeling fortunate on her own behalf and sad on Zoë's. Her old friend's sense of humour might still be wonderfully intact, but she was a far cry from the somewhat dreamy woman who had boasted of shared marital ideals and Pete's parenting skills a decade before, during the days of pre-school and pushchairs in the park. And yet the pair had seemed so close during her and Andrew's September dinner party, almost irritatingly so – eye-contact, arm-touching, laughing at each other's stories. But, then, a marriage was such a house of a thing, Sophie reflected affectionately, pausing outside her own front door: no one but the occupants really knew what went on inside.

As she stepped into the hall she was assailed by the strains of piano-playing, followed closely by a muted, less obviously tuneful noise floating from the direction of Olivia's bedroom. She found Andrew in the dining room, cocooned in his big silver headphones and conducting vigorously in front of a large book propped open on a music stand. When Sophie tapped him on the shoulder he spun round with visible irritation.

'Sorry . . . just wanted you to know I'm back. Goodness . . .' She put her hands to ears, rolling her eyes to the ceiling as a louder, different rhythmic pounding started up overhead. 'If Mrs Hemmel hasn't complained yet, she soon will . . . not that any single member of this household would hear the doorbell *or* the phone.' She laughed, stepping closer to offer her lips for a kiss and giving a playful tug to the wire sprouting out of the headphones.

Andrew smiled, looking sheepish, but also – she could tell from the speed with which he pecked her forehead – quite keen to be left alone. 'Good lunch? How was Zoë?'

'Great, thanks . . . At least . . . Yes, fine.' Sophie suppressed an urge to elaborate, out of a mix of loyalty to her friend and it obviously not being a good moment to talk. She squinted at the open pages of the score on the stand instead, the dense layers of dots and stalks, a foreign language, even after twenty years. 'You've been practising so much. This week is supposed to be a holiday, remember? You and Milly, you're like a pair of whirling dervishes at the moment – music, music, music.'

Andrew placed himself between her and the stand, pressing one hand protectively against the open pages. 'Rachmaninov's *Vespers*. I'm trying to work out if the choir are up to it.' He slotted the headphones back over his ears and then pointed his baton at the ceiling, asking in the too-loud voice of one who cannot hear, 'Please have a word with Olivia. She's been locked in there for hours with Clare and some boy, playing that hateful noise. It's not fair on Milly, it really isn't.'

Sophie put her head round the music-room door before going upstairs. 'All right, sweetheart?'

Milly, seated at the piano, her fingers flying, turned her head briefly and with an irritation so visible, so reminiscent of her father, that Sophie couldn't help smiling. 'What?'

'Nothing. Sorry to disturb.' Sophie closed the door softly and then paused as the music – Bach, of course (she had learnt that much over the years because Bach was Milly's favourite and the tune was something knitted and tricky and fast) – gathered momentum. What wasn't in doubt was that Milly's skill was extraordinary and growing by the week. Normally, the piano got short shrift when it came to practice, the cello being her first love, but throughout that autumn she had been giving it just as much attention, to the point where even Olivia had remarked on the fact. 'Bloody hell – she's better than me now,' she had observed grudgingly, adding for her father's benefit, 'and don't tell me she deserves it because I know that already.'

Sophie rapped twice on Olivia's bedroom door and leant against the wall to wait.

'Yes?' Olivia's head appeared a moment later.

'The music, darling, I'm afraid it's too loud. Both Dad and Milly are trying to practise.'

Olivia groaned. 'We'd just finished anyway.' She opened the door wider, revealing her friend, Clare, sprawled on the bed, and a boy with messy dark curly hair sitting cross-legged on the floor. He had a small gold ring stapled through one eyebrow and was dressed in a black T-shirt and low-slung skin-tight jeans that accentuated his long legs and narrow hips.

Sophie smiled at them both, before letting her eyes rest on Clare. 'Hi there.'

'Hi, Mrs Chapman.' Clare waved, then caught the boy's eye, looking as if she was trying not to laugh.

'And that's Harry,' said Olivia, pointing at her other visitor, who grinned and nodded and then, rather touchingly, clambered to his feet to shake Sophie's hand. Standing up it was even clearer how stick-thin he was and how pale, seen close to, with patches of unhealthy-looking red bumps across his chin and round his nose. 'Harry has his own band. We were listening to the demo.'

'Gosh – congratulations.'

'Thanks.' Harry grinned, revealing a flash of disarming adult charm, before shaking the heavy, overgrown locks of hair back over his eyes. 'Better make a move.' He bounced on the balls of his feet, looking first at Olivia and then Clare, who sprang obediently off the bed.

Sophie watched through the window as Olivia saw them out. It took a while, the trio hovering by the gate, saying she knew not what to each other, but laughing a lot, especially Clare, who showed off her even teeth and flicked her auburn hair whenever the Harry boy looked her way. He seemed not to notice, fidgeting constantly, crossing and uncrossing his arms, kicking the toe of his shoe at the pavement, rolling a cigarette, which he smoked with a vigorous nonchalance, holding it between his thumb and first two fingers, crinkling his eyes like a seasoned old man against the smoke. Watching him, Sophie found herself wondering who might have re-placed the percussion in her daughter's affections, hoping, ungenerously, that it was a creature rather more wholesome, and altogether less reminiscent of the oc-casional sorry soul expelled by Gareth for manifest use of illegal substances.

As the three hugged their farewells at last, displaying the physical closeness in which both her children seemed to indulge effortlessly with all their teenage friends, Sophie ducked out of sight and hurried to the kitchen to see if anything resembling an evening meal might be scrambled from the scanty contents of the fridge.

'That was Harry-as-in-Stapleton, by the way,' volun-teered Olivia, breezily, hoisting herself to sit on the kitchen table and plucking the last apple from the fruit bowl, which she began to eat – as always – in small circular bites starting from the stalk.

'You mean . . . ?'

'Doh . . . yes, as in the ones who spent August in this very house.' Olivia continued to nibble, swinging her legs, looking pleased with herself. 'Is that funny or what? He's got his own flat,' she continued with evident admiration, 'or, at least, he's sharing a place with a couple of the other band members so that they can concentrate on their music.'

'Blimey. He looked so young. I wonder what his parents think.'

'His mum is cool about it and he's not speaking to his dad.'

'Oh dear.'

'Why "oh dear"?' she sneered. 'It's called "real life", Mum, get over it.'

'I'll do my best,' retorted Sophie, drily, too eager for more information to risk the obvious, alienating, route of a reprimand. 'So how did you come across him then, if you don't mind my asking?'

'A gig . . . at this place we went to after Clare's eighteenth.'

'And are they any good, do you think, his band, whatever they're called?'

'The Skunks?' Olivia screwed up her nose, as if this was the first time she had given the matter serious thought. 'I'm not sure, to be honest, but, yeah, I guess they have potential.'

'Who has potential?' boomed Andrew, striding into the kitchen from a run-through that had clearly gone well, the headphones still bouncing round his neck.

'No one,' Olivia trilled, shooting a look at her mother as she slipped off the table and back upstairs, the half-eaten apple pinioned between her teeth.

Not the progeny of Beth Stapleton but of the ex-wife, Sophie reminded herself, absently dropping items into a supermarket trolley half an hour later, the fridge having proved empty beyond the wildest reaches of her creativity. And that one of her girls should come across one of the Stapleton boys was hardly a massive coincidence either, since Richmond was only a couple of miles downriver. On being told of it, Andrew had been only mildly interested, reserving his energies for some jaw-clenched criticism once Olivia was out of earshot, both for what he had been forced to hear of the band's demo and his impression of Harry Stapleton in general from a brief conversation before the three had disappeared upstairs. What did such 'friends' suggest about Olivia's blossoming powers of judgement? he wanted to know, adding darkly that it took only one kid to go off the rails for the rest to follow like lemmings.

Sophie had pooh-poohed his fears, but as her trolley filled, she found herself resolving to keep the closest possible eye on the situation. Harry Stapleton was interesting, clearly, a little wild and dangerous – hardly surprising, then, that Olivia should enjoy being drawn into his circle, especially given the amusingly star-struck state of her best friend. But he was also, plainly – as Andrew had so delighted in pointing out – no role model.

But Olivia, surely, would know that, Sophie reasoned, just as she would know that, having won her mother's faith and support, it would be unconscionable to adopt any sort of behaviour that would let her down.

But what she really didn't like, Sophie acknowledged, still mulling the matter over as she loaded her purchases into several splitting, overstretched plastic bags at the checkout (having forgotten, as usual, to bring her robust 'green' ones), was the sense that the appearance of Harry Stapleton in their lives brought his stepmother back into the frame too, just when Sophie had been doing such a good job of forgetting her. Minutely, remotely, like a blip on the edge of a radar screen – the woman lived thousands of miles way, after all – but for Sophie it was an unsettling reminder of how, thanks to the house-swap, the worlds of their two families would never again be absolutely distinct. There was an overlap now and always would be, like a Venn diagram – two immutable circles, sharing a slice of grey.

# 14

After much debate with himself, and against the advice of his wife, William had decided to keep his November visit to the UK a surprise. There was, he knew, a certain element of indulgence to the decision (the hero's welcome he would receive from Alfie, for starters), but there were other, more worthy reasons too, like not wanting to get Susan het up or put any pressure on his parents or – more importantly – on Harry, whose continuing hurtful silence strongly suggested that the child would grab any chance of ducking out of a face-to-face.

It was to be the briefest of visits too: Friday to Monday night, back on Tuesday, in time for a gritty-eyed day in the office and the arrival of his mother-in-law for Thanksgiving. All that week Beth had been immersed in shopping lists and recipes: an infallible version of a pumpkin pie (nutmeg, cloves, cinnamon *and* ginger, apparently) had been secured from one of her Pilates friends; cookbooks lay open round the kitchen, at pages detailing the intricacies of cranberry sauce, chestnut stuffing and the secrets of a perfectly roasted turkey. When William had pointed out – with somewhat acerbic incredulity – that there were still seven days to go, and all for an event scheduled that year to comprise a grand total of three attendees, only one of whom was noted for his large appetite, Beth had pouted like a little girl, asking what was so wrong about wanting everything perfect and why didn't he run along to England and leave her to get on with it?

And Thanksgiving was, without doubt, the best festival of the American year, William reflected, experiencing a pang of remorse for how quick he had been to put his wife on the spot, seeking to burst the bubble of her enthusiasm rather than enjoy it. What had got into him? An excuse for time off, a get-together over fabulous food, breaking up the dankness of November, all without the cumbersome attachment of presents or religious overtones. Judging from the dilapidated look of the street along which his taxi was crawling, he would be more than ready to embrace every aspect of such festivities by the time he flew home.

'You did say the Royal,' said the cabbie, glancing doubtfully at the sign of washed-out lettering dangling from the pockmarked wall of the building behind his smartly dressed passenger.

'Yes, indeed.' William peeled two twenties and a fiver out of his wallet, resisting the urge to explain himself further. The hotel was a lot seedier than the photograph on the Internet had suggested but, really, it hardly mattered, given the priority of keeping the trip cheap and needing nothing more than a pillow upon which to lay his head. Most importantly, he was a stone's throw from Harry and only a fifteen-minute walk from Richmond.

And there was something faintly exotic about the

sheer anonymity of it, William told himself, glancing up and down the dark street after the taxi had sped away, glad that he hadn't caved in to the temptation of phoning his parents, who would worry and want explanations and possibly even stress themselves with a rushed train journey south, all for a snatched meal and little possibility of reassurance. He was here to sort Harry out and nothing more. He had spent most of the flight planning what to say, how to win the boy round, now that enough weeks had passed for him to be certain that the letter, along with every other of his efforts since the end of the summer, had failed.

Led down a series of narrow, ill-lit corridors by the hotel's unsmiling, greasy-haired owner, William's spirits dipped. Stains of damp bubbled out of the walls and the air was layered with the stench of gas and cooked food. His room turned out to be a cubby-hole, the bed jammed between a shower box and a wardrobe sporting a splintered groove from collisions with the handle of the main door. On the plus side, it was warm, thanks to an electric radiator plugged in under the window, and when William gingerly checked under the bedspread there was no doubt that the linen was fresh. The mattress was thin and the pillow stuffed with what felt like foam rubber, but what could one expect for thirty-three pounds fifty?

William dropped his bag, kicked off his shoes and fired the TV remote at the television, which flickered obligingly into action. Stretching out as comfortably as he could, he channel-flicked several times through the various late-night options before settling on Stephen Fry being wry and self-deprecating from the corner of a deep leather sofa. William blinked sleepily. It was eleven fifteen local time, barely cocktail hour in New York, yet he felt he could sleep for years. There was no question of being hungry either, since he had snacked at Newark airport and eaten twice on the plane.

His mind obligingly withdrew from his surroundings, but then refused to shut down. Images and thoughts shuttled back and forth between his temples: of the continuing ardour in Beth's lovemaking – legs locked round his waist, her eyes wild, her tongue flicking between her lips as she came – as if intensity alone would be enough to ensure their new goal of conceiving a child; of Alfie during their most recent and not entirely satisfactory Skype session the previous weekend, his eyes large behind his new fashionable square glasses, a distinct teenage surliness starting to sour his tone – *French is gay, so why should I care if I get a C?*; of Ed Burke during the meeting that had been postponed so many times William had begun to wonder if it would ever happen . . . *I'm speaking to you as a friend, Will. Three months' pay, another for every year worked – as voluntary severance packages go, it ain't half bad. I'm not saying you should offer yourself, only that you should know what's on the table . . .*

A low-pitched loud vibrating noise had started up through the wall next to the bed. Hoover? Boiler? Shower pump? William opened his eyes. Stephen Fry had been replaced by an unfamiliar face, saying things he now couldn't even hear. He thought about calling Beth, but that would have been a challenge too, given the noise. Air, that was what he needed – preferably laced with nicotine, he decided grimly, reaching for his coat and giving the thin partition wall a mighty thump as he left the room.

Outside it was too cold to stand and smoke, so he set off at a brisk pace, his face shrouded in a mix of smoke and the steam of his own breath. Curlew Street came into sight a few minutes later, without any feeling that he had planned it. Number twenty-four took only a few strides to reach. A panel of buttons offered communication with the occupants of flats A, B and C, which meant D had to be the grey, ill-lit windows at the bottom of the wrought-iron stairwell to his left. William peered down into blackness. A bunch of junk mail was sticking out of the letterbox. What looked like a bed sheet had been clumsily pinned across the main window; through a break in its folds he could make out two lit, drooling candle stumps in a saucer, close to drowning in the hardening pool of their own wax.

William started down the steps, but then turned and strode away, not looking back – barely breathing – until he had reached the far end of the street. To doorstep the child at midnight, rouse him from sleep, a drunken stupor or something worse – what was he thinking? With such a start, no dialogue would have a hope in hell of success. And yet the need to see his eldest son now burnt like a fire in his chest – not just to set things straight but to pull him into his arms in a way that he once had so mindlessly, so easily, during all those early, careless years, when fatherhood had seemed more of a chore than a privilege. Close to tears, feeling like some desperate stalker, William pulled out his phone to seek consolation from Beth, only to remember that she would have embarked on her 'girls' night out' – a movie and a pizza, 'If that won't break the bank,' she had quipped, with the arch tone she now adopted for any subject relating to money, a masquerade of humour, designed, William knew, to stop him saying anything stern.

Standing alone in the street, fumbling with frozen fingers for a pocket in which to stow his phone, a wave of total desolation broke over him, squeezing the air from his lungs, making his heart pound till it hurt. Money, happiness, certainty . . . was it all slipping away *again*? No, God, no, he wouldn't let it. Not again. He tried to put the phone into his pocket, but missed. It clattered to the pavement, splitting in two as the back fell off. William dropped to his knees with a groan, scrabbling to retrieve the pieces. Glancing up, he saw an approaching woman avert her eyes and then hurry to cross the road. William hastily got to his feet, re-assembled the phone and carefully put it away. He was just 'dog-tired', he consoled himself, conjuring – by way of some comfort – a phrase Beth might have used. In his own parlance he was jet-lagged, juggling too many uncertainties, fire-fighting events in his life instead of taking charge of them. But it would pass. All things did in the end.

As his surroundings came back into focus, so did the pink neon sign of a bar some twenty yards further down the street. William plunged towards it, digging into his trouser pocket for his wallet well before he reached the entrance.

'Double whisky,' he growled, waving a ten-pound note once he had elbowed his way through the throng at the bar. Only after the first gulp of alcohol was safely tracking down his throat to his stomach, replacing the fire of despair with something altogether more bearable, did he turn to scan the room properly. And there – suddenly, unbelievably – was Harry. Or, at least, a version of Harry – skeletal in black drain-pipes, his hair so long it was a mess of curls, a thick silver ring stapled through one eyebrow. He was leaning against a far wall, engaged in what looked like an intense conversation with two girls, one slim and blonde, the other more rounded, with short, spiky auburn hair.

William's first knee-jerk reaction was a lightning bolt of pure joy, followed closely by something more akin to terror as it dawned on him that this encounter wouldn't do either – cramping Harry's style, making him feel cornered. Christ, the child might even think he had followed him from the dingy basement flat. Setting down the glass of whisky, William pushed off from the bar with the intention of edging his way discreetly back out into the street. But Harry, perhaps compelled by some sixth sense, was already looking over his shoulder. A moment later, ensnared in the slow-motion inevitability of all things disastrous but unavoidable, their eyes met. Disarmed, afraid, embarrassed, happy, William tried out a smile – a flimsy white flag of an effort that withered under the reply of his son's expressionless, remorseless gaze.

The pain of this silent exchange felt endless and beyond anything William could ever have imagined. It was broken only by the bar's double-doors swinging open and a fair-haired woman wearing a red anorak and clutching a large unfashionable handbag barging into the crowded room. Jaw set and eyes flashing, she made straight for the girls talking to Harry, tapping her watch, waving her phone – so clearly and unashamedly lost to the unsightly role of furious parent that William's heart instinctively went out to her. A few minutes later all three left the bar, the girls trailing behind, heads and bags hanging in defeat. At the same time, William found his heart going out to Harry too – purely as one man to another – for the public humiliation of the scene and the appalling ill-luck of having one's father there to witness it. He was still pondering how to express such sympathies, as well as the niggling sense that he had seen both the blonde girl and her mother some-where before, when he glanced up to find Harry at his side.

'I know why you're here,' he snarled, before William could speak.

'Yes, Harry, I hope you do.' William tried to touch his shoulder, but he twisted away, flinching.

'I've got to work. I was on a break.'

'You work . . . here? I mean . . . Wow . . . great. Good for you,' William gabbled. 'All I want is to make sure you're all right.'

Harry's scowl deepened. 'Don't pretend, okay? Don't pretend you've come all this way just to make sure I'm *all right*.' He put disdainful quotation marks round the words with his fingers.

'But I have,' William exclaimed eagerly, reading a tendril of hope in the sneering tone – a tone that seemed to suggest his son was still just a sulky kid feeling hard-done-by, that behind the ugly face-piercing and the posturing and the painfully bad complexion (where had that come from?) all he really wanted was to be cared about.

'You're here, I assume, because of Mum,' Harry growled, ignoring the interjection.

'Mum?' William bent his head nearer as the noise around them swelled. He thought suddenly of the father-son embrace he had envisaged, feeling the possibility of it recede like a silly dream. 'Mum?' he repeated.

'Yeah, because of her being ill.'

'No, Harry, I'm here because I couldn't bear another moment of letting you throw your life away. Because . . . What do you mean, "ill"?'

Harry had caught someone's eye over his shoulder and was gesturing with a thumbs-up sign and what struck

William as a hurtfully cheery grin. 'Gotta go, Dad,' he hissed, returning his attention to his father, the scowl dropping back over his features like a mask. 'See you around.'

'Oh, no, you don't.' William squeezed Harry's arm as he had tried to dive away, taking heart from the memory of the mother, guns blazing as she frog-marched her daughters into the street. 'Tell me what you meant – this instant. In what way exactly is your mother ill?'

Harry stopped struggling and lowered his eyes. 'I thought you knew,' he muttered. 'She said she was going to tell you. Seeing you here, I thought she must have.'

The hubbub seemed to shrink suddenly to a background hum. There were just the two of them and Harry looking at him properly at last, his face inflicted with a pain that William realized now had nothing to do with him. 'For fuck's sake, Harry, spit it out.'

Harry shook his head miserably. 'She's got cancer, hasn't she? She said she was going to tell you . . . That's why I . . . Look, I've got to go.'

'What sort?' Harry was starting to move away so William grabbed his arm again. 'What sort of cancer?'

'Breast.'

'Christ . . .' William released his grip, shaking his head in wonderment. 'But, Harry, I've still got to see you . . . talk to you . . .'

'I'm moving back home this weekend.'

'Moving home?' A spark of delight flew out of William before he could stop it.

'Yeah, but it's hardly for the greatest of reasons, is it, Dad? You might think I'm a waste of space but I figured *someone* should be around, shouldn't they?'

'Jesus, Harry, if I could . . .'

But this time he made good his escape before William could stop him. He reappeared a couple of moments later behind the bar with a tea-towel hanging out of the waistband of his jeans and a cocktail shaker tossing between his hands. William spent several minutes trying to catch his eye, but Harry merely blinked, keeping his expression blank, as if there was nothing to register, let alone avoid.

After downing a second whisky William gave up and stumbled outside. Stepping past the huddle of smokers at the entrance, he stopped to leave a hoarse, emotional message for Beth, saying how much he missed her but refraining from reporting the latest horrible twist to the situation in England. He had dug out his own, crumpled pack of cigarettes and was on the point of lighting up when he noticed that the car parked at the kerbside in front of him, whose ignition had been grinding in a series of failed attempts to fire, contained the fierce mother in the red anorak and the two dejected girls. A moment later the driver's window slid down and the woman stuck her head out in his direction.

'I don't suppose you're parked nearby with a handy set of jump leads, by any chance?' She tugged with evident irritation at the strands of hair that the wind was gusting across her face.

'I'm afraid not.' William approached, putting his cigarettes away. 'Flat battery?'

'I suppose . . . although it got me here, which is odd. And Volvos are so reliable normally, aren't they? And why do these things always have to happen at the *most* inconvenient times?'

'I wish I could help,' William offered lamely, deciding that it would do no good to confess his relationship to the boy from whom she had just extricated her daughters, but then proceeding to do so anyway. 'I only hope he hasn't been leading them astray . . . Oh, God, he has,' he groaned, seeing the rapid change in her expression.

'No . . . that is, I had these two on a promise, that's all – midnight tonight, two o'clock tomorrow night. Holidays are different but I like to try and keep a few rules for term time.' The blonde girl was murmuring something to her mother and leaning across to get a better look out of the open window. They had the same strong high cheekbones and wide blue eyes, except that the younger one's were set among heavily lacquered lashes and smears of dark eye-shadow. 'Sorry to have bothered you. I'll call the AA, or maybe a taxi,' she added, winding the window back up.

Dismissed, William stepped back. She tried the ignition again and this time the car started. He waved and she nodded. It was only as the Volvo pulled out of its parking space, revealing the small deep dent above the rear light and the memorable first three digits of its number-plate,

WOO – he had joked to Beth about it – that William finally recognized the vehicle he had spent four weeks driving that summer. The Chapmans, then. The mother and two daughters – or had the red-headed one been a friend? Yes, that was the more likely scenario, he decided, hurrying to the roadside to beckon the car back, but then losing heart.

The world was small – so what? William traipsed back in the direction of his hotel, fighting – amid all the other tumult in his heart – a faint sense of rejection that the revelation of his identity should have caused Sophie Chapman to flee rather than make conversation. Who could blame her? If he had daughters, would he want them to mix with Harry?

Sleeping fitfully under the thin duvet, it was this sad truth that haunted William the most, together with images of his son's altered angry, sickly, suffering face. Junk food, drugs – there was almost certainly something sinister going on. Pot? Ecstasy? He was too old and dumb even to know what there was out there, William reflected miserably, let alone what they called it.

And yet, most poignantly of all, the boy was moving back home, to be there for his sick mother. Tears seeped from William's closed eyelids, wetting the pillow so thoroughly that eventually, moaning in his sleep, he turned it over and hugged it to his chest instead. He woke with a start four hours later, his mind alert: two days simply wouldn't be enough. Even before he tackled the business of calling Susan he needed to get on to the airline and see about changing his return flight.

Greeted by the comforting warmth of the central heating and the still lingering aromas of that day's baking as she let herself back into the house, Beth breathed a heavy sigh of relief. She had been so dreading William leaving – being on her own, without even Dido now – and yet here she was, back from a thoroughly pleasant evening with her new friends, and all the good, positive thinking of the last few weeks still feeling safely intact inside. In fact, not long after William's departure, studying her calendar and the lists of things she had to do in his absence, she had momentarily set aside her loneliness to acknowledge a slow-burn glow of satisfaction in prospect. How much easier the Thanksgiving preparations would be without William parading his dry English wit in the background, teasing her for caring so much, conveniently overlooking the fact that it was precisely that care that produced so many of the things he loved.

Confessing as much to Patty and Cathy while they had waited in the theatre for the movie to start, large paper tubs of popcorn parked between their thighs, both women had laughingly chipped in with the shared opinion that husbands in general were a lot easier to love when they weren't around. But then it was great to get them back again too – especially for you-know-what, Patty had whispered, spraying sticky white crumbs as she giggled and casting a special look at Beth because of the thing they all knew about her now, the thing that made them like her so well.

Happiness was the weirdest, most wilful commodity, Beth reflected, enjoying the stillness of the house as she prepared for bed, recalling with some wonderment the low point she had reached just a few weeks before, on the day when the small disappointments of Sophie Chapman's robust email and the arrival of the ugly dress and tasselled boots had somehow snowballed into what had felt, for the first time, like a fight she might not win. With William choosing that night of all nights to lecture her about money and then to put communicating with his children above both her needs and that of their overcooked dinner, she had felt as if the world was tipping again, taking her balance with it.

But then, *whoosh*, something had happened – empowerment, determination, self-belief, *something* – triggered not so much by the sex on the chair in William's study (inexpressibly wonderful though that had been – beyond accurate recollection as it turned out, in spite of her efforts) as the onrush of sheer power that accompanied it; a power heightened by the occasional glimpses of William's computer screen throughout their sexual athletics – the flat, out-of-date family snap, twitching like a faded ensign. Her husband was hers, all hers. He wanted not just her body now but her kid as well. The hunger of that – the *need* in William – wasn't something Beth had fully appreciated until that night. It was raw, electrifying, addictive – a new level of connection that felt blissfully beyond the clutches of the ugly shed skin of their pasts. They had been getting along so much better ever since – almost like the old earliest days at times, when having enough of each other had felt joyously impossible and the future something to embrace rather than fear. Beth knew it was no coincidence that Uncle Hal had dropped from view in recent weeks too, along with any further urges to stir anxiety in the heart of Sophie Chapman. How could 'luck' be stolen, or space 'corrupted'? And as for feeling so envious and angry that she wanted to teach the woman some kind of lesson – the idea was so crazy in retrospect that she laughed to recall it.

Once safely in bed, Beth reached for her cell to listen again to William's late-night message from London, thrilling as she had the first time at the cracking intensity of his voice, the romantic growl of the final, treasured declaration of his love. She thought suddenly how wonderful it would be to collect all the lovely things he had ever said and store them in a box, just like the letters under the Chapmans' double bed: love in black and white – something to hang on to or consult if ever faith needed to be restored. Instead all she had was her head, Beth reflected wistfully, such a vast, unsafe place compared to a cardboard box, being full of closed avenues and spaces where things could be lost . . . She closed her eyes and breathed deeply, focusing on opening her ribs in the way Erica always reminded them in class. Calm . . . there it was. Easy when you knew how. She blinked her eyes open and dialled her mother, from whom a missed call had registered while she was in the movie theatre.

'Beth . . . hello, honey.'

'You sound sleepy, did I wake you? It's only nine with you, isn't it, or did I get the math wrong?'

'No . . . I mean, yes, it is only nine, but I'm afraid I'm already tucked up with my cocoa. I get so tired, these days, but then I wake real early too, which I hate. Old age sucks, I can tell you . . . but I'm so looking forward to my trip, dear.'

'Good, so am I, Mom. And everything is okay, then?'

'Oh, yes, everything's perfect.'

'So when you tried to ring me it was because . . . ?'

'Because they're saying there might be some early snow – in time for Thanksgiving. Did you see that?'

'No, I didn't.'

'In which case there could be a problem with my flight. Last winter they closed JFK for a couple of days, didn't they?'

'That was December and I think it was just a few hours. Look, Mom, I'm sure there won't be a problem, but I'll check out the long-range forecast tomorrow and email you, okay?'

'Thank you, dear, that would put my mind at rest. How's William?'

'Oh, he's wonderful . . . apart from being in London. His eldest is playing up – remember I wrote you about it?'

Diane said she did, but sounded uncertain.

'The kid is just pushing buttons, of course, but William can't see it.'

'Dear William,' Diane cried. 'I'm sure he does his best.'

'Yes, he does.'

'And being a good father isn't just about being *around*, is it now?'

'No, Mom, it certainly isn't,' Beth murmured, with some surprise: even such oblique references to her own early upbringing were extremely rare.

'Was there anything else, dear?'

Beth hesitated, detecting the familiar swift emotional withdrawal, the tacit desire to be allowed to put down the phone. There was something else, of course. There had been for most of her life, but she couldn't say it. She could never say it. And her mother's memory, she had noticed during conversations lately, was getting so patchy anyway. Who knew what she really remembered – or, indeed, what she had ever really known?

'No . . . except, that is, without William I guess I feel kind of *spare*,' she gushed. 'I love him so much, Mom, and he just left me the dreamiest message from England, saying how he couldn't live without me –' Beth broke off, not at all sure what she hoped to achieve by these disclosures, other than the need to hear them out loud herself. Her mother, she was certain, had never known such love. The years of drink had seen off any possible suitors. Now she lived off investments that Uncle Hal had made for her, in a condo that forbade pets, filling her time with medical appointments, magazines and the occasional game of bridge with neighbours, many of them with far narrower lives than she had.

'So you just make sure you hang on to this one, you hear?' Diane quipped, using a hateful, scolding, jocular voice, which made Beth wish she had kept her mouth shut.

'You bet I will. Goodnight, Mom. Don't let the bugs bite. I'll email tomorrow.'

After clicking off the phone Beth remembered to take one of the pills that now lived in the bathroom cabinet, instead of her bedside drawer, before putting out the light. She had thrown up her supper in one of the nicely sealed roomy bathrooms on the lower ground floor of the Mexican restaurant where she had gone with her girlfriends, but still liked the idea of keeping her digestive system on its toes, letting these metabolic enhancers zap calories that might have got left behind. She took a half sleeping tablet too, with just a sip of water to preclude any need to visit the bathroom during the night. Before closing her eyes she kissed William's pillow and then placed both the handset of the house phone and her cell side by side on top of it, wanting to be sure that either ring would penetrate even the soundest morning sleep.

As things turned out she was halfway through a banquet of a breakfast when William called: chocolate yoghurt, lox, bagel, cream cheese, blueberry muffin and coffee, served French style in a wide cup with steaming milk. Her stomach was so full it ached, but being able to binge openly was such a treat that Beth was determined to make the most of it. And the scale had been a joy that morning too – another two pounds lost in spite of the popcorn, the bulging fajitas and guacamole thick enough to stand a spoon in. It had to be the yellow pills, Beth reflected happily, conveniently forgetting the many mornings over the months when she had silently cursed the same tablets for making no discernible difference. She was still licking sugary muffin crumbs off her fingers as she picked up the phone. 'William, honey, I got your message, I miss you too . . . *sooo* much.'

'Are you okay? You sound like you're eating.'

'I am. A late breakfast. I'm being such a bad girl – neglecting my chores, just eating, sleeping, missing my baby . . .'

'What was the film like?'

'Oh, fine . . . you know the kind of thing, two girls, one guy, a *dog* . . . which was cute actually, except Patty says they used thirty different animals for the shoot – can you believe that? Anyway, then we went to Juanito's and then I came home. Mom called *again* – worried about snow this time, if you can believe it. She's definitely getting worse. I am looking forward to her visit and Thanksgiving and all but, I swear, the moment she steps off the airplane she's going to start driving me crazy for all the same old reasons. But, hey, that's moms and daughters the world over, I guess . . . But how are you, honey? How are things over there?'

'Mixed, to be honest . . . There's a bit of news, some good, some bad . . . '

'About Harry?'

'Yes, some of it about Harry. He's moving back home –'

'You see? Didn't I tell you it would all work out – that there was no need to go flying over there?'

'More amazingly – as I've only just learnt – he's decided to retake his A levels at this crammer place . . . '

'William, that is *fabulous*.'

'Yup, I know. He's still determined not to talk to me but, frankly, if he's prepared to have another bash at all three subjects I think I can live with being Public Enemy Number One for the time being. What's truly incredible is that the person we really have to thank for helping to bring about this turn of events is – of all people – one Olivia Chapman . . . '

Idly dislodging a blueberry from a muffin with her finger, it took Beth a few moments to absorb the fact that the name, which she had only half registered, was supposed to elicit some kind of a response. Her delight at the Harry turnaround was heartfelt, but sprang mainly from the way it would release William from the draining business of worrying about the boy all the time – thereby releasing her too, of course, from having to deal with the fall-out of that worry. 'Olivia . . . what did you say?' She pressed the berry flat against her front teeth and then rolled it onto her tongue.

'Chapman,' William repeated, 'as in eldest-daughter-of-the-Chapmans-whose-house-we-used-in-August. It turns out she and Harry have become friends and the mother, Sophie, teaches at this small sixth-form college that specializes in retakes –'

'Sophie Chapman?'

'Exactly. The very same. Thanks to petitioning from her daughter, she has got her boss to agree to take Harry mid-term with a view to –'

'You've met Sophie Chapman?'

'Yes – at least, briefly, last night, but I didn't know any of this until she phoned this morning.'

'How come you two met? Did you go to the house?'

'No, nothing like that – I was trying to see Harry and then . . . Look, it's a long story, but by total co-incidence I bumped into her and Olivia – and Harry come to that – in this bar late last night. In fact, on hearing who I was, she took off pretty rudely, but then she phoned this morning to apologize and explain all this business about WFC and how she's been trying to help.'

'WFC?' Beth pushed the muffin away, feeling she might do her vomiting there and then, all over the butter dish and the bowl of yoghurt.

'It's the name of the crammer – the sixth-form college – where Sophie Chapman teaches English. The point is . . .'

'William, I just feel very uncomfortable with this.'

William laughed uncertainly. 'Uncomfortable?'

'That woman . . .' Beth swallowed. The old fears had

stormed back, worse than ever. She bit her lip. 'You know I don't like that woman.'

William snorted, clearly incredulous. 'Beth, this has got absolutely nothing to do with what happened in the summer. You haven't even met Sophie Chapman and, I tell you, she couldn't be nicer. For a college of that calibre to let someone in mid-term – with such bad grades – is quite something. It was Harry's idea apparently, wanting to get his act together at last – which is just wonderful in itself – but Sophie Chapman is the one who has made it happen. It won't be cheap, of course –'

'So how can we afford it, then?' Beth snapped, pushing off from her chair and striding to the glass-panelled doors. The yard was now a wintry monochrome, the grass a dull green, the trees so stripped and skeletal that thick grey slats of the lake were visible between their branches. 'Or will Susan pay?'

When William eventually answered his voice was so painfully measured, so imbued with the determination to keep his patience, that Beth wanted to kick herself. Crazy, knee-jerk reactions, when everything between them had been so sweet – what kind of idiot was she?

'I haven't worked that part out yet. There hasn't been time. All that matters, as I'm sure you can appreciate, is that Harry appears to have a chance of getting back on track.'

'Of course,' Beth cried, the yard view dissolving in a blur of tears. 'Of course. Oh, William, I'm sorry, honey . . . sorry for being sharp. I just miss you so much.

Forgive me?' She could hear him breathing. She listened hard, wishing he would offer up what she needed to hear. 'You sound so close,' she murmured. 'I wish you were close.'

'But there's some other news too,' William continued softly, 'really bad, I'm afraid . . . Susan has been diagnosed with breast cancer.'

'Susan?' exclaimed Beth, whose few moments' preparation for yet more bad news had not taken her anywhere near William's ex-wife. 'Oh, dear God,' she murmured, aware of the need to imply sympathy while her thoughts lurched to an ugly certainty that Susan, being Susan, would milk the situation – for sympathy, money and anything else within reach. 'But at least that's one of the better ones,' she managed, doing her best to make the sympathetic tone convincing. 'I mean, for treatment and all . . . like with those new drugs and so on.'

'Indeed, it is. Thank goodness.'

'But how terrible for her,' Beth rushed on, wishing she could erase the insulting carefulness to her husband's tone, as if he had decided he was communicating with someone who had special needs, 'and for your kids too, of course.'

'The boys,' William said thickly, 'yes . . . but Susan's done well there – been straight with them, which can't have been easy. They seem okay about it. It's already made Harry sort himself out, which is unbelievable – more than I've been able to achieve.' He was silent for a moment. 'And she's no fool, Susan – she's already got

BUPA to agree costs, researched all the options, found a top oncologist and so on.'

'Good . . . Way to go, Susan.' Beth bit a piece off her lip and swallowed.

'But the most immediate point, my love,' William continued, switching suddenly to a much gentler, more soothing tone, 'as you might well already have guessed, is that with so much going on I see no alternative but to delay my return by a couple of days. I've told the office I won't be in until Friday and I've booked myself onto a flight for Thursday –'

'But that's Thanksgiving –'

'Yes, and it leaves at seven in the morning, so with the time difference I should easily make it home for the meal. I know it's not ideal, but life throws these googlies from time to time, doesn't it?'

'Googlies?' Beth whimpered, dropping her forehead onto the glass pane of the garden door.

'Cricket. A ball that looks like it's going to do one thing but then does another . . . The point is, given the situation, the least I can do is be around a bit longer to help out. Susan's got an appointment at the Parkside on Tuesday afternoon, which clashes with a rugby match for Alfie, so I've said I'll cover that. Then, of course, I need to see this WFC place and get the financing sorted. I've also arranged lunch with an old contact in the City – just to put my ear to the ground, see where London is compared to Wall Street . . .'

'Wow. Busy, busy, busy.'

'Sorry, Beth, but it's only two extra days.'

'Sure. And you need to be there – I see that.' When Beth lifted her head she saw that the greasiness of her skin had left an ugly oval smear on the glass. She rubbed at it with her elbow, but it only grew worse.

'I knew you'd understand.'

He was so obviously relieved that Beth almost felt as if she *did* understand. 'Mom and I will keep the turkey warm, don't you worry.'

'Sweet girl . . . sweet Beth . . . I love you.'

'I love you too,' she echoed, heartened only because he, too, sounded close to crying.

## 15

'We should probably invite the man for dinner or some-thing, shouldn't we?'

'Oh, God, surely not.' Sophie peered over the edge of her book. Andrew was standing in his boxers and a shirt, riffling with evident disconsolation through their over-crowded shared wardrobe. 'What are you looking for?'

'My black tie. Could it be at the dry-cleaner's?'

'No . . . at least, no, I don't think so.'

'So that's a maybe, is it?'

'Andrew, for goodness' sake, it's eleven thirty on a Monday night . . . '

'I'd like to track it down that's all – for the tour.'

'The tour? But there's still over two weeks to go.' Sophie returned her attention to her novel, shaking her head. Andrew had been in charge of numerous travelling music extravaganzas in the past – a school-choir com-petition in Toulouse, an orchestra trip to Hamburg and Munich, another to Russia. New York was obviously up there in terms of importance, but she still could not quite believe how all-consuming the project had become. Since half-term the intense sessions under the headphones, along with mountains of paperwork, had converted the dining room into a no-go area for the rest of the family. In addition, a things-to-pack pile had started growing on the floor of the spare bedroom. Daily, he quizzed poor Milly (inheritor of his own habitually last-minute approach to all matters practical) as to what she might like to add to it.

All of which was mildly endearing, but also *odd*, Sophie decided, losing her reading place again at the sight of Andrew balancing on a chair to rummage in the dusty storage cupboards above the rails on which they hung their clothes.

'Ha – found it!' He jumped clear of the chair, shaking the dust off a suit-carrier. 'Not the suit,' he added, in seeing her quizzical stare, 'but something to transport it in at least.'

'Good. I'm thrilled. Now, how about coming to bed?'

Andrew sneezed violently – four times in quick succession – at the dust-flurry he had created, then rummaged in a couple more drawers before complying. Once in bed, however, instead of reaching for his own book, *A Life of Herbert Howells*, recently borrowed from the school library, he tucked his hands behind his head in a way that Sophie knew meant he wished either to think or talk. 'But you'll be seeing him tomorrow, won't you?'

'No, Gareth is seeing him,' she corrected, a little dismayed that the subject of William Stapleton had not, after all, dropped out of view.

'You could invite him then, I suppose – just for a casual supper by way of a thank-you . . . We're not busy tomorrow night, are we?'

Sophie closed her book with a laugh of disbelief. 'All this from the father who thought Harry Stapleton was going to drag our daughter into the gutter . . .'

'Don't exaggerate. I didn't like the look of the boy. I still don't. But since it has happily become apparent that Olivia was influencing him rather than the other way around –'

'With *my* help,' Sophie reminded him archly. 'Credit, please, where it's due.'

'Yes, indeed.' Andrew rolled over and planted a kiss on her temple before resuming his thinking position. 'You've done well there – very well – reading the situation, staying on top of it, getting Gareth to give the boy a chance.' He nodded approvingly. 'But since his father has fallen into our laps, as it were, I don't understand your reluctance to show the man a little hospitality. It was a hell of a house, after all . . . and one hell of a holiday,' he added dreamily.

'Yes, it was.' Sophie turned onto her side and slipped her fingers between the buttons of his pyjama top, only to realize – when Andrew made no response – that the dreaminess had nothing to do with her. She withdrew the hand gently, marvelling not at the recent dwindling of all the rekindled physical intimacy with which they had ended their time in Connecticut but at the mysterious new ebb and flow of such patterns in their marriage, arriving and disappearing like tides, obeying forces that seemed, increasingly, to have little connection to anything over which she had any control.

A few minutes later Andrew's eyes had fallen shut while what remained of Sophie's sleepiness had evaporated under an adrenalin rush of frustration at the Stapletons, popping up every time she thought she had heard the last of them. She had seen Beth off successfully, only to find herself dealing with the messed-up Harry – a source of some worry until it had become sorely apparent that he was as smitten with Olivia as poor Clare was with him. A dear proverbial triangle, which Olivia had bashfully denied and then acknowledged as part of the reason behind her recent campaign to elicit her mother's help *vis-à-vis* Harry getting into WFC. It was a way of making up for not liking him more, she had explained. He was a different, interesting sort of friend, but for anything else Clare was *welcome*, she had added, with enough disgust in her tone for Sophie to know she was being told the truth.

So why fear William Stapleton? Sophie brooded, abandoning her book altogether and reaching carefully across Andrew to turn out his bedside light. In all their dealings the man had, after all, been nothing but gracious. A poor taste in wives was hardly a crime. And even if Beth had waved Carter's note in his face, William was hardly likely to refer to it over a bowl of spaghetti Bolognese, not with the Harry business, and being seated opposite the kindly hosts in whose very house he had spent four pleasant weeks that summer. And how distant the whole Carter business had grown anyway, Sophie reflected, hard to recall for anything now except how badly she had mishandled it.

In spite of such wise thoughts, a certain trepidation accompanied her to work the following morning. Making her way to the staff room after her first class had dispersed, she couldn't help casting a glance at Gareth's closed door, wondering if the interview with Harry's father was still going on or had already finished. It wasn't until the matter was far from her mind, displaced by a pile of marking, that a knock on the staff-room door was followed by the appearance of William Stapleton's head round the side of it, his thick dark hair jumbled in what looked like a carefully crafted state of dishevelment, his face flexing with comedic, exaggerated uncertainty.

'Sorry . . . I'm probably not supposed to come in here, am I?' He directed the apology at two of her colleagues, Gina Logan, a maths tutor, and Alain Labrousse, responsible for modern languages, both of whom were seated at the table nearest the door. 'I'm after . . . Ah, there you are.' He smiled with sudden obvious shyness at Sophie, who was already on her feet. 'I just wanted to say . . .' He slipped through the door and crossed the room quickly, self-consciously, on the balls of his feet. 'Sorry,' he offered again, speaking in a stage whisper and glancing over his shoulder at the other two, busy now packing away their books, 'I know I'm disturbing you. I just wanted to say thank you again for –'

'No need to thank me for anything – truly.' Behind him the door closed on Gina and Alain, leaving for their respective tutorials. As Sophie returned her attention to her visitor, the last of her apprehensions evaporated. On closer inspection it was plain that the hair wasn't styled into its rather wild shape so much as bent at odd angles from compression among bedclothes. He looked, more than anything, exhausted – his eyes red-rimmed and lost in creases of fatigue, his skin as pallid as his son's. He was also much taller than she had judged, either from the photos scattered around his home or the shadowy impression she had received in the dark outside the bar on Friday night. 'There's coffee, if you would like?'

'No, I'm fine, thanks.'

'Did it go all right upstairs? With Gareth . . . I mean, Mr Wainwright?'

'Oh, yes . . . splendid . . . all sorted. I'm so grateful – I can't tell you . . .' He combed his fingers through the mess of his hair, looking about him with a suggestion of desperation, as if the walls of the room and more of Gareth's tasteful prints might inspire the right lines of gratitude.

The exhaustion looked layered and deep, Sophie decided – quite beyond jet-lag. 'I'm the one who should apologize,' she offered kindly, 'for not introducing myself properly on Friday – I was just so cross with the girls and stressed out about the car –'

'Yes, you explained on the phone. It's quite all right. I would have done the same, I'm sure . . . At least, I hope I would. I admire anyone prepared to take a firm line with teenagers,' he added, to the accompaniment of such a grimace that it took Sophie a moment to register that she was being complimented.

'Look, Andrew and I would be delighted if you could come to supper tonight,' she blurted. 'I know you're only here for five minutes and you're probably fiendishly busy, but . . . well, there we are – the offer stands. We loved our time in Darien so much,' she added gently, forgetting her fears about what Beth might or might not have said, her heart going out to him as he laboured visibly with indecision at her offer, running one hand across his mouth while the other stabbed again at the hopeless disorder of his hair. 'The holiday of a lifetime,' she pressed on diplomatically, assuming the agonizing was to find a polite way of saying no. 'We were just so sorry about –'

'Did you say tonight?' His face was calm suddenly, the eyebrows raised, as if surprised by his own conclusion. 'Actually, that might work pretty well . . . if you're sure?'

'Of course,' Sophie cried, making a mental note to add mince, onions, mushrooms and spaghetti to the list of things to swoop round the supermarket for on her way home from work.

'This trip to London was only supposed to be for the weekend but it's all turned a bit hectic –' He broke off as his mobile sounded from the confines of his trouser pocket. 'Sorry . . .' He plucked the phone out and gave a quick glance at the screen before turning it off.

'It must be hard,' Sophie ventured, wondering at the identity of the caller – so swiftly despatched – and speculating whether it might have been the American wife. 'I mean, living abroad, away from your sons.'

'It is.' He looked at her then – into the heart of her, it felt – his bloodshot eyes so ablaze that for a moment Sophie had a vivid image of the man literally exploding into fragments in front of her, in a spontaneous combustion of all the nervous energy that seemed to be bursting to get out of him. 'That's why what you have done for Harry means so much,' he added, blinking as the moment had passed.

'Nonsense,' Sophie countered briskly. 'They hatched it themselves – Harry and Olivia. I've done nothing except ease the way – although he'll have to work hard. Make no mistake about that.'

'Good, I'm relieved to hear it. Retakes won't change the world, but it's a start, at least, a step in the right direction – hopefully one that will get him into a university next year. You're English, aren't you? Shakespeare, the Romantics – Christ, the lucky bugger.' He shook out his overcoat, which had been draped over his arm, then fed his arms into the sleeves and shrugged it on over his shoulders. 'I suppose you know he likes Olivia,' he remarked, once the coat was in place. 'I mean, really likes her.'

Sophie pressed her lips together, hiding her surprise. 'I had sort of gathered, yes, but . . .'

'She doesn't like him?'

He was smiling now, but Sophie felt a sort of vicarious awkwardness at having to confirm the rejection of Harry's emotions on her daughter's behalf. 'Yes . . . at least, of course she likes him – they're tremendous friends – just not in that way. Clare on the other hand . . .'

'Clare? Is that the red-haired girl? Oh, I see.' He had dropped his phone into his pocket and started doing up the buttons of his coat. 'Funny, isn't it,' he murmured, 'people liking the wrong people? It starts so young and never seems to end.'

Sophie glanced at him sharply, her stomach twisting, but there appeared no hidden agenda to the remark – indeed, from what she could tell, it had been made more for his benefit than hers. He looked much better in the coat, which seemed to sit naturally with the collar up, ruffling the ends of his overgrown hair. It was clearly an expensive wool and of a sufficiently dark blue to draw attention to the fact that, within the wrinkles of fatigue, his eyes were a strong, deep brown, flecked with green. 'Yes, I suppose it does.' Sophie stretched the words out, puzzling even more at the man in front of her – so clearly not to be feared and yet so not what she had expected either from the sleek, affluent home or the monstrous wife. 'I'll see you out now.'

'Yes, please – I've taken up more than enough of your valuable time.' He glanced up at the staff-room clock and grimaced. 'I'm already running late.'

'Shall we say eight o'clock, then? You know the address, of course . . .' Sophie turned for the door but he didn't follow.

'I say, that burglar of yours – did they get him?'

'Pardon? Oh, goodness, you had that to deal with, too, didn't you?'

'Beth was mistaken for you, that was all. It freaked her out,' he chuckled fondly, 'but it was no big deal. Did they get him? That's all I wanted to know.'

'Thank you so much for asking and, yes, they did, thank God. Just a sad lost child, really. He's awaiting trial, or something. I haven't had an update for a while.'

'Brilliant. Good. See you at eight o'clock, then. Assuming I survive my day.' William strode ahead of her and held the door open, insisting with a sweep of an arm that she be the first to exit into the hall.

'You have a lot to do, I expect,' Sophie murmured, somewhat disarmed as she stepped past.

'Too much,' he growled. 'Lunch with an old adversary in the City, rugby-watching my thirteen-year-old, trying to coax more than a scowl out of his middle brother, getting the cold treatment from my eighteen-year-old and – as if such delights weren't sufficient – having to be more than usually nice to my ex-wife because she is *ill* . . . '

'Oh dear, I'm sorry to hear that,' Sophie muttered, somewhat taken aback that a merely polite enquiry should have triggered such an outpouring of information. They had passed Reception and were at the door, which she had swiftly opened.

'Breast cancer . . . I told Mr Wainwright as well. There's a fair prognosis and so on – but I thought it best that the college should know, in the circumstances.'

'Of course. I'm so sorry. How very difficult for all of you.' Sophie pulled her cardigan more tightly round her as a sharp wind gusted up the path. 'Especially Harry . . . and his brothers. Three boys, then, is it?'

'That's right.' The blaze was back in his eyes and he was tugging at his lower lip again with his teeth. 'What's that quote . . . ? "Sorrows come not in spies . . ."'

'"When sorrows come, they come not single spies, but in battalions."'

'That's the one. Thanks. That's rather how it's been lately. It's been decades since I was in Harry's shoes – my *Hamlet*'s a little rusty.' He held his hand out to clasp hers but then pulled her towards him so he could plant a kiss on both her cheeks. 'You – your beautiful daughter – this college – it was the help Harry needed. I thank you both from the bottom of my heart.'

'The man is a complete wreck,' Sophie reported to Andrew an hour later, catching a moment to phone between tutorials. 'I said eight o'clock for dinner – I hope that's okay. I'll have fed Olivia by then – I'm sure she won't want to be dragged into adult small-talk round the dining-room table. Milly, of course, is on that field trip.'

'Oh, God, you asked him to dinner.'

'You told me to,' Sophie shrieked, keeping her hand over the mouthpiece even though she had taken the precaution of putting on her coat and stepping onto the front steps of the college so she could have the conversation in private.

'Yes, yes, I did, but now I've had to schedule an extra rehearsal. Believe me, we need it.'

'But how can I cancel?' she wailed. 'Oh, Andrew, this

just isn't fair. And how can you have an extra rehearsal without Milly? I thought she was the best of all of them?'

'She is. But the others need it. I'll be back by nine thirty – ten at the very latest. Just go ahead and eat – put mine on a plate in the oven to keep warm . . . Sorry, Sophie, love.'

'Bloody hell, Andrew.' Sophie snapped off the phone and stormed back to work, slamming the door so hard that even Gareth, coming down the stairs in the hope of having a word about their new student and not usually swayed from a chosen course of action, decided to seek out a cup of coffee instead.

To: annhooper@googlemail.com
26 November
From: chapmanandrew@stjosephs.sch.org.uk
Subject: NY Tour

Dearest Ann,

I just had to write and say (tempting fate notwithstanding) that – as of this very evening – we have just had the most excellent rehearsal yet. That old adage about high expectations producing the best results is so true. They are still way off on some details – not to mention the odd note! – but there is heart to their performance now, that magical component that is so hard to put one's finger on although, by golly, you know when it's there. We were minus Milly (geography expedition to Lulworth Cove), which seemed in

some weird way a positive thing – perhaps because she's
so good it puts some of them off. Anyway, I can't tell you
how pleased – how relieved! – I am. After all your hard
work it would be unforgivable of us to arrive with a
second-rate show.

As to your getting Stanley Hart to be one of my referees . . .
words fail me. If I had known that a man of such potential
influence and prestige was sitting blowing into a trumpet
during all those rehearsals in August I might have been too
intimidated to pick up the baton! But then, like so much
recently, I feel as if events have gathered a momentum beyond
my control and the wisest – the only – course of action is to go
with the flow. I might not succeed, of course, but am certain
now, thanks in a large part to your encouragement, that it
would be nothing short of idiotic not to try. The only thing
gnawing at me is whether or not to tell Sophie. It feels
unnatural to keep something so potentially significant to
myself but I have this (no doubt childish and irrational) fear
that to tell her BEFORE might somehow jinx things . . .

I'm tempted to pick up the phone and get your advice, Ann,
wise, capable counsellor that you are. I might yet do so, but
not now, as the rehearsal ran even later than I had
anticipated. I can hear the school caretaker pacing the
corridors, while poor Sophie has had to do a single-handed
job of entertaining William Stapleton – over here seeing his
sons, one of whom is a friend of Olivia's and has just signed
on to resit his A levels at Sophie's college. Small world or
what?!

In haste therefore, but with love as ever,

Andrew x

PS Twelve days and counting . . .

Walking briskly across the school car park a few minutes later, Andrew waved at the caretaker as he emerged from the gym. 'Sorry, Bill – no rest for the wicked.'

'No worries. Goodnight, Mr Chapman. I hope that wife of yours has got something nice and warm waiting for you.'

'Oh, she has,' Andrew fired back, aware suddenly, as he swung out of the gates, that he was hollow with hunger. Spaghetti, Sophie had said. No matter how congealed, it would be wonderful. A glass of red wine, a quick despatch of their guest, and he would tell her. He *would* tell her. He slapped the steering-wheel. Keeping it to himself was becoming increasingly hard. And if it was all going to come to nothing then why not share the lovely growing anticipation with her while he was still in the delicious thick of it, with everything to play for and nothing lost? Milly had spilt all her secret plans of going to the Juilliard earlier in the week and Sophie had been unhesitatingly – hearteningly – thrilled, catching his eye as she dropped kisses onto their youngest's high ponytail, saying how kind of Meredith to be so encouraging and informative and that if Milly had set her heart on something she had every right to see it through.

By the time Andrew arrived home, he was virtually

groaning out loud with the weight of his own hopes. To blurt them to William Stapleton as well as his wife seemed entirely reasonable. When Sophie appeared in the hall, he stumbled towards her, arms outstretched, the words ready to pour out of him, but she pressed her index finger to her lips, pointing at the sitting-room door.

'What?'

'Ssh . . . Goodness, you're so late, I was worried something had happened.'

'No, the rehearsal ran on – I'm sorry. Is he still here?'

'Ssh. Yes. In there.' She gestured again in the direction of the sitting room.

'Why are you whispering?'

'See for yourself.' She stepped past him and pushed open the door. William lay curled up on his side on the sofa, his head on one of the old grey velvet cushions and a duvet tucked round him. 'I went to make coffee and when I came back he was like that – dead to the world. I tried waking him, but it was like he was drugged. He came round for a second but then dropped off again.'

'So you got him a duvet.'

'I didn't know what else to do.'

Andrew frowned, torn between attempting to wake their guest himself and eating his supper. His stomach throbbed it was so empty. 'If it was me, I'd much prefer to be woken,' he admitted, whispering in spite of himself.

Sophie stared at the sofa, shaking her head helplessly. 'Me too. But I tried, honestly. You have a go.'

Andrew went nearer and gingerly touched William on

the shoulder. 'Hey, mate.' He gave the arm a proper squeeze and then shook him, all to no avail. 'Blimey.'

'See?' Sophie murmured, with some triumph.

They retreated to the kitchen where Andrew wolfed his plate of lukewarm pasta while Sophie gallantly sat opposite him, fighting yawns and reporting on the discussions she had had with their guest: the ex-wife with cancer, the difficulties with Harry, the embarrassing, endless gratitude about her assistance over securing the place at WFC. Andrew exclaimed at the high drama of it all while inwardly mourning the demise of his own plans for conversation. But it was clearly no evening for big announcements – at least, not ones so badly in need of a positive response. By the time his glass and plate were empty Sophie's face was crumpled with fatigue, her eyes glassy.

Having carried out all the rituals of locking up, he arrived upstairs to find her already in bed with the pillow tucked round her head. 'Just five minutes,' he murmured, reaching for the Howells biography and then reading for far longer, since the chapter covered the composition of the electrifying 'Take Him Not For Cherishing', which his own little troupe had delivered with such heart-rending verve that very night. The simple coincidence made the hairs on Andrew's arms stand on end. Reading on, through a description of a triumphant visit of Howells to New York, he felt, not for the first time and with mounting excitement, as if some benign, irresistible force had taken over the helm of his life, steering him towards things and places of which he – for years – had hardly dared dream . . .

The whine of the burglar alarm brutally pierced what had been the deepest of sleeps. Andrew sat bolt upright, as if electrocuted, while Sophie floundered next to him, knocking over her alarm clock and then her glass of water.

'Fuck.'

'I'll go.'

'Careful for heaven's sake.'

They were fumbling in the dark like blind people, Sophie to rescue items drowning in the spilt water, Andrew for his dressing-gown. Having got as far as their open door, he paused, slapping his palm to his forehead. 'But of course, it's him, isn't it?'

'Who?'

'Our sleeping *guest*.'

'Who?' echoed Olivia, appearing on the landing behind him, shivering visibly in the skimpy vest and underpants that passed for nightclothes.

'William Stapleton – he stayed the night. Go back to bed – I'm on it. And it's my fault anyway, for being dozy enough to set the bloody thing –'

'Andrew – for God's sake – just get down there and turn it off,' Sophie wailed, 'or Mrs Hemmel will call the police for us. And you get back to bed,' she called after Olivia, who was already scurrying in the direction of her room, hugging her bare arms.

Andrew found William standing forlornly in front of

the alarm panel pinned to the wall of the cupboard under the stairs. His overcoat was on the floor next to his feet and he had pushed the sleeves of his sweater up to his elbows in the manner of one embarking on demanding physical toil. 'Christ, I'm sorry. I knew this number once. Although to be honest we never used it.' He stepped away as Andrew approached, dropping his chin to his chest with a groan of relief once the noise stopped. 'I can't apologize enough – and to pass out on your sofa like that . . . what you must think . . . *Christ.*'

'It's fine. Nice to meet you.' Andrew grinned, holding out his hand. 'Not exactly how I pictured our first encounter, but there you go. I'm the one who should apologize, for missing dinner.'

William gripped his host's fingers briefly, still shaking his head in mortification. 'I was trying to leave quietly.'

'And I don't know what I was thinking, setting the alarm. We never used to bother, but we had this break-in – Ah, you heard about that, of course . . . but look here,' Andrew urged, changing tack as William began pulling on his coat. 'It would be absurd to leave now. We have a spare room . . .'

'No, I couldn't, honestly.'

'Don't be ridiculous, man. It's two o'clock in the morning. Get some sleep upstairs. We'll all be up bright and early tomorrow. And I won't reset the alarm,' he joked.

William dug savagely at his eyes with his thumb and third finger. 'The jet-lag – I've never known it so bad. I can't think straight.'

'How about a Horlicks or hot chocolate or perhaps some tea?' interjected Sophie, peering timidly round the banister post. 'I've got some camomile and even rosehip, I think. I'm going to have one,' she prompted, tightening the cord on her silk dressing-gown as she turned for the kitchen, leaving the men to look at the floor and their watches and then at each other.

'Oh, God, I cannot believe the trouble I'm causing.' William groaned, dropping his head into his hands. 'Beth will kill me when I tell her . . . '

'Nonsense, it's no trouble,' Andrew assured him, a little irritated by such dramatic reactions. 'We're in your debt, after all, as I trust Sophie has made plain. A hot drink and the spare bed is the least we can offer in re-compense – though I'm going to pass on the tea. Soph always needs it to get back to sleep, but I never do and I'm bushed.' He offered a hand for a formal farewell, tipping his head towards William graciously. 'In case our paths don't cross tomorrow morning, let me say it has been a pleasure to meet you. Our holiday in your house was truly splendid – quite literally a turning point for both of us. Darien, New York . . . we loved it. In fact, I'm returning to New York in under two weeks.'

'Sophie mentioned that – with your choir. You should look us up if you have the time.'

'I doubt I will, sadly. Maybe you could come and listen to one of the concerts? Get Sophie to give you the website.'

Andrew was grateful to be able to escape upstairs.

Before falling asleep – as he knew he would, instantly – he switched Sophie's bedside light on for her, taking the precaution of placing it on the floor, well away from the still damp wood.

## 16

Twigs and desiccated leaves dusted the pool cover, fluttering to new positions as the wind gusted round the yard.
A few feet behind Beth, across the polished, rug-strewn
pine floor, her mother was at full beam, laughing co-
quettishly at Carter's jokes and oozing praise for Nancy's
daytime drama, which she had never seen. Preparing for
the cocktail party had taken her most of the afternoon:
she had retreated to her room after lunch, emerging only
once – her thin grey-blonde hair swollen with heated
rollers – to ask for a nail file, and then reappearing a
couple of hours later, attired in a cream wool skirt suit
that disguised the old-lady thickening of her torso while
being short enough to show off her still slim legs. She
stood with her weight on one foot while she talked to
Nancy, sticking the other out with the casual poise of a
young girl, belying the discomfort of the narrow pumps,
which had been the object of much profanity during the
course of their slow walk between the two front doors.
The stem of her wine glass twirled between her fingers.
No spirits, these days.

Beth squeezed the stem of her own glass, longing for
William. Drinks with their elderly neighbours – he would
have made it funny, made it okay. She blamed her mother,
allowing herself to be yodelled at by Nancy the day

before, during the course of her daily 'constitutional' round the yard, clad – beneath her dreadful old squirrel fur coat – in boots and sweatpants, as if such clothes assured the modest physical effort the status of real exercise. The summons to a 'pre-Thanksgiving cocktail party for a few friends' had been the result – impossible to refuse, Diane had claimed, breathless but clearly delighted as she shook her feet out of her fur-lined boots, as if the stay with her daughter was taking shape at last. Her disappointment at William's absence had been palpable to the point of insulting. Because she saw so little of the pair of them, she claimed, although Beth suspected darker reasons connected to the myriad deflections that William's presence provided. His sweet, flattering mother-in-law small-talk seamlessly removed the need for Diane directly to address her daughter, or indeed any other potential awkwardness in the world.

Perhaps because of her mother's extreme sartorial efforts, Beth had found herself deliberately dressing down for her neighbours' party in soft Italian leather slides, loose black velvet pants and a light pink top that was more of a T-shirt than a blouse. Twisting in front of the mirror, she decided she liked the inherent rebelliousness of being so casual, not to mention the chance to show off the new tight toning of her upper arms, the result of some recent nightly workouts that made her mother's strolls round the yard even more laughable than they were already. The outfit had lifted her spirits, as did a vague curiosity at seeing the lovelorn Carter.

Minutes after crossing the threshold, however, all the curiosity had evaporated. Carter was sad, fat, old and blighted – or so it seemed that night – with an irritating propensity to tell everyone the same stories. Three times already Beth had heard him regale different guests about the wonderful work he was doing on a once-abandoned script, deploying on each occasion a pretentious quote about being 'a prophet new-inspired' while drawing elaborate air-circles with his cigar.

Worst of all, Carter made Beth think of Sophie Chapman. Studying her neighbour, trying to imagine what possible physical appeal his portly, ageing frame might hold, she decided the Englishwoman had to have been playing some sort of sick game, leading the poor man on, probably. And now she was in London, with William. Since their phone call Beth had worked hard at not minding – not thinking – about William and Sophie's paths crossing, but it hadn't been easy. She couldn't shake off a horrible sense of inevitability about it, a sense of doom. The woman was beginning to feel like gum on the sole of a shoe, sticking fast every time she thought she'd scraped it off.

'Muscle testing, the doctor calls it . . .' said the curvaceous blonde, who had been dominating her small group by the patio window. Beth tried to look interested. The speaker had long thick platinum bangs that knocked into fortress eyelashes every time she blinked. Her cheeks were plump and smooth, her lips soft and bee-stung.

'Or quack, depending on your point of view,' interjected

the man standing next to her, whom Beth guessed to be the husband. He offered a companionable wink at Beth, folding his arms in preparation to hear out the rest of the story. He was lean, with the lined ruddy face of a sailor.

'The body holds memories of trauma . . .'

He jerked a thumb at his wife, bending nearer Beth. 'That's Lindy, I'm Art. She's big on alternative stuff.'

Lindy was clearly used to ignoring spousal interruptions. '. . . so they test muscles to see exactly where the trauma is stored. My friend Martha had an aching face so bad no one could help her. Turns out it was all to do with finding her father dead when she was seven.'

'Driven to despair by a toothache – well, I think we can all relate to that.' Art looked to Beth for support at his own wit, drawing a sharp glance at last from his wife. Beth smiled, sneaking a glance at her watch. Twenty more minutes and they would leave. What was she doing with these horrible old people anyway? Darien was supposed to be full of young couples with families, not these has-beens.

In England, Beth comforted herself, William would already be asleep, getting closer each minute to his early flight back to JFK the next morning. She turned to catch her mother's eye, but Diane was talking animatedly to a tall, thin man in tartan pants and cream loafers, looking enthralled. There was a strident ring in her voice, loud enough to be heard above the hubbub of the room, loud enough for Beth to know it was time to go home.

Three days in, and the visit from her mother had been following exactly the pattern Beth had jokingly foretold to William: fun at first – chatting over coffee, saying the right things, the novelty of meeting imbuing both of them with a fresh willingness to reach out to the other – until gradually the quieter, tenser business of unsaid things and irritation had begun to exert its hold. After the coffee and a tour of the ground floor Beth had shown Diane to the larger of the two spare rooms, tugging the heavy compact wheeled suitcase up the stairs behind her. Her mother had swooned gratifyingly at the hand-stitched bed-quilt (bought by Beth in a moment of wild, exquisite exuberance the day before) but then looked about her with dismay, rubbing her arms theatrically against the cold. The entire house had been kept at greenhouse temperatures ever since, although Diane had shown little acknowledgement of the fact, spending most of the time wrapped in a voluminous, ugly home-crocheted shawl and making a big deal of pushing her TV chair right up against the radiator. She talked enthusiastically of helping Beth in the kitchen, but would then park herself stiffly on a chair while her daughter did the work, sighing at every glimpse of the wintry windswept garden next to them and throwing out wistful comments on the magical warmth of both the climate and fellow inhabitants of her home state.

'You know, Hal has had both knees done now,' Diane remarked suddenly, once they were safely outside, wrapped up in their coats and scarves, farewells and holiday greetings completed, offers of chaperoning politely declined.

Beth adjusted the angle of the flashlight, illuminating the twenty-yard stretch of smooth asphalt drive ahead, the ghostly sentinels of the trees on either side. Halfway down, a speck of something dark floated across the path of the beam – a leaf or an animal it was hard to be sure.

'So it's difficult for him to get about. And I think he's lonely in that rest home.' She had linked her arm through Beth's, as if they were two companionable old ladies, hobbling home.

'Life is difficult for a lot of people,' Beth murmured, biting her left cheek till she tasted blood, telling herself that if she waited long enough the subject, like a bad odour, would fade away. Doing the walk the first time, the light had been dusky. Now the dark had thickened. Beyond the beam of the flashlight the drive might not have existed at all. The wind had picked up and the trees were swaying and whispering like a Greek chorus. Alone, she might even have been afraid.

'Now, Beth, that's just unkind.'

Her mother, thanks to the wine no doubt, was in no frame of mind to be spooked. The rule about one occasional glass of wine – held to for years (from what Beth had seen and there was no reason to believe otherwise) – had that night been stretched to three or four. There had been another rule too, just as old, which was that Hal never got talked about so directly, that he was for the occasional reference in emails, or in passing

323

conversation – a sub-clause, never the subject.

'I am many things, Mom, but unkind? No, I don't think so.'

Diane snorted tipsily. 'Well, you're in a strange mood. And have been all week, if you don't mind my saying. And you're skinny too, like a stick. Trust me, men – William – they don't like that.'

'Oh, and you would know what men like, wouldn't you, Mom?' said Beth, so softly that when there was no reply she wondered if Diane had even heard. She felt something like regret spill into the silence. The slight crunch of their footsteps sounded desperately loud suddenly – loud and empty. Here was the chance to talk for which a small, deep part of her yearned and yet her first, defensive, reflex had been to shun it. The doubt that such a conversation could ever lead anywhere good was too great; and the reference to her weight had made her mad. 'William likes me,' she said in a spiky voice, 'I can assure you of that.'

'Good, dear. I'm sorry if I spoke out of turn. I'm just tired, I guess . . . these darn shoes. It doesn't look that far but it sure feels it.'

'You're doing great, Mom,' Beth encouraged stiffly. 'We're nearly there. If we cut round through to the yard this way it's quicker.' Beth went first, holding branches out of the way. Emerging onto the lawn at last, there was just time for a momentary panic at the sight of the ground-floor lights blazing when a tall figure, moving under a cloud of cigarette smoke, boomed: 'Are you burglars or my two favourite women in the whole wide world?'

Beth dropped her mother's arm and ran. William cast the cigarette away and threw his arms open to greet her, issuing quick-fire explanations of changed plans and flights between kisses.

'Oh, I have so needed you,' she moaned.

'Me too,' he whispered, transferring her to one arm and then holding the other out to welcome Diane. 'Where have you been hiding that glorious coat? You look fabulous . . . and frozen. Let's get you inside. I found some soup and boiled it – was that okay? I was starving but not sure what I was allowed to eat. I've never seen the fridge so full or been more terrified of touching any of it . . . Food, food everywhere but not a bite to eat. Where on earth have you two been anyway? There I was, imagining my presence might be appreciated, busting to make my arrival a surprise, and you two girls are out – partying, by the look of things . . . Can't turn my back for a minute.'

So William, jovial from the bottle of wine with which he had unwisely fought jet-lag and wiled away the time, herded them gently inside. Thrilled, both talking at once, Diane and Beth unfurled like flowers in the warmth of the kitchen. Beth took charge, laying the table with cutlery and snacks and being so irreverent about Carter and Nancy's dreadful drinks party that William laughed till his eyes streamed. Watching him, she felt her love swell till the seams of her heart strained to bursting. All the absurd dark fears fell away. Who said absence made the heart fonder? Absence was crap. William made sense of her life. She needed him right next to her, always.

For the next two nights William slept with an intensity that plumbed new depths, even for him. A dreamless, thick oblivion, he surfaced from among the bedclothes each morning like a diver kicking up for air, gasping, his limbs leaden. Meeting the challenge of Thanksgiving – conversation, merriment, feasting, more feasting – was an act of sheer willpower that never quite reached the point of being truly enjoyable. Having planned to spend Friday in the office, he pulled out, reasoning that the place would be half empty and the week was shot anyway. With all that had been going on, this chance to spend four full days at home felt like some God-given oasis, a beach upon which he could throw himself, while the troubled waters of the outside world lapped at his heels.

It helped that Beth's shriek of surprised pleasure in the garden on Wednesday night evolved into a state of loving attention the like of which he had never known. The bad phone conversation had worried him, but there were no difficult interrogations about his time in London, no guilt-tripping. When he apologized for the third night in a row for not yet having the energy even for sex, she responded with a tender stroking massage of his neck and shoulders, saying, what rush was there, after all, when they had the rest of their lives? Every morning – even on the holiday, when there was a lot to do – she let him lie in till eleven and then appeared with a tall glass of freshly squeezed grapefruit juice, a cup of Earl Grey tea and his preferred sections of the *New York Times*. On Sunday these treats were accompanied by a gift, propped against the juice glass, of a small watercolour – smoky rings of oranges, reds and browns circling a gash of blue. 'It's called *Trees in the Fall*. That's supposed to be the lake in the middle and that tiny smudge down there I'm calling Dido,' she joked. 'It *was* a jasmine bush, but I kind of lost control. You like?' She knelt down by the bed and rubbed the tip of her nose against his.

William carefully set the juice and tea out of harm's way and then pulled her next to him on the bed. 'I love it and I love you.' He nuzzled her hair, which felt softer and thicker than he remembered and smelt faintly of peppermint. 'But I do have one complaint.' He pulled away to study her face, pretending to look serious. 'How dare you give me a present when you know I have nothing for you?'

Beth smiled, nestling closer. 'You gave me that perfume, dummy.'

'Yes, from Duty Free at Heathrow – it hardly compares.'

'But you missed me – didn't you? – and that's like a present.'

Her breath was warm on his neck. 'Now that's what I call being royally let off the proverbial hook.'

'But you did, didn't you . . . miss me?'

William responded by pulling her on top of him, noisily crushing the newspaper among the bedclothes.

Between kisses Beth peered worriedly through the

curtain of her hair at the door. 'But what about Mom?'

'What about her?'

'Honey, it's, like, *lunchtime* – she could come upstairs at any moment . . .'

But William wasn't to be so easily deterred. And what was there to worry about anyway? Beth reasoned, closing her eyes with pleasure in spite of herself as William's hands began to travel more widely over her body. If Diane was misguided enough to open their bedroom door she would be bound to close it again pretty quickly . . .

'Beth? What is it?'

She had stopped – or, rather, the world had stopped, freezing her with it, tongue, hands, hips. Freezing too, an image of her mother's face at another door, another bedroom, twenty-three years before.

'Darling?' William levered himself into a sitting position. 'Heavens, but you have got *so* thin.' He ran a palm across her stomach and up over her ribcage, shaking his head. 'I mean, I'd noticed you'd lost a bit obviously, but this . . . sweetheart, this is too much, surely.'

'Like I said, I missed you, baby . . . It put me off my food. I've been pining.' The room was back in focus, the blood in her veins pounding. Beth lifted her hips off the bed, pushing the stony flat of her stomach against his palm. 'Don't stop,' she urged softly.

William obediently sank on top of her, tenderly clearing the wisps of hair off her face.

A couple of hours later they were in their favourite

weekend brunch diner with Diane, tucking into plates of eggs and hash browns, knees brushing companionably under the small rustic table. Beth had gone for a side order of waffles and maple syrup, which she ate with finger-licking enthusiasm, shooting William looks of affection and reassurance, her cheeks popping with food. The power of the sex hung between them still, like an invisible cord, a secret.

Diane, perhaps sensing it, was subdued. With only a day to go until her departure, she had been showing visible signs of distraction anyway, agitating about her travel plans, plainly more focused on the place she was going to than the place she was in. Watching her across the table, fussing with her paper napkin, making un-inspired efforts at conversation, William felt little inclin-ation to cajole her into a state of happier inclusion. Four straight days of playing the gallantly attentive son-in-law – much of it through the fog of jet-lag – felt already like qualification for sainthood. In fact he was longing for her to be gone, so that he and Beth could talk properly – capitalize on this latest, much-needed close-ness, make proper plans for the coming months, instead of chasing conversational hares that, with Diane, always seemed to arise from concerns about the weather and half-baked ideas connected to celebrity panel shows on the TV.

When they got home William announced, with apologies, that he needed to spend a couple of hours in his study. After a week away and with Monday morning looming, it was time, he knew, for one of his grand reckonings – columns showing incomings and outgoings, factoring in ever-decreasing estimates as to the bonus. Not the pleasurable exercise it had once been, he hoped it would at least produce a glimpse of the much-needed light at the end of the proverbial tunnel, as well as imbuing him with the vital sense of still being on top of things, good and bad. And he had promised to Skype the boys too, he explained from the sitting-room doorway, prompting a throat-clutch of cooing admiration from Diane who was settling herself in front of the television.

'Such dear creatures,' she cried. 'I'll never forget them at your wedding, so adorable in their tuxedos. Give them my love.'

'And mine,' echoed Beth, who was on the sofa, trying to shake some shape into the layers of newspaper she had retrieved from the bed upstairs.

'Such a shame they've been giving you trouble,' Diane added, 'but then that's kids for you. And you do *such* a good job, William – I've said so many times, haven't I, Beth dear?'

Beth nodded, not raising her head from the paper.

William hurried off to his study, swallowing his irritation. Less than a day and the woman would be gone. Surrounded by papers a few minutes later, calculator in hand, he experienced a swoop of longing for his sons – one of those that came from nowhere, as vicious as a horse-kick. Setting aside the statements, he switched on the computer instead. It was an hour before the agreed time, but one of them might be online – Alfie, probably. William shook his head wistfully at the thought of his youngest's growing addiction not just to games, these days, but to all the avenues of chatter available between social websites.

He had had a stab at a serious talk with Susan about it, suggesting she restrict Alfie's screen-hours, or keep a closer eye on them at the very least – but it had been hard, with the fact of her illness now hovering over all their conversations, as invisible and unwelcome a guest as the tumour itself. To be harsh, to criticize anything, had felt cruel, impossible – even given the way Susan, to her credit, had been breezily dismissive of anything to do with her illness, pooh-poohing the ugly shopping list of treatments ahead of her and William's complaints at not having been informed earlier.

But it had got Harry back on track, hadn't it? she had pointed out slyly, on William's final visit to the house, reinforcing the sorry fact that not even the horror of cancer had the power to offer either of them a path back towards any form of blameless affection. And she clearly relished the whole business of Harry still refusing to communicate with him, as if there had been a competition for their eldest's affections and she had won it, with the dramatic trump card of her health. Perhaps to demonstrate this victory, she stood guard during the course of his farewell bear-hugs to Alfie and George (the usual golf-ball in his throat made worse by the dim, angry thump of Harry's drums from the basement), not only folding and refolding her arms with impatience, but tapping her foot. *Tapping her foot.* As if his love – their love – was trivial enough to warrant rushing. As if it was a mere irritant, with no power to do good.

Finding no sign of life from any of his offspring online, William pushed back his chair and ventured out into the hall. He needed the bathroom and – given the presence of Diane – had decided to seek out the privacy of his own upstairs. As he made his way down the hall, he could hear bursts of canned laughter coming from the TV. Some dreadful sit-com, no doubt, he mused darkly, in which things like missing one's kids and sick ex-wives and money worries could be simplified into matters of hilarity, knots to be untangled, always with certain, positive outcomes. At the top of the stairs he stopped, his train of thought disturbed by a noise, coming not from the direction of his and Beth's room, or the spare that Beth had allocated to Diane, but behind him, in the recess of the landing that housed the smallest of their four bedrooms.

Frowning to himself, William turned on his heel to investigate, quickening his pace as the noise came again, definitely human, like choking or crying or . . . William stopped in the doorway of the bedroom, fearful suddenly of catching his mother-in-law in some depressing, private expression of personal aggravation. The door of the en-suite bathroom was slightly ajar. Gingerly, quietly, he crossed the carpet and pushed it a little wider with his fingertips. As he did so the toilet flushed and Beth turned, wiping her mouth with a square of tissue. She started so guiltily on seeing William that his thoughts flew at once from any first assumptions about food poisoning or genuine sickness to what – for him – seemed the only other possible conclusion; a joyful conclusion bolstered by a sudden dim, sleepy memory of hearing retching during one of his long morning lie-ins. That Beth continued to stare at him, wide-eyed, apparently lost for words, only made him more convinced. 'Darling . . . why didn't you tell me?'

'Tell you?' she echoed faintly. She looked dazed, her face bleached of colour.

'That you are . . . surely . . . ?' He dropped his eyes to her stomach, which she was pressing with the palms of both hands. 'Beth, my love, are you pregnant?'

'Pregnant?'

There was a sound behind them, something between a growl and a laugh. 'Oh, I don't think so.'

'Mom . . . no.'

'Surely it's best he knows.'

'There is nothing *to* know.'

William looked between the two women, his head swivelling like an automaton. Beth was animated now, the colour back in her cheeks, her hands busy – dropping the piece of tissue into the toilet, running her hands under the tap, drying them on the hand towel, a smooth, expensive rectangle of embroidered white linen that Diane had given them as a wedding present, William remembered suddenly and uselessly, part of a set towards the furnishing of their new home.

'Bethan, honey,' Diane murmured, 'I guessed this was happening . . . I guessed and it isn't right.'

Beth spun round, leaving the hand towel to slither off the rail to the floor. 'Don't call me Bethan. And who are you, *Mother*, to talk about what is *right*?'

'Would one of you please tell me what is going on here?' William begged, his mind reeling, yet dimly aware, beneath the confusion, that in some other parallel life he might even have been faintly entertained by such circumstances – his sweet, eager-to-please wife having the courage to snarl reprimands at her irritating, pampered mother. And she was called Bethan, which was a surprise. How could he not have known her real name?

He was still pondering the oddness of this alone when Beth pushed past him and began trying to usher Diane out of the bedroom. 'This entire conversation ends here. This is William's and my home and you have no right . . . '

Diane resisted, folding her bony arms tightly across her chest, gripping the edges of her crocheted shawl so hard her knuckles bulged as purple as grapes. William saw in the same instant a strength he had never guessed at, a strength that made him think of the heavy-drinking husband with whom this same old lady had spent her married years, of what that might have taught her. 'But you are sick, Beth,' Diane declared, jutting the sharp V of her jaw at her daughter. 'You are sick and he should know that, at least.' She jerked a thumb at William and then turned to address him directly. 'She had it real bad in her teens . . . *real* bad. There were relapses later, but I thought it was done with. It's bulimia,' she added, when still William did not speak. 'I'm so sorry she didn't tell you. She should have.'

William continued to look, stupidly, from his mother-in-law to his wife, his heart – his loyalty – lurching towards Beth, who was standing in the doorway of the bedroom shaking her head. Suddenly he saw how big it looked – far too big for her neck. There were sinews and veins standing out on either side from the sheer effort of supporting it. Why hadn't he seen those till now? What else hadn't he seen? 'But we've been trying for a baby . . .' he blurted, halting not at the sudden knowledge that he was clinging to the most unlikely of explanations for his wife's vomiting, but at the look those words prompted between mother and daughter – a look of such dark, complicit intensity that the sense of their past rushed at him again. They had a world, a history – thirty-six odd years – of which he knew nothing.

'And there's something else she should have told you.'

'No, Mom, no . . .'

'About the bulimia?' said William, hoarsely, glancing at Beth for confirmation. As he did so another, worse, realization crystallized in his mind. It was in the glare of Diane's eyes, the sharpness of her voice. Beth couldn't have a child. She was infertile.

'Yes, about the bulimia,' Beth said breathlessly. 'Like I

told you this morning . . . when I'm sad, when things get me down, I don't eat so well as I should.' She began to cry, streams of silent tears spilling over the edge of her eyes. She stepped in front of Diane, blocking her. 'I tried to tell you, William.'

'Tell me what? That you could never have a baby?' He spoke very softly. Behind her Diane was tiptoeing away towards the stairs. William wanted to call her back. There was still something else, he was sure of it, something unsaid, unexplained. But Beth was weeping and William knew he had a duty to her, a duty that mattered more than the white-hot shock of being almost too angry to speak. 'Not wanting kids was never a choice, was it?' he managed. 'Because you knew you couldn't, is that right?'

Beth nodded, sliding herself between his arms.

William held her lightly, resting his chin on her head, looking at the open door. 'You were never on the pill, were you?'

She jerked her head from side to side, keeping her nose pressed into his shirt.

'Those yellow pills were something else entirely . . . something to do with keeping the weight off.' William was gathering speed now, gathering pace, the anger pushing out of his mouth, between his gritted teeth. 'All this time you've been letting me believe . . . letting me want . . . letting me hope . . . '

'I didn't know how to tell you, William, I'm so sorry . . .' Her voice was thick with spittle.

William had his arms round her still, but his throat was

hot and dry. He knew he should feel sorry for her. He *did* feel sorry for her. But a bigger, stronger thought was that she had lied to him. All that drama of throwing her supposed contraceptive pills in the bin – of pretending to *take* them, for Christ's sake – not to mention all the whispered urgings about conceiving while they made love, what kind of sick charades had she been playing? 'We'll get you help,' he growled, loosening his arms so that they circled but barely touched her.

'I don't need help,' she said, in a small voice. 'I know what to do. I've been here before.'

'Good. Right. Well, at least we're clear on something.' He let go of her and ran his hands back through the sides of his hair, tipping his chin to the ceiling. A small beetle-like creature was making its way through the bobbles of paint, labouring slowly, doggedly, like some lone explorer traversing the wastes of the Arctic. 'I can't believe you kept all this from me, Beth. I just can't believe it.'

She reached out for his hand, rubbing his fingers, her head bowed and sniffing like a little child.

He tugged the hand free, folding his arms. 'Are you sure there isn't anything else? Anything I should know?'

'Nothing. There's nothing.' She looked up then, her eyes fierce.

'Okay.' William sighed. 'I've got stuff to do downstairs. And I need a little time . . .'

'Time?'

'To take this on board.'

'Okay. Of course. Just forgive me, William, please. If

you don't forgive me I'll die ... I truly will, I'll die.'

William sighed. 'Enough of the drama, Beth, please. You should talk to your mother. She was doing the right thing, trying to help – you should make your peace.'

A cry escaped her then – a high gargle from the back of her throat – but she checked it at once, pressing her hands against her mouth. 'You're right. I will. Of course I'll talk to her. Right now. I love you so much, William – please try to see it that way. Not telling you I couldn't have kids was because I was afraid you'd no longer love me.'

William paused at the top of the stairs, stroking the reddish chestnut wood of the banister. 'But what is love without truth, Beth?' The words were no more than a murmur, but she heard them and looked so forlorn in response, so like a lost waif of a little girl, her face swollen, with her big bony head and the bushy thickness to her hair, that William relented, beckoning her back into the circle of his arms. For a few moments they clung to each other on the edge of the top stair, their heads and hearts thrumming with their separate fears; two souls drowning – or perhaps keeping each other afloat, William told himself, pressing her fingers to his lips and holding them there as they descended the stairs.

That night, Beth felt Dido creep onto her belly, kneading the emptiness inside with the wide springy pads of her paws. But then suddenly Hal was there instead, and the baby too, the one that had finally taken root after months of rushed, dry pumping under the clamp of her uncle's gripping hands, so tight that in the morning sometimes there would be a ring of small bruises – blue as flowers – round the tops of her arms.

For a few suffocating instants Beth was back in the thick of it, pinned under the weight of the hefty legs, the moist, pungent breath wheezing obscenities into her mouth and ears. Fighting for air, blinking tears, she glimpsed her mother's face over his shoulder – just that one time – a mere slice, between the door and the jamb: one eye, half her nose, a section of cheek, roughly rouged. One glimpse, one eye . . . but that was all it took to bear witness. One eye, one time.

When Hal rolled off the baby was there again, the small ugly bulge of it, and Dido too, landing on Beth's chest this time, working the soft, soothing pressure of her paws across the ridges of her collarbone. But then something startled her and the cat leapt away. Gone for good this time, Beth knew.

And then the instruments arrived, probing, digging, removing, clumsily enough to leave infection as well as pain, an infection that ensured she would never need such an operation again. Clouds had silver linings, Hal had said, which was when Diane had thrown the bottles away and said they could manage alone.

## 17

The choir tour left on the first Friday in December, four days before the end of term. With no early class that day, Sophie offered to drive her family to school, Olivia for regular lessons and Andrew and Milly for embarkation on the coach, which was already parked outside the gates when they arrived, its chugging engine creating a sense of urgency, even though a good half-hour remained until the official time for its departure. Sophie double-parked while Andrew and Milly leapt out, tugging their bags from the boot. She then swung into the school car park to drop Olivia and find a space for the car before return-ing on foot to the roadside to give her husband and daughter a proper farewell.

By the time she got back out into the street, however, most of the choristers were aboard, including Milly, while Andrew was surrounded by parents and the staff accompanying him on the tour, busy consulting clip-boards, shuffling papers and ticking names. Standing on the pavement, freezing – in spite of her coat – in the morning cold, the ritual of a proper farewell denied her, Sophie felt a sort of panic. *Separation anxiety*, she scolded herself, the phrase popping into her head from nowhere. Once they were gone she would be fine.

She *wanted* them gone, she reminded herself wryly,

her mind flicking back to the irksome state of suspension that had been hanging over her household for the last couple of weeks. Andrew, obsessing about every detail, seemed to have entered some kind of parallel universe. Never before – not even during their earliest years, when his whole life had revolved around music (composing it, listening to it, singing it, trying to earn money from it) – had Sophie felt so much like a powerless spectator, with nothing to offer by way of reassurance, or assistance, even as a sounding board. And something about Milly had been snagging at her heart too – caught up in the maelstrom of extra rehearsals on top of all her other commitments, nurturing premature ideas about American music colleges, when most of her friends weren't thinking beyond what to wear for the imminent flurry of sixteenth-birthday parties and revision for GCSE mocks the following term.

Locating her youngest daughter in a window seat towards the back of the coach, Sophie immediately felt a little better. She was chatting animatedly to her companion, a sweet dimpled Chinese girl in the year above – famous for being a fiend on the violin. Milly's auburn blonde hair, a little wild as it always was straight after washing, was pinned off the sides of her face with butterfly clips, one of which was already working its way loose towards her ear. Sophie waved madly. A little too madly. Catching her eye, Milly smiled, offering a flutter of fingers, before resuming her conversation with her neighbour. Sophie turned to seek out Andrew instead, now standing with one foot in the open door of the coach and talking to the head, who had emerged to see the expedition off. Other parents were milling along the pavement, hand-signalling or mouthing instructions and farewells up at the windows.

Sophie moved nearer the front of the crowd, watching for a chance to catch Andrew's eye. He had on his old charcoal grey wool overcoat – still smart after well over a decade – and a green tartan cashmere scarf she had given him one Christmas slung loosely round his neck. It brought out the blue of his eyes and made one notice how gingery blond his hair still was, instead of how receded and thin. New York was in the grip of a cold snap, he had reported gleefully that morning, chomping noisily on his cornflakes and punching the newspaper, as if wind-chill factors of minus ten could only add to the joys of the trip. Sophie, altogether less enchanted, had responded by tunnelling in the winter-woollies drawer in the spare bedroom, emerging not just with the scarf for Andrew but a hat for Milly – a knitted one with ear-flaps that she had been very keen to wear the year before. Handing the items over (to an I'd-rather-die look from her daughter), she had found her thoughts skipping back suddenly to the morning of her and Andrew's departure for Connecticut; her mysterious low spirits, the dark silence between them, the awaiting heatwave – how the world had turned since then. And how wonderful to know that it could.

'You take care,' she instructed, brusque because they

were surrounded, when Andrew came over at last. She dusted a speck off his left lapel. 'Good luck – break a leg, whatever works.' They kissed lightly, like siblings.

'Thanks.' He thrust his hands into his pockets, shooting her an odd, boyishly nervous grin. 'You should get off – you look freezing.'

'Call when you get there.'

'Yup, of course.' A moment later he had melted back into the crowd, exchanging handshakes and good wishes as he threaded his way along the pavement.

When the coach, after a final head-count of its occupants, finally moved off, Sophie ran alongside for a few yards, waving again at Milly who – as if the reality of the leave-taking had sunk in – knelt on her seat, frantically blowing kisses off the palms of both hands. 'I love you,' Sophie screeched, glad that her daughter was too far away either to hear the words or to see the tears storming her eyes.

'Hard, isn't it?' said a kindly fellow mother, blowing her nose.

'Bloody awful,' Sophie agreed grimly, hurrying back to the car. On the radio a woman was talking about Christmas, how it wasn't too late to make a pudding or too early to start on a cake. Sophie did her best to concentrate, determined to shake off a sadness that felt far bigger than the muddle of goodbyes warranted, as if the trip was for months instead of a mere two weeks. Cake and pudding – it could be a project for the weekend, she decided, along with the Christmas quizzes she was planning for her students. She had already bought a couple of bags of sweets to lob round the room as prizes. She would have to watch Harry Stapleton, though – make sure he didn't hog all the answers, not to mention the confectionary.

The thought of her new pupil was a pleasing distraction. Harry was shaping up nicely, thank God. What with all the dodgy history – not just Harry's, but hers with the Stapletons in general – Sophie had felt the pressure of her position keenly. And she wanted Harry to succeed for his father's sake too. That he was a decent man had become even more evident during the course of their unplanned dinner *à deux* and William's ensuing overnight stay. Their talk over camomile tea had ended up lasting hours and seemed, by the end, to have covered every topic that could matter to the world. When Harry was late or difficult, Sophie would find herself recalling William's exhausted face and frank outpourings at her kitchen table that night, aware of the bite it added to the challenge of keeping the boy on track. She found the physical resemblance between the two disarming as well, especially since Harry's face had plumped out a little and lost most of its blemishes: the dark hair and chocolate eyes, the strong nose and wide triangle of a face – all of it was so weathered on the father and so striking and clear-cut in the son that the pair could have been a before-and-after duo warning against the damaging business of being alive.

Which wasn't to say Harry was anywhere near a

completed project. He was late and sometimes lazy. His essays, though often original, were too short. He liked either to ignore or to dominate the class, parading – if in the latter mood – a blasé intellectual confidence with which he knocked down established ideas with wild but cleverly plausible theories of his own. Sophie had thrown a book at him twice, once asked him to leave the room and on several occasions made him apologize to fellow pupils. It was of no cause for regret to her whatsoever that the friendship with Olivia seemed to have gone into retreat, while Clare, perhaps because she needed Olivia as a conduit, perhaps because she missed the gigs (Harry having declared his musical career 'on hold'), had apparently transferred her affections to a fellow student called Mickey, whose only musical ability was a reputation for being able to make a passable sound of a saxophone through his nose.

Sophie wrested her attention back to the radio presenter, now singing the praises of marzipan. 'Almonds are packed with goodness . . .' Andrew and the girls liked the stuff well enough and it kept the cake fresh, of course, but the very thought of it made her gag. She switched the radio off, noting as she did so a scruffy young man sitting on a low wall in front of the riverside pub at the top of White Hart Lane. She had reached the roundabout, one of the small painted white lumps that made it hard to know who had got there first. Slowing the car to a crawl, she craned her neck out of the window to get a better look. He had his hands in the pockets of a padded black coat and his legs stretched out in front of him, showing off what were clearly new, very white trainers. His face was a mere shadow inside a voluminous hood – pulled out from a separate garment worn underneath the coat – impossible to identify with any certainty. And he was larger than she remembered too, larger and *longer* . . .

Sophie sped away, only just managing to slow in time for a reckless mother tugging a recalcitrant toddler across the road. In the rear-view mirror she noticed the youth get up and saunter in the opposite direction, rolling on the thick rubber soles of his new shoes. Maybe it wasn't him, then. Maybe it wasn't him and she was an idiot, letting a blue mood get the better of her.

She worried always about the wrong things, Sophie scolded herself, kicking her front door shut a few minutes later, but then rooting out a Victim Support leaflet anyway. An hour and several phone calls later, clutching crime-reference numbers and yet more leaflets she had unearthed from a drawer, she found herself digesting the news that the young criminal whom she, Andrew and several others had identified at the police station a few months earlier, was indeed at large, his young age having secured him the punishment of community service rather than a custodial sentence.

'Care in the community,' commented Gareth, drily, once Sophie – for want of any audience at home – had paced his office, expostulating. He poured a glass of water from the jug that lived on his desk and pushed it at her.

'But what is the *point*? That's what I want to know,' Sophie wailed, swigging the water and already feeling a lot better. 'All that effort to get the bloody child before a judge . . . '

'You said it – a *child*, so it would have been a juvenile court –'

'He didn't *look* fifteen, I can tell you.'

'But, then, sometimes that's the trouble, isn't it?' Gareth pointed out mildly, making a steeple of his hands and peering at his employee over his fingers. 'They are only kids but because they look like men people forget that and mishandle them accordingly. And where would we all be, anyway, if youngsters stopped getting a second chance?'

'Of course, you're right.' Sophie dropped into a chair with a sigh, smiling now. 'If he's learnt his lesson it's the best outcome. I'm just in a ranting mood. I've been dying for Andrew and Milly to disappear on their bloody tour – the pair had grown insufferable – but since waving them off this morning I've felt terrible. Bereft . . . *something*.'

'You must come to ours one evening in that case. Bring Olivia. I'll get Lewis to call you with a date.'

Sophie pretended to look pleased, knowing Olivia would hate it.

'And talking of youngsters and second chances,' Gareth continued, 'I'm halfway through signing off on the reports and so far your lot are looking pretty good, including Harry Stapleton.'

347

'Yes, I'm pleased with him.' Sophie drained the last of her water. 'The only real worry I have is our Spanish friend.'

'Indeed.' Gareth slipped on his glasses and studied a row of marks across the top of one of the pieces of paper among the orderly piles arranged across his desk. 'But it's early days and the parents are happy and money is money . . .'

'Except it almost doesn't seem fair to charge, does it, when he tries so hard and gets nowhere? I say a word one way and he repeats it another. It's as if he's deaf as well as stupid.'

Gareth burst out laughing. 'My dear Sophie, if I'm to consider taking you on as a business partner, you're really going to have to be (a) more ruthless and (b) more tactful about the fodder by which we earn our bread and butter.'

Sophie started to laugh and then stopped, forgetting for a moment to close her mouth. 'What did you just say?'

'Less easily dumbfounded would be good too. I've been dropping enough hints, for heaven's sake.' Gareth chuckled, getting up from his chair and giving her a companionable pat on the shoulder as he crossed to the window. 'You knew I was entering the bid for next door. Well, as of yesterday, that bid has been accepted.' He turned his back on the window to face her, looking, with his arms clasped behind his back and his steady gaze, like a life-sized version of one of his family portraits. 'The college is going to double in size and I need someone to help me run it. Someone I can trust. Someone who's bright and efficient and – I hope very much – now in a position to consider working full-time . . .'

'Ohmygod.'

'Hmm. Still not the most promising of responses, but it's a start. Look, think about it, okay?' Gareth cast another fond glance at the garden of his new property, a jungle of abandonment swamping a rusted swing, before returning to his desk, where he leant against the front edge with his legs crossed, facing Sophie. 'It's very early days, of course – a long-term plan – but, honestly, I couldn't think of anyone I'd rather have at my side. I would be more in charge of the business side of things and you would be head of studies. It goes without saying that I'd need you full-time and your earnings would escalate considerably . . .' Gareth hesitated, studying his immaculately manicured small hands. 'Sophie, I'm painfully aware that a few months ago I was leading the charge not to put too much strain on you. Yet here I am – selfish bugger – throwing all that to one side, because . . . well, frankly, you seem so beautifully recovered, so impressively on top of things –'

'I am,' Sophie cried, finding words at last. 'I am, but –'

'As I have said, the idea is at its earliest conception,' Gareth continued hastily, fearing a refusal. 'In due course, if you're amenable, there will be contracts, small print, numbers – a proposition to get your teeth into and bully me about.'

'Oh, heavens, Gareth, stop there. Thank you, but I need to think. Thank you.' Sophie got up and squeezed both his hands in hers before hurrying from the room.

She took her time after leaving WFC that afternoon, dawdling in the supermarket for something a little different for her and Olivia's dinner and then speed-walking for two of the six bus stops on her route home. She didn't think about what Gareth had said so much as let it wrap itself around her – so unexpected, so warming and wonderful, to be wanted like that, to be thought worthy and useful. Accepting it or not felt, for the time being, beside the point. Although, once she had waited for a bus, then succeeded in leaving her shopping bag on board, she did find herself wondering if the sort of upgraded full-time role Gareth envisaged would entitle her to a parking space – a treasured perk currently reserved for Gareth and Alain (who walked with a stick), thanks to council restrictions on the number of parking permits granted per household in residential roads. She could wave goodbye to buses and envying Andrew bouncing off to work in the Volvo. She could buy her own little second-hand car, a Beetle or a Mini – she had always wanted one of those.

'Cool,' was Olivia's response, a verdict delivered with endearing wide-eyed enthusiasm, but then abandoned so quickly for other, apparently more pressing, matters between her laptop and the television that Sophie found herself facing up to the fact that Gareth's proposal had come at a highly suitable time. Her daughters' need of her – in any concrete sense – was shrinking. As it had to. As it should. On hearing of the lost shopping bag, Olivia went on unwittingly to reinforce the point by offering to take charge of supper that night, proudly rattling off a stalwart pasta recipe (tinned tuna, tinned sweetcorn, chopped ham) that Clare had apparently taught her the previous weekend.

'You put your feet up,' she commanded proudly, opening cupboards and pulling out tins and saucepans. 'Watch telly or listen to the radio or something.'

Sophie laughed, remaining in her kitchen chair but pulling up another on which to rest her feet. The gloom of the morning felt a million miles away. Her life was entering a new phase – she could *feel* it, as clearly as if she was turning the handle on a door. 'I'd rather talk to you.'

'Oh, yes?' Olivia eyed her mother suspiciously over the edge of the fridge door. 'Do we have ham?'

'Half a packet – past its sell-by date, but only just. If it doesn't smell it's fine.'

Olivia pulled a face and handed the packet to her mother. 'You smell it, then.'

'It's fine.'

'You didn't smell it!'

Sophie put her nose near the peeling plastic of the packet and inhaled deeply, pronouncing it delicious.

The ham spat as Olivia stirred it round the frying pan – far too much oil: Sophie knew without looking just as she knew not to say. She was also a little uncertain about the appeal of combining meat and fish in the same dish.

'Clare and I have decided to spend our gap year in Australia and Thailand,' she announced breezily, once they were eating. 'There are these amazing full-moon parties, apparently, when thousands of people gather on the beach. And I was thinking it would be cool to drive across America as well – buy a car one side and sell it on the other.'

'Fantastic,' Sophie declared, suppressing a motherly knee-jerk reaction of pure horror. The pasta concoction was sticky, but very tasty. 'You'll need to earn quite a bit of money to manage that lot, though.'

'Yeah, I know. Harry's bar work pays so well I thought I might try and get something similar – starting as soon as my exams finish in the summer,' she added, with a hasty glance at her mother. 'With a day-job too, that should earn enough, shouldn't it?'

'I would think so.' Sophie smiled encouragingly, knowing that such plans would probably be modified many times during the course of the coming months. She felt, in the same instant, a guilty spurt of relief that Andrew wasn't there to pour scorn on such wild, hazy travel schemes. Still raw about Olivia abandoning the idea of a conservatoire, he was being as harsh with his elder daughter as she had ever known him, not just at home but at school. One of the essays poking out of her music file the other day had had such thickets of red biro scrawled across it that it had been hard to decipher whatever Olivia had written underneath.

As for Olivia's gap-year plans, the time for parental involvement might arrive, but not for a while yet. She was good at parenting, Sophie remembered suddenly – William Stapleton had said so, several times, during the course of their late-night talk over tea.

They had finished the pasta and Olivia had retreated to the sitting room with a bowl of ice cream when the phone rang. Sophie was washing up – alone at her insistence, by way of a reward for the cooking. Wet-fingered, she plucked the receiver off its wall slot and wedged it between her cheek and shoulder.

There followed the unmistakable click of a long-distance connection. 'No lost passports, I hope,' she quipped, reaching for a drying-up cloth.

'Sophie?'

'Yes . . . who is this?'

'Don't hang up.'

'Carter?' Sophie grabbed the phone off her shoulder, her voice shrinking from a cry to a whisper by the second syllable.

'I know Andrew's over here, so I know it's safe to talk.'

'But it's not,' she hissed, peering down the corridor, where Olivia's elbow was just visible, resting on the arm of the sofa, through the open door of the sitting room. 'More importantly, I have nothing to say to you. Absolutely nothing.' Sophie put down the receiver, but the phone rang again. She quickly picked it up, cut the call dead and then left it off the hook. Trembling, she returned to the washing-up. But within a few minutes the hand-set was beeping – an ear-piercing signal cleverly designed to alert its owners to the fact that it had been left out of its cradle. A few more moments and Olivia, surely, would be moved to leave the sofa and investigate. Gently, as if handling an explosive, Sophie replaced the hand-set and folded her arms to wait.

Next time she caught it halfway through the first ring. 'And how on earth would you know that Andrew is in America anyway?'

'Beth knew and she told Nancy when they met in the mall . . .' She could hear the smile in his voice, as if there was nothing for either of them to worry about, no risk in the world. 'You know how women get to talk.'

'Beth Stapleton?' Just saying the name made Sophie's throat dry. Andrew was in America, after all. Who knew what the woman was planning to do. 'Remember that *stupid* note you put in that book?' she hissed. 'Well, you should know that Beth found it.' She had turned her back to the sitting room and had her palm cupped over the mouthpiece to prevent her words travelling anywhere other than into Carter's ear. 'What were you *thinking* writing such a thing? After Beth found it she emailed me, threatening to tell Andrew . . . Christ, you have *no idea* what you've put me through, Carter. And now phoning like this . . . you have no right. I want nothing from you, do you understand? *Nothing.* Except for you to leave me alone. I thought I'd made that plain.'

'Hey, sweetheart, slow down. You're mad – I under-stand that – but surely the occasional brief phone conversation can do no harm? As to Beth finding my *billet-doux* – that's too bad, but not so terrible either . . . though, by the way, how the hell did *that* happen?'

'I don't know,' Sophie admitted quietly, miserably, checking again on her daughter's elbow. 'I threw it away, I swear.'

'But you know what? I don't give a damn what my neighbour thinks or doesn't think and neither should you. People meet for a reason, Sophie. We met and it was real special. What we had – it meant so much to me. Fifteen days, was it? Fifteen days but it was like *for ever* . . . and I mean that in the best possible way. You were so sad, Sophie, remember that? You were sad and I made you happy. Didn't I make you happy? And you helped me too – that's partly why I'm calling. You broke my heart, sure . . .' he paused to release a bitter laugh '. . . but out of that – somehow – I've started writing again. I've been longing to tell you, Sophie. An old script I'd thought worthy of the trash – I've rewritten the whole thing, got a director interested. I was dead, sweetheart, dead. You – my feelings for you – brought me back to life.'

'Carter, I'm glad. And, yes, you helped me, but please, I've got to go.'

'Okay, but don't worry, least of all about Beth Stapleton. So what if she talks?'

'So what?' Sophie echoed disbelievingly.

'What happened, happened. It will all work itself out. Life does that – finds its own route for each of us, often not what we had planned. You and I were meant to meet, that's all I know.'

'Don't call again,' Sophie pleaded. 'If our friendship meant anything, promise me that at least.'

'But, honey, you're in my heart for ever –'

Sophie put down the phone. The elbow had moved. Moments later Olivia was standing beside her. 'Are they okay, then, all the way over there in the "Big Apple"?' She spoke in a mock American accent, putting quotation marks round the words with her fingers.

'They . . . Oh, yes, fine . . . At least, I think so – the line was funny.'

'Dad fretting as usual, is he?' Olivia sauntered over to the fruit bowl, picked out a banana, peeled off its label and put it back again.

'You know Dad. And Milly was there . . . I had a word with her.'

'Yeah, right . . . You okay, Mum? You look kind of . . . weird.'

'I miss them . . . you know.'

Olivia hesitated, her eyes briefly widening with surprise. 'Me too, sort of.' She went back for the banana, screwing up her nose in distaste as she bit off the top. 'Not long, though, is it?' She peeled away the skin and dropped it into the bin, shooting her mother a quizzical look.

When the phone went again, Sophie felt the blood drain from her face. Olivia was still there, watching her closely, eating her banana.

'Milly . . . darling . . .' Sophie gasped, trying to disguise her relief.

'Say hi from me,' Olivia mumbled, through a mouthful. She traipsed back out of the kitchen, casting her eyes skyward by way of silent disdain for the evident neediness in her sibling, requiring a second home phone call within the space of five minutes.

'Bed by eleven,' Sophie called lamely, aware that she was merely seeking comfort in the habit of the command rather than meaning it. She then embarked on an interrogation about the choir's transatlantic journey, which astonished even Milly (fresh from a paternal warning about the cost of phone calls) in its thirst for detail.

# 18

The cold in New York that December contained for William the distinct suggestion of hostility. Clamping his briefcase to his chest and tipping his head against the icy cut of the wind as he trudged the ten blocks from Grand Central to his office each morning, he had begun to feel not only unprotected and old but unwanted, as if the city itself had turned against him. Beth, in her new state of loving, glassy-eyed penitence, had taken to slipping hand warmers into his gloves and tucking the flaps of his scarf inside his overcoat as she said goodbye. But the moment he was away from the false blast of the car and train heaters it made no difference. His eyes ached and his nose ran. The cold slithered up his trousers and down his neck, folding itself round his torso and legs like an extra layer of icy skin.

It was absurd, of course. It was only weather. And not even the coldest snap lasted for ever, William reminded himself, fighting this now habitual onslaught of negative feelings as he laboured down Fifth Avenue on the penultimate Thursday before Christmas. A hardy group of Salvation Army musicians had gathered under the awning of a department store and were trumpeting carols. On the opposite side of the street a classically rotund Father Christmas was shaking a bell and rattling a collection box. Foam snowdrifts, fairy lights and nylon Christmas trees adorned every window. No city did Christmas better – William had always thought so. The buzz, the tackiness, the shopping frenzy, it all fed off the compressed occupation of Manhattan like wild-fire through dry bush.

Arriving in front of a display of glittering reindeer, he paused to wipe his streaming eyes with the back of a glove, wishing his sons were going to get a proper chance to enjoy the festive atmosphere, instead of arriving at the end of December, as he had recently (sympathy compounding the usual guilt) agreed with Susan. Beth was already gushing with plans for what they could all do – movies, ferry rides, skating, catching a hockey game – how she would make sure it was the best New Year's ever, but William wasn't so sure. Entertainment for teenagers was a tricky business, especially during the anticlimactic aftermath of Christmas. And the prospect of fielding Alfie's grilling on how plans were going for the installation of a swimming-pool by the summer didn't fill him with much joy either.

As William tossed a handful of change into the Salvation Army bucket a flyer was pressed into his hands by a woman in pink ear-muffs. 'Treat yourself, mister.' She grinned, revealing long smooth teeth.

William found himself smiling back. Everyone was braving the inclement weather, after all, most of them with far more to complain about than him. Thinking of the boys was a reminder that he had still to buy their plane tickets – he had reserved a brand new credit card for such necessities. It would be brilliant to see them (all three of them, he still hoped), whatever the time of year. And what was the big deal about being cold anyway? Hadn't he been just as frozen every day of a skiing holiday on a glacier in his twenties, not to mention during a memorable early happy Christmas on a Scottish island when he and Susan had been snowed in and the boiler responsible for heating their cottage had broken down?

William walked on with more of a lift in his stride, keeping an eye open for a pavement bin in which to drop the flyer, now flapping awkwardly between his gloved hands and his briefcase. But then a tug of wind blew the paper up straight for a moment and his eye was caught by the word 'Chapman'. William stopped, forcing his fellow rush-hour walkers to stream round him, like river water round a rock, many of them muttering volubly at the inconvenience. The flyer was a promotion for the concert Andrew's school choir were giving the following evening in St Thomas's, New York's one and only cathedral. Entry was five dollars, with a retiring collection for a charity supporting Peruvian street children. William studied the details, savouring amazement at such a thing finding its way into his hands.

He wouldn't go, of course. He wasn't musical and Beth wouldn't want to. She knew about the St Joseph's music tour because he had told her that Andrew had told him. But any reference to the Chapmans – even in relation to Harry's turnaround – was still liable to elicit such pained looks from his wife that William had lately taken to avoiding them altogether. Without the dreadful implosion at the end of her mother's visit he might have been tempted to press Beth for a more thorough explanation as to why this should be so, given that the Dido was business was long done with and the Chapmans' kindnesses towards him had been exceptional. But he hadn't the energy or heart. All his strength – all Beth's – was now focused on the painstaking, brick-by-brick business of rebuilding trust. A labour of love, literally, for both of them, since while Beth might have been dishonest, the reasons for that dishonesty – a fear of his reactions if presented with the truth – William recognized as falling squarely upon his shoulders. Children had never been part of their original commitment. He had allowed sentimentality to sweep him away, boxing Beth into a corner as a result.

The business of forgiving had therefore been taking place on both sides; and hard as William had found it at times – Beth was as needy and clinging as he had ever known her – a detached, self-congratulating part of him had also been rather relishing the effort for the proof it offered of how committed he was to his second shot at marital happiness. They were, as the platitude went, *working at it*. Two bare, forked souls stripped to the core, as the Bard might have said, facing each other properly for the first time, all the early heady flush of love spent, the masks torn away, with nothing left to be but true and tender.

And Beth, most importantly, was allowing food to stay in her stomach. In response to William repeating the suggestion that she seek medical help, she had even insisted on incorporating him into her morning ritual of climbing on the scales. 'Anything but doctors,' she murmured each time, closing her eyes so that he had to be the one to read the verdict on the dial out loud.

Pushing through the revolving doors of the high-rise that housed his employer – and several others – William dropped the flyer into a waste bin. As he did so his phone beeped with a message: Just to say I love you Bx

William quickly typed Me too x before joining the swarm of office workers moving across the foyer. There were many such messages these days, all of them much appreciated, all of them needed. His elevator was full and silent. One woman blew her nose. A man coughed into a handkerchief. The small space smelt of damp fabric, damp skin. When the doors slid open for his floor, William, momentarily pinned to the back wall, fantasized about staying there. He could ride to the top and down again as the sole occupant; the rebel, with air to breathe.

Instead he elbowed his way out, turning left for the coffee machine as usual. He nodded at familiar faces, clamped to phones or bent over desks, working with a humourless intensity that seemed to have shifted to a new level since his week away. Ed Burke, having taken the same week off, had not come back and the rumour-mill was at full stretch – a breakdown, gardening leave, divorce, early retirement; every possibility had been feasted on and picked clean. William had tried phoning his old mentor's cell a couple of times only to be greeted by the answering machine.

When William got to his desk, there was no sign of Kurt, and Walt, his younger, muscle-bound neighbour, was staring at his screen, rubbing his freshly shaven jaw and shaking his head.

'Cheer up, it may never happen.'

'That's where you're wrong, buddy. It *has* happened.'

William tipped his chair sideways to peer at Walt's PC, laughing out loud when he saw playing cards instead of share prices. 'That bad, eh?'

'We're screwed. All of us. No bonuses. Not one dime. It's not official but Lou says so and Lou is always right. We're fucking screwed, I tell you. Great fucking Christmas present, right?' He carried on clicking his mouse, glaring as he moved his cards.

To William's surprise, he felt very calm. He sipped his coffee, scalding his lips, then carefully prised off the lid for it to cool down. He turned his computer on, going not to the S&P 500 or NASDAQ, but the spreadsheet he had assembled of all his personal accounts. Seeing the numbers, the terrible numbers, a dim notion about life as an equation – a balance of opposing forces needing equilibrium – suddenly crystallized into wisdom. There had been too much going on to see straight, too many elements pulling in different directions, but now, like some unwittingly well-aimed blow to the head, Walt's news had brought him to his senses.

The calmness stayed with him all day, buoyed by the clear path that had opened up in his mind. Walking the ten blocks back to Grand Central, it wasn't the cold that made him hurry so much as an eagerness to get home and share his revelation with Beth. They were on a new road together anyway, newly raw and honest – for that reason alone it was perfect timing. And then on the train, as if some invisible deity had his hands clasped in relief that William had seen the light at last but wanted to preclude the possibility of him changing his mind, Susan rang.

'I can't really talk, I'm on the train.'

It didn't matter, she said, since all he had to do was listen. Another lump had appeared, she went on to explain, in a tone of manifest irritation, under her arm this time, which meant she was being advised to have her lymph nodes out as well as the tumour. 'Add on the joys of chemotherapy and radiotherapy and it's going to be a helluva new year.'

'Christ, Susan, I'm so, so sorry . . .'

'Oh, God, don't be dramatic, please, William – it doesn't suit you and makes me angry. I'm only telling you because you got so shirty about not being "kept informed" before. Lymph nodes can be lived without – I've looked them up. Swollen legs seem to be the main problem. Support tights in the summer, that sort of thing. Since my legs don't warrant displaying, these days, it hardly matters. My op's booked for the week after Christmas so, timing wise, our new dates for the boys' visit works perfectly. Although it seems only fair to warn you that Harry is still saying he won't go . . .'

After the call, William found his thoughts drifting to the length of time it had taken to fall out of love with Susan – the drip-drip business of disappointment and misconception disintegrating over years into the mess of infidelity and, finally, the slow, grisly traffic-accident of divorce. It occurred to him for the first time how ghoulishly ironic this was, given that falling *in* love (at the wedding of mutual friends – they had been in each other's hearts, and underwear, by the end of the day) had been so speedy. It was surely no coincidence that his courtship with Beth had been contrastingly steady and slow. Indeed, instigating that first meeting in Starbucks had, for William, been merely a bit of fun – checking his charm levels.

But afterwards, the smell of her had stayed with him – a soft, enticing, womanly perfume – along with the faint mocking look in her dark eyes, as if there was nothing he could tell her that she didn't know already. On their first proper date – a cripplingly expensive lunch overlooking Rockefeller Plaza – he had been spellbound by the jutting triangle of her collarbone, visible between the open buttons of her cardigan. She was so slim and the bones looked so strong; it had seemed a marvellous combination of delicacy and power, suggestive – he grew certain, as the day wore on – of untold alluring personality traits. It was nonetheless several weeks and many hours of conversation later that they had sex, and a good couple of months after that before William – world-weary cynic of a divorce, as he believed himself to be – capitulated to the acknowledgement that he appeared, once again, to have fallen in love with a fellow human being.

'You're early.'

She was breathless, a towel slung round her neck, wisps of hair sticking to the sheen on her face.

'Exercising?'

'Yes, but only because it makes me feel good,' Beth gabbled, fighting so hard not to look guilty that it tore at his heart. 'Pilates moves mainly – it's too darn cold to run. We're having a special dinner – salmon in filo pastry. I've made it myself.'

'Clever girl.' William kissed her, pulling her close and sliding his mouth onto her neck.

'Hey, I should shower first.'

'I love the smell of you, don't you know that?'

Beth flicked her towel at him, laughing. 'Yeah, right, my *clean* smell. I'll go shower.' She spun on her heel, still so thin, William noticed sadly, seeing how the tracksuit bottoms hung straight off her waist, without the interruption of undulations from her stomach or bottom. The scales said she had gained eight pounds but, really, it was hard to see where.

Halfway up the stairs Beth stopped and leant over the banisters, tossing her hair off her face. 'I've decided I'm going back to work – I mean, it makes sense, now, doesn't it? But I want to do something totally different – and local, like, say, working in a bookstore or a gift shop, or even . . . well, I've been thinking maybe I could become a personal trainer or something. Would that be so crazy?' She frowned suddenly, as if sensing the weight of William's still unannounced decision, crouching inside his chest now like a ticking bomb.

'Of course not – all good ideas. Now get under that shower, I'm starving. And I've got some stuff to talk through too,' William yelled up the stairs, the eagerness bubbling out of him. 'Big stuff.'

He felt as if he was floating after that – not really doing things but filling time, waiting: cutlery on the table, pouring a glass of white wine and getting a glass for Beth, but not pouring it yet so that it would be nice and chilled, just as she liked it. Catching sight of the cat-grooming box, he carried it down to the basement and then sat at the kitchen table, flicking through the Metro section of the *New York Times*.

Beth appeared after what felt like an age, in loose black harem pants and coral turtleneck sweater, her hair black and sleek from the shower. He poured her wine and then began to talk, hesitantly at first but gathering conviction as the stark truth of their situation and the good sense of his remedial plan poured out of him.

And it went beautifully, for a while. With her quick fingers, Beth rolled out her pastry and made neat parcels of it full of herbs and salmon. At everything he said she nodded – the absence of any bonus, the scale of their debts. Even when he got to the part about selling up and the hefty differential between a luxury property in Connecticut and a terraced house in west London, her head kept bobbing. He went on to tell her more about the lunch he had had with the ex-colleague in the City – the sniff of a job at his old bank in London. 'It would only be for a couple of years – just to get our finances on an even keel until we could afford to live here again. And, of course, so I can be there for the boys while Susan fights her way back to full health. They've found another lump – under her arm. No one needs to do much research to know that's bad.'

William waited. The smell of cooking fish was wafting out of the oven. His mouth watered it was so good. Beth had transferred her attention to vegetables – eggplant, haricot beans – washing, drying, slicing, using for each task a slow, deliberate manner that suggested her primary absorption was with the irrefutable sense of what he had been saying.

Before responding she looked up, carefully steering a coil of hair round her ear with the hand that held the knife. 'But surely . . .' she frowned, laying the knife down and crossing her arms '. . . surely your parents could look after the kids, couldn't they? If Susan gets real sick, I mean.'

William stared at her, his mouth dry, the end of his love roaring in his ears. He had been prepared to fight for it, for them. He had, truly, been in for the long haul. But in one sentence she had destroyed it all. The prudent slow-burn of their courtship made no difference; neither did the probable fact of his culpability in ever having allowed her to believe that his sons could be in some way separate rather than central to his life. She hadn't the remotest clue of their importance to him and never would. A child of her own was the one thing that might have rectified that; the one thing they couldn't now do.

A moment could be the crescendo of years, but still pass in a flash. Turning away as Beth resumed her chopping, William was aware of just such a moment having passed. His feelings had changed. A piece of elastic, stretched inside him to breaking point, had snapped. And there was no going back.

Emerging into the street after his interview, Andrew blinked at the garish streetlights, blazing on all sides like fireworks. The city had still been veiled in misty afternoon sunshine when he had gone in. Only an hour and it was like stepping back out into another world. It was noisier too, with the rush-hour in full swing. The long tunnel of the street was thick with vehicles edging homeward, the pavement a mass of hurrying people, their faces half buried under hats or coat collars. Horns, sirens, shouts — what did he want to join such a place for anyway?

No sooner had the thought formed than Ann, in her white-fur-rimmed hat and scarlet coat, stepped out of the mêlée.

'Not good?'

Andrew shook his head, astonished that she should know – that she was there at all. 'No, I don't think so. Thanks for coming. You shouldn't have.'

'I thought you might need a drink,' she replied drily, taking his arm and steering him into the crush. 'How bad was it, anyway?'

'There were three of them and one didn't like me. I'm sure he didn't like me.'

'Curly grey hair, big eyebrows and droopy jowls?'

'That's the one.'

'Arnold Bloomberg – he wouldn't smile if it was the last thing to save the world . . .'

'Look, Ann, I don't feel like celebrating.' Andrew gently prised her fingers off his arm. 'There is nothing *to* celebrate . . . For most of it I was a stammering idiot. I'm so sorry after all your hard work,' he added bleakly.

'My God, you *do* need a drink,' she cried, seizing his arm again and increasing her pace.

'But I should get back to the hotel. The children . . .'

'I thought it was a night off?'

'It is.'

'And you have two members of staff helping run the show.'

'I do.'

'Okay, then. We're going to the Algonquin – not what it was in its heyday but still worth a visit. I've taken the liberty of inviting a few others – I hope you don't mind – Larry, Francesca . . . and even Geoff said he might

370

make it. Hey, there's a cab.' She put two fingers between her lips to produce a piercing whistle that turned several heads as well as summoning their ride.

'In that case I might ask Meredith to join us,' Andrew muttered, once they were inside, the firework lights of the city streaking by. 'The dear girl kindly brought a whole group to the opening concert last night and I was too busy to say a proper thank-you. If that's okay?'

'Sure it is. The more the merrier. Hey, cheer up, you.'

'Sorry, but I had such high hopes.' Andrew pressed his hands between his thighs, keeping his gaze out of the window as dreadful memories of his lack of fluency surged back at him.

Ann sighed. 'I know you did, Andrew, I know. So did I, on your behalf.' She took off her big hat and placed it on the seat between them. 'But you know what?' She shook her hair out and slapped his knee – so hard it stung. 'You've just arrived in New York with the dearest, most wonderful school choir I have ever heard, getting a standing ovation on your very first appearance, *if* you can be bothered to remember. Besides, it's nearly Christmas . . .' she picked up the hat and playfully slotted it onto his head '. . . and right now we're going to have a cocktail. Just one, but it's going to taste *so* good.' She licked her lips, adding a denser shine to the scarlet. 'Now, then, daiquiri or highball, that's the question.'

Andrew tweaked the hat half over his face, pulling a comical expression, but only because the situation demanded it. 'A margarita for me, lady,' he quipped, aiming for something between Frank Sinatra and Humphrey Bogart, while inside the bleakness swelled. If he'd blown the job it was going to take a lot more than a cocktail to recover his spirits. They'd be in touch, they had said, 'in due course'. When they shook hands his had been clammy.

But worst of all had been the walk down the corridor away from the room containing his panel of interviewers, with the distant lovely strains of boys' voices at singing practice echoing in his ears – music scholars all, as he had once been. Faint and ethereal, the sound had woven its way round the patter of his footsteps, like an elegy for blasted hope.

## 19

It wasn't until Sophie found herself driving in circles round the school car park that she realized she was nervous. With the holidays in full swing there were acres of tarmac from which to choose a space. The school buildings, locked and unlit apart from the occasional blink of security lights, looked soulless and sinister in the afternoon dark. A convivial atmosphere was brewing nonetheless among the other early arrivals, gathered in a cluster near the gates, busy winding down windows or getting out of their vehicles to share the excitement of the wait. Sophie performed a final slow loop, before pulling up at a distance sufficient to preclude the necessity of joining in.

She was excited too, of course, especially at the prospect of seeing Milly. The tour, by all accounts, had been an unqualified triumph – sell-outs for every concert, a two-minute standing ovation after the Kennedy piece in the cathedral – but Milly, even while reporting these successes, had sounded increasingly small-voiced and exhausted. In a last contact before take-off she had texted to request her favourite meal for supper on the day of their return, a fabled creation of Sophie's known in family parlance as 'chicken slop'. Sophie had all the ingredients ready in the fridge, along with the supermarket chocolate mousses of which Milly had been known to eat three in one sitting.

The nerves were on account of Andrew, or rather Carter, who, in spite of her pleas, had called again twice. He was merely 'communicating', he had insisted both times, seizing the chance to nurture a friendship that meant the world to him. After days of dreading the ring of the phone, Sophie had come to her senses and recognized that the simple – the only – sure route out of the situation once and for all was for Andrew to be informed of it. Discovery by any other method (and the chances of that, in spite of her efforts and the passage of time, seemed doomed never to recede) would be so much worse. Zoë had been right: she should have made a clean breast of things from the start. But with that chance lost, all she could do was make the best of the situation as it stood. A sexual embrace with someone who had befriended her at a time when she had been feeling hugely vulnerable was hardly the most heinous of crimes, at least not in the context of twenty years of watertight fidelity. And now that same someone was stalking her – that was, surely, far worse, and something for which she needed Andrew by her side. Just the fact of that alone – Sophie grew certain – would win him round.

Once fixed, this resolve had twisted inside her for every remaining day of the tour, curdling the simpler business of looking forward to the homecoming and a family Christmas. It had seemed, too, to cast an insidious shadow over her and Andrew's brief transatlantic phone calls. Nothing she said felt quite apt or right, while Andrew, perhaps picking up on her mood, and understandably preoccupied, had sounded increasingly remote. Trying to talk on the final night, what with her nerves, and Andrew clearly anxious to get off to the tour farewell dinner, had been so laboured it had been a positive relief to put down the phone.

When the coach appeared at last, hissing and puffing to a standstill by the kerb, Sophie's first instinct was to hold back. She hovered by the school gates while the other parents surged forwards, crowding the door. Then Milly, hair streaming, rucksack bouncing, bowled into her out of the throng, and she forgot what there had been to fear. The task of her imminent confession felt tiny suddenly – easy – especially when Andrew ducked under one of her arms, asking impishly if he might be allowed to join in.

Once home, there was the chicken slop and gifts: from Milly a set of fridge magnets of New York landmarks for her, and a T-shirt imprinted with a large half-eaten apple for Olivia; from Andrew a mug commemorating the tour for Olivia, and a tea-towel stitched with *Home Sweet Home* for her, its cellophane wrapping still bearing the price sticker of $4.99.

'Because home is wherever we are, right?' He caught Sophie's eye across the table.

She nodded vigorously, her heart skipping a beat. She would get her 'confession' over with that night, she decided, after they had made love; strike while the flame of reunion and intimacy was still warm. *The truth will set you free*, as the odious Beth Stapleton had, for her own warped reasons, once pointed out.

And yet the chicken stuck in her throat. Andrew seemed almost manically happy to be home – in a way that was putting her on edge rather than relaxing her. Milly, in contrast, wilted through the course of the meal, speaking less and less, drooping on her elbows and then finally placing her cutlery in defeat over her half-eaten food. 'Sorry, Mum . . . I'm just so . . .'

'Bed. Come on.'

She allowed herself to be led upstairs and then asked Sophie to wait while she peeled off her clothes and cleaned her teeth.

When she was under the covers Sophie perched on the bedside and nuzzled her cheek. 'Glad to be back, by any chance?'

'Oh, Mum . . .'

Sophie looked down in amazement as her daughter lunged for her, tears spilling down her cheeks. 'Being a musical prodigy is an exhausting business,' she soothed, squeezing herself onto the bed and manoeuvring until Milly was pinned under her arm. 'Here.' She pulled a clean tissue out of her cardigan sleeve and kissed the top of Milly's head. 'Sleep, that's all you need.'

'I don't want to go to the Juilliard,' Milly mumbled, in a thick voice.

Sophie laughed. 'Well, that's okay –'

'Don't tell Dad.'

Sophie twisted to look down at her daughter, frowning. 'Why ever not?'

'He won't like it. He wants me to go there.' She sniffed and gulped. 'Because of Meredith.'

'Meredith?'

'I like London, Mum, I want to stay here . . . go to the Royal College or whatever.'

'Of course, of course,' Sophie murmured, stroking Milly's hot forehead with the tips of her fingers. 'It's years away yet and, besides, I'm not sure how I would have coped if you'd bombed off to New York.'

'Really?'

'Really. I just thought you admired Meredith and wanted . . .'

'I don't admire her.'

'Okay.'

'She came to all the concerts but I don't like her. And don't tell Dad because . . . because he won't understand that either.'

Mystified, concerned, agreeing to everything, Sophie slid off the bed to fetch a glass of water and a fresh tissue. By the time she got back Milly was asleep – flat on her back with her mouth open, her lips and nose still reddened from crying.

Downstairs a second surprise awaited her in the form of Andrew standing in the hall in his overcoat. 'I thought we'd go to that wine bar.' He dangled the door keys.

'Gosh . . . right, then. That would be nice.' Sophie

glanced at Milly's suitcase, open and overflowing with dirty clothes. 'I'll just put a load into the washing-machine.'

Andrew blocked her way. 'It can wait, surely.'

'Yes, of course it can. I'll tell Olivia –'

'I've told her.'

'I should comb my hair. I look a sight.'

'You look fine.' He unhooked her coat from the rack behind the front door and thrust it at her. Outside it was so cold that Sophie rushed back to grab Milly's ear-flapped hat before catching up with Andrew in the street.

'I lost that scarf by the way.'

'Never mind.'

'I kept thinking it would turn up, but it never did.'

They walked briskly, side by side, hands in pockets. It was nine o'clock by the time they reached the wine bar – an erstwhile Victorian pub stripped back to its beams and given a mezzanine level for those wanting to eat. There were a few diners but, even though it was Friday, most of the ground level of bar stools and leather chairs was almost empty. Andrew strode to the best of the corner seats, summoned the waiter with one look, then ordered the most expensive red wine on the list before they had even sat down. Sophie watched in wonderment. The success of the tour had clearly instilled a new forthrightness in him, a confidence she had never seen before. He was riding high and it showed.

'There's something I need to tell you.'

They had chinked glasses and taken sips. The wine

was rich and smooth, coating the throat even after it was swallowed. Andrew was leaning forwards, legs open, rolling his wine glass between his palms.

Sophie sat a little straighter, balancing her glass on her knee. 'Me too, as it happens.'

Andrew did not seem to hear. He started talking fast, glancing at her but in that way she didn't like, when he was seeing his own train of thought rather than her face. 'In New York I went for a job interview. Headmaster of St Thomas's Cathedral School. I never thought I stood a chance . . . I would never even have known about the vacancy if it hadn't been for Ann. She's been amazing. That charity choir and orchestra of hers, it was stuffed with the most incredible people and they liked me, liked what I did in August, which helped, but Ann's networking on my behalf was what must have swung it. New York's like that, you see, so much more about who knows who than we dare to be over here. I applied back in November, but I didn't tell you because I didn't want to get your hopes up – or mine. And then the interview was so tough – I was certain I'd ballsed it up – but, of course, Cambridge counts for a lot, as did all those years of music-festival stuff afterwards with people they'd heard of, not to mention the practical business of being a deputy head and ten years of running the large music department of such a well-known school . . .' He paused for breath, his eyes shining. 'I'd given up on myself, Sophie, I really had. But they've offered me the job. They bloody have.' He pressed his fist into his mouth, biting his knuckles and then blinking slowly, as if digging deep for the effort of bringing her into focus. 'It will be an upheaval, I know, for you, for the girls, but financially it will be fantastic. Accommodation comes with the post, so we can let the house, not burn any bridges – and, of course, with Milly and Olivia doing their GCSEs and A levels in the summer, it couldn't be better timing. Then there's Milly's passion for the Juilliard – talk about Fate . . . Christ.' He shook his head, adding, when still Sophie had not said anything, 'You're upset I didn't tell you, aren't you?'

Sophie stared back dumbly. She didn't know what she was. Not having been told was indeed a shock but not nearly as unsettling as the fact that even now, in the telling, it had not seemed to occur to Andrew to factor her – her needs – into the decision on any level. She had married a man who was dreamy and driven, she knew that, but she had never, until that moment, thought of him as arrogant or selfish. 'Yes, I suppose I am . . . sort of upset.'

'Headmaster of the only cathedral school in New York,' he galloped on. 'Sophie – can you *believe* it? I'm still pinching myself. Thank God for that house-swap, that's all I can say, and Geoff for instigating it and Ann and the Stapletons and – bloody everything.' He tipped more wine into his glass and drank deeply. 'Don't tell me you're not pleased,' he said, putting down his glass. 'Please don't tell me that.'

'Of course I'm pleased . . . I'm thrilled . . . for you.'

'Ah, now we're getting somewhere. But there's a "but",
isn't there? I can feel one coming on . . .' He cast his eyes
skyward, as if seeking patience – inspiration – from the
glittering ball of a lampshade suspended above their
table. 'It wouldn't be until the summer at the earliest – I
have to give at least a term's notice – so it's not as if there
won't be loads of time to prepare. Sophie, after the year
we've had – all your trouble . . . I thought you'd be
pleased. It was New York, after all – the holiday - that
sorted you out, wasn't it? Given that alone, I would have
thought you'd leap at the chance to live there. I thought,
God help me . . .' he studied his wine glass, clenching his
jaw, his expression darkening '. . . I *thought* that this –
coming here – would be something of a celebration.'
When still Sophie did not speak he flung himself back
in his seat, shaking his head in bewilderment. 'Come on,
then, out with it – the *but*.' He held out both hands,
curling his fingers towards his palms in the manner of
one inviting an adversary to fight.

Sophie looked up at the studded silver globe over their
heads. Some invisible jet of air had started it spinning,
taking reflected bits of her and Andrew with it. There
was a new hardness to him, a curt impatience. It was like
being talked at by a stranger. And the *volte-face* on Ann
– where had that come from? A minor matter, perhaps,
but its significance felt huge. And yet while Andrew had
been talking a lot of things had fallen into place too – the
intensity of the preparations for the New York trip, the
manic energy since tumbling off the coach, as well as

deeper realizations connected to his hunger for this job, his ambitions for their daughters and his view of her. 'But Ann is so silly,' she murmured. 'I thought we thought Ann was silly . . . didn't we?'

Andrew rolled his eyes. 'What has that got to do with anything? I – we – misjudged her. Ann has been un-believable – clever, helpful, tireless.'

Sophie pushed away her wine glass and shifted her weight forwards so that she was sitting on the edge of her chair, both feet squarely planted on the ground. She pressed her toes into the soles of her shoes, instinctively seeking further stability. She had never opposed Andrew before – at least, not on anything big. She had been the muse, she reminded herself, the peacemaker, the homemaker . . . until her illness. But he hadn't liked that, had he? she remembered suddenly. Her low spirits – that had been the start of all the trouble. 'There isn't one "but",' she said, trying to keep the tremor from her voice. 'There are at least four.'

'I'm not turning it down.' He folded his arms. 'I can't turn it down. Sophie, please don't ask me to turn it down.'

Sophie met his gaze. She felt rotten inside, close to tears. 'But what about me? I don't want to live in New York . . .'

'But in August you were so happy there –'

'That was Connecticut –'

'Well, we'll live in Connecticut, then – I'll work some-thing out.'

'But St Joseph's – you're going to be head . . .'

'Says who? You want me to pin my life on a rumour? And this is *so* much better – in another league.'

'Olivia has set her heart on an English university –'

'Olivia is nearly *eighteen* – are you telling me she won't like visiting New York in her vacations?'

'Milly doesn't want to go to the Juilliard any more.'

'Nonsense.'

'It's not nonsense. She told me tonight, sobbing – in pieces – worried about how angry *you* would be –'

'Don't be ridiculous.'

'She said she wanted to go to the Royal College after all, that she didn't like Meredith . . .' Sophie stopped. The colour had drained from Andrew's face. 'Odd, I agree, but –'

'You said something to her,' he growled, 'you must have done.'

'Why would I do that?'

'Music – you feel threatened by it, that's why. You always have. Because you can't do it.'

They looked at each other, the air around them vibrating.

'And Gareth has offered me a job,' Sophie pressed on, in a shrunken voice. 'He's bought next door and is expanding the college and wants me to be a partner and head of studies – he's drawing up contracts and everything.'

'There'll be loads of chances to teach in New York.'

'Not like this . . . This, for the first time in my life,

would be a *proper* job. And there's something else.' Sophie dropped her eyes to the wine bar's scuffed parquet floor. Feeling like a person stepping blindfold off a cliff, she proceeded to tell him about Carter. They were so in the thick of it by then, so past any point of return, that to stick to her resolve of total honesty seemed the only thing to do. The American's unwanted attentions weren't a factor in themselves, she explained – certainly not now that Andrew knew how they had come into being – but they certainly weren't an incentive either for hurling herself back across the Atlantic.

Sophie wasn't sure what she expected – hurt, astonishment, disappointment, requests for ugly details. But nothing prepared her for the slap of Andrew's palm across her face.

The waiter started, then looked away. Sophie sat motionless, her cheek throbbing.

So she was avoiding an old lover, Andrew snarled, once they were out in the street. So she had treated him like shit and seduced a total stranger. No wonder she had enjoyed the house swap – no bloody wonder. He would go to New York without her. He didn't need her. He didn't need anyone capable of behaving like that.

He walked fast. Sophie ran alongside, gabbling: breathless explanations, pleadings to be forgiven, to be understood, to be allowed to accompany him to America as his wife, his slave . . . anything. All her rationale for resistance, even Andrew's cruel words – seemed, in this new crisis, remote to the point of insignificance.

But something in Andrew seemed to have been un-leashed. At their front gate, with Sophie drained of words at last, her face blotched with tears, he stopped, allowing her a moment of hope. She said his name – a last begging sob. He gripped the gate latch, not looking at her. He had once thought her special, he said, his voice brittle. He had once thought her special and different. Because of Tamsin. Because of Tamsin he had dared to believe that Sophie might offer the same faultless devotion to a husband.

Without another word he strode into the house, fetched the spare-room bedding and set up camp on the sofa.

Why the sofa? Why not the spare bed? Sophie was too crushed, too shocked even to ask. Upstairs alone, wide awake, she learnt that guilt had a taste beyond the reach of toothbrushes or mouth-swilling. She had a wonderful husband, yet she had driven him away. What a fool, what a bloody fool. Several times she crept downstairs to peek into the sitting room, fighting the urge to drop to her knees and howl. He looked so peaceful, curled on his right side, knees and arms bent, one hand tucked under his cheek. How was that possible, to look so peaceful, to *sleep*?

Turning wretchedly for the stairs, she thought of William Stapleton occupying exactly the same spot a few weeks and a lifetime before. What would Andrew make of the full truth of that night? she wondered bitterly. Her and William talking late, an extraordinary intimate exchange of life-thoughts and life-stories, somehow made possible by the quiet of the kitchen and the innocent steam of their tea. William's woes – the torment of being stretched between two families, his ex-wife's illness – had made her wince with *Schadenfreude* and sympathy. In return, she had spoken of her own hiatus – the fog of negativity – that had descended earlier in the year. She had even referred, obliquely, to the business with Carter – the restorative kindness of a stranger, the paradox (so ironic in retrospect) of it strengthening her marriage. Instead of flinching, William had nodded, as if such twists in a life were entirely to be expected, entirely normal. With the result that Sophie had slipped back to bed that night with the lightest of hearts, feeling not only purged but forgiven, marvelling not for the first time that so sweet a man could be even remotely allied to a creature who had been so ready to use the same information to cause her distress.

Inspired by the memory of that sense of forgiveness now, Sophie made her way back down to the sitting room. Andrew had shifted onto his other side, facing the back of the sofa. She touched his shoulder, stroked it; then his cheek. He knew she was there – she was sure – he had to; but still he didn't move.

For the final climb of the stairs Sophie's pace was slow, her limbs leaden. The girls, sealed along the passageway behind their own bedroom doors, felt like part of a previous existence, a lost paradise.

He had drunk too much, she consoled herself next, blinking in the dark. That was why his reaction had been so extreme, so cruel . . . The remarks about music – about Tamsin – they weren't from the Andrew she knew. The wine had been strong and he had been exhausted, that was it. Jet-lagged, just like William that time. The Carter thing had touched a nerve, but she would make him see sense. In the morning she would explain it all again and he would understand and be glad. She would turn Gareth's offer down and go to New York, as she should have agreed to from the start.

But when she awoke the only trace of Andrew was the imprint of his head on a sofa cushion. In an envelope propped next to the telephone was a short message: *I need to think. Please don't call. I have taken my suitcase and a few things.*

# PART THREE

## 20

Beth tugged the last of the baubles off the tree and dropped it into the box, along with a shower of pine needles. Deprived of its decorations, the sorry state of the plant was laid bare, a poor dry browning version of its once verdant self. A ten-foot Norwegian Blue – it had cost the earth. When she had said she was going to Florida the tree was the one thing the realtor had strongly recommended leaving in place until the traditional January deadline. Even with Christmas having passed, such touches helped close a sale, the woman had explained in the singsong nasal voice that made Beth want to press her hands over her ears. Buyers inclined towards houses in which people appeared to have lived happily, she had gone on, adding, with an indelicacy so cruel that Beth decided it had to have been unintentional, that in these hard times the empty property of a separating couple needed all the help it could get.

But waking that morning to the eerie creak of the for-sale board swinging in the bitter January wind, Beth had found herself unable to concentrate on her packing with the tree presiding – as it seemed to – over the ground floor. The glittering show, the suggestion of celebration – it was too much. She hadn't dismantled so much as attacked it, twisting and snapping branches in her haste to get every ornament, every last trace of tinsel, out of her sight.

Once the job was done, she picked up the box and took it out into the yard, leaving it first by the trash and then transferring it to the small cordoned-off area on the edge of the garden near the kitchen where William, in happier times, had lit the occasional bonfire. She was kneeling, icy fingers cupped in mounting desperation round a weak flickering blue flame of an old gas cook-out lighter, when her concentration was broken by the noise of a car pulling up in the drive. William. Could it be William, in spite of everything? Beth dropped the gas lighter and flew, hearing already the words he would have ready for her: *I was wrong. Of course I haven't stopped loving you. Of course I understand why you lied. My sons matter less than you and always will. I'm coming back to New York, back to our idyllic life together. Life without you has no meaning . . .*

But it wasn't William, it was Ann Hooper, in a stunning calf-length red overcoat and suede boots with fur trim. At the sight of Beth she held her arms open, as if genuinely entertaining the unlikely notion that Beth might consider running into them, rather than stopping in astonishment that so faint an acquaintance (born out of an only slightly firmer friendship between their husbands) should come calling three days into this already hateful New Year without warning or invitation. She had come to gloat, Beth guessed bleakly. Nancy had done the same the week before, making a thinly veiled effort to disguise the fact by announcing that she and

Carter were off on a three-week vacation, then producing a tray-bake and a bottle of sweet wine while she fished for details behind the for-sale sign and what had gone wrong.

A life in pieces – a *real* life: what better entertainment was there? Beth's defence to Nancy had been to lie, using the poignant, palatable fiction already offered to her other local friends that her and William's relationship had buckled under the insupportable strain of trying for a child. William hadn't been able to share her maternal yearnings, she had expanded to her neighbour, tears pricking her eyes, thanks to unhappy experiences of parenting during his first marriage.

It was only when Nancy flexed the thin arcs of her eyebrows in a show of not entirely buying this story, probing for further elaboration, that Beth had dug deeper into her armoury and slung out the fact of her knowledge of Carter's relationship with Sophie Chapman. She was sorry, she told Nancy, but it had been eating her up for months and sisters had to look out for each other, didn't they?

Oh, the *Englishwoman*, Nancy had trilled, taking the hint, gathering her things to leave, batting the air with her manicured nails between attending to the buttons on her coat. Of course, she had known about *that*. With Carter, she always knew: he was an open book, not so much a bastard as a foolish old goat who got crushes. During his scriptwriting days it had been actresses. The English girl was one in a long line. They were always one-sided things, meaning nothing and leading nowhere.

Air kisses of farewell, unnecessary advice to serve the wine chilled and reheat the tray-bake had followed, leaving Beth to ponder the fine line between thespian skill and a show of truth. Whatever lay behind the display, she had experienced a grim twinge of admiration at Nancy for managing it. Who, after all, was anyone beyond what they tried to be? If only William had understood that they might still be together. But among the torture of being told he no longer loved her, that the marriage had been a mistake, that selling up was the only way to rebalance his finances, that he wanted to return – alone – to face the responsibilities awaiting him in London, there had been the stinging accusation that he had never really *known* her, that the person he thought he loved simply *didn't exist*.

Ann dropped her arms, her face creasing with concern as Beth approached. 'Aren't you cold, my dear? Out here without a coat and so . . . but my goodness, *so* slim.'

'Ann, I'm real busy, if you don't mind . . .'

'Oh, Beth, please don't think I'm intruding. I was just so sorry to hear about you and William and since I was in the area I thought I'd drop by, just to see how you were doing . . . to ask if there was anything –'

'I'm fine, really. William and I have had some issues, that's all. But there's still a good chance we'll work them out. Choosing to live out here wasn't right, I can see that now. Darien is a place for families rather than couples . . . Look, Ann, I appreciate you coming, but now, if you'll excuse me, I have a lot of packing to do. I leave for Florida this afternoon. Some time out with my mom – after the Christmas I've had, I'm kind of in need of it.'

'You weren't on your own for the holiday, were you?' Ann's voice spilt incredulous dismay.

'I wanted to be. Like I said, there's been a lot to do.'

Ann eyed her doubtfully. 'And you're sure there's nothing I can . . . ?'

'Certain, thanks.' Beth hugged herself, rubbing her arms, not because she minded the cold, but in the hope of encouraging her visitor to leave.

Ann obligingly opened her car door but then paused to stare wistfully past Beth's shoulder at the house. Its elegance was irrefutable, but in the grey wintry light, with the towering surround of trees, its lemon walls and white shutters looked somehow inappropriate and washed out, like a shell removed from the glowing waters of a rock pool. It was even colder out here than in the city; a weird, dry cold that caused each intake of breath to burn her throat and nose, as if strep germs and all sorts of other horrors were busy trying to burrow into her bloodstream.

'It's a tragedy, that's what it is,' she declared briskly, completing her manoeuvre into the car. 'Two wonderful people, a wonderful house – the Chapmans *loved* it . . .' She paused, leaving the car door open while she tugged off her gloves, plucking the thin expensive leather off the end of each finger. 'But, unbelievably, they've split up too now. It's all just too sad for words.'

'Excuse me?' Beth stepped closer, thinking she must have misheard.

'Oh, yes, it's heart-breaking.' Ann placed the gloves carefully on the passenger seat and twisted her head to give Beth's sudden show of interest her full attention. 'Andrew has been offered the most amazing job – head of St Thomas's Cathedral School, in New York – but Sophie has refused to accompany him. There's someone else apparently. Andrew's heart-broken.'

'Someone in England?'

Ann hesitated, wary suddenly of the alertness in Beth's tone. And there was a faint whiff of alcohol coming off the woman too, which was disconcerting. The news of the Chapman separation was something she was still digesting, mulling over its implications. 'No one knows for sure. Andrew's not the sort to talk. But he has certainly hinted that that's the case and it wouldn't make sense otherwise, would it? Twenty years together, he gets the job of a lifetime and she bales out. But, then, I've never been entirely convinced that Sophie knew quite how lucky she was with that man . . .' Ann pressed her lips into a tight line. 'But none of this is helping you, Beth dear, is it? So I'll be on my way. Good luck with working things out. And get inside this instant – you're blue.' She shook her head ruefully as she slammed the door.

Beth stood in the drive for several minutes after the sounds of the engine had died away. She was numb now rather than cold. Not even her fingers would flex, or her elbows, or her neck. A large part of her wanted to stay that way for ever, rooted, frozen, unburdened by the need ever to move – ever to do anything – again.

*Someone else*. It wasn't possible, was it? But the thought had its hooks in and wouldn't let go. There was a symmetry to it, somehow; an inevitability she had sensed right from the start, stepping back after the horrible house swap into the altered world of her once happy home, smelling the Englishwoman's scent, smelling the danger of her. The Carter flirtation had been both a warning and a red herring. *Someone else*. When William had called on Christmas Day sounding happy, in spite of all his protestations of concern for her – begging, at one point, for her to jump on a plane to her mother's – the thought even then had dimly crossed Beth's mind. *Someone else ... Sophie Chapman ...* It wasn't such a great leap. And weren't such leaps precisely what brought most relationships to an end? One dying because another had started; that was how it was, an endless chain.

Beth swayed as the house came in and out of focus. She wished she had followed her instincts during the Christmas phone call and asked William straight out, given him some of that honesty he was so keen on. But then, she reasoned bleakly, he would only have said no. Her husband was a practised philanderer, she reminded herself. How many other women had there been with Susan? Three? Four? And those were only the ones he had confessed to. And what about the repellent Henrietta back in August? What would have happened then if she hadn't been there, reminding him of his marital state? Once a line was crossed, it was easier to cross again. That was the sordid truth. Hal's assaults had taught her that if nothing else, the first having taken place after a build-up of months and months, the rest following almost daily, as repetitious as the greedy compulsion of a rutting beast.

When Beth moved at last, her steps were slow and stiff. Shuffling back into the house, she selected an old coat of William's from the pegs under the stairs and plunged her face into it. The smell of him was unbelievably distinct – skin, man, cologne. She would have bottled it if she could. Slipping the coat on and carefully rolling up the too-long sleeves, she made her way down to the basement. The shelves were crowded but neatly arranged, just as she liked them to be. Tenderly she traced her fingers along the familiar objects, recalling their uses and origins and William's teasing of her meticulousness as they had shared the task of stowing them away. He would have married her for her powers of organisation alone, he had joked, snatching a box out of her arms so he could get hold of her for a proper kiss.

The canister of gasoline took some finding nonetheless, having been shifted somehow – by William no doubt – to the back of a top shelf behind several dusty tins of gourmet cat food. Dido. Beth waited for the pain, but none came. There was too much other stuff now, all of it so huge, so exhausting.

Back upstairs, she tipped the tree on its side and lugged it out of the house to join the box of decorations, leaving in her wake a thick trail of pine needles through the hall and across the yard. For good measure she then fetched several other things as well – a couple of kitchen chairs, bags of clothes, rugs. A few minutes later, thanks to the entire canister and one lit match, she had produced a roaring fire. She stood close, holding out her hands to the heat, which stung her frozen fingers. The tree caught first, spitting, releasing the rich scent of pine. Soon flakes of ash were floating like snow, dusting her hair and shoulders. Beth took a step closer, blinking the water from her eyes, licking the dryness from her lips. What did the Hindus call it? *Suttee*. That was it. A wife throwing herself on the pyre of her husband. And William was as good as dead to her, wasn't he? Her one big shot at happiness, lost.

But the smoke thickened suddenly, releasing a choking, acrid smell of melting nylon and plastic. And the fire was probably too small for so grisly a task. Beth took a step back, coughing violently. Dizzy from the smoke and lack of food – she couldn't recall her last meal – she staggered back into the house and slammed the door. The violent noise, the silence afterwards, helped bring her to her senses. There was packing to do all right, she saw suddenly, but not for Florida. For London. The obviousness of this decision exploded in her head with such clarity it hurt. Since when had she gone down without a fight? If Sophie Chapman was to be her nemesis then so be it. But the least William could do was admit that to her face. He might not love her, but she still loved him. If not knowing her was the problem then that was easily sorted. He wanted to *know* her, did he? Well, oh, boy, she'd let him have it. From Hal's trips to her bedroom to the botched termination – he could have all of it. In person. Face to face.

Beth ran around the house, grabbing things out of drawers and cupboards and dropping them into suitcases, her new plans fizzing inside her head. Showdown time, guns blazing – oh, boy, it would be glorious. He'd feel guilt at the very least. How sweet would that be? She would catch him unawares, maybe *with* Sophie – yes, that would be perfect. She could engineer that, surely, with a little imagination, a little steady thinking . . . if she could just lay her hands on her laptop and get into her emails.

Beth put her hands to her head as the bedroom walls began to spin, slowly at first and then faster, like a carousel. She wasn't cold now, she was sweating. Feeling her way round the bed, she steadied herself sufficiently to open one of the windows. A fantastic wall of icy air hit her face. She breathed deeply, moaning aloud with relief as her head cleared again and the room stabilized. She inhaled slowly, tasting smoke this time, but even that seemed to do her good.

One message, that was all it would take, one clever composition, to engineer the perfect showdown. But she needed a drink first. Water. She was parched. And then maybe a drop more of William's malt, which had, for several days now, been doing an excellent job of steadying her nerves. The room had come back into focus but she felt off-balance still, as if lucidity might desert her at any moment. It was quite a task she had set herself, after all: exposing the ugliness, after a lifetime of trying to forget it. Even the hardiest stoic would have felt giddy. Beth pushed off from the window-sill and made her way downstairs, opening more windows as she went.

It was only once she was settled on the bed with the computer on her lap, tumbler in hand, that she noticed she was still wearing William's coat. Crazy woman. She laughed out loud. No wonder she had gotten hot. But the house had cooled down so much she kept it on. The draughts of smoke-tinged air seemed to be getting stronger too, shaking the window as they blew in. Beth pulled the duvet over her legs and hurriedly logged on, remembering as she did so that there were two emails to write, not one. Her mother . . . How could she have overlooked that, even for a moment? The change of travel plans – Diane, of all people, needed to know. And the other stuff too, the stuff that had fermented for more than twenty years. If she was going to tell William she had to confront her mother, too, even if it was only by written rather than spoken word. Did that make her a coward? Beth hesitated, her skin goose-bumping.

A shadow – Hal – had appeared in the corner of the room, by the closet. 'Yeah?' Beth sneered, staring right at him till he sank back into the wall. The room was growing misty, but her resolve stood firm. She had reached a *tipping point*, that was it. It might have taken more than two decades, but here she was, no going back. And it felt good.

Sipping from the bottle of malt, which she had taken the precaution of bringing along for refills, Beth began to type, happy to use the fingers of one hand for the fact of it slowing her down, giving her time to pick her words.

'So, how long will you be gone for tonight?'

'Not long – it's only drinks. A surprise for William's birthday, the email said. If you must know, I really don't want to go at all.'

'So why are you?'

Sophie peered into the shopping trolley, checking on the safety of the bottle of champagne that had prompted this daughterly interrogation. That she had agreed to meet Beth Stapleton in a friendly social situation was a matter of almost as much wonderment to her as the fact that Andrew's early-morning abandonment of the sofa – three weeks and four days before – seemed to be proving permanent. After a couple of nights in a hotel he had taken a short-term let on a flat in Richmond. Ever since, he had made exemplary arrangements to spend time with the girls – including Christmas Eve and Boxing Day – but was continuing to refuse to discuss anything with Sophie beyond terms for their separation. Such was Sophie's betrayal of his trust, he said, that forgiveness – a rethink on their position from any angle – remained out of the question. During their most recent conversation he had informed her that he had appointed lawyers, submitted his formal resignation to St Joseph's and planned to leave for his new life on the east coast as soon as the summer allowed.

So the Carter business had been her undoing after all, without any help from Beth Stapleton, had been Sophie's first thought on spotting the American woman's email that morning, wondering – with bitter indifference – whether she was to be subjected to any more of the vindictive threats. Instead, much to her astonishment, she had found herself reading a pleading, garbled invitation to co-operate in a small surprise celebration of William's forty-fifth birthday at an address in Sheen. It had been an unnecessarily long composition too, so lacking in punctuation and ordered thought, so full of confusing descriptions of the logistical complications concomitant upon the project – rejigging flights, being between a home that was for sale and another that had yet to be bought, the supreme importance of keeping it all secret – that by the time Sophie had laboured to the end she had found herself in a state of baffled pity.

The decision to accept had been purely on account of William. Because she liked him. And because it seemed the least the man deserved was a pleasant birthday surprise organized by his wife. But Sophie was aware of an undeniable curiosity too – sharpened by the now flailing state of her own relationship – to meet, at last, the twisted oddity that was Beth Stapleton, a woman whom she sensed had once truly, mysteriously, hated her but who was now, in this most recent missive, gushing gratitude for all the help Sophie had provided to Harry and William, and begging – no less than three times – *for the two of us to be friends*.

'Mum, I asked *why* you're going and you still haven't said.'

Sophie threw a sheepish smile at her younger daughter. 'Maybe, if I'm honest, because I'm not in the sort of mood where I care much *what* I do. And maybe because the email was sort of desperate. They're between homes, apparently – she said William's been renting somewhere over here to help out while the ex-wife is ill and Beth's trying to sell the place in Connecticut so she can go to Florida from what I could gather. It all sounded a bit of a mess and I feel sorry for them.'

'What – they're selling that *sick* house we stayed in?'

'Milly, don't say "sick" when you mean "wonderful".'

'Why?'

'Because "sick" is a horrible word for something nice.'

'But why are they selling that house?'

'I told you, I don't know. There was quite a lot of what she said that didn't make sense. And we haven't seen Harry lately to get a proper low-down, have we? Or his father, for that matter. In fact it was news to me that William was over here.'

Sophie picked up a packet of sliced salami and then hesitated, studying the trolley, which was already far fuller than she had intended, thanks to her daughters plucking items off the shelves every time her back was turned. With the start of the spring term, they had taken the chance of stocking up on stationery as well as the usual items of toiletry – pens, pencils, pads, highlighters, rulers, rubbers, files; there was enough equipment to start their own school. Sophie had scolded them for it, but only lightly since they were all three still too dazed to do anything but go through the motions of such rituals. The cost wasn't something she could muster much worry about either, not since Gareth's written offer of employment – rushed out, she was sure, to give her a much-needed boost, and containing numbers that made her giddy.

'Can we try this?' Milly cried. 'It's on special offer.'

'It's cream cheese – you hate cream cheese.'

'But it's got apricots in.'

'You'll still hate it. Now, find your sister and tell her we're heading for the checkout. If she wants anything else she can pay for it herself.'

Milly obediently put back the tub of cream cheese and sloped off, so easily quietened, these days, that Sophie's heart ached to see it. Olivia's anger had been far easier to deal with – Sophie had told her everything and they had had some shouting matches as a result, clearing the air to as good an understanding of the situation as either of them could manage. But her younger child had reverted to a state of clingy self-doubt – sucking the ends of her hair and dodging efforts to talk, stirring in Sophie the urge to smother her with hollow reassurances she was in no position to give.

The fact was Andrew had gone and that could not be made up for, no matter how violent the urge to try. Zoë's brand of assistance had been to say that he had always been pompous and uncompromising and Sophie should rejoice at being shot of him. At least Pete had *wanted* to work things out, she had claimed proudly, happy to refer to the virtues of her own marital hiccup now that she believed it safely past. Andrew, in contrast, had an evil, selfish side, she said, culling evidence from every distant quarter she could think of.

Sophie accepted all such well-intentioned remarks without being able to take from them any real comfort. Rejoicing on any level was out of the question. A terrible year had come to a terrible end. And it was her fault. Andrew had loved her and she had driven him away. By being self-centred, stupid, selfish. Hunting for a shoe that morning, she had spotted the box of his treasured letters of courtship under the bed and read every single one, desperate enough to be glad that the snooping, odious Beth Stapleton had had her fill of them too. To have even so dubious a witness to those early wonderful feelings made them seem, briefly, more real.

Olivia and Milly were joshing and giggling by the time they found her at the checkout. Having taken charge of loading the boot, they clambered onto the back seat together, taking turns on some game on one of their phones. The return of their once effortless primary-school closeness had been one of the rare, unexpected consolations of the last four weeks. They had been particularly thick that day, conferring behind closed doors and hands at every opportunity.

They were five minutes from home when Milly blurted, 'I wasn't going to say anything, but Ollie thinks I should.'

'What's that?' Sophie glanced in the mirror, more concerned with a black sports car that had been pressing at her rear bumper ever since the supermarket.

'It's about Dad.'

'Oh, yes?' Sophie pressed her lips together, tightening her grip on the steering-wheel as the black car roared past.

There was a long silence before Milly spoke again. Next to her Olivia rolled her eyes and mouthed silent encouragements. 'Dad and Meredith . . . they . . . at least I think they . . .' She glanced imploringly at her elder sister who batted one hand in the air, in the manner of one trying to urge someone on.

'Meredith?' Sophie let out a whoop and then swallowed it. 'Meredith?' she repeated hoarsely.

'Milly saw them, Mum,' added Olivia, 'late at night in the hotel.'

'Twice. I saw them twice. They held hands.'

'But she's so . . .' Sophie faltered as her thoughts – the grey scenery of west London – dissolved into a blur.

'So it can't just be what you told us – about what happened with that man liking you – can it?' Olivia exchanged worried looks with her sister. The business of being concerned for their mother's emotional state was still new, and while it had its horrible side it was also proving undeniably interesting. During the period when Sophie had been so run-down the previous year Olivia and Milly had felt like nothing but irritants, useless, deliberately locked out. But with this far greater calamity, the opposite seemed to be going on. In fact, their mother was now so unnervingly open at times – shouting, crying, talking – it felt as if they were three grown-ups going through the same awfulness together.

'You were right to tell me that, Milly, thank you,' Sophie managed at last, her voice high and tight. Having parked, she left them to empty the car and went upstairs. The box of letters was still on her dressing-table, her fingerprints fresh in the dust on the lid.

She sat on the bed, the box on her lap. Meredith. A new muse, a musical one this time. And younger, of course. They were always younger – at least, they were in the stories one read, the stories that happened to other people. Andrew was an artist, after all, an artist with a big ego that needed feeding. She had loved that once, when that ego had needed her. Now it was feeding off someone else . . . someone younger, more talented. No wonder he had been riding so high after the tour – the fancy wine, the fancy job. But seizing upon her stupid fiasco of a misdemeanour with Carter, that was the cruellest thing of all. All that self-righteous guff about not being able to forgive her . . . Sophie clutched the box, denting the cardboard with her fingernails. He had been looking for a way out, that was all; a way that would allow him to blame her.

Sophie lifted the lid off the box and slowly, methodically, tore each letter in half. When the box was empty she tore that too before dropping the whole lot into the waste-paper basket. Crossing to the window, she stared down at the garden, at its most brutal in its January guise, brown but for the holly bush by the back door and the rhododendrons along the back fence, looking too sparse ever to manage budding again. Except that they did. They always did. With the branches so bare, she could see clearly the section of fencing that had been mended after the break-in. Andrew had wanted to put a roll of barbed wire along it, hidden in the undergrowth; but someone somewhere had said that wasn't allowed, that such measures meant they would run the risk of future intruders taking them to court.

The boy intruder . . . Sophie shuddered. Something had indeed been broken that day, something beyond fences and wallets. A loss of equilibrium, of belief. They had failed each other and never recovered. And yet the boy himself could not be blamed, since the ingredients for implosion, she could see now, had been there all along, just waiting for the right spark. Sophie had seen their criminal a couple of times now – once talking and smoking with friends, once scrubbing graffiti off a wall. Community service. She had walked past slowly, daring a smile that had been ignored.

Downstairs, Sophie shook the contents of the waste-paper basket into the kitchen bin, then tied the bag and carried it outside, pressing it as deep as she could into the wheelie-bin. As she tried to close the lid a gust of wind blew it back out of her hands. A sob escaped her, the shock rippling out at last. Her hair blew across her mouth, sticking to her teeth.

Meredith: the skinny soprano with a remarkable voice; at least, they had all said it was remarkable – all Andrew's fawning friends, clustering round after the charity concert, jostling to congratulate, to shake his hand. Not being musical, Sophie had recognized she was in no position to disagree. But there had been a tremor to the girl's voice that she hadn't liked, an affected warble, which, for all its supposed tunefulness, had made Sophie think of a sound in search of itself rather than one certain of its destination.

In the kitchen the girls were subdued, talking in hushed voices, unpacking the bags with exaggerated care. When they saw Sophie they exchanged a nervous glance.

'It's okay,' Sophie said softly. 'I'm okay. The truth can hurt but it's always best. Thank you so much for telling me, Milly. It was brave and right.'

'Will you still be going to your party?'

Sophie nodded, smiling. 'Oh, I think so. A glass of champagne is just what I need. I'm going to have a bath first, though.'

She ran the water to within a few inches of the rim and lay under it, her eyes closed. There was no rejoicing. But there was definitely relief – at the pieces fitting, at the lifting of all the self-blame. That Andrew had been prepared for her to bear that alone – to hide the truth of his own back-sliding – hurt more than anything. And the accusation about Tamsin . . . and her own lack of musical talent . . . The bastard, the bastard, the bastard. Sophie surfaced, gasping, crying, snorting water and steam. Meredith, New York, the choir school could have him. They were welcome.

In anticipation of her daughter's arrival that evening, Diane had retired early and slept late. After phoning in a grocery order at the mall, she instructed the Mexican girl who cleaned to do a special job. The girl was neither smart nor educated and, with Diane's woeful Spanish, anything out of the ordinary always took time.

'*Mucha limpia!*' Diane cried several times, jabbing a finger between a photo of Beth on graduation day and the apartment in general, while the girl, who was called Bienvenida, looked on impassively. '*Mi hija* – she come,' Diane added, desperate to prompt a spark of comprehension. '*Muy especial – por favor.*'

Exhausted, she fell into her TV chair for the afternoon, watching a courtroom drama followed by a series tracking the fidelity of married celebrities. The girl was a noisy worker – thumping, scraping, squirting – and Diane was glad when she was gone. After the celebrities she dozed and then woke to find the TV screen filled with grieving relatives of slaughtered soldiers. The more prescient of those killed had left farewell letters to their loved ones. Snippets of these moving documents were read out by the narrator of the programme over slow-motion footage of exploding bombs and processing coffins draped in the American flag.

*If you are reading this then I am long gone . . .*

*If you are reading this the only thing that matters is for you to know how much I love you . . .*

Soon Diane was reaching for the box of anti-viral tissues on the table next to her. They had a smell she didn't like but were supposed to be the new best thing for fighting disease. On screen, by way of a finale, one brave mother read the valedictory endearments her dead nineteen-year-old son had composed for her, straight to camera. Her voice was strong but her eyes were hollow, and her mouth flexed every time she paused, as if it knew an altogether different script that it would have howled from the rooftops if it could.

Diane hung on until the credits rolled, then paid a visit to the bathroom, using toilet roll this time to blow her nose. Passing her computer *en route* to the kitchen, she made a mental note to check her emails, but then forgot about it until she had fixed herself a soda and sunk back into her chair. By then her eyes were heavy and her legs ached. And she should enjoy her peace while she could, Diane reminded herself, with Beth's arrival just a few hours away. She shifted sideways, releasing a small, stinging belch of flatulence. Soda always played instant havoc with her innards but she loved it so.

Bethan, between men again. Diane closed her eyes. Her daughter would be hard work. She always was when she had messed up. Aged thirty-eight and still running to Mom. And from dear William too this time – such a prize. Diane had had to fight down envy on many an occasion. Not a man to dick around with, as she had warned, and yet her dear daughter had done just that – letting the poor guy believe she could have kids, of all the unnecessary things – and then starving herself back to a stick with her disgusting vomiting tricks. She had even had the cheek to try and cast some blame Diane's way this time, citing the unpleasant scene in the upstairs bathroom after Thanksgiving as evidence that she – her own mother – had *wanted* the relationship to fail . . .

As if. Diane snorted softly, almost asleep now. She had borne a head-case of a child and that was the sore truth of it. Fat or starved, getting herself pregnant by some kid of a class-mate, the illness after the termination, screwing up every decent adult relationship that came her way – there had never been a time when Beth hadn't made life difficult. Her punishment was picking up the pieces.

A few feet from her elbow, the screen-saver of palm trees and blue sky that had come with the computer shimmered like a reflection in a pool. Beth's email (the last she had managed, huddled on her bed in William's coat in the smoky house) lay beneath it, a shouted angry note of a thing, and yet as silent as a letter under a doormat.

On the way, in spite of her bottle of champagne, rolling itself into an unhealthy frenzy on the passenger seat, Sophie stopped at a sell-everything corner shop to buy flowers. They could be for Beth, she decided, leaving the queue to snatch a greetings card (lavender fields rolling down to a monastery) from the meagre dog-eared selection on offer and, at the last minute, a biro as well, since she wasn't sure there was one in her handbag and didn't want to keep the queue waiting while she rummaged to check. She wrote birthday greetings to William pressing on the steering-wheel inside the car, signing the card, after some thought, *Sophie and the girls*, and scrawling one large cross underneath, to show friendliness but not too much. The etiquette of kisses – such things mattered, she suspected, to a woman like Beth Stapleton.

The rented Sheen house was grey brick, terraced, with a small slatted wooden porch over the front door. Having slowed to locate the number, straining her eyes in the dark, Sophie sped on past, her courage failing. It had been quite a day after all. Quite a day. She could simply go home, drink wine alone, compose stunning put-downs for her next conversation with Andrew, then take one of the pills that Dr Murray had given her to ease the passage into sleep.

But life went on and here was a chance to prove it, she scolded herself, pulling into a parking slot in a parallel street and retracing her route on foot, keeping the champagne under her coat to deter muggers (her mind flitting to such possibilities, these days, without a second thought). When she arrived outside the house, it looked so quiet – one upstairs light on – that yet again, Sophie had to fight the urge to flee. It was a surprise party for a forty-five-year-old man, she reminded herself, hardly an occasion for blaring music and balloons pinned to gateposts. There wasn't a gatepost anyway, just a gap between a straggly hedge no higher than her hips. Sophie strode through it, rehearsing greetings for the American woman and flexing her face in preparation for what she hoped would be an impregnable smile.

She was halfway down the path when an outside light flicked on. A moment later the front door opened and a bicycle appeared, pushed by a dishevelled boy in a padded anorak and wire-framed spectacles. Behind him another boy – clearly older, much taller, darker-haired and full-bodied – pushed a second, larger bike, which had two helmets looped over its handlebars.

'Dad,' shouted the younger one at once, twisting back towards the door, 'there's someone here.'

'I think you must have the wrong house,' muttered the elder one, glancing with evident doubt at the flowers and bottle, which Sophie had taken out from the protection of her coat.

From somewhere a man who had to be William, although it didn't sound like him, shouted back, 'Tell whoever it is to go away.'

'It's a surprise,' Sophie explained to the two boys, lowering her voice and grinning conspiratorially. 'Organized by your stepmother. I'm obviously the first to arrive. You must be George, right? And you're Alfie? I'm Sophie Chapman – it was my house you guys borrowed last summer. I teach at the crammer where your brother is –'
She broke off as the two continued to exchange glances,

416

clearly less rather than more reassured with every word. 'I teach Harry?' she prompted.

'I'd better get Dad,' growled George. 'Here, Alf, hold this.' He thrust his bike at his younger brother and disappeared back inside the house. Alfie dropped his gaze to the ground, clearly miserable at having been left in charge.

'Surprise parties are often a *bad* idea,' Sophie ventured, trying to cheer him up. 'I mean, you have to be in the mood to party, don't you? You can't just do it because someone else wants you to, can you?'

Alfie raised his eyes, nodding slowly. His brother's bike chose that moment to teeter from the balanced position in which he had been keeping it upright, slipping from his grasp. Sophie dived to catch it, dropping the flowers and the champagne on the scrubby grass and then managing to trip herself so that both she and the bike ended up in a tangled mess on the ground.

Alfie watched, appalled and then relieved when Sophie burst out laughing.

'Your wine's all right anyway,' he offered solemnly.

'Phew – that's the main thing.' Sophie held his gaze as she struggled to her feet, teasing out a dimpled smile. She had the bike upright and was dusting the dirt off her coat when George re-emerged.

'Thanks.' He seized the handlebars, glowering at his brother and thrusting one of the helmets onto his tousled head, so roughly that Alfie yelped. 'Dad's coming. We better be off back to Mum's.'

'You're not staying for the party?'

George shook his head. Alfie, the helmet now pinned at a roguish angle, pointed at her leg. 'You're bleeding, look.'

Sophie glanced down to see a rip in her tights and a bloody gash. 'So I am. Only a bit, though.' She picked up the bottle and the flowers. Two of the most spectacular members of the bunch had lost their heads in the tumble. She tried to conceal them behind a sprig of greenery and watched with something like envy as the two boys pedalled off into the dark. The evening had barely started and already it felt doomed. The front door was wide open now, but the hall was so dim that it seemed wrong to do anything but wait. She stayed in the square of yellow cast by the outside light, self-consciously twirling her bouquet, picking at the price sticker, which appeared to be one of the annoying variety designed never to come off properly. William was probably in the bath, she decided, as the minutes ticked by, and Beth must have popped out to buy provisions – secret parties invariably demanded such last-minute manoeuvres.

When William appeared at last, a shadow in the darkness of the hall, she darted forwards and then stopped, flooded with fresh doubts.

'Sophie, it is you. Thank God.' His voice was gritty, tortured. 'I couldn't take anyone else.'

Sophie approached cautiously, some instinct prompting a feeble effort to hide her gifts behind the bulk of her handbag. 'Is Beth out?'

'Beth?' He looked horrified.

'She invited me,' Sophie stammered, 'an email – a surprise drinks party for your birthday, she said . . . William, you don't look well. Look, I'll go – I'm so sorry, obviously something's gone wrong, some misunderstanding –'

'No, don't . . . Jesus, this is unreal. Totally unreal.' He tugged at his hair with both hands. It had been cut very closely and stuck where his fingers left it, pointing skywards.

'Not a good birthday?' Sophie prompted, in a lame attempt to lighten the mood. 'I was just saying to Alfie – at least I assume that was Alfie – how rarely surprise parties end up pleasing their targets –'

'This email, when did it arrive?' he blurted, looking stranger than ever.

'Today – this morning. At least, that's when I read it.'

'So she sent it yesterday?'

'Yes, I suppose –'

'And it asked you to come here now – tonight – for my –' He clamped his hand to his mouth, stifling whatever might have remained of the sentence.

'Yes, for your birthday.' Sophie felt weary suddenly – caught in something she had neither the energy nor the desire to understand. The shock of the Meredith news swung back at her. There were too many crossed wires in her own life to start negotiating anyone else's. 'Look, I'm going to take off now. Here. These are for you and Beth with my best wishes.' She held out the bouquet and bottle. 'There's a card too here somewhere

'. . . shit – unless I left it in the car.' She managed, with some difficulty, to frisk her handbag, but found only her car keys, which she seized and jangled by way of underlining her intention to depart. 'I'll put the card in the post, okay? William?' Her arms ached from holding out her ridiculous gifts.

'Beth has died, Sophie. She has died. There was a fire.'

Sophie dropped her arms. 'What do you mean, a fire? What sort of fire? Where?'

'Darien.' He gestured with his hand, as if America lay round a bend in the street.

'God, how unspeakable . . . how utterly unspeakable. William, I am so, so sorry.'

He hadn't moved from the doorstep and she was still on the patchy grass, caught in the big square of light. The cut in her leg had started to throb, like a faint pulse, reminding her she was alive. A few houses away a dog started barking – high-pitched and frantic.

'I'll go.'

'No, for Christ's sake, no.' He lunged for her, seizing her elbow and then dropping it quickly as if ashamed. 'Come in, please, if you can bear it. I want to hear exactly what Beth said – this email . . . I had no idea . . . ' His voice had shrunk to a monotone, all the emotion fenced in. Checking she was following, he led the way down the narrow hall into a large back living room that had clearly involved the demolition of several original walls. 'Last I heard she was going to her mother's for a few months – Florida – until the house sold. We'd had it on the market since the split.' He opened a cupboard and took out two smeared, thick-glass tumblers. 'I'm going to drink whisky. What I'd really like is a cigarette, but I've given up.' He spun the lid off a bottle of Johnnie Walker. 'Will you join me? Or I could open that, if you like.'

Sophie glanced down at her bottle of champagne, visibly frothing from its adventures and beaded with condensation. 'Hardly . . . I'll have whisky too, please.' She rid herself of the bottle and flowers, dumping them next to a double sink that bulged with dirty crockery. The kitchen area was small, an L-shape, with nowhere to sit or perch. She backed out of it and lowered herself into one corner of a stained dark green sofa parked next to a vast television. She could see their reflections in it: a sombre fair-haired woman sitting a little stiffly, a dark-haired man at the kitchen counter behind her, pouring drinks. They could have been any old couple, sharing a companionable evening in a messy back room. 'What did you mean, "split"?'

William poured a half-inch of whisky and downed it in one, silently, grimacing as he swallowed. Bringing the bottle and both glasses, he threw himself into the other end of the sofa in the manner of one beyond caring for his own physical comfort. 'We separated. The beginning of December. Or, rather, I left.' He poured more whisky, into both glasses this time, and handed her one. 'Which makes her death . . . Christ, this is such a mess, Sophie, I'm so sorry, drawing you in like this . . .' He stared at her over the rim of his glass as he drank deeply again, reminding her of the first time she had looked properly at his face during his visit to WFC, the blaze of suffering in the handsome brown eyes. It was there again now, but so much worse. Having emptied the glass, he slammed it down on the small weathered coffee-table next to them. 'So now I feel about as bad as it's possible to feel . . .' He dropped his face into his hands.

'This fire,' said Sophie softly, 'what happened?' She could feel the weight of her own problems receding, no match for such calamity. 'If you feel able to talk . . .'

'They're not sure yet.' William sniffed and coughed, his Adam's apple wild as he fought to compose himself. 'It appears . . .' He blew out, a low, slow whistle of air. 'It appears that she was burning stuff in the garden and somehow it got out of control. Our neighbours, Nancy and Carter – but you know them, of course – were away, so it was a while before anyone alerted the emergency services. And now the insurers say they need to do a thorough investigation in case –' He broke off again, pressing the side of his glass against his mouth to calm the tremble in his lips. 'In case it was deliberate.'

'You can't be serious?'

He nodded. 'Sadly, yes. You see, financially, Beth and I had got into some trouble. We were in a rush to sell. From that point of view the fire was convenient.' He started a ghoulish smile but it collapsed. 'The insurance, while nowhere near the sale value, will go a long way to getting us – me – off the hook.'

Sophie laughed sharply. 'But you don't burn your

422

house down for money and kill yourself in the process, do you? I never heard anything so ridiculous.'

'I think it's just the house they're suspicious about, not Beth . . . but she did have problems,' he blurted, 'I mean, really big problems. It's why I left – why I had to leave. I can't go into it now, but it was as if I had married a . . . a façade. Nothing I thought about her turned out to be true . . .' William shook his head, adding thickly, 'None of which stops me feeling like a total bastard now.'

Sophie sipped her whisky, weighing up the value of revealing her own glimpses of Beth's unbalanced mental state, and at the same time pondering the oddness of having been one step ahead on such a matter. She and the American woman had never met and yet, thanks to the house swap, threads of their lives had become enmeshed. She and Beth had known things about each other, big things, all of them more dangerous somehow for their lack of context. But William needed reassurance, she realized, glancing at the forlorn figure huddled at the other end of the sofa, and Beth – poor troubled dead soul, with no recourse now to defend herself – deserved the gentlest handling.

'William?'

He looked up, blinking.

'Don't make things worse by blaming yourself. It seems clear to me that Beth, with this party business, was hoping to extend some sort of olive branch, mend bridges and so on.' Sophie paused, wondering suddenly if she would ever, in their new, horrible circumstances, get Andrew to extend the same courtesy to her. 'I mean, that's quite something,' she pressed on, 'arranging a surprise gathering that involves a round trip of four thousand-odd miles. You should take heart from that, William. She must have loved you very much, and while I can understand that should make you sad, it's also rather wonderful.' Sophie reached across the space between them and squeezed his hand.

William kept hold of it, stroking her fingers. 'Thank you, Sophie. I knew you'd be good, after the talk we had that night, I just knew.'

Sophie glanced at him, taken aback. 'Yes, it was special for me too.'

'Did you tell Andrew, in the end, how late it got? You said you might not.'

She shook her head.

'Where is he anyway? Didn't Beth invite him too?' William threw an anxious glance in the direction of the hall.

'Andrew couldn't come –'

'Right. Fine. And if the doorbell goes we're not answering, okay?'

Sophie nodded, holding out her glass for a refill, her mouth dry. 'Who else did she know to invite?' she asked hoarsely.

William shrugged, pouring more whisky. He kept hold of Sophie's hand as he did so, shifting the grip so that her fingers were interlaced in his rather than the other way round. 'She died of smoke inhalation.' He had locked his gaze on a patch of wall above the TV. 'Which is better, I suppose, than the alternative.'

They sat in silence for several minutes, long enough for Sophie's fingers to grow slightly moist in his grasp. A small insect flew at the bulb above their heads, snagging in the folds of the shade. 'Andrew left me,' she said at length, the admission sliding out of her as she had known it would, as it had to. 'The difficult patch I told you about that night – it turned out to be terminal.'

William stared at her, his eyes, through the glaze of alcohol, soft with sympathy and dismay. 'Why, for heaven's sake?'

Sophie shrugged. 'Maybe he, too, decided I wasn't the woman he thought he had married . . . that I was a "façade".'

'Bollocks to that. You're a . . . special woman . . . Fucking special.'

Sophie almost smiled. He was seriously drunk, she knew. And she wasn't far behind. 'Turns out he met someone during our time at your place – and then again on that tour . . . although I'm not sure of the details. He won't tell me. But I can't help thinking, looking back, that maybe it *was* my fault, for taking my eye off the ball – all that self-obsessing I did, daring to have my own little mid-life crisis, never expecting,' she let out a tipsy sneer of a giggle, 'that dear Andrew would choose the same bloody month to have one too. She's a singer. Prettier . . . younger, of course. He's got a job there – in

New York. Headmaster of some cathedral school. He's been plotting it for months. He pretended he wanted me to go with him, but he didn't really. In February he's going over to sort things out and then he'll leave England permanently in the summer.' Sophie tried to swallow but suddenly her tongue seemed to be in the way, huge, blocking the release of air. 'It hardly compares to what you,' she gasped, 'with poor Beth –'

'Shush. Don't talk. Come here.' William held his arm out and she crawled under it. Overhead the fly ricocheted one last time against the hot bulb and flew off, taking its angry buzz to another room.

# 22

New York, that February afternoon, was forbidding. The sleet and wind didn't fall so much as drive at horizontal angles, as if pummelling for gaps in the population's armoury of winter clothes. Tumbling into the warm, brightly lit foyer of Geoff and Ann's apartment block, shaking the ice particles out of his hat, and a scarf he had had the foresight to buy at Heathrow, Andrew felt like a soldier escaping a battlefield. The city took energy, there was no denying that. But twenty-four hours in and he was still buzzing – up for anything.

As he waited for the lift, he thought of Meredith, her long, fine-boned body curled into his after they had made love that morning, her fabulous chestnut hair like flames across his chest. She had agreed to the continued need for secrecy like a lamb, putting such a good supporting case about not wanting to shock her parents that by the end Andrew had been almost worried. Could she really love him that much if she was so easily – so willingly – able to bury their relationship from sight? The governors of St Thomas's had been behind his own reasoning about continued discretion, their grave, formal dismay at the news that he would be taking up the post without a wife not being an obvious invitation to reveal that he

427

had embarked on a relationship with a twenty-six-year-old music student.

The dust would settle, Andrew assured himself, stepping into the lift. It was just a question of playing his cards right, allowing time to pass. Once he was in the swing of the job and the separation from Sophie old news, then – and only then – would it be right to brave the glare of social limelight with his exquisite, gifted darling Meredith at his side. The age-gap would no doubt cause a raised eyebrow or two at first – until it became apparent what a great couple they were, how integrally tuned to each other's needs, how beyond the trivialities of whatever number of years either of them had so far spent on the planet.

Meredith said she had sensed the pull between them right from the start – during their first encounter over small-talk and orange juice in August. For Andrew it had taken a little longer, not out of any private doubts so much as the sheer terror of acknowledging something so momentous, so life-changing. He had ended the Connecticut holiday certain that they were excellent friends, but it was only when Meredith had had the guts to knock on his hotel bedroom door on the night after Ann's impromptu cocktail gathering at the Algonquin that he had capitulated fully to other, stronger, instincts. The rest of the trip had passed in a blitz of similar secret encounters, each more intense than the last, each confirming – in both their eyes – that they were old souls whose paths had been destined to coincide.

Looking back, Andrew still didn't know how he had found the wherewithal to tell Sophie about the cathedral-school headship in the manner that he had. If she had leapt at the idea of living in New York, he wasn't sure what he would have done, beyond the certainty that it would have involved seeing Meredith anyway, carrying on an affair, probably, until his marriage collapsed under the pressure of it. As it was, Sophie's sordid, sorry holiday-romance confession had fallen into his lap like a miracle, even if things had got a little messy later on.

While the lift moved upwards, taking its time, Andrew flicked open his phone. There was a message from Meredith, along with the decidedly unflattering photo she had taken of him in the hotel room that morning, sitting up in bed looking horribly close to his age – lined, balding, white, flabby. Andrew chuckled, but deleted it instantly. His grabbing at food, as he did these days, had resulted in the beginnings of an annoying paunch. He had vowed to get rid of it the moment he left England for good. When he blurted as much out loud, Meredith had sweetly, if a little disconcertingly, written a list of gyms in the Midtown area on the top page of a small fluorescent-pink pad, carefully tearing it off and stowing it for him in the back flap of his wallet.

Andrew continued scrolling, hoping for a message from Milly. He had sent her two texts before boarding, saying goodbye, asking if there was anything she wanted him to buy during his visit. Olivia, mute since the Meredith business had come out, might well be lost to him, but Milly, in spite of having been the one to bring matters to a head, was showing distinct signs of thawing. And he would never give up on her, Andrew vowed, never. She needed a bit more work, that was all, reassurance of her importance to him, concrete plans for visits – they would work it out somehow.

He snapped his phone shut and stepped out of the lift. Sixteen years of love and closeness and music couldn't just stop, not with someone as warm and open as his younger daughter. Technology – emails, phones – would always offer a lifeline. And he had heard about something called Skype recently, which sounded worth investigating. Visual and verbal contact across thousands of miles – a colleague at St Joseph's with a back-packing twenty-year-old had said it was the only reason he and his wife ever managed a decent night's sleep.

Andrew strode along the passageway, unconsciously clenching his fists. He had a lover who loved him, he reminded himself, turning on his heel with a hiss of irritation when it became apparent he had gone the wrong way. A lover with alabaster skin and a voice to rival an angel's. How could he have imagined he would ever achieve lasting happiness with a woman who was tone deaf anyway? A woman with a sneaking preference for Abba to *La Traviata*. A woman, who – in their final months at least – had bestowed sexual favours like some devilish opponent in a chess game? A woman who flirted with fat Americans the moment his back was turned. A woman busy, no doubt, poisoning his daughters against him at that very moment . . .

By the time he reached Geoff and Ann's door he was in something of a lather, in spite of having removed his coat.

'Andrew.' Ann took a step back, beaming at him before they kissed. She wore high heels and a clinging, low-cut bottle-green dress of such obvious distinction that Andrew wondered, with some dismay, whether he wasn't to be the only dinner guest. He tried to peer at the long dining table to see how many places were laid, but a Japanese screen of white silk had been erected to partition it away. 'This is a *celebration*,' Ann declared firmly, waving at him to follow her into the leg-bend of the sitting room. 'I've made margaritas. Geoff is running late . . . So, what's new?' She threw him a look of wifely forbearance. 'It was margaritas, wasn't it, that time at the Algonquin?'

'Er . . . yes, it was.'

'You so had me going, that night, you naughty man, telling me it was all over, that the interview had been a disaster. And now look at you,' she exclaimed, spinning round and clapping her hands. 'The new headmaster of St Thomas's Cathedral School of New York. Are you still pinching yourself? And *why* are you staying at that stupid hotel? That's what I want to know. Didn't you think I would look after you well enough?'

Andrew smiled uncertainly, aware that under the glare of Ann's energy some of his own New York buzz was in danger of draining away. 'My priority had to be being near the school . . . I've already had one meeting there, and there are several more to go.'

'But I could have driven you downtown whenever you wanted,' Ann cried. 'In fact, I declare myself officially *offended* and you are going to have to work really hard to make it up to me.'

An oval plate of canapés had been set on the long glass-topped coffee-table, along with several spindly-stemmed cocktail glasses, their rims crisp with salt, and a large stainless-steel cocktail shaker. Ann seized the shaker and then quickly put it down, crossing to join Andrew, who had drifted over to the wall of windows. The park, behind the icy rain, looked grainy and caged.

'Nice to be inside, huh?' She spoke softly, placing a hand on his arm. 'I knew you'd get the appointment, Andrew, I just knew. A more deserving, fitting candidate it would have been hard for them to find . . . and as for Sophie, I just want to say –'

'Nothing – please, if you don't mind, Ann.'

She stopped, mouth open, a flash of something like hurt in her eyes. 'But of course, forgive me.' A few minutes later they were seated on the leather sofa, toasting his success with their cocktails and talking through the logistics of his imminent move across the Atlantic. Ann fired question after question and Andrew tried to enjoy supplying the answers, wondering all the while how long Geoff would be and whether it would be rude to ask. Under pressure from his companion, he had soon eaten so many morsels off the plate next to them that Ann excused herself to fetch more. Watching her stride away, her wedge heels thwacking in a way that comically belied the elegance of the green dress, Andrew found himself recalling Sophie's goggle-eyed incomprehension that he should have been won round by the wife of his oldest friend. *We think Ann is silly, don't we? I thought we thought Ann was silly.*

In the kitchen Ann made herself breathe deeply. Geoff would be ages yet. Geoff was always ages so long as business wasn't concerned. Five minutes meant twenty. One hour meant two. 'Andy won't mind,' he had joked on the phone. 'He knows me well. And, Christ, we're going to have the bastard on our doorstep every day of the year soon enough.'

Oh, she hoped so. She really hoped so. Leaving the canapés, Ann tiptoed into her dressing room to check her face, running a comb through her hair and then spraying a cloud of perfume and stepping into it. She had left the newspaper article about the fire on her dressing-table, but now wondered whether to produce it. He knew of the Stapleton tragedy, obviously. She herself had told him about it by email. But Ann didn't feel she had wrung enough from the subject yet, especially not her own private trauma of probably having been the last person to see Beth Stapleton alive. She wanted to tell Andrew all the terrible poignant details – the smell of alcohol on the woman's breath, the emaciated appearance that had torn at her heart as she drove away. And

433

the extraordinary business of the cat returning too, padding round the smoky ruins, she was longing to get to that, to see the tremble of wonderment in his face.

Taking the cutting, she hurried back along the corridor to the sitting room, only to find herself staring at two heads over the back of the sofa instead of one.

'Honey, I'm home,' Geoff cried, in a mocking voice, raising one arm, before resuming his conversation with Andrew.

'I didn't hear you.'

'Maybe that's because I have a key.' Geoff winked at Andrew. 'Hey, do we have anything to eat with this stuff?' He raised his other hand, which contained his cocktail glass. 'It's got quite a kick.'

Ann sloped back to the kitchen and retrieved the re-stocked plate of salmon-and-cream-cheese rolls. Spotting the newspaper article as she set the plate down, Geoff snatched it from her hands and launched into a discussion about the tragedy with Andrew, covering everything from Beth's pitiful state to the miracle of Dido's return and concluding with a dramatic tale about a client's dog walking back across two states after a separation. 'The animal chose the husband!' Geoff exclaimed, slapping his thigh, and then sliding seamlessly into full buddy-client mode, telling Andrew that every aspect of his capacities both as a friend and a divorce lawyer were entirely at his disposal. 'Anything you want – if Sophie plays hard-ball – anything you need, I'm your man.'

And what had *she* wanted anyway? Ann scolded

herself, sinking deeper into her chair as the conversation between the two men continued. Andrew's attention. Andrew's admiration. Andrew's gratitude. Her husband's oldest friend had never really liked her and then he had. That was the simple truth of it. As the weeks ticked by and the news of his separation from Sophie had sunk in, she had found herself in a state of suppressed excitement, wanting more. Wherever it led.

But now, suddenly, it didn't feel like it would lead anywhere. There had been something – a connection – but it had passed. Had he used her? Was that it? Ann watched their guest closely, feeling an unlikely fluttering of empathy for Sophie, who presumably knew better than anyone what it was to have had and lost the glow of Andrew's attention. And there was a faint mark on his neck, she noticed, bluish, like a bruise, sitting just above the collar line of his shirt. It made her think of Meredith and the rumours, rumours that she herself – with mounting vexation – had quashed. For when Andrew had referred in the past, during their close patch, to the 'pull' of New York, he had meant her, hadn't he? Hadn't he meant her?

'Any more of this stuff, babes? It's going down rather well.' Geoff waggled the empty cocktail shaker at his wife, still so focused on Andrew that he didn't bother to look at her, not even when she took it from his hands.


'Your throw.'

'Oh, crumbs, what do we need?'

'At least five.'

Sophie closed her eyes and flung the dice so hard that it bounced off the kitchen table and landed on the floor. When it proved to be a six, a vigorous debate ensued as to whether the throw was valid. Alfie, who at his own insistence was playing solo, got particularly heated, while George and Milly, smugly certain of a third victory in a row, announced that the adults were welcome to cheat if it made them feel good. Whooping at their cheek, William retrieved the dice and handed it back to Sophie, saying he had every faith his partner could repeat her achievement within the confines of the table.

Sophie closed her eyes again and threw a one. The children erupted into explosive celebrations, toppling a full glass of orange juice across the Cluedo board. Merry mayhem ensued, all the merrier for the fact that – thanks to a power-cut – the game was being conducted by candlelight. Indeed, without the power-cut the game would never have been embarked upon, since Sophie would either have taken the girls home or allowed them to remain clustered round the television watching an old *Batman* DVD with William's sons. And that un-likely scenario had only come into being because of the monsoon-like deluge – starting as Sophie pulled up outside the house – which had scuppered William's grand, impromptu plan of a joint half-term outing to an amusement park. Younger children might have been induced to pull on wellies and Pac-a-macs and make a go of it, but their five had shaken their heads gravely and retreated, in tacit agreement, to the old green sofa. They would stay for twenty minutes, Sophie had conceded, after being shouted down at an initial suggestion of simply going home.

The twenty had somehow stretched to thirty, then sixty, and then – with Alfie making chocolate brownies and Harry producing the DVD – the entire afternoon. The storm blew the power cable when the film was within minutes of its climactic end. The fun of candle-lighting ensued, after which William had reached for the Cluedo box and the two eldest, exchanging looks of horror, had escaped to the pub.

Things going wrong turning out right, Sophie mused, holding the dripping board out of the way while four pairs of hands mopped at the spillage with squares of kitchen paper and tea-towels. Andrew's decision to spend half-term in New York had upset the girls badly, even from the vantage-point of their being deeply upset already. While they claimed not to want to spend time with him anyway, their father's voluntary absence over the holiday seemed to have laid bare for them the starkness of the choice he had made, the vastness of its geographical implications. After two straight days of separate, silent misery pulsing out from behind their closed bedroom doors, William's suggestion of Thorpe Park on the phone that morning had arrived like a blessing. Persuading her daughters to see it that way had been the challenge.

But she had done it. And here they were, happier,

better, without even having gone near a rollercoaster. Their anger with Andrew would burn out, Sophie knew. She would do what she could to ensure that it did. She loved them too much to do anything else. In the meantime the world would continue to turn, taking them all with it, changing them. Maybe Andrew would marry Meredith and produce some more musical offspring. Or maybe the pair would implode in an egotistical frenzy, proving to be as mismatched by temperament as they were by age. She didn't know. Best of all, she didn't care.

Sophie took the board to the sink, groping round the taps for a J-cloth. Behind her the children, still dabbing at dripping murder weapons and sodden pads of clue-notes, were continuing the debate about the game. Milly, perhaps on a spurt of delayed filial loyalty, was expressing doubts about the decision on Sophie's six. George said a cocked dice always had to be replayed and they had been right to apply the same rule. Alfie kept pleading for them to forget the whole thing so they could start a new game.

William squeezed a sponge into the sink. 'What we did – that night – I want to do it again.'

'Ssh. We were drunk and miserable and mad.'

'I know. I want to do it again, not drunk, not miserable . . . maybe mad, though. The mad was good.'

Sophie turned to him, widening her eyes in silent reprobation.

'I want to make love to you until your eyes pop.'

She looked away, stifling a squeak of indignation. 'They did not pop . . .'

'Yes, they did. It was fantastic.'

'Ssh, William . . . It's too much, too soon.' Sophie glanced over her shoulder. 'And the children . . .'

'The children know anyway.'

'No, they don't,' she hissed, disentangling herself from the sponge that William seemed to be using to rub at her hands rather than the Cluedo board. 'There's nothing to know anyway.'

'Oh, yes, there is. And the children know it. Children always do, though they don't let on. We'll have to keep an eye on Milly and George,' he murmured, managing to brush his lips over her ear as he reached across the sink, 'or it might start to feel like incest.'

Sophie blushed, glad of the dark. She pushed away from the sink but William managed to keep hold of her hand for a moment longer, kissing the tips of her fingers, in spite of them dripping with juice and dirty sink water.

The pleasure of his touch slid up Sophie's arm and into her heart, where it stayed throughout the next, more riotous, game (interrupted this time, rather to everyone's dismay, by the lights coming on), and for the rest of the evening, through the return of the pub-goers, the pizza-ordering, the final throes of the DVD and Susan phoning to change plans and report on her latest, encouraging, appointment with her oncologist. Even during the eventual innocent cheek-pecks of farewell on the doorstep it was still there, so intensely that Sophie took the precaution of pinning her eyes to William's shirt lapels rather than his face. Too much too soon, as she had told him. It was important to be sensible.

But could the girls possibly know? She stole glances at her daughters' closed expressions once they were all in the car. It certainly felt very silent, but then it was bound to – being just the three of them again, after the riot of the afternoon. Milly had commandeered the front seat, while all she could see of Olivia was a slice of her profile in the rear-view mirror, staring studiously into the dark. Good silence then, Sophie decided, trying to think about the danger of flitting foxes rather than the graze of William's cheek stubble on her lips.

'Weird about the cat,' said Milly, after a while.

'Totally,' agreed her sister.

Sophie swerved slightly, in spite of there being no sign of a fox, flitting or otherwise. They knew. Oh, God, they knew.

'I mean, like, *spooky* weird.'

'Is William going to have it?'

Sophie cleared her throat. 'It's not been decided. He says he's offered, but there's a possibility it might go to the mother, in Florida. I'm just glad the wretched animal was okay after all.'

'It would be funny, though, wouldn't it,' chirruped Milly, 'if it *did* come over here? I mean, you always said you were afraid it might have run away because it didn't like you. So if it lived over here with William you could find out once and for all, couldn't you . . . when . . . if you visited to see if it liked you? '

'But not for six months,' Olivia interjected, by way of a rescue, 'because of quarantine, remember?'

Sophie drove as steadily as she could. Six months sounded good to her. Even if things went well with William, she knew she would always rather dread the cat.

# 23

Diane was ready long before her car and driver arrived. She hovered by the condo's glass entrance doors, checking and rechecking the contents of her bag and making small-talk with the concierge. Outside the heat shimmered, a layer of fine muslin laid upon the day. The previous year she had hired a vehicle and driven herself, but she had been younger then, braver. Miami felt far away now, at the end of a long path of frightening hurdles – busy traffic circles, divided highways, overpasses, thundering eighteen-wheelers – and the woman capable of negotiating such obstacles was long gone.

'You say a happy birthday to that brother of yours from me, you hear?' commanded the concierge, holding open the door for her when the car drew up at last. 'Here, let me get that,' he added, seeing the weight of the bag, which instead of her usual purse was a large dark blue leather shoulder grip Beth had purchased for her many years before.

'Oh, I've got it, Sidney, thank you.' Diane kept both arms curled protectively round the bag and stepped out into the heat. She barely left the condo, these days. Because of Dido she had had to move to one that cost more but wasn't quite as nice. Bienvenida, thankfully, had moved with her. The girl came three times a week now and performed more chores, including keeping the cat tray clean and going to the mall to run errands.

The car was smooth and air-conditioned to an icy cool. Diane watched the world slide by, thinking of the gruelling, surreal effort of the last big trip she had made, five months before, to New York, to organize the cremation and blessing of her daughter's remains. She had been relieved at the turn-out: colleagues from Beth's work days, local friends, Nancy and Carter – and William, bless him, stiff and dignified in his long dark coat, his eyes burning coals. Throughout the ordeal the dear man hadn't left her side. He had been particularly good with his erstwhile neighbours too, whose repeated apologies for not having been around when the fire happened had quickly begun to ring hollow when it transpired that the pair had been in Hollywood securing a deal for some film-script Carter had written. Smug delight beamed from their every pore. Jennifer Aniston was in the running, they said, along with Jack Nicholson – old guy meets not-so-old girl – and it was to be a sizzling *Lolita*-style tale for the middle-aged. They had put their house in the hands of a realtor on the back of it and were moving to the west coast.

William. Her ex-son-in-law. On coming face to face, Diane had been momentarily afraid. Beth's insane, tragic, final email to her had screamed in her head: Hal must suffer for what he did . . . all those years, with you standing by . . . why, Mom, why? But the truth sets you free so I will tell William. William will know and he will understand. It was one of the few pinpricks of light in an otherwise very dark time that Beth had clearly done no such thing; that, in spite of the heroic efforts at resuscitation by Darien's volunteer firemen, her daughter had taken her pitiful ravings to the grave. An email to Sophie Chapman was all William knew of the final dreadful hours: Beth had been planning to come to London by way of some sort of birthday surprise, he had explained to his mother-in-law, offering a look of such simple, regretful sadness, that Diane had envied him.

Her own feelings, alas, could never be so straightforward – not now, with that demented nonsensical screech of a final message branded into her memory. Discovered the day after the phone call from Stamford Hospital, when she was still so dazed – sleepless, in the thick of grieving – Diane had deleted it after just one reading. Indeed, she would have *un*read the entire miserable three lines if she possibly could, erased them for ever from the faltering hard disk of her seventy-three-year-old brain. As it was, she had stabbed repeatedly at the delete button, her fingers sliding in her tears, her heart leaping with wild jealousy for the bereaved military mothers she had watched on the TV a few hours and an eternity before, treasuring final sentiments that parents had every right to hear from their offspring – that they were loved, that they had done their best.

Yet even with the hateful message eradicated, the computer had felt tainted. So much so that, on her return from the north, Diane had stowed it at the back of a cupboard and upgraded to a much smaller, lighter machine – a laptop – that could be battery-charged and carried from room to room. She had taken to watching DVDs on it at all hours of the day and night, picking favourites from a job-lot of golden oldies that Bien-venida, with astonishing insight, had picked out for her from the Netflicks summer sale. Digitally – magically – washed through with colour, the films' innocent stories and familiar protagonists, Fred Astaire, Frank Sinatra, Humphrey Bogart, Audrey Hepburn, Gloria Swanson, had become for Diane the best, most comforting friends, ready always to distract her from the darkness that so often now seemed to be lurking beyond the screen.

Hal was in his room, slumped in a wheelchair, a camel blanket covering his knees. He was dozing, chin on chest, adding an extra crease to the now permanent roll of flesh around his neck. Once thickset and muscular, the persistence of ill-health in recent years had turned him into a bulging bag of a man, shaped more by the furniture that housed him rather than the structure of his own skeleton.

'You came.'

'Happy birthday.' Diane placed a kiss on top of his head and eased the gift she had brought out of the blue leather grip, making sure she didn't disturb the urn of ashes she had wedged alongside. She had taken the precaution of sealing the urn's lid with tape – four thick white strips – but even so, the bottom of the bag felt worryingly gritty, as if some of Beth's dust had seeped out. Cremation had been a tough choice: burning some-one who had died in a fire – it didn't seem right. But then common sense had won out: it was the only way of having a ceremony in Beth's chosen home state – near her friends – while at the same time allowing Diane to take the remains with her to Florida, for eventual burial or safe-keeping as she chose.

Hal pawed weakly at his parcel. He looked terrible, even given Diane's mental preparation to expect the worst, factoring in the toll of the knee operations and the increasingly dark, monosyllabic answers he had been giving her over the phone. His hands trembled and his nails were too chewed to get any leverage under the sticky tape. Eventually Diane reached into his lap and pulled up an edge of the tape herself to get the process rolling. Like a useless kid, she decided, sitting back to watch, swallowing irritation at the thought – never far from her mind – that this selfsame irksome, short-tempered and increasingly self-pitying creature had paid for every day of earthly comforts she had ever known. The cheques had started soon after she had asked him to move out, small at first but then increasing steadily as his business investments took off.

Inside the wrapping paper, under layers of white tissue, were a blue crew-neck jumper and black sweat-pants, both picked out by Bienvenida (following a brief-ing from her employer) at the best of the men's clothing stores in their local plaza.

'One for smart and one for casual,' Diane pointed out,

feeling the need to make up for her brother's mumbled thanks. She folded up the gift wrap and then shook out the pants as if seeing them for the first time, which wasn't far from the truth. 'I thought these would be useful when you're doing all that rehab —'

'There is no rehab. I've stopped going. There's no fucking point. I'm nearly at the end of the road, Diane.'

'Hal, really —'

'There's a padre here and we've been doing a lot of talking.'

There was a knock on the door and a young woman in a crisp white uniform asked if they would like any refreshments. 'I've brought Hal's favourite cookies,' trilled Diane, returning the trousers to Hal's lap and plucking a small white paper parcel from her voluminous bag. 'So, yes, dear, I guess we'd like some tea. Hal, would you like tea?'

He shook his head.

'Just me then, please, dear.'

After the door closed, Diane walked over to the window, crossing her arms and squeezing herself to rein in the anger. Telling her how sick he was all the time . . . how self-centred could the man get? Not showing gratitude, not offering one iota of acknowledgement at the monumental effort she had made getting herself over there — a three-hour round trip — putting on a bright, brave, birthday face when all she really wanted was the numbing solace of bourbon and her own bed.

So his knees hurt, did they? Well, poor baby. Diane

focused on the landscaped garden through the window. Spread outside Hal's room was a large, rich green lawn, studded with attractive pebbled walkways and benches for rest-stops. Beyond that lay a huge oval lake, fringed with bulrushes and sporting a cute wooden latticed bridge over its narrowest point. Underneath, alligators cruised – timid ones, according to the people who ran the care home, and yet during the walks she and Hal had had over the years (how many was it? Three? Four? Five?), glimpses of the reptiles surfacing like floating planks or slithering into the water from the undergrowth had never failed to make her blood run cold.

'My time, Diane . . . it's running out,' Hal croaked behind her. 'My heart, it races so, I can't think straight half the time.'

Diane turned slowly, summoning patience. 'I'm sorry to hear that, Hal, but when I spoke to the doctor just now, he said –'

'Nothing. He knows nothing. How can any human know truly how another feels?' He slammed his palm against his chest, with the passion of a soldier saluting his country. 'Only the Lord knows that.'

The gifts had slipped off his lap onto the floor. Diane slowly bent to pick them up, aware of the resistance in her own increasingly frail and faltering body. Hal might be five years older than her, but she was full of mysterious pains, too, these days, perhaps not so far off the end of the road herself. Yet her brother had been the one constant in her life, looking out for her. She had to stick

by him. The medical ailments had started viciously, re-
lentlessly, the moment he had finally given up work.
Before the knees it had been hips. Before that, thyroid
problems, a hernia and cataracts.

'How are you anyways?' he asked dully.

Diane cleared her throat. 'You've always been so
good to me, Hal, and I want you to know how much I
appreciate —'

'I asked how you were, woman.'

Diane folded the sweater and pants and laid them
neatly on the end of his bed. 'I'm bearing up, thank you,
Hal. I have the cat, which is some comfort . . . but I
already told you about that . . .'

'Yeah, and I thought you hated the darn thing.'

'Oh, I never minded Dido.' Diane laughed a little
wildly. 'Although I have to confess, she *is* clawing the
place to shreds, which does make me wonder whether
I shouldn't have accepted that kind vet's offer of re-
homing in the Darien area. Or William — he said he
would have her,' she continued, gabbling now, glad of
having alighted upon a subject on which she had so much
to say. 'The girl who cleans for me keeps suggesting we
get the claws removed — they can do that, you know —
and I would in a trice if only I couldn't help remembering
that Beth —' Diane caught her breath as the grief, like
nausea, washed through her.

'I brought the urn, Hal,' she gasped, crossing the room
to pick up the blue leather bag and clasping it to her
chest. 'Beth's . . . remains . . . I thought I wanted them

near but I can't look at them a day longer and I didn't know what . . . or where . . . and so then I had this idea that we could drive out together and pick a spot on the beach – you and me – a quiet place where we could, you know, cast them into the sea, like people do . . . Hal?' Diane could feel her chest pumping against the bag. She took a step nearer the wheelchair. 'Hal, it's not too much to ask, is it? People do it all the time. Ashes into water.' Whispering the last words, she drew the urn out of the bag. It was ceramic, a smooth dark blue. The man at the funeral home had helped her choose it from a catalogue. The lid was snug and good.

'Jesus, Diane, it's my fucking birthday.'

'I know, Hal.' She stroked the smooth clay, loving its cool. 'I know and I'm sorry. I would have saved this for another visit, but I didn't know when that would be. It's hard for me to get out, these days, Hal. I can't manage the drive and car-hire is costly and I tire so easily . . .'

Her brother's head had sunk deeper into his thick neck, like a tortoise trying to retreat into its shell. He was shaking his head, shielding his eyes with his hands. 'I'm not sure I'm ready for this . . .'

Diane could see the time had come to be stern. Why was he making it so hard? She had lost a daughter, for Christ's sake. All he had lost was a niece, a niece with whom he had never got along anyway; a niece who, in his own words, had 'disgraced the family' and whom Diane had obligingly spent a lifetime not forcing down his throat. If anyone had suffered emotionally over their rift, it was her.

'Hal, I'm the one trying to hold it together here,' she pointed out, her voice brittle. She cradled the urn to her chest. 'Bethan – Beth,' she corrected herself, remembering how much the full name had been hated, 'was my daughter, remember? And literally the only thing that's been helping me through these past months is the fact of how ill she was before she died. She had been drinking again, Hal – they're certain that's why the fire got the better of her. And she was back on one of her starvation kicks – her wrists were like sticks.' Diane snapped her mouth shut. Her nose was running badly. She dabbed at it with the back of her hand, digging deep for composure. 'Her marriage had folded,' she continued more smoothly. 'She was a mess. In fact, I think a part of her probably wanted to die. And though I miss her, I keep reminding myself of that.' Calm now, liking how this sounded, Diane was disappointed to see her brother's face do the white, hard thing it did when he was going to say something hurtful.

'I fathered that child, Diane.'

She took a step back but he said it again, leaning towards her, gripping the arms of his wheelchair as if preparing to launch himself out of it. 'Beth's child,' he hissed, 'the one that made her so sick when it was removed. Not that boy we blamed. Me. You know it. You've always known. You just won't say it. You never would. But I'm going to die soon, Diane, and I need to confront it . . . to atone. The padre has been helping me.'

The girl in the white uniform came in with a tray but Diane did not see her. She moved towards her brother but forgot the urn. It slipped from her hands and rolled across the carpet. She had thought she was safe with Hal, of all people. Everyone needed someone and she had always had Hal. He had been her protection, against penury, against pain, against herself, against the truth. The disgusting truth. She flew at him, teeth, nails, spitting. The tea girl rang a bell and other people came into the room, all trying to pull her away.

Diane fought on, smacking at his wide, bald head, snapping her nails as she tore at his clothes. And she wept. She wept and would not stop – howls that swelled her lips and wore the skin off her throat; so heart-rending that the padre, summoned to help restore calm, confided later to a fellow pastor that it was as if the devil himself was pouring out of the woman's soul, ripping her entrails as it went.

# 24

Dear William,

Thank you so much for your Christmas card and letter. It was very thoughtful of you to write.

You had so much good news. I am happy for you. You deserve contentment, William, I always thought that. That you could not find it with Beth is not something I want you ever to beat yourself up about. She had coped with many difficulties – some you know of and others, happily, you have no need of knowing – and I'm afraid that in the end they all caught up with her.

I am so glad you have found someone else. You didn't say who she was or how you met, but I am certain Beth – wherever she is! – must be happy for you too. She loved you so much, William, and when you love someone all you want is for them to be happy, isn't that right?

It has been a very difficult year for me. I fell sick in the summer and then my brother, Hal, passed away in the fall. But he was a wealthy man and as his only surviving relative I have been able to move into a luxurious gated residence in the Keys. There are views of the sea on both sides, a private pool and beautifully maintained gardens. I am lucky enough to have my own live-in housekeeper – a dear, Mexican girl – who takes care of my every need. And Dido's too, of course! Thank you for the offer of *shipping her to the UK, but she is a much happier cat since we left the condo. She can take or leave me (she always could), but she adores Bienvenida — and I am doing my best to win her round!*

*When I say ill, I mean I had something of a breakdown. I see a therapist now and that helps. For, as I am discovering, one is never too old to start to try and make sense of life. And having someone to talk to — someone who won't judge — is such a comfort, especially if, like me, you are short on friends and have made a darn mess of so many things.*

*You might be interested to know that I finally got around to laying Beth's remains under the brightest of the bougainvillaea in the gardens here. I didn't make a fuss of it — just tipped them out and watered them in — not even the landscaper knows! But it makes me happy to have her nearby.*

*Say well done to Harry for me. They are such great kids, William, I am sure they must make you very proud.*

*It goes without saying that you should all visit if ever you find yourselves coming this way. Maybe you are planning a house swap in Florida with your new girlfriend?!*

*Warmest wishes and Happy Holidays!*
*Diane*

# Acknowledgements

One of the pleasures of writing this book was that it took me across the Atlantic by way of research. So a huge thank-you, first, to my husband, Mark, for our very enjoyable spring trip to soak up the sights of New York; and second, to my dear friend and 'co-researcher' Gilly, who helped me explore Connecticut the following November. What made that second visit so invaluable was the kindness of my old friends Monica and Simon Gill, who showed us round the area and their beautiful Darien home, not minding my notebook and endless lists of questions. The plot took several swerves as a result of their crucial input.

Back home I sought further 'American' advice via the always welcoming and wise conduit of ex-Connecticut resident Greg Barron and his sister-in-law Eve Sundelson Barron – both of whom compiled wonderfully detailed and informative emails on any subject I cared to raise. Greg, a fellow novelist, also performed the generous favour of proof-reading the manuscript to weed out any howlers *vis-à-vis* my American places and people.

For 'musical' advice, I must thank Richard Mayo, who gave me all the facts I needed to hammer out the career path of Andrew Chapman, while Sara Westcott stepped in – as always – to offer help on matters medical.

Finally, I want to use this page to express my debt of gratitude to Field House at St Edward's School and its incomparable housemaster Richard Murray. A champion of literature and most excellent friend and custodian to the children in his care – to work with such peace of mind as a parent was a luxury indeed.